LINDA LAEL MILLER

B.J. DANIELS

COWBOY
Homecoming

ISBN-13: 978-1-335-77328-9

Recycling programs for this product may not exist in your area.

Cowboy Homecoming

Copyright © 2019 by Harlequin Books S.A.

The publisher acknowledges the copyright holders of the individual works as follows:

Big Sky Summer
Copyright © 2013 by Linda Lael Miller

Cowboy's Redemption
Copyright © 2018 by Barbara Heinlein

www.HQNBooks.com

Printed in U.S.A.

CONTENTS

BIG SKY SUMMER

Linda Lael Miller

For Larry Readman, aka the Canadian Wrangler.
Thanks for taking such good care of my horses.

CHAPTER ONE

WALKER PARRISH, WEDGED into the middle of a third-row pew, with old ladies wearing gauzy hats and floral dresses packed in tightly on either side, risked a glance up at the church ceiling, just to make sure it wasn't fixing to fall on his head. He resisted a nervous urge to loosen his tie—for him, like churchgoing, tie wearing was reserved for funerals and weddings. This occasion, fortunately, fell into the latter category.

The small sanctuary seemed charged with excitement; folks chatted in whispers, the organist was tuning up for the wedding march, and the groom, Sheriff Boone Taylor, stood tall up front, just to the right of the simple altar, looking eager and scared shitless, both at the same time. Like the majority of men around Parable, Montana, Boone lived in jeans, cotton shirts and boots most of the time, and he looked a few degrees past uncomfortable in his rented tux.

Hutch Carmody and Slade Barlow, half brothers and Boone's closest friends, stood up with him, hardly recognizable in monkey suits of their own. Both married men, and cowboys to the core, they kept an eye on Boone, as if ready to catch him by the elbows if his knees buckled, but wry grins twitched at the corners of their mouths, too. They were enjoying this, most likely figuring that if they'd had to get up in front of the whole county and plight their troths, Boone shouldn't be spared the ordeal, either.

Walker fixed his gaze on Hutch, remembering the last time he'd set foot in this tiny church—a June day, much like this one, with birds chirping in the trees and warm breezes sweeping up the aisle from the open doors of the entryway—and felt the hinges of his jaws lock down. Back then, almost two years ago now, Hutch had been the bridegroom, not best man. And Walker's kid sister, Brylee, the only blood kin he could—or would— rightly claim, had been the bride, shiny-eyed and full of bright hopes, wearing the kind of gown women start dreaming about when they're little girls.

Just when the organ cue sounded, on that other day, the bridesmaids having already taken their places up front, as endlessly rehearsed, and Walker had swung one foot forward to march Brylee between the rows of pews jammed with people, Hutch had suddenly broken rank with Boone and the minister and walked midway down the aisle, where he stopped.

"Hold it," he'd said in a sheepish but nonetheless de- termined tone.

He'd stopped the wedding, called it off, right then and there, shattering Brylee's fairy-tale dreams and maybe souring her forever on the subject of marriage.

While a part of Walker had been relieved—he'd never thought Brylee and Hutch Carmody were a good fit—the memory of his sister's humiliation still stung like a thistle stuck in his hide. If he hadn't been so busy trying to keep Brylee from doing something stu- pid, he'd have punched Carmody in the mouth, church or no church.

Which was part of the reason he didn't trust the rafters to hold. He tossed another wary glance toward the ceiling.

The Reverend Walter Beaumont was officiating, and he took his place, book in hand, resplendent in maroon robes and a long gold scarf of some kind. Most times, the preacher dressed Western, like most everybody else, but today he looked as serious as an Old Testament prophet about to lower the boom on a gathering of unrepentant sinners. He looked like Morgan Freeman and sounded like James Earl Jones, so everybody got ready to listen.

Beaumont cleared his throat.

The organist struck the first rousing chord, and the congregation settled in to watch the show. Walker suspected some of them were, like him, wondering if history was about to repeat itself. The thwarted Carmody-Parrish wedding was, around Parable County, anyhow, the stuff of legend.

Tara Kendall's twin stepdaughters, now living with her, were barely teenagers and served as flower girls, happily scattering rose petals in their wake as they fairly danced up the aisle, both of them beaming and obviously enjoying the attention of the guests.

Joslyn Barlow, married to Slade and in a noticeably advanced state of pregnancy, soon followed, wearing an elegant lavender maternity dress and carrying a bouquet of multicolored flowers in both hands.

Walker noted the electric look that passed between Joslyn and her husband as she took her place opposite the three men dressed like tall, rangy penguins.

Kendra Carmody, Hutch's beloved—the woman he'd thrown Brylee over for—came next, sleek and classy in pale yellow and also carrying the requisite flowers.

Hutch winked at her when she came to a stop beside Joslyn, and a fetching blush pinked her cheeks.

Next to join the march were Boone's two young sons, wearing suit jackets and slacks and little bow ties. Each of them carried a satin pillow with a gold wedding band nestled in the hollow, and the smaller boy stopped a couple of times along the way, seeming to forget the procedure. He showed the ring he was carrying to Opal Dennison, and she smiled and gently steered him back on course.

This brought an affectionate twitter from the assembly, and the clicks of several phone cameras slipped in between the notes of organ music.

Walker grinned as the older boy finally backtracked and herded his little brother the rest of the way.

Then it sounded, the loud, triumphant chord signaling the imminent approach of the bride. Walker felt a pang, again reminded of Brylee's ill-fated wedding, but the truth was, he was glad for Boone and glad for Tara Kendall, too.

Widowed several years before, Boone had been one of the walking wounded for a long time, doing his job but clearly unhappy. He was a good sheriff and a fine man, and Walker liked him.

The bride, a glamorous city slicker hailing from the Big Apple, had come to Parable some time before, reportedly to reinvent herself after a nasty divorce. It had been a while before Boone and Tara got together, considering that they'd evidently disliked each other on sight, but they'd finally gotten past all that. And, wisely, Walker thought, they'd agreed on a fairly long courtship, just to make sure.

And now their big day was finally here.

There was a churchwide shuffle as the guests rose, turning to watch the bride start what probably felt like the longest short walk of her life.

Boone's brother-in-law, Bob, escorted Tara, but he was pretty much lost in Tara's glow. She looked like an angel bride in her billowing lacy dress, and her smile was clearly visible behind the rhinestone-studded netting of her veil, as were the happy tears sparkling in her eyes.

Walker felt a catch in his throat, wishing her and Boone well without reservation, but at the same time wanting that kind of joy for his disillusioned kid sister. She'd been invited to this shindig, right along with him, but Brylee stayed away from weddings these days. She stayed away from too many things, in his opinion, working crazy hours, too worn-out to say much when she did turn up, long after all her employees had called it a day and gone home. Even then she immediately retreated to her apartment in the main ranch house, her rescued German shepherd, Snidely, following devotedly at her heels.

Realizing he'd gone woolgathering, which was unlike him, Walker was a little startled when Casey Elder appeared beside the organist, music sheet in hand. She wore a blue choir robe and almost no makeup, and her shoulder-length red hair, usually tumbling around her face in spirals, had been pinned up into a sedate knot at her nape.

Inwardly, Walker allowed himself a grim, silent chortle.

This was a side of Casey he'd rarely if ever seen, despite the tangled and chaotic history they shared. She could still pack arenas and major concert halls, even after fifteen years as a professional entertainer, and she'd never recorded a song that hadn't gone straight to number one on all the charts and ridden there for weeks on end. Her videos were legendary, full of fire and smoke and color, and she was as famous for her flashy style as she was for her voice, always astounding in its power and range. A thing that spread its wings and took flight, soaring like a soul set free.

Onstage or on camera, she wore custom-made outfits so bejeweled that she glittered like a dark Montana sky full of stars, a one-woman constellation, and between her looks and the way she sang, she took every member of every audience captive and held them spellbound until the moment she retreated into the wings after the last curtain call. Even then, the magic lingered.

Walker wondered if Casey's legions of fans would even recognize her the way she looked today, all prim and well scrubbed. He shook off the riot of reactions he felt whenever he encountered this woman, up close or at a distance, and kept his face impassive when she started to sing.

She'd written the song, all about promises and sunrises and sticking together no matter what, especially for Boone and Tara. The organ played softly in the background, a gossamer thread of sound supporting that amazing voice.

By the time she finished, the old ladies on either side of Walker were sniffling happily into their lace-trimmed hankies, and Walker felt the need to blink a couple of times himself.

Casey retreated as swiftly and silently as a ghost, and the ceremony began.

The truth was, most of it was lost on Walker. He sat

there in a daze, Casey's song reverberating inside him like a sweet echo.

Boone moved to stand tall and proud beside his bride, and the reverend began his speech.

Vows were exchanged, promises made, and the light of Boone's and Tara's separate candles bonded into a single flame, strong and steady, barely flickering. They slipped rings onto each other's fingers, their faces shining.

Walker, a man in a daze, took it all in, like a dream, with Casey's remarkable voice for a sound track.

The reverend pronounced them man and wife in a tone of rumbling jubilance, and Boone gently raised Tara's veil, smoothed it back and kissed her with a tenderness that struck even Walker's tough cowboy heart like the plucking of a fiddle string.

The organ erupted again, joyous thunder, startling Walker out of the spell Casey had cast over him, and Mr. and Mrs. Boone Taylor came down the aisle together, both of them beaming, cheers breaking out all around them.

Patiently, Walker waited for the guests to file out into the afternoon sunshine, scented with flowers and new-mown grass and fresh asphalt, glad the wedding was over and equally glad he'd put on scratchy duds and shown up.

Now all he had to do was put in an appearance at the reception, eat a little cake, shake Boone's hand and kiss Tara's cheek, nod to this person and that one, and make a subtle escape. The to-do, which would probably resemble a small circus, was to be held in Casey's massive backyard, about the last place Walker wanted to hang out, but there was no avoiding it, since he was representing Brylee as well as himself. If he was lucky, he might manage to steal a moment or two with Clare and Shane while steering clear of their mother.

Clare and Shane. Casey's children.

His children.

Finally reaching his truck, a big rig with an extended cab and plenty of horsepower for hauling trailers loaded with rodeo stock, Walker swung up into the driver's seat and immediately dispensed with his tie, which was starting to feel like a noose.

The road in front of the church was plenty crowded, and it took a while to get into the flow of traffic, all headed toward Casey's mansion on Rodeo Road.

Walker spotted the nuptial limo up ahead and smiled in spite of his increasing case of the jitters, because Boone's and Tara's heads and shoulders were sticking up through the open sunroof, and both of them glowed as if they'd had sunshine for breakfast. It was good to be reminded that that kind of happiness was possible, short of heaven itself. With one broken marriage behind him, besides his long and tempestuous relationship with Casey, Walker tended toward skepticism when it came to love and romance. The kind that lasted, anyhow.

A mild glumness overtook him as he drove at a parade pace, and he was tempted, more than once, to zip out of the procession onto a side street, head home to his horses and his bulls and his regular clothes, and skip the whole second act. If only he hadn't been cursed with a single-minded—some would say cussed—nature, the kind that compelled a man to do what he thought was right, whether that happened to be his personal inclination at the time or not.

So he endured, pushing on until the line of cars and

trucks finally snaked onto Rodeo Road, and Casey's house loomed ahead, big as a mountain. He found a parking spot—no small feat in itself—and walked two blocks to the mouth of the long white-gravel driveway, blending in with the wedding guests and the throng of new arrivals who wouldn't have fit inside the church.

Everybody was dressed up in their best, toting wrapped presents and covered casseroles and flowers cut from their gardens.

Walker felt a little self-conscious, showing up empty-handed, but that passed quickly. Brylee had taken care of the gift-giving end of things, signing his name and her own to the card, and whatever she'd sent was sure to be just right for the occasion.

Rounding the side of the house with the others, Walker was amused to see that he'd guessed right—Casey's yard did indeed have a carnival-like atmosphere, with paper lanterns strung on every branch of every tree, a silver fountain flowing with chocolate instead of water, a massive canvas canopy arching above a couple of dozen tables. There was a bandstand, too, a temporary dance floor, an open bar and, incredibly, a genuine carousel for the little ones.

Obviously, this party would go on long after Boone and Tara had cut the cake, posed for the pictures, danced the customary waltz and lit out on their weeklong honeymoon. Rumors varied as to the destination—Vegas, Honolulu and Cabo were all in the running—but the bride and groom were keeping that information to themselves.

In a town where almost everybody knew everybody else's business, folks kept what secrets they could.

Walker was taking in the Casey-like spectacle of the

whole setup when Shane turned up, handsome in his slacks and white dress shirt, though he'd gotten rid of his tie and suit jacket at some point. At thirteen, the boy was growing up fast—every time Walker saw him, he was a little taller, or his feet were a size bigger, or both.

"Hey, Walker," Shane greeted him, grinning. While his sister resembled Casey, with her auburn hair, milky complexion and green eyes, Shane looked pretty much the way Walker had at his age. Strange that nobody seemed to notice that and put two and two together.

"Hey," Walker replied. "Looks like this is going to be quite a party."

Shane nodded. "Mom's going to sing later," he said, "and the whole town could live for a year on the food the caterers are setting out."

Walker's throat tightened. He was tough, raised a ranch kid, no stranger to hard work *or* hard knocks, but hearing Casey sing at the wedding had nearly dropped him to his knees, figuratively, anyhow. Listening to her repertoire of greatest hits might just kill him.

"I can't stick around too long," he said, his voice coming out gruff. "I've got things to do out at the ranch—" He fell silent then, because of the way Shane's face fell. Although the kid probably had no clue that Walker was his biological father—Casey had made sure of that—there had always been a bond between him and Shane just the same. Walker was the avuncular family friend, the guy who usually turned up for Thanksgiving dinners, birthdays and sometimes Christmas. Casey refused to accept child support, but Walker had been putting away money for his son and daughter for years just the same.

"Oh," Shane said, looking bleak. Familiar with the

operation, he knew what it took to run a spread the size of Timber Creek, where Walker raised cattle, along with bulls and broncos for the rodeo circuit.

He'd spent a week or two on the ranch most summers, along with Clare, and he knew there were plenty of capable ranch hands to take up the slack when Walker wasn't around.

Walker, aching on the inside, grinned and laid a hand on Shane's skinny shoulder. "I guess I can stay for a while," he conceded. Clare and Shane had had tutors, growing up on the road as they had, and attending school in Parable for the past year had been a new experience for them. Adaptable and confident, used to traveling from place to place in a well-appointed tour bus or a private jet, they'd thrived, even before the move to Montana.

Shane lit up. "Good," he said, and he stuck pretty close to Walker for the next fifteen minutes or so before he noticed the flock of giggling girls watching him from the sidelines. "My public," he quipped, making Walker laugh.

"Go for it," Walker told him.

He meandered toward the bar, stopping every few feet to speak with somebody he knew, and finally scored a cold beer. Boone and Tara and the rest of the wedding party were busy posing for pictures, both amateur and professional, and he watched for a while, envying his friends a little. Between them, the newlyweds had four children: a ready-made family. What would it be like if he could claim Shane and Clare publicly as his own? If they called him Dad?

Never gonna happen, cowboy, he reminded himself silently. *So get over it.*

Walker took another long pull on his beer. How, exactly, did a man "get over" not being able to acknowledge his own flesh and blood?

He felt a stab of annoyance at Casey for insisting that Shane and Clare were *her* children, and hers alone, as though she'd somehow managed not just one Virgin Birth, but two. Heat climbed his neck and made his collar feel tight, so he set the bottle of cold beer on a side table, half-finished. Maybe it was the alcohol that was causing this fit of melancholy; best leave it alone for the time being.

He'd barely made his way through the crowd of thirsty wedding guests clustered around the bar when he came face-to-face with Kendra Carmody.

"Hello, Walker," she said. She was a Grace Kelly blonde, classy and smart and soft-spoken, and Walker could certainly see why Hutch loved her, even though his sympathies were, of course, with Brylee.

"Kendra," Walker said with a polite nod. He had nothing against the woman; she was no home-wrecker, and even Brylee knew that. When it came to Hutch, though, neither Walker nor his sister was quite so broadminded.

"I'm sorry Brylee couldn't be here," Kendra told him, and he knew by the look in her pale green eyes that she meant it. Parable and Three Trees, just thirty miles apart, were the kind of communities where people just naturally included everybody when there was something to celebrate, put right or mourn.

Walker sighed. "Me, too," he said honestly. He wasn't about to make excuses for his sister; Brylee was a grown woman, and she had her reasons for avoiding social occasions—specifically weddings—that made her uncomfortable.

Kendra smiled, touched his arm. "Anyway, it's good to see you," she said.

After a few polite words, they parted, and Kendra went on to greet other guests. Once, the big house had been hers, but a lot had changed since then. She and Hutch lived on Whisper Creek Ranch, had two daughters and planned to add several more children to their family.

Once again, Walker put down a swell of pure envy. Okay, so maybe he didn't have everything he wanted—kids, a wife, a home instead of just a house. Who did? He liked his life for the most part, liked breeding and raising rodeo stock and ranching in general, and besides, nothing good ever came of complaining. For him, it was all about keeping on.

CASEY ELDER WIGGLED her toes in the soft grass, glad to be barefoot after spending most of the day in high heels and pantyhose, both of which she hated. Her blue cotton sundress felt airy and light against her skin, too—a big improvement over that heavy choir robe she'd been talked into wearing when she sang at the wedding.

She smiled and nodded to passing guests, keeping to one side of the moving current of people, sipping champagne from a crystal flute and indulging in one of her favorite activities—watching Walker Parrish from a safe distance.

He was one fine hunk of a man, in her opinion; tall, with broad shoulders and a square jaw, movie-star handsome with his green-gray eyes and that head of glossy, deep brown hair, always a mite on the shaggy side.

He was completely unaware of his effect on women, it seemed, which only made him more intriguing.

Casey's feelings for Walker were complicated, like everything in her life. She knew she could fall in love with him without half trying—hadn't she done precisely that numerous times over the years, only to talk herself out of it later? She was practical to the bone— *too* practical to open her heart to the one man on earth with the power to break it to bits.

As if he'd felt her gaze, Walker turned his head and their eyes met.

She nodded and lifted the champagne glass slightly. *Here we go,* she thought, wishing he'd walk away, hoping against hope that he'd weave his way through the crowd toward her instead.

Her breath snagged on a skittering heartbeat when Walker started in her direction. A sudden dizziness struck her, as though she'd stepped onto the rented merry-go-round only to have it start spinning fast enough to blur.

Once they were face-to-face, Casey tried hard to keep her cool, though part of her wanted to tumble right into those solemn, intelligent eyes of his and snuggle into a warm corner of his heart for the duration. "Hello, handsome," she said softly.

He didn't smile. "You did a real nice job with that song," he told her. "The one you sang at the wedding, I mean."

Casey raised one shoulder slightly, let it fall again. "I've had lots of practice," she said. Just for a moment, she let her eyes stray toward the wedding party, still posing for pictures over by the gazebo, and felt a tiny pinch of sorrow at the base of her throat.

When she looked back at Walker, she saw that he'd been watching her face the whole time, and hoped he hadn't guessed that, happy as she was for Boone and Tara, both of whom deserved the best of everything, she happened to be feeling just a tad sorry for herself at the moment.

"They're lucky," Walker observed quietly, inclining his head toward the bride and groom, who were clowning for the cameras now.

"Yes," Casey agreed, barely suppressing a sigh. She knew her friends had traveled some twisting, rocky roads to find each other, and she was ashamed to admit to herself that she envied Tara all that was ahead—not just the wedding night and the honeymoon, but the solace and shelter of a committed marriage, the sex and the laughter, the babies and the plans. Fiercely independent though she was, Casey sometimes longed to be held and loved in the depths of the night, to share her joys and her worries and her children with a man who loved her, instead of always playing the brave single mother who could more than manage on her own. "Very lucky."

To her surprise, Walker cupped a calloused yet gentle hand under her chin and lifted her face so he could look straight into her eyes. For one dreadful, wonderful moment, she actually thought he might kiss her.

He didn't, though.

His expression was so serious that it bordered on grave. Whatever he was about to say was lost—probably for the best—when fourteen-year-old Clare bounded up, beautiful in her peach-colored dress chosen especially for the wedding. She was still coltish, horse crazy and ambivalent about boys, but the woman she would become was clearly visible in her poise and lively personality just the same.

Faintly, Casey heard a few of the local musicians tuning up, but the sight of her daughter, so beautiful, beaming up at Walker in pure delight, almost stopped her heart in midbeat. *Don't turn into an adult,* Casey pleaded silently. *Not yet.*

"You *have* to dance with me," Clare told Walker. The child didn't have a shy bone in her body, and anyway, both Clare and Shane had always been close to this man, and to Brylee, as well.

Boone and Tara, with the photo session finally behind them, were standing in the middle of the dance floor, looking like the figures on top of some celestial wedding cake.

Walker smiled down at the daughter who thought of him as a beloved uncle, and in that moment Casey caught a glimpse of a place deep inside him, that part of his soul where he was this child's father, not just a loyal and trusted friend of the family.

"Let's wait a couple of minutes," he said, taking Clare's hand and squeezing it lightly.

Somehow, Casey found her voice. "The bride and groom always have the first dance, honey," she told Clare. "It's tradition."

Clare's emerald eyes sparkled with mischief and spirit. "Okay," she agreed good-naturedly, still looking up at Walker with something like hero worship. She bit her lip, then blurted out eagerly, "When I get married, will you give me away? Please, Walker? I wouldn't want anybody else to do it except you."

Casey lifted her chin, swallowed. "That's a ways

off," she said somewhat weakly. "Your getting married, I mean."

"I'd be proud to walk you down the aisle," Walker told his daughter, "when the time comes." He paused, eyes twinkling, and one corner of his mouth crooked up in a grin, the way it did when he was teasing. "Of course, it all depends on whether or not I like the yahoo you choose for a husband."

Clare laughed, clinging to his arm and clearly adoring him. "If I like him," she reasoned with confidence, "you will, too."

Walker chuckled and kissed the top of the girl's head. "You're probably right about that, princess," he agreed.

Boone and Tara owned the dance floor, waltzing slowly, closer than close, lost in each other's eyes.

Casey's own eyes scalded, and she looked away quickly, afraid Walker or Clare would notice, but they, like everyone else, were watching the newlyweds.

As prearranged—Casey knew her showmanship—hundreds of snow-white rose petals drifted down on Boone and Tara like a velvety, fragrant first snow, spilling from a net strung up in the high branches of a venerable maple tree.

The guests were impressed, gasping in delight, and Boone and Tara looked up, smiling, Tara putting her hands out to catch some of the petals in her palms.

Casey started the applause, her throat thick with emotion, and the rest of the company joined in.

In the interim, the makeshift band launched into a twangy ballad that opened the dance floor to all comers, while Boone beckoned for others to join them. Clare practically dragged Walker onto the floor, and seeing how happy Clare was to have his full and laughing attention, Casey felt the starch go out of her knees. She made her way to the porch steps and sat down, willing herself not to blubber like a sentimental fool.

There, in the shade, amid all that celebration, she thought of the lies she'd told, right from the beginning. Sure, she'd been young and scared, wanting Walker a lot but wanting her then-blossoming career even more, back then at least. She'd told Walker the baby she was carrying belonged to another man, someone he didn't know, and at first, he'd believed her. They'd broken up, as she'd planned, because Walker was a proud and decent man, but the grief she felt after losing him was something she hadn't reckoned on, consuming and painful as a broken bone.

Casey had done what she always did: she'd carried on. Barely showing even when she was near full term, she'd been able to camouflage her pregnancy, from the fans and the media, anyway, by wearing flowing gowns and big shirts.

But a year later, she and Walker had met up again, and they'd both lost their heads and conceived Shane.

Knowing Walker wouldn't buy the same story twice, Casey called him from the road when the second pregnancy was confirmed.

Nobody's fool, Walker had soon figured out that the redheaded baby girl, just learning to toddle around on her own, was his, too.

All hell had broken loose, and the battle was on.

Walker wanted to get married immediately, but his cold rage was hardly conducive to romance. They'd wrangled back and forth over the children for a couple of years, though they never got quite as far as the courtroom, and finally, they'd forged a sort of armed truce.

Unwillingly, Walker had agreed to go along with Casey's story—that both Clare and Shane were test-tube babies, fathered by an anonymous sperm donor—as long as he was allowed regular visits with both children.

For a long time, it worked, but now—well, Casey could feel the framework teetering around her, and she was scared.

Kendra sat down beside her on the porch step just then, touched her arm. Her friend was the only person on earth, besides Casey and Walker, of course, who knew the truth about Clare's and Shane's births. Oddly enough, it had been Walker who'd told her, possibly out of frustration, rather than Casey herself.

"It's not too late to fix this, you know," Kendra said gently, bumping her shoulder briefly against Casey's. She was watching as Clare persuaded Walker to dance with her just once more, her gaze soft with understanding.

"Has anybody ever told you that you're too damn perceptive sometimes, Kendra Carmody?"

Kendra smiled. "I might have heard it once or twice," she replied. Then her smile faded and her expression turned serious. "Things like this have a way of coming out, Casey," she said, nearly in a whisper. "In fact, given how famous you are, it's a miracle the story hasn't broken already."

Casey wiped her cheeks with the back of one hand, sat up a little straighter. "What if they don't understand?" she asked, barely breathing the words. "What if Clare and Shane never forgive me?"

Kendra sighed, then countered with a question of her own. "Do you want them to hear it from somebody else?" she asked.

CHAPTER TWO

THOUGH IT WASN'T quite dark, lights glowed yellow-gold in the kitchen windows of the ranch house when Walker pulled in, and that raised his spirits a little, since he was grappling with a bad case of lonesome at the moment. Leaving Clare and Shane and, okay, Casey, too, had that effect on him, especially at that homesick time around sunset, when families were supposed to gather in a warm and well-lit room, laughing and telling each other all about their day.

Not that long ago, his ancient, arthritic black Labs, Willie and Nelson, would have been waiting in the yard to greet him, tails wagging, gray-muzzled faces upturned in grinning welcome and the hope of a pat on the head, but they'd both passed on last fall, within a few weeks of each other, dying peacefully in their sleep as good dogs deserve to do. Now they rested side by side in a special spot near the apple orchard, and Walker never got through a day without missing them.

He swallowed hard as he left the truck behind, heading for the house. He'd raised Willie and Nelson from pups, and Brylee had been urging him to replace them, but he wasn't ready for that. For the time being, he'd rather share his sister's dog, though Snidely went everywhere with his mistress, which meant he wasn't around home much.

Walker let himself in through the side door, which opened into the spacious, old-fashioned kitchen, his suit jacket slung over one shoulder, and was heartened to find Brylee there. Blue-jeaned and wearing a T-shirt with the motto Men Suck on the front, her heavy brown hair pulled back in a ponytail, she was splotched with flour from head to foot.

Snidely kept watch nearby, curled up on a hooked rug.

"Hey," Walker said, addressing both of them, draping his jacket over the back of a chair.

Snidely lifted his head, sighed and rested his muzzle on his forelegs again.

"Hey," Brylee said, careful not to look at Walker. She'd been baking bread, probably for hours. The air was scented with that homey aroma, and pans full of rising, butter-glistened dough waited, assembly-line fashion, on the counter nearest the stove. "How was the wedding?"

Walker wanted a beer and a quiet chat with his sister, but he had to get out of his suit and head for the barn and stock pens, to make sure the chores had all been done. With six ranch hands working the place year-round, though, the task was more habit than necessity. "It was a wedding," he said, pausing. He wasn't being flippant; the church variety was always pretty much the same, that's all—white dress and veil for the bride, nervous groom, preacher, organ music, crowded pews, tons of flowers.

Every line of Brylee's slender body looked rigid as she absorbed his reply, and she kept her back to him. Whenever somebody got married, she folded in on herself like this, keeping frenetically busy and pretending it didn't matter.

"So it went off without a hitch, then?" she asked, her tone so falsely airy that a crack zigzagged its way down the middle of Walker's big-brother heart. Brylee wouldn't have wished what had happened at *her* wedding on anybody, but she always asked that same question after every new ceremony and she always seemed to be braced for the worst.

"I'd say it was perfect," Walker answered gently. He'd retrieved his jacket from the chair back, but beyond that, he hadn't moved. His feet seemed to be stuck to the kitchen floor.

Brylee looked back over one flour-coated shoulder, offered a wobbly smile that didn't quite stick to her wide mouth. "That's good," she said, blinking once and then turning to the dough she was kneading.

"What's with all the bread?" Walker asked.

"Opal Dennison and some of the other ladies from her church are holding a bake sale tomorrow, after the second service," she replied with brave good cheer, though her shoulders slumped slightly and she was careful to keep her face averted. "To raise more money for the McCulloughs."

Young Dawson McCullough, seriously injured in a fall from the now-demolished water tower in town, had worked on the ranch since he was big enough to buck hay bales and muck out stalls, after school and during the summer, and he was practically a member of the family.

"And you're the only woman in the whole county who signed up to bake bread?" Walker asked lightly.

Brylee stopped, stiff along her spine again and across

her shoulders. She kept her head up, but it looked like an effort. "Don't, Walker," she said softly. "I know what you're trying to do, and I appreciate the thought, but, please—don't."

Walker sighed, shoved a hand through his hair. He opened his mouth, thought better of saying more and closed it again, went on through the kitchen, along the corridor, past the dining and living rooms, and into his spacious first-floor bedroom, where he peeled off the suit and kicked off the dress shoes and put on worn jeans, a lightweight flannel shirt and boots.

The relief of being himself again was enormous.

Brylee was lining up what looked like the last of the doughy loaves on the oven racks when Walker came back through, on his way to the door. She didn't acknowledge him, but Snidely got to his feet and lumbered along after him, outside, across that wing of the porch that wrapped around the house on three sides, down the steps.

"Women," Walker told the dog in an exasperated undertone. "Brylee could have her pick of men and what does she do? She pines after the one that got away."

Tongue lolling, Snidely wagged his tail as he ambled companionably alongside.

Walker was glad to have the company. "The worst part is," he went on, relieved that nobody on two legs could hear him prattling away to a German shepherd, "she's just being cussed, that's all. Deep down—but not all *that* deep down—Brylee knows damn well that she and Hutch weren't right for each other. By now, the honeymoon wouldn't just be over, they'd have crashed and burned."

Snidely offered no insight, but, in that way of faithful dogs, his mere presence was soothing. He paused to lift one hind leg against a pillar of the hitching post, then trotted to catch up with Walker at the barn door.

Walker flipped on the lights lining the long breezeway and stepped inside, pausing to check on each horse in each stall, making sure the electronic watering system was working and there was hay in every feeder.

Mack, his big buckskin gelding, occupied the largest stall, the one across from the tack room, and he nickered a greeting when Walker stopped to offer a quiet howdy. All the horses, Mack included, had been properly looked after, but Walker had had to see that with his own eyes if he expected to get any sleep. Same with the bulls and the broncos, some in the pastures and some in the holding pens behind the barn.

He sighed again, rubbed the back of his neck, still itchy from the starch in the collar of the dress shirt he'd worn earlier, and adjusted his hat, even though it didn't need adjusting. With his head full of Casey Elder and the two children they should have been raising together, he'd probably toss and turn the whole night and wake up cranky as an old bear with a nettle between its toes.

Snidely, standing close, thumped the back of Walker's right knee with his swinging tail, as if to remind him of the here and now.

Walker chuckled and leaned down to ruffle the dog's ears, and then the two of them went on to check on the bulls snorting and pawing the ground in their steel-girded pens, the broncos grazing in the nearby pasture. Across the Big Sky River, the lights of the ranch hands' cabins and trailers winked in the shadows of early evening, casting dancing reflections on the water. Voices drifted over—children playing outside, determined to wring the last moment of fun from a dying day, mothers calling them inside for baths and bedtime, men smoking in their yards while they swapped tall tales and laughed at each other's jokes.

The sounds were ordinary, but they lodged in Walker's chest like slivers that night. He tilted back his head, looked up at a sky popping with stars and wondered how a man could live square in the middle of a busy ranch like Timber Creek and still feel as though he'd been exiled to some faraway planet with a population of one.

Snidely lingered, but it was plain that he wanted to head back toward to the house and Brylee, and Walker figured the dog had it right. God knew, standing out here by the river, listening in on all those family sounds, wasn't doing him any good.

"Let's go," he told Snidely, and started back.

By the time they reached the house, Brylee had the kitchen cleaned up, about two dozen loaves of bread wrapped up in foil and ready for tomorrow's bake sale, and was actually sitting down at the table, sipping from a cup of tea while she waited for the stove timer to ring so she could take out the last batch.

She'd pulled herself together while Walker was out, and he was grateful, because he never knew how to comfort her when she got into one of these jilted-bride moods.

"I kept back a few loaves for you," she told her brother, smiling a genuine Brylee smile when Snidely walked over and laid his chin on her lap so she could stroke his long, gleaming back. "One in the breadbox, two in the freezer."

"Thanks," Walker said, hanging his hat on its peg next to the door and proceeding to the sink to roll up his sleeves and wash his hands the way he always did when he'd been outside. He remembered their father doing the same thing in the same way, and their grand-dad, too. There was a certain reassurance in that kind of quiet continuity.

"I guess you must have seen Casey and the kids today," Brylee said easily.

"I saw them," Walker said.

"And?"

"And what?" Walker grabbed a dish towel and dried his hands, his motions brisk.

Brylee chuckled. "Whoa," she exclaimed. "Touchy."

"You're a fine one to talk about being touchy," Walker pointed out, frowning at her.

Brylee held up both hands, palms out. "Okay, fair enough," she conceded. "It's just that I'm allergic to white lace and promises." Her hazel eyes, set wide above high cheekbones, twinkled, and she reached back to free her hair from the rubber band that had held it in place, shaking her head a couple of times so her curls flew around her face. Before the wedding-that-wasn't, Brylee's hair had tumbled past her waist, but she'd had it cut to shoulder-length afterward, which was better, Walker supposed, than getting a tattoo or having some-thing pierced.

"You might want to get over that," Walker remarked, walking over to the fridge, opening the door and taking out a can of cold beer.

"Are you going to make a speech?" The question was mildly put, but it had an edge to it nevertheless. Brylee narrowed her eyes, her cheeks flushed from an afternoon spent baking bread in a hot kitchen. "Because you're the *last* person on earth, Walker Parrish, who has room to lecture anybody about their love life."

He hooked one foot around the leg of a chair at the table, scraped it back and sat, plunking his can of beer down on the red-and-white-checked cloth and regarding her steadily. "Who said I was fixing to give a lecture?" he asked coolly.

Brylee flashed him one of her wide, toothy grins. The woman was a walking advertisement for orthodontia now, but as a kid, her pearly whites had gone every which way but straight down. "It isn't as if we don't have this conversation every time there's a wedding anywhere in Parable County."

"What conversation?" Walker took a long, thoughtful draft of his beer. "You said you were allergic to white lace and promises, and I said you might want to think about getting over that. Where I come from, that doesn't qualify as a conversation."

Brylee rolled her eyes. For somebody who'd probably been down in the mouth all day, she'd certainly perked up all of a sudden. "I come from the same place you do," she reminded him. "Right here on this ranch."

"Is this discussion going anywhere?" Walker asked, suddenly realizing he was hungry. The only food he'd had since lunch, after all, was a slice of white cake, a few pastel mints and a handful of those tiny sandwiches held together by frilly toothpicks.

She reached out then, rested her hand briefly on his forearm and then withdrew it. "I know you worry about me, Walker," Brylee said softly. "But I'll be all right. I really will."

"When?" Walker wanted to know.

"Things take time," she hedged, making her big

brother wish he'd left well enough alone and talked about things like the price of beef or the weather or, better yet, nothing at all.

"How much time?" he asked, because they were already knee-deep in the subject and wishing he'd kept his mouth shut in the first place wouldn't help now. "It's been a couple of years since you and Hutch parted ways and, far as I know, you haven't so much as looked at another guy since then, let alone dated."

Brylee propped one elbow on the table and rested her chin in her palm, regarding him with a sort of tender amusement. "I'm running a business, Walker—a *successful* business, in case you haven't noticed—and that keeps me pretty busy."

"Too busy, if you ask me," Walker grumbled.

"I didn't ask you," Brylee reminded him sweetly. Her brow furrowed in a slight frown, quickly gone, and another twinkle sparked in her eyes. "Are you afraid I'll wind up an old maid, and you'll be stuck with me for good?"

An image of Brylee sitting on the front porch in a rocking chair, her hair gray and pinned back in a bun, wearing a church-lady dress and knitting socks, flashed into Walker's mind and made his mouth twitch upward at one corner. "Heck, no," he teased. "I'd just park you in some nursing home and get on with my life."

Brylee didn't laugh, or even smile. Her expression was sad, and she gazed off into some unseeable distance. "What if we *do* end up all alone when we're old?" she murmured. "It happens."

"I reckon I'll wait a decade or two before I start worrying about that," he said. There had to be things he could say that would encourage Brylee, get her off the sidelines and back into the rough-and-tumble of life, but he was damned if he knew what those things were.

Like quicksilver, Brylee's mood changed again. The timer on the stove made a chiming sound, and she pushed her chair back to stand, dislodging Snidely's big dog head from her thigh. All hustle and bustle, she picked up a couple of pot holders and started taking tinfoil loaf pans out of the oven and setting them on the waiting cooling racks. "You're right," she said, as though there had been no lag in their verbal exchange. "Let's wait twenty years and figure it out then."

Remembering that he was hungry, Walker stood, went to the breadbox on the counter, a retro thing coated in green enamel, took out a loaf and set it on the counter while he rummaged through a nearby drawer for a knife. "It's a deal," he agreed, proceeding to open and close cupboard doors until he found a jar of peanut butter and one of those little plastic bears with honey inside. The bottle was sticky and the cap was missing, and honey went everywhere when he squeezed too hard.

"Honestly," Brylee scolded, elbowing him aside, constructing the sandwich and shoving it at him, then wiping up the mess with a damp sponge.

Walker grinned at her efficiency. "You were born to pack lunches for a bunch of little kids," he observed.

"Gee," Brylee said, *"thanks."*

"I only meant—"

"I *know* what you meant, Walker," she broke in crisply.

He bit into the sandwich, chewed, swallowed. "Well, *excuse* me," he said, pretending to be wounded.

"Shut up and go to bed," Brylee told him.

"I'll do that," Walker replied, thinking that they must

have slipped into a time warp and been transported back to their teens, when they couldn't be in the same room without needling each other.

She made a disgusted sound and thumped the tops of a few loaves with one knuckle. She'd be up for a while, waiting for the last batch of bread to cool off so she could wrap it.

Walker saluted her with a lift of his sandwich and headed for his room, shaking his head as he went. He wondered when he was going to learn. Ninety-five percent of the time, reasoning with a woman, especially when that woman happened to be his kid sister, was a waste of breath.

IT WAS ALMOST midnight when the last guests took their leave and the carousel finally stopped turning.

Surveying her backyard, empty except for the caterer's helpers and the guys taking down the big canopy and dismantling the dance floor, Casey was reminded of her childhood and the feeling she got when the carnival moved on after its yearly visit, leaving a bare and somewhat forlorn patch of ground behind.

"Mom?" Clare stood at her elbow, barefoot but still in her party dress. She was already taller than Casey, and so was her brother, and she had the elegant carriage of a young woman. "You okay?"

Casey turned her head, smiled at her daughter, thinking that if she loved her kids even a smidgeon more, she'd burst. "I'm fine, sweetheart," she said. "Just a little tired." She paused, enjoying the night air and the sky full of stars and the bittersweet remnants of a happy day. "Speaking of which—shouldn't you be in bed by now?"

Named for Casey's late grandmother, Clare resembled the woman more with every passing year. Now she made a face. *"Mom,"* she said, "I'm almost *fifteen* and, anyway, it's Saturday, so I can sleep in tomorrow."

"We're going to church," Casey reminded the woman-child. "There's a bake sale after the eleven o'clock service, and I promised Opal I'd help out. And you won't be fifteen for another eight months."

With a dramatic sigh, Clare turned and started across the darkened sunporch, toward the kitchen, and Casey followed with some reluctance, turning her back on that big sky full of stars.

"Well," the girl argued, since teenagers couldn't go more than ten minutes, it seemed to Casey, without offering up some kind of back talk, "you didn't promise Opal that *I'd* help, did you?"

Shane stood at one of the sleek granite-covered counters in that gleaming, cavernous kitchen, eating leftover wedding cake with his fingers. He gave Casey a look of good-natured guilt, shrugged once and reached for another slice.

"You're disgusting," Clare informed him.

Shane stuck out a crumb-covered tongue and made a rude noise.

"Yuck," Clare wailed, drawing the term out to three times its normal length. "*Mother,* are you just going to stand there and let him act like a baboon?"

Casey pretended to consider the question. "Yeah," she said finally, with a little grin. "I guess I am."

Shane laughed in obnoxious triumph, snorting more crumbs. The three dogs, clustered around him, waited eagerly for scraps.

Clare made a strangled, screamlike sound of truly theatrical proportions and stomped off toward the rear stairway, bound for the sanctuary of her upstairs bedroom, a private preserve where Shane was not allowed.

"That's enough cake," Casey told her son. "Have the dogs been outside?"

Shane nodded, his mouth full, and dusted frosting-sticky hands together. Once he'd swallowed again—actually, it was more of a gulp—he answered, "Only about five times. Rockford ate a crepe paper streamer and part of a balloon."

Rockford, the baby of the chocolate-Lab trio, gave a mournful little howl of protest, as though objecting to being snitched on.

Casey walked around, took a gentle hold on the dog's ears and looked him over closely. "He seems all right," she said.

"He'll be okay," Shane confirmed nonchalantly. "He already barfed. That's how I knew what he ate."

"Ewwww," Casey said, taking her son by the shoulders and steering him toward the stairs. "Be sure to wash up before you turn in for the night," she added as he followed the trail blazed by his older sister.

The dogs trooped after him, the way they did every night.

Doris, the cook and housekeeper, poked her head out of her apartment off to the side of the kitchen, wearing face cream and curlers and a pink chenille bathrobe. "Is the party over?" she asked pleasantly. It was, of course, a rhetorical question; Doris had to have heard all the goodbying and the slamming of car doors and the crunch of gravel in the driveway. She'd stayed until nearly ten, socializing, then retired to shampoo and set her hair so she'd look good at church the next morning.

"Yep," Casey replied with a smile. She locked the

back door, set the alarm and padded over to the counter to brew a cup of herbal tea. The stuff helped her sleep—usually.

Doris nodded a good-night and retreated back into her nest, shutting the door softly behind her.

Casey lingered in the kitchen for a few minutes, sipping tea and listening to the familiar sounds overhead—the dogs' nails clicking on the hardwood floor of the upstairs corridor, Shane laughing like a villain in a melodrama, Clare calling him a choice name and slamming her bedroom door hard.

With a sigh, Casey crossed the kitchen—it seemed to cover two acres, that room—and, reaching the foot of the stairs, flipped off the lights.

Shane was still baiting Clare from the hallway when Casey reached the second floor, and Clare made the mistake of opening her bedroom door and calling him another name, which, of course, only egged him on.

Casey whistled shrilly through her teeth, the way Juan, her grandparents' gardener and all-around handyman, had taught her to do when she was eight. The sirenlike sound was an attention-getter, all right, and it had served Casey well over the years, not only with the kids, but with the band, the road crew and every dog she'd ever owned.

"The fight is over, and I'm calling it a draw," she announced with authority when both Clare and Shane stared at her, startled, along with all three of the dogs.

"Dickhead," Clare said to Shane in an undertone.

"Pizza face," Shane shot back.

Casey put her hands on her hips and puckered up to whistle again.

The mere threat made them both retreat into their

rooms, the dogs ducking in ahead of Shane, probably keeping a low profile in case they were in some kind of trouble themselves.

"My sweet children," Casey said wryly, and went on to her own room.

Actually, the word *room* fell a little short of accurate description—the place was the size of a small gymnasium, or one of those swanky penthouse hotel suites that take up a whole floor all by themselves.

Again, she had that sense that things had shifted. Everything *looked* the same—the fancy antique bed rescued from some crumbling Italian villa and sporting a museum-quality painting of nymphs frolicking with various Roman gods on the gilded headboard, the massive dresser, the couch and chairs and elegant marble fireplace, the expanse of floor-to-ceiling windows specially made to give her a sweeping view and, at the same time, ensure her complete privacy.

It was just plain too big a space for one lone woman, but at least it didn't have wheels, like the tour bus, or a reception desk downstairs, like a hotel. This was the home she'd hungered for all her life.

Oh, yes, she'd wanted this house, she reminded herself, wanted to park herself and the children somewhere solid and real and finally put down some roots. So what if she and Clare and Shane sometimes seemed to rattle around in the place like dried beans in a bucket? She hadn't bought the mansion because it was grand, so she could play lady of the manor or live in the style to which the public probably believed she was accustomed; she'd bought it because it was *big,* with room for the band and the backup singers and the roadies and a host of other staffers who came and went. Downstairs, there was a soundstage for filming videos *and* a recording studio, both of which she used constantly.

Try fitting all *that* into a three-bedroom, split-level ranch, she thought, glancing at her reflection in the big three-way mirror, encircled with lights, above her vanity table.

Vanity was certainly the operative word for that setup, Casey reflected with a shake of her head as she turned away and set her course for the bathroom. Like the rest of the house, the room was almost decadently luxurious—the shower stall could have accommodated a football team, and she'd seen backyard hot tubs smaller than the mosaic-lined pool she bathed in.

Shutting the door—it was a habit one developed after years of living in a bus—Casey washed her face at one of the three gleaming brass sinks, brushed her teeth and finally pulled her dress off over her head, tossing it dutifully into the laundry hamper, along with her underwear, before pulling on flannel boxer shorts and a T-shirt commemorating her most recent European tour. Once again, she faced her own reflection.

Wearing the shirt should have made her feel nostalgic, she supposed, since that tour had been a record breaker, every concert sold out months before she and the gang had flown over a dark ocean in a jet with her name emblazoned on its sides to visit the first of twelve cities. She'd loved singing in front of huge audiences—thrived on it, in fact—and instead of wearing her out, those performances had energized her, flooded her system with endorphins, provided a high no drug could have matched. Unlike some of her colleagues in the music business, she'd never burned out, had a breakdown, played the home-wrecker or floated into rehab on a wave of booze and cocaine.

So why didn't she miss all that excitement and attention and applause? She supposed it was because, for her, life was and had always been all about singing and plucking out new tunes on her favorite guitar, the scarred and battered one her grandfather had given her for Christmas when she was around Shane's age. She'd done what she'd set out to do, pursuing her goals with near-ruthless resolve, but somewhere along the line, she'd noticed that her children were growing up faster than she'd ever thought possible. All too soon, she'd realized with a road-to-Damascus flash of insight, they'd be heading off to college, starting careers of their own, getting married and having children.

Figuratively blinded by the light, Casey had finished the tour, called Walker and asked him if he knew of any houses for sale in his part of Montana. Suddenly, she wanted her children attending a regular school, saluting the flag every morning and making friends their own age. And she'd wanted Clare and Shane to see a lot more of Walker, too, though she hadn't been sure why and still wasn't, considering the effort she'd gone to to keep the truth under wraps.

If he'd been surprised by this turn of events, Walker hadn't given any indication of it. He'd said he knew a real estate broker—who turned out to be Kendra, now a dear and trusted friend to Casey, like Joslyn and Tara—and before she could say *Jack Daniel's,* she'd found herself smack-dab in the middle of Parable, Montana, taking one good look at this house and promptly signing on the dotted line.

Since then, Casey had had plenty of second thoughts,

though she'd never actually regretted the decision to settle in a small town where it was still safe for kids to go trick-or-treating on Halloween, where everybody knew everybody else and people not only went to church on Sundays and then had breakfast over at the Butter Biscuit Café, but voted in every election.

It was living in close proximity to Walker Parrish that made her question this particular choice. By doing so, she'd put the secret she'd guarded for years in obvious jeopardy.

Frowning thoughtfully, Casey left the bathroom, crossed to her big, lonely bed and switched out the lamp on the nightstand.

Was it possible that, on some level, she'd *wanted* the truth to come out?

CHAPTER THREE

IRRITABLE AFTER A restless night, Walker spoke briefly with his longtime foreman, Al Pickens, leaving the orchestration of yet another fairly routine workday on the ranch to him. Climbing into his truck, the backseat jam-packed with boxes of Brylee's homemade bread, each loaf carefully wrapped in shining foil and tied with a ribbon for the church bake sale, it occurred to Walker—and not for the first time—that he was more of a figurehead than a real rancher.

Sure, he ran things, made all the major decisions, personally hauled badass bulls and even badder broncos to rodeos all over the western United States and parts of Canada, led roundups and rode fence lines here at the homestead, signed the paychecks and paid the bills. But, in point of fact, his crew was so competent that they could manage without him, any day of the week.

He headed for Parable, a thirty-mile drive, with his windows rolled down and a worn Johnny Cash CD blaring out of the dashboard speakers, tapping out the familiar rhythms on the steering wheel with one hand as he drove. There were some days, he thought wryly, when nothing but songs like "Folsom Prison Blues" and "A Boy Named Sue" could keep a man's mind off his problems.

When he reached the same small clapboard church

he'd sat in the day before, watching Boone and Tara tie the proverbial knot, the Sunday services were still going on. He found a parking place in the crowded gravel lot, and not without difficulty, as the Reverend Walter Beaumont was a popular preacher.

Since the day was warm and the congregation wouldn't spring for air-conditioning, the doors were propped open, and the voices of those gathered to make a joyful noise before the Lord spilled out into the sunshine, curiously comforting simply because the words of the old hymn were so familiar.

Spotting the booths set up in back of the church—members who had probably attended the early service were out there lining up goods for the bake sale—Walker briefly recalled the Sundays of his youth. His mother had branded the whole idea of religion as pure hypocrisy—and, in her case, that was certainly true—but their dad had carted him and Brylee off to a similar place of worship over in Three Trees every single week until they reached the "age of reason," that being, by Barclay Parrish's reckoning, twelve.

Life had its rough patches, the old man had quietly maintained, and, in his opinion, a person could take the dogma or leave it, but over the long run, they'd be better off believing than *not* believing. If nothing else, he'd figured, Walker and Brylee would lead better lives just for trying.

Brylee had continued to attend services, on and off, but Walker had gone his own way when he was given the option. He wasn't a believer *or* a nonbeliever—it seemed obvious to him that nobody really knew what the celestial deal was—but he was grateful for the training and the Bible verses he'd had to memorize for Sunday school just the same. Those lines of Scripture had a way of popping into his mind when he needed them.

Opal Dennison, soon to be Opal Beaumont since she was engaged to the preacher, beamed at him from behind one of the booths. A tall, handsome black woman, Opal carried herself with an easygoing dignity and served as matchmaker and mother confessor to half the county. Rumor had it that she'd been directly involved in hooking up not only Boone and Tara, but Hutch and Kendra Carmody, and Slade and Joslyn Barlow, as well.

A part of Walker tended to turn nervous whenever he encountered Opal—he might suddenly find himself married if he wasn't careful.

She approached as he was opening the back door of the truck and reaching in for the first box of Brylee's homemade bread.

"Mercy," Opal marveled, her eyes widening a little at the sheer bounty. "Talk about the miracle of the loaves and fishes. Without the fishes, of course."

Walker grinned at her. "Brylee got a little carried away," he said, recognizing this as an understatement of no small consequence. "Where do you want this?"

Opal pointed out a nearby booth, consisting of a portable table covered with a checkered vinyl cloth and shaded by an old patio umbrella with its pole held in place by a pyramid of cinder blocks. A charitable frown creased her forehead as she walked alongside Walker, subtly herding him from here to there in case he got lost between the truck and the backyard bake sale. "I didn't see Brylee at the wedding yesterday," she said before adding in a confidential whisper, "I worry about that girl."

Walker set the first box down on the appointed table

and started back for another. Opal stuck with him, marching along in her sensible shoes and her flowery dress, which she'd probably sewn herself.

"Me, too," he admitted, thinking admissions like that one came all too easily with Opal. She did have a way about her.

Picking up the second of three boxes brimming with wrapped and beribboned loaves, Walker raised an eyebrow and grinned. "You keeping attendance records at weddings these days, Miss Opal?" he asked.

She laughed. "I've got what you might call a photographic memory," she explained, sunlight glistening on the lenses of her old-fashioned eyeglasses. "It's a God-given gift—if anybody's missing from anywhere, I know it right away." She paused, ruminating. "It's time that sister of yours got her act together, as far as love and marriage are concerned. And *past* time she put what happened with Hutch Carmody behind her once and for all and moved on."

"I couldn't agree more," Walker said on the return trip to the booth.

"Not that you're doing all that great in the love department yourself," Opal observed, benignly forthright. "You're not getting any younger, you know. Living out there in that big house, all alone except for your sister and her dog—haven't you noticed just how happy your good friends Slade, Hutch and Boone are these days?"

"It would be hard to miss that," Walker allowed with another grin, this one slightly wicked, "what with Joslyn and Kendra coming a-crop with new babies and all."

Opal smiled widely, and mischief danced in her eyes. "That's just the way it should be," she said with confidence.

Walker set down the box of bread and returned to his truck for the last one.

Again, Opal accompanied him every step of the way, there *and* back again.

"I wouldn't dream of arguing with you, Miss Opal," Walker said as they covered the final leg of the journey.

"Good," she answered, "because you wouldn't win."

He laughed, tugged at the brim of his hat, intending to bid her farewell and get out of there, reasoning that if he headed straight for the Butter Biscuit Café, he might beat some of the after-church rush, especially since it was safe to assume a large portion of folks from the other local denominations would gravitate to the bake sale.

Opal caught hold of his shirtsleeve. "Don't you go rushing off. These other ladies and me, we could use some help setting up extra tables."

Walker suppressed a sigh. He couldn't turn Opal down—that would go against his grain and she knew it—but he did narrow his eyes at her so she'd know he had his suspicions concerning what she might be up to.

She just laughed and pointed him toward a half-assembled booth with boxes of fresh strawberries stacked all around it. It was no big surprise when Casey Elder came out of the church kitchen carrying a tray loaded with shortcake to go with the strawberries. Seeing Walker, she stopped in midstep, rummaged up a smile and then marched straight toward him.

"Hello, Walker," she said sweetly.

Walker had set his hat aside and crouched to wrestle with a table leg that refused to unfold. That put him at a physical disadvantage, the way he saw it. "Casey," he replied with a brief nod and no smile. After all, this woman and her stubborn streak had cost him the better part of a night's sleep—and not just this once, either.

Her mouth quirked up at one corner, and she cast a glance in Opal's direction before meeting his gaze again. "This must be some kind of record," she said. "Walker Parrish setting foot on church property twice in two days, I mean."

He got the table leg unjammed with a hard jerk of one hand, straightened, hat in hand. Walker rarely made small talk—there wasn't much call for it on a ranch, working with a bunch of seasoned cowboys—and he didn't have a quip at the ready.

He felt heat climb his neck and throb behind his ears.

Opal whisked over and, with a billowy flourish, spread a cotton cloth over the rickety table before vanishing again. Casey set the tray of shortcakes down with a knowing and possibly annoyed little smile.

"I'm sorry," she murmured without looking at Walker.

The interlude gave him time to recover some of his equilibrium, and he was secretly grateful, though he wasn't sure to whom. "For what?" he asked calmly. Oh, yeah, Mr. Suave-and-Sophisticated, that was him.

"Giving you a hard time just now," Casey answered, meeting his gaze but keeping her hands busy fussing with the cellophane covering all those little yellow rounds of shortcake. "It was nice of you to help with the table and everything."

Walker felt his Adam's apple travel the length of his throat and back down again, like mercury surging in a thermometer, and hoped his ears weren't glowing bright red. He was a confident man, at home in his own hide and stone-sure of his own mind, but something about this ordinary exchange made him swear he'd reverted to puberty in the space of a few moments. "That's all right," he managed, apropos of whatever. The appropriate answer, of course, would have been something along the lines of *You're welcome*.

Everything seemed to go still around him and Casey as they stood there, looking at each other in the shade of half a dozen venerable oak and maple trees, the new-mown lawn under their feet. Birds didn't sing, and the voices of the bake-sale ladies and the congregation inside the church faded to a mere hum. Right then, Walker would have bet the earth had stopped turning and the universe had ceased expanding.

There was so much he wanted, needed, to say to this woman, but his throat was immovable, like a cement mixer with its contents left to dry out and form concrete.

Fortunately—or *un*fortunately, the jury was still out on that one—church finally let out and people spilled into the yard, streaming colorfully along both sides of the building and through the rear doors, too.

It was Shane who broke the spell, jarring the whole of Creation back into a lurching motion with a happy "Hey, Walker—can you have breakfast with us, after the bake sale is over? Doris is making stacks of blueberry pancakes, and there are always too many—"

Clare appeared at her brother's side, equally insistent. "Please?" she added. "Mitch will be there, too, and he's probably planning on bugging Mom about going on the road again. You could run interference!"

Mitch Wilcox, Walker knew, was Casey's longtime manager. He'd never really liked the man, though there was no denying Wilcox was the best at what he did. Whatever that was.

Casey had regained her composure—if she'd ever lost it—while Walker was still trying to get his vocal cords to come unstuck.

"You'd be welcome," she said, gently amused, her smile making Walker feel light-headed and very much off his game. "And you *don't* have to 'run interference.' I can handle Mitch Wilcox just fine." With that, she sent a mildly reproving glance in Clare's direction, but the girl was undaunted, all her attention focused on Walker's face.

"Say you'll be there," Clare wheedled, guilelessly wily.

"Yeah," Shane put in. "'Cause if I have to eat your share of the pancakes on top of mine, I'll probably puke or something."

"Shane," Casey warned sweetly, "this is no place for that kind of talk."

"Sorry," Shane said, clearly unrepentant.

Walker knew it would be better to refuse the invitation, especially since it hadn't been Casey's idea, but, looking into the hopeful faces of his children, he couldn't bring himself to say no. "All right," he said gruffly, finding that his voice had gathered some rust in the past few minutes.

"The bake sale will wind up in an hour or so," Casey said. "After that, we'll be heading for home, and Doris will be ready to put brunch on the table." She checked her watch, the plastic kind sold from kiosks in shopping malls. "Stop by around one-thirty?" she concluded.

Walker nodded and was just turning to walk away when he nearly collided with a smiling Patsy McCullough. Her young daughter wasn't in evidence, but Dawson was beside her, seated in his wheelchair, grinning up at Walker. Just behind Patsy's right shoulder stood Treat McQuillan, Parable's chief of police and most irritating citizen.

The look that passed between Walker and Treat was deadly, though brief.

Once upon a time, when he was still working as a sheriff's deputy, Treat had crossed a line by putting a hand on Brylee in the Boot Scoot Tavern, demanding that she dance with him.

She'd indicated that she'd rather not, but Treat hadn't taken no for an answer. He'd made the mistake of trying to drag Walker's kid sister onto the small dance floor, really just a table-free space in front of the jukebox, since the establishment was nothing fancy, and Walker had clocked him for it. For a while afterward, Treat had made a lot of noise about pressing assault charges against an officer of the law, but in the end, he and Walker had come to a gentlemen's agreement, the details of which Walker couldn't exactly recall. Treat hadn't filed a complaint with his boss, Boone Taylor, and he'd mostly kept himself out of Walker's way.

None of which meant he wasn't as sneaky as a rattlesnake curled up in a woodpile, ready to strike when the right opportunity presented itself.

Dawson, a handsome kid with dark hair and inquisitive blue eyes, broke the silence by asking, "When can I come out to Timber Creek and ride a horse again?"

Out of the corner of his eye, Walker saw a stricken look cross Patsy's thin face.

"You just say the word, cowboy," Walker said to the boy, hoping his smile covered the sorrow he felt whenever he thought of the way Dawson had been before he'd climbed that damn water tower and fallen nearly fifty feet, doing permanent damage to his spine.

"You know he can't ride a horse," Treat growled. As always, he was on the peck, beating the brush for something he could get all riled up over.

Patsy, a plain, hard-worn woman in a cotton dress, eased herself between Treat and Walker and offered up a feeble smile. "What Treat means is," she warbled nervously, "we wouldn't want Dawson to get hurt—"

Dawson groaned angrily.

"Patsy," Walker said, ignoring McQuillan the way he ignored flies when he was shoveling out stalls, "I wouldn't let anything happen to your boy. You can be sure of it."

"I know," Patsy allowed after a fleeting glance over her shoulder to gauge the heat of her escort's temper, followed by a longer, softer look down at her son. It was clear that she loved the boy, felt torn between protecting her child and letting him spread his wings as far as their limited span permitted. "I guess it would be all right," she went on, still focused on Dawson. "As long as Mr. Parrish was right there with you the whole time and all."

Dawson's face, cloudy before, busted loose with a dazzling smile. *"Yes!"* he said, punching the air with one triumphant fist.

Walker, who had been holding his hat until then, carefully placed it on his head, gave the brim a slight pull for Patsy's benefit, a tacit signal that he was done here and he'd be going on his way now. Treat simmered behind her, but for once he had the good sense not to offer an opinion.

"I'll be in touch in the next few days," Walker said, grinning down at Dawson.

"Thanks," Dawson replied, almost breathless. "I'll be waiting to hear from you."

Walker said goodbye and meandered through the milling congregation, making his way back to his truck. He had just short of ninety minutes to kill before turning up at Casey's place for the pancake feed, but he wasn't about to pass them hanging around a bake sale.

CASEY SMILED AND served strawberry shortcake to a long line of eager customers, Clare obligingly squirting canned whipped cream on each plateful before handing it over, Shane making change from a cigar box balanced on the seat of a folding chair.

By the time the sale was over—the men of the congregation had been volunteered by their wives to clean up afterward and stow away the folding tables and other gear, since the women had done most of the baking and selling—Casey was more than ready to go home, have a few unhurried cups of coffee and enjoy another of Doris's incomparable Sunday brunches.

And never mind that the pit of her stomach felt jittery, hungry as she was, because Walker would be joining them.

It was crazy—she'd had two children by the man, after all, and though they hadn't been intimate in a long time, there was no part of her body Walker Parrish didn't know his way around—but she was as jumpy as a wallflower suddenly elected prom queen.

Walker had that effect on her, even now.

"So what's this about needing somebody to keep Mitch from talking me into booking another concert tour?" she asked when she and the kids were buckled into their respective seats in her unassuming blue

SUV and rolling in the direction of Rodeo Road. "In the first place, I gave you two my word I'd stay off the road until further notice, and, in the *second* place, I've never, in my whole entire life, had any trouble standing up to Mitch Wilcox or anybody else."

Clare, whose turn it was to ride shotgun, flicked a glance at the rearview mirror, the next best thing to making eye contact with her brother, seated in back. The exchange wasn't exactly guilty, Casey noted with some amusement, but there was clearly some collusion going on there. Considering last night's row in the upstairs corridor, by no means an unusual occurrence, unfortunately, it was almost a relief that brother and sister seemed to be on the same page, however briefly.

Neither of them spoke, though.

Casey sighed, keeping her eyes on the road ahead. By now, she knew every street in Parable and most of the ones in Three Trees, too, to the point that she could have driven them in her sleep, but you never knew when somebody might run a stop sign, or a dog might dash out into the road.

Careerwise, Casey was a card-carrying risk taker, but when it came to her children, she didn't take chances.

Unless you counted lying to them for their whole lives, she thought with a slight wince.

"Fess up," she said. "What's going on here?"

"Walker looked like he might say no," Clare finally answered. "To breakfast, I mean."

"Ah," Casey said knowingly. The knowing routine was sometimes an act; her kids were smart, and they confounded her more often than she'd have liked to admit. This time, though, she would have had to be in a coma not to pick up on their motivation.

"You could have invited him yourself," Shane put in, addressing his mother and sounding slightly put out, as though he thought she'd been remiss. "It wouldn't kill you to be nice to Walker, you know."

Casey waited, sure there was more and unwilling to share her suspicion that being too nice to Walker Parrish might *well* kill her, because he had the power to break her heart.

"Did you see Walker talking to Dawson McCullough?" Shane asked, still fretful. "I heard him say Dawson could come out to the ranch and ride horses with him."

A pang struck Casey's heart. Did Shane envy the attention Walker had paid the other boy?

"I saw," Clare told her brother, none too sympathetically. "Get over it, dweeb. Dawson's in a *wheelchair,* in case you missed that, and he used to work for Walker sometimes, before he got hurt. They're friends."

Casey let the "dweeb" remark pass, and Shane maintained a glum and resentful silence the rest of the way home.

When they pulled into the driveway, Mitch Wilcox's rental car, a white compact, was parked beside the guest cottage, and he was already lugging suitcases over the threshold.

How long, Casey wondered, was her manager planning to stick around? He'd called to say he'd like to "drop by," and once he'd emailed his arrival time—Mitch had flown in from Nashville—Casey had replied that she and the kids would be out when he got to Parable, but she'd leave the key to the cottage under the doormat. He was to go ahead and make himself at home.

Evidently, he'd taken her at her word. From the looks

of his luggage, he wasn't just making himself at home; he was moving in.

Yikes.

Twenty years older than Casey and several times divorced, Mitch was still an attractive man, with his tall, graceful frame and full head of silver-gray hair. It would be easy enough to figure him for a catch, Casey supposed, provided you didn't know him the way she did.

He set his bags down and waved as Casey parked the SUV. The kids got out of the rig immediately. Shane sprinted toward the house so he could let the dogs out to run in the yard for a while. Clare approached Mitch with one hand gracefully extended, like a princess welcoming a visiting dignitary.

Casey walked slowly behind her daughter, nervous now that Mitch had actually arrived. Most of the time, when he made plans to visit, he had an agenda—an offer to appear in a TV movie, perhaps, or some other "huge" opportunity she'd be a fool to turn down, but he was also prone to canceling his travel plans at the last minute. She'd hoped this would be one of those times, and for all the bravado she'd shown in the car, for the kids' benefit, she was uneasy.

Mitch wasn't one of the most successful managers in the music business because he wasn't persuasive. The man could sell sand in Morocco or mosquitos in Minnesota. And she was feeling oddly vulnerable just now.

"Try to contain your enthusiasm," he teased, planting a light kiss on Casey's cheek. "I'm the bearer of good news."

Casey smiled and folded her arms, then wished she hadn't. Folded arms were classic body language for *Don't convince me, I'm feeling too convincible,* and

Mitch was more than shrewd enough to read her. In fact, he was a master at it.

"Get settled in," she said cordially. "Doris is back from church by now, and she's about to start stacking serious numbers of pancakes."

Mitch laughed. "Wonderful," he said. "I'm starved. They served three peanuts, two broken pretzels and a cup of bad coffee on the plane—and that was in first class."

"Poor you," Clare said, linking her arm with Mitch's. During the years on the road, he'd been like a grandfather to Casey's kids, and they were both fond of him, though not in the way they were of Walker.

Another tide of guilt washed through Casey's beleaguered soul with that thought. What would her children say, what would they think of her, if they ever found out that Walker, the man they adored, was their father? On one level, they'd both be thrilled, she surmised, believing, as they did now, that they didn't have a dad at all. And then they'd be furious—with her. She'd been the secret keeper, the villain of the piece, the one who'd raised them on lies, however well-intentioned. The one who'd robbed them of what they probably wanted most—a father.

She must have turned a little pale just then, because Mitch narrowed his wise blue eyes at her and asked with concern, "Are you feeling all right?"

Clare was already tugging Mitch toward the house. Mostly, she was eager to get out of her church clothes and into shorts and a T-shirt.

The three dogs clamored across the sunporch floor and shot down the steps like fur-covered bullets, overjoyed by the heady return of freedom and the presence of their significant humans.

"I'm fine," Casey said, moving to head off the dogs. If she hadn't, they'd have knocked poor Mitch to the ground in their exuberance.

Mitch looked skeptical, but he didn't refute her statement.

Doris, who attended a different church, was back in her regular clothes and all smiles and bustling busyness. She'd set the big table on the sunporch with fine china and the best crystal, and well-polished silverware gleamed at each place.

"Walker's coming to breakfast, too," Clare said happily. "I'll get another place setting."

With that, she zipped into the kitchen, and Casey indulged in a proud moment, because her children hadn't been raised to expect Doris or anyone else to wait on them or do their bidding. They cleaned their own rooms and washed their own clothes, for instance, though Shane was admittedly less of a laundry expert than his sister.

Doris said hello to Mitch and gave Casey a wry look. "Walker, is it?" she asked. "Imagine."

Casey wondered, not for the first time, how much her cook/housekeeper had guessed over the years, and looked away quickly, pretending to straighten the perfect bouquet of spring flowers in the center of the table.

"Do my eyes deceive me," Mitch inquired, "or did I actually see a genuine merry-go-round in the yard?"

Doris had already hurried back to the kitchen, and Clare returned with a plate, silverware and a glass for Walker, which she carefully placed, Casey noted, opposite the place where she normally sat.

"We had a wedding reception here yesterday," Clare chirped in explanation. Miraculously, in the short time she'd been out of sight, she'd swapped out her dress for denim shorts and a tank top—probably raiding the laundry room and changing there. "Mom likes to make sure the little kids have something fun to do whenever she entertains."

Outside, wheels ground up the gravel driveway. The dogs barked out a happy chorus, and Shane called out his usual "Hey, Walker!"

Clare abandoned the table to rush out and join the welcoming party.

Mitch, meanwhile, arched one neatly trimmed gray eyebrow and remarked quietly, "I *wondered* if he wasn't part of the reason you decided to settle in Podunk, Montana."

Casey blushed. "He's a friend," she said, sounding more defensive than she might have wished. "A *good* friend."

Something sad moved in Mitch's eyes, there for a millisecond and then gone again. "Yes," he said, almost sighing the word.

Casey watched through the screen enclosing the sunporch on three sides as her children and the dogs ushered Walker toward the house, surrounding him like an entourage. Both Clare and Shane chattered fit to wear off his ears, but he didn't seem to mind. In fact, he looked as happy as they did.

Casey's stomach clenched, a not entirely unpleasant sensation but an alarming one nonetheless.

If—*when*—the secret was out, Clare and Shane wouldn't blame Walker for the deception. They'd place the onus on Casey herself, and rightfully so. Dread filled her, even as the old, ill-advised excitement sang in her veins and made her nerve endings crackle. Had she been lying so long that she didn't recognize the truth when she encountered it?

She *wanted* Walker Parrish, and not just as a friend, either. She wanted him as a man, as a lover. Heat surged through her as she remembered their times together, alone and lost in each other while the world flowed on past, like some oblivious river.

Walker looked up just at that moment—luck wouldn't have had it any other way, Casey figured sadly—and when their glances connected, the planet slipped off its axis for the length of a heartbeat.

She went to the screen door, opened it and smiled her most cordial smile, the one she wore for guests and special fans. "You made it," she said, that being country for *hello*.

Walker's smile, slow and cowboy-confident, made her heart skitter. "Good to see you again, Casey," he said, as though it had been days or even years since they'd last met, instead of an hour and a half.

The kids and the dogs and Walker all spilled onto the sunporch, forming a crowd.

Walker looked at Mitch.

Mitch looked at Walker.

And, finally, the two men shook hands.

Was she imagining it, Casey asked herself, or had she just heard the sound of antlers locking in combat?

CHAPTER FOUR

CASEY FELT AS jumpy as a cat crossing a hot griddle, with Walker seated across the sunporch table from her, consuming a respectable stack of Doris's pancakes, Shane at his left elbow, Clare at his right. Both kids actively jockeyed for his attention, and he managed to strike a remarkably diplomatic balance, taking in every word of their chatter and weighing it all, somewhere behind those calm green-gray eyes of his.

Poor Mitch might have been invisible, at least as far as Clare and Shane were concerned, and they didn't spare their mom a whole lot of notice, either.

Casey wasn't bothered by this—she understood their yearning to connect with this man they didn't know was their father—but the guilt was another matter. She'd always been able to rationalize keeping the secret, out there on the road, far from Walker and the place he called home, but now she didn't have a constant round of concert tours and other distractions to serve as buffers. The reality of what she had cost these children, and this man, all the while thinking she was doing the right thing, keeping them safe, was now up close and personal, in her face, a table's width away. Denial, she realized, required distance—in close proximity to Walker, she might as well have been trying to spin plates on top of long sticks.

Once, amid the chatter of his children, Walker looked over at her, caught her gaze and held it, somehow making it impossible for her to look away. And what she saw in his eyes only reinforced the conclusion she'd already reached: that there was a crisis coming, an inevitable collision of deception and truth, and there *would* be casualties. That she stood directly in the line of fire was a given—and the least of her worries. Casey's greatest concern was the havoc this revelation would wreak in the lives of her children and, yes, in Walker's, too.

Yet again, the question pealed in her heart like sorrowing church bells announcing a funeral: *What have I done?*

Exhibiting surprising sensitivity, Mitch, sitting beside Casey at the table, reached over to squeeze her hand lightly. Another person, she thought with a stab of regret, who hadn't been fooled. Mitch—and how many other people?—must have known all along that Walker was more than a family friend. Very possibly, her longtime manager had merely been pretending to believe Casey's claims that the children's fathers were anonymous donors. He'd been willing, for whatever reason, to play a small part in her private soap opera.

An achy warmth enfolded her heart just then, and she gave Mitch a grateful glance, which he acknowledged with a wink.

"So can we, Mom?" Shane's eager voice jarred Casey back into the present moment. "Please?"

Flustered, Casey felt color bloom in her cheeks. She'd missed whatever had been said before, and now everyone at the table would know she hadn't been listening.

Walker came to her rescue in a way so offhand and easy that she could have kissed him—which, of course, was something she'd already been obsessing about anyway, for very different reasons. "We'll head out to the ranch and do some horseback riding," he recapped, "and I'll bring the kids back here after supper, if that's okay with you."

Casey swallowed, offered a wobbly smile and a nod of assent. If she'd heard the original request, she might well have refused it, if only to avoid being alone with her manager for a while longer. She wasn't afraid of Mitch, far from it, but she didn't feel like her usual scrappy self, either. Whatever he planned to propose—Mitch never showed up when she was off the road without a specific reason, generally one that would fatten his fee—she would honestly consider, and probably refuse. She knew her mind, and she was certainly no pushover, but the exchange was going to take more emotional energy than she could spare at the moment.

Both Shane and Clare cheered uproariously now that she'd given her permission, drowning out any possibility of conversation, and all three dogs got to their feet, suddenly alert, barking out a chorus of canine excitement.

"Can they come, too?" Shane asked Walker, big-eyed with hope, referring, of course, to the Labs.

"Sure," Walker said gruffly. How could anyone miss the love in his face, in the roughness of his voice, as he returned his son's gaze? And how had *she* managed to ignore the wide-open spaces of Walker's heart—a heart big-sky expansive enough to hold not just his children, but a trio of chocolate Labs clamoring to join the festivities?

By comparison, Casey thought sadly, she was the Grinch, with a ticker the size of a walnut.

Chaos reigned as the meal ended and Clare and Shane rushed to clear the table and load the dishwasher—always their shared responsibility—each racing to be the first one finished, evidently, laughing and elbowing each other out of the way, good-naturedly for once. The dogs, clueless but wild with delight, only increased the mayhem.

"This is giving me a headache," Mitch said, quickly retreating to the guesthouse.

On the one hand, Casey was glad he'd gone, because it was hard enough to think with Walker sitting there looking so unspeakably good, the dogs barking, the kids carrying on. On the other, though, she was, however briefly, alone with Walker.

And that sparked a kind of delicious terror inside her.

"You and I need to talk," he told her quietly, in a tone that held regret as well as finality. "Soon."

Casey's heart had shimmied up into the back of her throat and lodged itself there, beating so hard that she felt submerged in the sound of blood pumping in her ears. She merely nodded, unable to speak.

Walker's expression was not unkind, but it was obvious, from his tone of voice, that he wasn't going to give an inch of ground, either. He'd reached critical mass, the proverbial hundredth monkey, and this time there would be no going back, no reasoning with him, no changing his mind.

He meant to claim Clare and Shane as his own, once and for all, and publicly, whether she wanted him to or not.

Once the children and the dogs had all been loaded into Walker's pickup truck, the figurative floodwaters slowly subsided, and Casey could, at last, hear herself think.

She brewed a cup of tea and went downstairs to the soundstage, turning on a single lamp, the only light in the huge room besides the green, blue, yellow and red LEDs blinking back at her from various pieces of high-tech equipment.

Casey opened the battered guitar case she'd first glimpsed under a glittering Christmas tree when she was still a child herself, reverently lifted out the instrument on which she'd played her first, stumbling chords, picked out the initial uncertain notes, made her earliest attempts at composing songs. Eventually, after many incarnations, some of those tunes had become hits, catapulting her to fame.

Remarkable.

The guitar fit comfortably in her arms, and she smiled sadly as she looked down at the open case—both Clare and Shane had taken backstage naps in that unlikely cradle, as tiny babies, bundled in denim jackets on loan from the band or the roadies, nestled among rolled-up souvenir T-shirts or blankets brought in from the bus.

Remembering, Casey's heart turned over again.

She began to play softly, feeling her way into the sweet flow of music that had always been her solace, her hiding place. Even before she'd learned to play the guitar or any other instrument, she'd sung along with the radio or her grandparents' stereo system. According to family lore, she'd tackled singing first, and talking later on.

There, in the music, her private refuge, if only for a

little while, she lost her fears and her worries and her doubts, and her everyday self with them.

THE TRUCK WAS a rolling uproar—both kids talking at once, the dogs scrambling to change places every few minutes, like some canine version of the Keystone Cops—the wind whipping past open windows and swirling inside to jumble it all into primordial chaos.

Walker loved it, but his delight in Shane and Clare's company was bittersweet, too. In a few hours, it would be time to say goodbye and take them back to their mother and her world, the one they knew so well—and he had no place in.

It was something of a relief to see Brylee's rig parked in the driveway when they pulled in at the ranch house—Walker, grimly independent all his life, suddenly felt the need for his sister's moral support.

She stood on the steps of the side porch, blue-jeaned and wearing a flannel shirt over a T-shirt, battered boots on her feet, her smile as wide as the Big Sky River that flowed through Parable, through the middle of Three Trees, and rolled on by Timber Creek Ranch, in a hurry to reach the distant coast. Her dog sat obediently at her side, tilting his large head to the right, ears perked in curiosity as he took a silent roll call and found himself up two kids and three dogs from the norm.

Walker had no more than stopped the truck when Shane and Clare both tumbled out, hitting the ground running like just-thrown riders racing for the fence at the rodeo, with a pissed-off bull hot on their heels. The Labs, quieter now, followed, probably trying to gauge Snidely as friend or foe.

Brylee met the kids halfway, and the three of them

ended up in a huddle hug, laughing and jumping around like happy fools on a trampoline.

Walker hung back, taking it all in. It was a scene he wanted to remember, etch into his heart and mind, so he could come back to it when he felt the need, and savor the sight and the sounds.

Snidely greeted the Labs with some sniffing and some cautious tail wagging and, as quickly as that, the dogs were all friends. They dashed off to explore the wonders of a genuine barnyard on a genuine ranch, Brylee's faithful German shepherd leading the pack.

Brylee's eyes were gleaming with happy tears when the hugging and jumping finally subsided long enough for everybody to catch their breath.

"What a terrific surprise!" She beamed, apparently crediting Walker with the working of this particular miracle.

Brylee loved Clare and Shane; she considered them her honorary niece and nephew—if only she knew— kept their most recent pictures taped to the refrigerator in her apartment kitchen, was forever sending them texts or emails or small gifts.

"Opal said to thank you for all that bread," Walker told his glowing sister, oddly uncomfortable in the face of all that joy.

"Every single bit of it got sold!" Clare put in. "Mom said the bake sale took in a small fortune."

"Good," Brylee said, slipping one arm around Clare's shoulders and one around Shane's and giving them each a squeeze. Her eyes were full of questions, though, as she studied Walker's face.

"We're going riding," Shane said to Brylee. "Will you come with us?"

Brylee, still looking at Walker, raised one eyebrow in silent question.

"Absolutely," Walker said. When, he wondered, was the last time he'd seen Brylee looking so happy?

Anyhow, they all ended up in the barn, choosing which horses they wanted to ride—Walker steered the kids toward the gentler ones—saddling up, leading the animals out into the penny-bright sunshine of a Sunday afternoon in summer.

Brylee, like Walker, had been riding since before she could walk or talk, but as far as he knew, she hadn't done more than groom her trusty black-and-white pinto gelding, Toby, in months. She'd told Walker once, in a weak moment, that some things, like certain kinds of music and the company of her horse, touched places so raw inside her that she had to back away.

Recalling this, Walker was heartened to watch his sister instructing Clare and Shane, who were fair riders but lacking in experience, as easy in the saddle as if she'd been born there. This was the old, spirited, devil-take-the-hindmost Brylee, the one Walker knew best and loved without reservation.

With Brylee leading the way, Clare alongside on Tessie, the four of them headed for the foothills rippling at the base of Big Sky Mountain like ruffles on a fancy skirt. Walker followed on Mack, while Shane bounced cheerfully beside him, riding chubby, mild-mannered Smokey.

The four dogs brought up the rear, behaving themselves and sticking close to the band of horses and riders, though not so close they were in danger of being kicked or trampled.

"This is great!" Shane said enthusiastically, his backside slapping hard against the saddle as Brylee eased Toby into a slow trot and the other horses followed suit.

Walker laughed. "You're going to be mighty sore tomorrow if you don't get in rhythm with that horse," he told his son.

His son. He wanted to shout it from the mountaintop: *my daughter, my son, my children.*

"I'm *trying,*" Shane answered, smiling fit to light up the whole county.

Walker showed him how to stand up in the stirrups—sometimes that helped a rider get in step, so to speak, with his mount—but the boy's legs weren't quite long enough to reach.

When they got to the creek, some fifteen minutes later, Walker got off Mack, walked over to Smokey and adjusted the stirrups to suit Shane.

"I guess I'm sort of out of practice," Shane said, keeping his voice low so Brylee and Clare, who were having a fine old time girling it up, wouldn't overhear.

"That'll be easy to fix," Walker assured him. "It's been a while since you and your sister came for a visit, after all, and my guess is, you haven't had many opportunities to ride horses in the meantime."

Shane studied him solemnly, swallowed once. "I wouldn't mind being here more often," he said, choosing his words with such obvious care that Walker's heart hurt a little. "If you wanted me—us—Clare and me, I mean, hanging around and stuff."

Careful, Walker counseled himself, because his most powerful instinct was to gather the boy in his arms, tell him how much he wanted Shane and Clare to play bigger parts in his life. How very much he wanted to tell them they were his, try his damnedest to make up for lost time, hear the world call them by their rightful surname, which was Parrish, not Elder.

"You can hang around as much as your mom will allow," Walker finally replied. "How's that?"

"She'll say you're busy and we'll be underfoot," Shane answered with bleak certainty.

Walker's throat hurt. He cleared it, in order to speak. "I reckon that part of it is my call," he said cautiously. Then, after a long pause, he added, "Suppose I have a talk with her?"

Shane brightened, but his delight faded as quickly as it had appeared. "You can try," he said. "Mom's pretty hardheaded, though. Everybody says so."

Walker chuckled, a rusty sound, saw-toothed enough to draw blood, the way it felt coming out. "That's true," he allowed gently, "but I reckon she's had to be a bit on the hardheaded side to raise you and your sister into the people you are, and build a world-class career at the same time."

Shane appeared to consider this, but in the end, Walker suspected, the finer points went over his head. He was only thirteen, after all, in that in-between place, neither boy nor man, an ever-changing sketch of the person he would become as he grew to manhood. "I guess," he said, sounding unsure.

"Are we going to ride or stand around and yammer?" Brylee interceded, the smile on her face seeping into her voice. She hadn't dismounted, and neither had Clare.

Walker laughed, shook his head and swung back up into the saddle, the reins resting loosely across his right palm. "You ready?" he asked Shane in a quiet aside.

Shane nodded, proud and determined. "Ready," he confirmed.

They rode for another hour, until the dogs started lagging behind, tongues lolling, signaling that, as Walker's dad used to say, they'd had about all the fun they could stand for one afternoon.

Back at the barn, Brylee and Clare continued to chatter while they unsaddled their horses and put them away in their stalls. They talked while they brushed the animals, too, and the whole time they were feeding them.

"How come women talk so much?" Shane asked innocently. He and Walker had been performing the same tasks as Brylee and Clare right along, but only a few words had passed between them. It wasn't that there wasn't anything to say—working together, side by side, was its own kind of communication, rendering speech unnecessary.

"I have no idea," Walker answered in all honesty. "I guess females are just wired that way."

"Maybe," Shane agreed. "Mike—that's my mom's lead guitarist—says girls think if things get too quiet, somebody's mad at them."

Walker weighed the pros and cons of that theory. "That's a little on the simplistic side, I think," he said. "My guess is, strong women—like your mom and Brylee and Clare—don't worry too much about whether or not anybody's mad at them. They're too busy doing the things they figure they ought to get done."

Shane nodded thoughtfully, and Walker would have given a lot to know what was going on in the boy's mind just then. What had it been like for him, on the road with Casey and the band for most of his young life? Had he ever felt scared, facing new places and new people at every turn? Did he ever wish he could just light somewhere, attend regular school, make friends and play on the softball or soccer team?

He didn't really know Shane, or Clare, for that matter, and that realization, oft-visited though it was, shook him, made him feel wistful and pissed off and a whole passel of other things, too. He clamped his jaw down tight so he wouldn't say it, wouldn't blurt out the facts. While it was probably right, the claim that the truth set people free, it was *equally* true that it could scorch the earth, destroying everything in its path, leaving nothing but rubble in its wake. It could break hearts.

Maybe, he reflected glumly, it was already too late to rectify the situation without doing more harm than good.

He was fairly sure Casey believed exactly that—and she might be right.

"Spaghetti for supper?" Brylee asked when the horses were taken care of. Two ranch hands were already busy feeding the rest of the livestock and attending to other end-of-the-day chores.

The kids approved of the suggestion loudly and with vigor, but Walker remained pensive, thinking of all the time they'd wasted, he and Casey and the kids. And while he figured he could love the woman if he was ever fool enough to trust her that much, right about then, if she'd been handy, he'd have read her the riot act from start to finish, and then started all over again just in case she'd missed anything.

Whatever happened between him and Casey, Walker thought, he was through playing games, through watching from the sidelines while his children grew up, through with the lies and the pretending and all the other bullshit.

If the four of them—he and Casey, Clare and Shane—couldn't be a family, well, so be it. It wasn't an uncommon problem, in the modern world—folks dealt with it, did the best they could.

All Walker could have said for sure as he fed and watered all four dogs on the side porch, the sounds of laughter and cooking and table-setting rolling out through the screen door between there and the kitchen, was that he was *done* doing this Casey's way.

Yes, there would be consequences. He'd just have to find a way to work through them, the way a man worked through a hard winter or a long-term heartache.

MITCH FOUND HER, eventually, probably drawn by the faint strains of her guitar and a song that wouldn't quite come together.

Companionably, Casey's manager sat down on the bottom step, rested his elbows on his knees and his chin in one palm.

"You and the cowboy," he began. "Is it serious?"

Casey stopped playing, placed her guitar gently back in its case, lowered the lid and snapped it closed. "By 'the cowboy,'" she replied, "I assume you mean Walker?"

"Don't try to throw me off, Case," Mitch said with a note of sadness in his voice. "We've known each other too long for that."

Casey looked away. "Walker is a—friend," she said, because the first person she told about her relationship with Walker was *not* going to be Mitch Wilcox, no matter how much she respected him and appreciated all he'd done for her over the years. No, Clare and Shane had to hear what she had to say before anyone else and, after them, Brylee. This was, after all, a family matter.

"If you say so," Mitch agreed, still seated on the stairs. Out of the corner of her eye, Casey saw him spread his hands in a gesture of helpless acceptance. "I'm not here to talk about Walker Parrish."

"You could have fooled me," Casey replied sweetly, though the joke fell a little flat, flopping between them like a fish out of water.

"I care about you, Casey," Mitch went on in a concessionary tone. "And about the kids, of course." With Mitch, Clare and Shane were always an afterthought. A logistical problem. "That's why I'm here—in Parable, I mean."

She looked straight at him then, dread leaking into her soul through the holes in her heart. "What?" she asked, somewhat stupidly.

"I care about you," Mitch repeated.

A silence fell, very awkward and pulsing with all sorts of nebulous meaning.

"I care about you, too," Casey finally replied.

Mitch seemed to relax slightly, and a grin spread across his face. "Then maybe there's a chance," he said.

"A chance for what?" Casey had no clue, though later she would reflect that she ought to have known where this conversation was headed. In some ways, she'd always been aware of the undercurrent in her association with Mitch.

He looked affably hurt. "I know you're not in love with me," he said carefully, "but I'm proposing all the same. You're tired and burned out, Casey. You need someone to take care of *you* for a change."

She blinked, unable to believe what she was hearing. Yes, she'd suspected once or twice that Mitch had a "thing" for her, but it came and went. Every few years, he got married, then divorced, then married again. Each time that happened, she'd shaken her head in confused concern, but she'd never entertained the idea of joining the lineup.

"You're a good friend, Mitch," Casey said, trying to be gentle and, at the same time, firm. "I'm grateful for all you've done for me, careerwise, but you're right, I don't love you."

"Love is overrated," Mitch offered with a casualness she knew he was putting on for the sake of his pride. "Where has the fantasy of happily-ever-after gotten you so far, Casey? Two children, no husband—all the money and fame in the world can't make up for the loneliness you're bound to feel when Clare and Shane grow up and go off to live their own lives."

Casey blinked. *Where has the fantasy of happily-ever-after gotten you so far, Casey?* Was Mitch implying that she'd been in love before and wound up with a broken heart? True or not, that was private turf—no trespassing allowed.

"Where has *what* gotten me so far?" she demanded, feeling testy and dizzy and very disoriented, as though she'd wandered onto the set of a play with a worldwide audience and didn't know her lines. This was the stuff of her nightmares—going onstage, finding herself unable to sing or play her guitar or even think.

"Let's take the gloves off," Mitch said with a lightness that made her want to cross the room and slap him across the face—hard. "I know Walker Parrish is the father of your children, Casey—" He paused, raised both hands, palms out. "Don't deny it, please. Shane looks just like him, and Clare bears a resemblance, too, though you have to look more closely to see it."

"I don't believe this," Casey said, although she *did* believe it. Like Job, the thing she had most feared had come upon her. "That's just—speculation, Mitch. *Dangerous* speculation. What do you think gossip like that could do to Shane and Clare?"

Mitch simply looked at her for a long moment, his expression maddeningly tolerant and even gentle. "Stop," he said. "I'm not going to blow your cover, Casey—I love you, and I love the kids. But after all the years we've worked together, I think I deserve the truth."

"I think you need to leave now," Casey said evenly.

"I'm not going anywhere," Mitch replied flatly and without rancor. "Not before you agree to marry me, anyway."

She gaped at him. "Marry you?"

"It's not as if I'm the Elephant Man or the Incredible Hulk," Mitch pointed out. "I've been your partner, Casey. Your mentor and your advisor and, most important, your friend. Maybe I can't offer passion and all that other fairy-tale malarkey, but I understand you. And I can give you companionship, security, a good name—"

"A *good name?*" Casey broke in, incensed. She'd come in for her share of trash talk, having two children without benefit of marriage, but she was damned if she'd apologize for doing her honest best. Besides, this was *her* business, not Mitch's. Friend or not, he didn't have the right to pry or make judgments—especially not with *his* marital track record.

"Maybe I could have been more tactful," Mitch allowed.

"I doubt it," Casey observed sharply. She was glad

she'd put her cherished guitar away, because if she hadn't, she might have been tempted to smash it over Mitch's head. "No, Mitch. That's my answer. *No*. And, furthermore, I'd appreciate it if we could pretend this conversation never took place."

"In that case," Mitch said, looking broken, "perhaps this is the time to offer my resignation as your manager."

"That might be for the best," Casey said, shaking on the inside, solid on the outside. If it hadn't been for Mitch, she might never have gotten past playing in cheap bars and opening for loser bands in third-rate venues, yet while she certainly owed him a debt of gratitude, she did *not* owe him her soul.

Mitch said nothing after that. He simply set his jaw, got to his feet and headed back up the stairs. Fifteen minutes later, after she'd crept into the vast kitchen to brew another cup of tea with shaky hands, Casey heard the rental car start up and saw her old friend driving away—probably for good.

"Oh, hell," she told the two cats curling around her ankles. They kept a low profile when the dogs were around, but invariably appeared when Casey needed comforting.

Doris opened her apartment door. "Did you say something, dear?" she asked.

Chagrined, Casey shook her head, managed a lame smile. "That was a lovely breakfast you prepared for us," she said. "Thank you."

Doris looked benevolently suspicious. "Are you all right?"

"Why do you ask?" Casey retorted, teasing. "Because I complimented you on your cooking skills?"

"No," Doris said, "because Mitch Wilcox just drove out of here like the devil himself was on his tail, and I haven't seen hide nor hair of Clare or Shane since breakfast. The dogs, either."

Casey felt her shoulders slump a little. "The kids are with Walker," she admitted, "and the dogs went along for the ride."

"I see," Doris replied, her tone and expression annoyingly cryptic.

No, you don't see, Casey wanted to argue, knowing all the while that she didn't have a leg to stand on. *I'm about to lose the two most important people in my life, possibly forever, and I've got nobody to blame but myself.*

"I'm *fine,*" she said instead.

"Of course you are, dear," Doris agreed charitably and without a shred of sincerity. "Do you need anything? Because if you don't, I'll just watch my Sunday-night programs and then turn in early. Mondays are always crazy around here."

From Casey's viewpoint, *every* day was crazy around Casa-Too-Grande, but it was a good kind of crazy.

"Good night," Casey said.

Doris replied in kind and ducked back into her private quarters, closing the door softly behind her.

Casey stood in the middle of her massive kitchen, in the heart of her massive house, and felt as bereft as a lone polar bear on an ice floe. Was this what it all came down to—after all her work and her struggles, all her hoping and believing, all her trying and failing and trying again?

Loneliness was loneliness, after all, even in the midst of luxury.

Basically, it was the story of her life. As a child, she'd rattled around in her grandparents' stately pile, haunting the vast, echoing rooms like a little ghost searching for the doorway to heaven. If it hadn't been for Lupe, the housekeeper, and Juan, the gardener as well as Lupe's devoted husband, he of the whistling expertise, she might have gone days without anyone saying a word to her.

How was it that she'd come so far, only to wind up right back where she'd started?

CHAPTER FIVE

THE CRITTER, SITTING forlorn and slat-ribbed in front of the supermarket, well away from the automatic doors, looked like a wad of dryer lint with legs and eyeballs. Walker, parking his truck, considered the dog as he shut off the engine and got out, noticing how people came and went without so much as a glance in the animal's direction. Even in a good place like Parable, some folks had a tendency to look the other way, pretending they didn't see a problem when they didn't have a solution handy.

Walker Parrish, for better and sometimes for worse, was constitutionally incapable of turning his back on trouble—the old man had seen to that, not by preaching, but by saying a few well-placed words and setting an example. *When you see trouble, boy,* Barclay always said, *don't you walk away thinking someone else will deal with it. Roll up your sleeves, put some steel in your spine and wade in.*

So, having no other choice—at least, not one he could live with—Walker approached the stray slowly, careful not to startle it. From the looks of him, this fella had already experienced his fair share of trouble, and more besides.

"Hey, there, lintball," he said affably, keeping his distance.

The dog scooched—Brylee's word, apt in this instance—backward on his skinny hind end, as if trying to hide himself in the shadows between the blue-metal mailbox and the DVD vending machine, probably expecting to be kicked or chased off, or both.

"You sure are ugly," Walker commented, still as a pond on a windless day, his gaze fastened on the dog's upturned and patently sorrowful face. A few minutes earlier, as he was leaving Casey's place, Brylee had called him on his cell phone and asked him to stop by the store for milk, some lightbulbs and a certain brand of flowery shampoo, and he'd agreed. He hadn't been looking forward to setting that ultrafeminine bottle of shampoo on the counter—the brand that apparently inspired orgasms in the models in the TV commercials—for the checker to ring up and maybe even run a hold-it-up-and-yell price check, but he supposed he ought to be grateful she hadn't asked for tampons.

The dog made a throaty, whimpering sound and moved, ever so slightly, toward Walker.

Walker crouched, put out a hand. "Come on over here, boy," he said. "I won't hurt you."

Meanwhile, people went into the store, and others came out. Walker and the dog remained invisible, it seemed.

Tentatively, the critter crept forward and gave Walker's knuckles a wary sniff, then a brief lick, before retreating again.

Though saddened to see any living thing in such a fix, Walker was also glad to have a distraction. Before making the stray's acquaintance, he'd been all churned up on the inside, full of things he intended to say to Casey the first chance he got. Of course, there hadn't been an opportunity when he took the kids and the dogs home, mainly because they'd sort of hovered, his son and daughter, like reporters waiting outside a courthouse for a big verdict to be handed down by the grand jury.

Between Brylee's shopping list and this hard-luck dog, Walker had other things to think about, and that was a good thing.

"Wait here," he told the critter, standing up straight again, scouting around for anybody who looked as though they might have dumped a helpless animal in the last little while. Considering the sorry shape the dog was in, it had probably been at least a month since he'd been run off or abandoned or simply wandered away from home and gotten lost.

Hoping the latter was the case, Walker went inside the store, tracked down the lightbulbs and the milk and the embarrassing shampoo, adding a large bag of kibble, a couple of plastic pet bowls and a toy skunk with a squeaker inside to his cart just before taking his place in the express-checkout lane.

The woman in front of him surreptitiously counted the number of items in his cart and seemed disappointed to discover that he was under the limit.

When Walker's turn at the register came, he asked the twentysomething clerk about the dog out front. Did she have any idea who it belonged to?

The clerk, someone he didn't know since he lived closer to Three Trees than Parable and generally did whatever shopping he couldn't avoid there, shook her head and sighed. She had a strange haircut, some kind of Mohawk, and wore too much eyeliner, giving her the look of a beleaguered raccoon, though he figured she was probably a nice enough person on the whole.

"You could take him over to Marti Wren—she runs Paws for Reflection, the shelter," the clerk suggested. "She'll take him in if she's got the kennel space."

Walker absorbed this information as if it were new, nodded, handed over a bill and accepted change. "Thanks," he said, noncommittal. He knew Marti—she was a good woman with a generous and caring heart— but somehow leaving the lintball with her or anybody else didn't sit well. Just how many times could a creature be dropped off someplace without giving up all hope?

Outside, he noted that the dog was still in his hiding place. The animal's brown eyes glowed luminous in the gathering darkness, patient as those of a suffering saint.

Walker stowed his purchases in the truck, drove it up close to the front door and got out, leaving the engine running.

"I reckon you'd better come with me," he told the dog.

Miraculously, the dog seemed to agree. He low-crawled out of his shadowy nook, like a soldier hauling himself through a hail of gunfire on forearms and elbows, dragging the rest of his body along with him.

Walker opened the passenger door, and the four-legged saint eyed the interior of the truck, rummaging up his last shred of faith in human nature to take one more chance.

Hoping the creature wouldn't bite off one of his ears, Walker lifted him off his unsteady feet and set him inside, to ride shotgun.

The dog trembled, but if he had any fight left in him, he held it in reserve.

No collar, Walker noted after double-checking, which meant no tags or other visible identification and almost certainly no microchip.

"You're gonna be fine from now on," Walker told his newly acquired sidekick. In this small thing, if not the larger terrain of his life—namely, the realm occupied by Casey and his unclaimed children—he could make a pronouncement like that one, without qualification, and know he'd be able to follow through.

It was something, anyway.

The newcomer rode quietly all the way to the ranch, though Walker wasn't sure whether he was glad to find himself in safe company or simply resigned to a whole new kind of nothing-much.

Twenty minutes later, Brylee put a hand to her mouth when Walker carried his quivering protégé into the kitchen in both arms, like a shepherd bearing a lamb back to the flock. Snidely, snoozing in a corner of the room, looked up, yawned and went back to sleep.

"What on earth happened to that poor thing?" Brylee asked, quietly alarmed, eyes full of compassion and a fair portion of righteous indignation, going by the way she jammed her hands onto her hips and jutted out her elbows.

"That's anybody's guess," Walker answered mildly. He passed Brylee to head into the laundry room; she shuffled ahead to turn on the water in the big sink next to the washer and search the cupboards for Snidely's grooming supplies.

Gently, Walker soaked the dog with the sprayer and scrubbed him repeatedly, unable to raise any suds at all until after the third rinse. Brylee, meanwhile, crooned to the dog as the animal huddled shivering in the laundry sink, enduring.

Once most of the dirt was gone, the critter looked less like a lintball and more like an actual dog, a midsize mixed breed of questionable lineage. He was black, it turned out, floppy-eared and slightly cross-eyed, with no visible injuries or illness, and no spare meat on his bones, either.

While Walker toweled the dog dry, Brylee went back to the kitchen, where she could be heard explaining this new turn of events to Snidely and asking him to be nice.

Walker smiled at that, but when he and the former lint-wad joined the others, he would have sworn Snidely had understood Brylee's kindly lecture and decided to abide by her suggestions. He sniffed at the painfully thin wayfarer; then, amazingly, walked over to his bed, one of several placed at various household locations in case of sudden dog exhaustion, picked up his favorite toy, a red plastic fire hydrant, with his teeth, brought it back and set it carefully at the black dog's feet.

"Isn't that sweet?" Brylee marveled.

"It's weird, that's what it is," Walker commented, wondering if he was hallucinating or something. In his experience, dogs might tolerate each other's presence, but they tended to be territorial about their possessions and their food.

Brylee dismissed Walker's remark with a wave of one hand. "What's his name?" she asked.

"Damned if I know," Walker said. "I just found him outside the supermarket, remember? And he hasn't shared any information."

Brylee made a wry face, then shook her head once,

in case the face hadn't expressed her low opinion of his intelligence clearly enough. "You're being deliberately obtuse," she cried with despairing good humor. "This dog needs a *name,* so he knows there's a place for him in the scheme of things. He'll need a veterinary checkup, too, and maybe some special vitamins to build him up."

"Thank you, Dr. Doolittle," Walker said.

Brylee's whole face lit up. "That's it!" she cried jubilantly. "We'll call him Doolittle!"

Walker chuckled. "Whatever," he said, studying the dog's unimpressive countenance. "It's probably a pretty apt handle, considering what he's likely to contribute around here, which won't be much."

"Wrong," Brylee argued on a swell of conviction. "Doolittle might not herd cattle or guard against marauding intruders, but he'll be *excellent* company, and that's worth something, isn't it?"

"I reckon it is," Walker concluded as the dog gazed up at him in wary adoration.

"Did you get the shampoo and the other things I asked for?" Brylee asked. So much for the greeting-card moment.

"In the truck," Walker said, starting for the side door, meaning to bring in the small bag containing the items he'd bought at the supermarket.

Doolittle, he soon learned, wasn't about to let his new master out of his sight. As Walker left the house, that dog stuck to his heels like a gob of chewing gum on a hot sidewalk.

Walker brought the dog food in first, then the bowls and the toy, but Doolittle, hungry though he surely was, wouldn't be distracted by the offer of a square meal. He clearly intended to go wherever Walker went, period.

Laughing, Brylee said she'd get the last bag herself and left the house.

Walker opened the kibble bag, scooped some into one of the plastic pet bowls and set it on the floor. While Doolittle sniffed the food suspiciously, as though it might be booby-trapped, Walker filled the water bowl and put that down, too.

Doolittle was thirstier, it turned out, than he was hungry. He lapped up that whole bowl full of good country well water and looked up at Walker, asking for more as clearly as if he'd spoken in plain English.

Walker refilled the bowl and Doolittle drank most of that, too, before turning to the kibble.

Snidely watched the whole scene with quiet interest for a few moments, then ambled over and casually reclaimed his fire hydrant.

Brylee came in with the small shopping bag, set it on the counter. Watched fondly as Doolittle munched away on his supper.

Walker, remembering that the front of his shirt was soaking wet from washing the dog in the laundry sink, held the fabric away from his chest and frowned with distaste.

Brylee laughed, not in the halfhearted, forced way that had become a habit with her, but for real. Until they'd gone horseback riding with the kids earlier that same day, Walker hadn't heard her let go. It was about time.

"Give me the shirt," she said, holding out one hand. "I'll wash it next time I run a load of whites."

Walker undid a few buttons, then got impatient and peeled the garment off over his head, mussing up his hair in the process. Then, bare-chested and mildly self-conscious about it, he went to his room to find a T-shirt.

Doolittle immediately stopped eating and followed.

In his bedroom, Walker rummaged through the antique blanket chest and made a square, tidy pile for Doolittle to sleep on, over by the fireplace. While the dog checked out the bed and all corners of the room, Walker pulled on an old T-shirt.

When he went back to the kitchen, Doolittle accompanied him.

Brylee and Snidely had retreated to Brylee's apartment by then, so Walker locked the side door—nobody came to the front entrance except for the UPS man and those hell-bent on spreading the Good News, whatever reception they might receive.

"Looks like it's just you and me," Walker told the dog.

He got a can of beer out of the fridge, popped the top and turned one of the kitchen chairs around to straddle it, resting an arm across the top of its ladder-back.

Doolittle returned to his bowl of kibble and resumed his supper.

And thoughts of Casey and the kids, held at bay for a short time, flooded back into Walker's mind, like rising waters taking out a flimsy dam. He took a long drink of beer, swallowed and waited for the foam to settle in his stomach.

"Beware of redheaded women," he told Doolittle, who paid no discernible attention to the advice.

"WHERE'S UNCLE MITCH?" Clare asked long after she and Shane and the motley crew of dogs arrived home. She stood on tiptoe, peering out the kitchen window, having noticed, finally, that the guesthouse was dark and the rental car was gone.

Casey, seated at the table in her flannel pajama bottoms and a band shirt, her legs curled beneath her on the chair, tossed off her answer. "He got called back to Nashville," she said. *Liar,* accused her conscience, which refused to be suppressed for another moment. "Or something like that."

Shane, sitting across from her and sipping hot chocolate, made a snorting sound. "Good," he said. "He wants to marry you, Mom, and that would be a serious bummer."

Casey's mouth nearly dropped open. "What would make you say such a thing?" she practically gasped.

Clare turned around at this, all ears, but she kept her face expressionless. She looked like a hurricane trapped in a barrel, full to bursting with opinions that were bound to bust loose.

"He *asked* me," Shane said, pausing to pretend he was gagging, "for permission to propose. Said I was the 'man of the house,' and it was only right to consult me before he made his pitch."

"He asked me, too," Clare put in, looking indignant, "even though I'm not the *man of the house.*"

Casey was aghast—and furious with Mitch. She tried to speak, but all that came out was a sputter reminiscent of a lawn mower failing to start when the cord was pulled.

"*Did* Mitch propose, Mom?" Clare pressed.

Casey closed her eyes. A headache flashed across her brain and then rolled back and forth between her temples. "Yes," she said. "After a fashion, he did."

Both kids were staring at her when she opened her eyes again.

"And you said—?" Shane prompted, pale except for the circles of defiant red splotching his cheeks.

"I said no, of course," Casey informed her children, somewhat indignant that her answer to such a question wasn't perfectly obvious.

Clare beamed and punched the air with one fist, like a cheerleader celebrating a Hail Mary score on behalf of her team, with only seconds to go before the final buzzer sounded.

"Now I won't have to run away," Shane said matter-of-factly, and with measurable relief.

"You were planning to run away?" Casey demanded. That was one of her worst fears, that Clare or Shane would take off on their own sometime, in a fit of adolescent angst, and she wouldn't know where they'd gone. Running away from home was dangerous enough for any kid, but for the children of a celebrity, it was asking to be abducted, held for ransom and God only knew what else. The mere idea made her queasy.

"Only as far as Timber Creek Ranch," Shane replied lightly. Then his expression changed, in the blink of an eye, and he looked thoughtful. "Do you think Walker wishes Dawson McCullough was his son?"

The question struck Casey like a bolt of lightning from a clear blue sky. She couldn't have answered to save her soul.

Clare did it for her. "No, dork brain," she told her brother, her tone and manner none too charitable. "Walker's a realist. He's into what is, not making stupid wishes that have a snowball's chance of coming true."

Casey spent a few moments groping for her lost equilibrium. It wasn't what Clare had said that troubled her so much as the *way* she'd said the words *stupid wishes*. She'd sounded so jaded, so cynical.

Was this the same child who, as a little girl, wished on stars and believed unquestioningly that the tooth fairy and a legion of guardian angels and Santa Claus always kept tabs on her and her brother, whether they were rolling along some highway in a tour bus or calling yet another hotel suite home?

Casey wanted to weep for that long-ago Clare, confidently hanging up her stocking wherever Christmas Eve happened to find them, assuring her younger brother that it was dumb to worry. Hadn't Santa Claus always caught up with them before?

"I'm not a dork brain," Shane told his sister heatedly. "And you're not supposed to call names, horse face!"

"That's enough," Casey said wearily. "Off to bed, both of you. Tomorrow's a whole new day."

"It's only nine o'clock, Mom," Clare protested.

"It feels like midnight," Casey responded, briefly closing her eyes again and squeezing the bridge of her nose between a thumb and forefinger. The headache wasn't letting up.

"Can I cruise the net for a while at least?" Shane asked, shambling to his feet, which seemed to be growing twice as fast as the rest of him, and causing all three dogs to leap to attention, ready for adventure.

Casey had employed experts to keep track of the sites Clare and Shane visited on their computers, blocking the unsavory ones, but, compared to her, the kids were superhackers. They could probably sail right past any barrier they came across online.

"Watch TV instead," she said. "Or, here's an idea. Read a book."

Shane groaned like a prisoner sentenced to solitary confinement, though he, like Clare, was an avid reader. He'd devoured all the Harry Potter books, not to mention *The Hobbit* and the *Lord of the Rings* trilogy and a lot of similar tomes.

"Take the dogs out first," Clare commanded her brother. "If you don't, they'll pee in the house—or worse."

Shane scowled at Clare, but he took the dogs outside.

"When did you stop believing that wishes can come true?" Casey asked her daughter, the moment they were alone in that vast kitchen. She hadn't consciously decided to raise the question—it had simply popped out of her mouth.

Clare looked too skeptical for someone so young. "Every year when I blow out the candles on my birthday cake," she answered, "I wish for a dad." She paused and spread her hands, apparently indicating the absence of said father. "Obviously, I've been wasting my breath, at least on the wish front, since I was five."

Casey willed back the tears that would have filled her eyes if she'd allowed them to get that far. *Bucking up,* that had been her grandfather's term for overriding inconvenient emotions.

Sometimes, it was hard to do.

"Oh, honey," she said when she could manage even that much.

Clare lifted one slender shoulder in an offhanded semblance of a shrug, then crossed to Casey, leaned over and kissed her on top of the head. "Everybody has to grow up sometime," she said, and vanished up the back stairs, bound for her bedroom.

Forty-five minutes later, when the kids and the dogs were finally showing signs of staying put behind their doors, Casey drew a deep, quavering breath, picked up the phone and scrolled until Walker's number appeared.

She speed dialed before she could back out, and waited through one ring, then two, then three. Her heart pounded the whole time, and a little voice in her head repeated, *Hang up, hang up, hang up...*

Finally, Walker answered, his voice a sleepy rumble. "Casey?" he muttered.

"Were you asleep?" Casey asked.

"No," he said. "Which isn't to say I wasn't trying."

She carried the cell phone into the cavernous living room, spoke in a whisper. If ever there had been a time when privacy was vital, this was it.

"You were right," she forced herself to say. And, man, it wasn't easy.

Walker was silent for a long moment, then he let out a slow, quiet whistle of exclamation. "Who is this, really?" he joked.

"You know damn well who it is," Casey retorted, unamused. "And there's no need to make this any harder for me than it already is."

"Say your piece," Walker said generously. "The part that comes after *You were right,* I mean."

He was loving this, Casey thought, tight-jawed. "We have to tell Clare and Shane the truth."

"Babe, you're not going to get any argument from me on that score."

Casey scrubbed away tears with the back of one

hand. *Buck up,* she told herself sternly, but it didn't help much. "The question is, how?"

"In plain words," Walker said.

"What if they hate me?" Casey fretted, pacing.

"They might be angry for a while," Walker told her, gruffly gentle. "But hate you? That'll never happen."

"I thought I was doing the right thing," Casey lamented.

"I know," Walker replied, tough and tender at the same time, like any cowboy worthy of the name. "In time, I think Clare and Shane will understand that."

"In time," Casey echoed, miserable.

"Don't build this up into more than it is, Case," Walker advised. How different it was, when he called her by that shortened version of her name from when Mitch did the same. "I'm not going to hang you out to dry by putting all the blame on you. I just want my kids to *know* they're my kids, and that I love them. They don't have to take sides, like this was some kind of war."

"That doesn't mean they won't," Casey said in anguish as she paced the darkened living room. "Take sides, I mean. You'll be the hero, and I'll be Darth Vader."

"Not if I don't play the hero, and *you* don't play the villain."

Casey frowned, working her way through that somewhat-cryptic sentence. "You'll stand up for me?" She hardly dared hope for that.

"Of course," Walker said without hesitation. "You're their *mother,* Case. And you've been a good one. Clare and Shane will get through this. We all will."

"Do you really think so?" It was lame, but Casey couldn't help asking.

"Have I ever told you about *my* mother?" Walker countered.

"Not really," Casey said. Whenever she and Walker had been alone together, back in the early days anyhow, they hadn't talked about anything or anybody. They'd been too busy making love.

Making babies.

"Remind me to do that sometime," Walker said. Something about the masculine timbre of his voice wrapped itself around Casey like an invisible caress.

Casey agreed that she would, but the fact was, she couldn't think that far ahead, couldn't think beyond the expressions on her children's beloved faces when she dropped the bomb.

Oh, by the way, she imagined herself saying, *Walker is your biological father. Sorry I didn't mention that sooner.*

"How are we going to do this?" she asked in a frantic whisper. Just then, she missed old-fashioned phones, the kind with cords you could twist around your fingers.

"Very carefully," Walker answered. "Did it ever occur to you that Clare and Shane might be *happy* to find out they were conceived in the usual way, instead of in a test tube?"

Casey recalled what Clare had told her in the kitchen, about all those ungranted birthday wishes, and felt such a stab of painful regret that she nearly doubled over. "I'm so scared," she confessed.

"You don't have to do this alone," Walker promised.

"When?" Casey was pacing again. "When are we going to tell them, I mean?"

"I think you and I ought to discuss it first," Walker

said reasonably. "In person. So we can present a united front and all that."

Casey felt a rush of purely unfounded relief. "Walker?" she ventured.

"What?"

"Thank you."

"For what?" He sounded honestly puzzled.

"For not using this situation as a weapon to beat me over the head with," Casey answered. "Some men would, you know."

"I'm not 'some men.' And you'd do well to remember that, Casey."

As if she'd ever been able to forget, for as much as a second, how unique Walker Parrish really was. He was a passionate man, with a strong body and stronger opinions, but, for the sake of his children, he'd kept a secret he didn't want to keep. Now, after years of dutifully playing the avuncular family friend—he'd never made any bones about his misgivings—he wanted to "present a united front." He was willing to defend her, to take on as much of the blame as necessary.

And that was no small thing.

"Good night," she said.

"I'll be by tomorrow," he replied.

"What about the kids?" Casey worried. "They'll be around—"

"They can stay with your housekeeper or that manager guy, if you trust him."

"Mitch is gone," Casey said, without meaning to offer up the information in the first place. "He and I had—words."

Walker was quiet for a long moment. Casey could tell he wanted to pursue the subject further but, to his everlasting credit, he didn't. "Well," he finally said, "that leaves the housekeeper."

"Right," Casey said. "That leaves Doris."

"I'll pick you up before breakfast," Walker finished up. "We'll have something to eat over at the Butter Biscuit, and then we'll head out here to the ranch, saddle up and ride."

"It's been a while," Casey reminded him.

He chuckled. "A while since what?" he asked, his voice raspy and so thoroughly male that it made her nerve endings sizzle.

Casey blushed. "Since I rode a horse," she said with emphasis.

"Glad we cleared that up," Walker teased. "I might have thought you meant it's been a while since we made love."

Casey had no reply. What could she say, after all? That her whole body burned for his touch? That, after two pregnancies and a load of heartbreak, she'd probably fall under his spell all over again, given half a chance?

"See you in the morning," Walker said after a few beats of eloquent silence.

"See you in the morning," Casey confirmed, all but sighing the words.

"WALKER'S HERE," SHANE ANNOUNCED, peering out through one of the sunporch windows as the familiar truck rolled up the driveway.

"He is?" Clare asked breathlessly, hurrying over to see for herself.

Casey, seated at the table with a cup of coffee in

front of her, sighed. "He and I are going out for break-fast," she said.

Both kids turned their heads, stared at her over their shoulders.

"Can't we go along?" Shane wanted to know.

"Not this time," Casey said mildly.

"What are we supposed to do?" Clare inquired dramatically. "Starve?"

Casey stifled a chuckle, which would have come out sounding more like a sob, the way her emotions were behaving. "Doris will feed you," she said as Walker's truck door slammed and the dogs, a beat or two behind the times, uttered a few tentative woofs. "And, anyway, it's not as if you're helpless."

Clare folded her arms and looked stubborn. "What's going on here?" she demanded.

"Nothing you need to worry about," Casey replied lightly. *Yet.* "The people from that rental place are coming to pick up the carousel today. If they show up while I'm gone, make sure they don't trample any of the flower beds like they did when they delivered the thing."

Clare blinked. "What kind of answer is that?" she persisted.

"The only kind you're going to get," Casey answered. Walker was almost to the porch steps by then, looking unfairly handsome in his usual getup of jeans, boots and a starched Western shirt.

The kids didn't lobby Walker to override Casey's decree and let them come along on the outing, which surprised her a little. She hadn't spoiled Clare and Shane, but she hadn't raised her children to give up easily when they wanted something, either. They were scrappers, as she was, and they rarely kept to the sidelines.

Walker greeted them quietly, then patted each of the eager dogs in turn.

"I brought Doolittle along with me," he told Casey solemnly when the dogs and the kids backed off a little. "He's kind of mulish when it comes to being left behind."

"Doolittle?" Casey asked.

"My dog," Walker said with a tilted grin and a note of pride in his voice. "He did consent to ride in the backseat," he added. "But it took some fast talking."

CHAPTER SIX

WALKER PARKED DIRECTLY in front of the Butter Biscuit Café. Casey, riding in the passenger seat, was turned halfway around, reassuring Doolittle that he'd be just fine waiting in the truck until they got through eating.

Doolittle had warmed to Casey right off, and he proved to be surprisingly tractable over the issue of temporary separation. It must have been Casey's celebrated charisma.

"See?" Casey said to the dog, pointing toward the broad window, through which tables, part of the counter and quite a few customers were clearly visible. "We'll sit right there, where you can see us the whole time."

Walker was not a fanciful man, but the gentle way Casey talked to Doolittle, and the way the dog seemed to respond, moved something inside him—something that had been rusted over and stuck fast for a long, long time. "You're talking to a dog," he pointed out reasonably, pushing open the driver's side door.

"What's wrong with that?" Casey asked, just as reasonably, sitting tight while Walker rounded the truck to open her door.

Facing her now, Walker shoved his hat to the back of his head and grinned. "Nothing, I reckon," he said, thinking that he might have to grip the metal doorframe just to keep from falling right into Casey Elder's impossibly green eyes.

She smiled back at him, a little wistfully, he thought, unsnapped her seat belt and squeezed past him to stand on the sidewalk. That fiery red hair of hers, pulled back into a ponytail, gleamed in the morning sunshine, and she looked like a teenager in her jeans, ordinary boots and blue cotton top.

Walker moved Doolittle from the backseat to the front so the critter could put his paws up on the dashboard and peer through the windshield, should he choose to do so. He left a window rolled down partway, too, so there would be plenty of air, and he and Casey walked toward the entrance to the restaurant, side by side but not quite touching.

Looking back, a little confounded because he'd expected some whining and carrying on, Walker saw Doolittle gazing placidly out at him, forefeet resting on the dashboard of the truck, as he'd imagined the scenario moments before, but without the yowling, droopy ears and long-suffering countenance.

"He'll be all right," Casey told Walker with a soft smile as he opened the door to the Butter Biscuit and held it for her. He'd told her all about finding Doolittle outside the supermarket while they were making the short drive over to the café, and she'd gotten all misty-eyed listening to the story.

Inside, Essie, the portly proprietor, seated them immediately, directly in front of the main window, as Casey requested. They settled into the booth across from each other, fiddling with their menus, suddenly shy now that they were inside, with folks sliding curious and furtive glances their way.

Casey looked out the window and waggled her fingers at Doolittle, who was watching them from the truck, just as she'd instructed him to do.

"I guess he believed you," Walker said, having decided on the special, whatever it happened to be that day. He had enough on his mind, thanks to this woman, and didn't need even one more decision to make, however mundane it might be.

Casey turned to face him. "Of course he believed me," she said with a little grin. "Would I lie?"

The next moment, one of awkward silence, reminded Walker of a mammoth caught off guard by the Ice Age and freezing so fast that it never got a chance to chew the grass in its mouth.

Casey looked mortified, and somehow smaller than she was.

Walker, deciding to spare her the obvious answer to her question, cleared his throat diplomatically and said, "I hope you're hungry. The portions are big here at the Butter Biscuit."

Casey swallowed visibly and, for a moment, her eyes shone emerald behind a sheen of tears. She blinked rapidly as Essie approached with the coffeepot in one hand, her order book in the other and a stub of pencil riding above her right ear.

"What'll it be?" Essie asked. She probably thought she was being subtle, but Walker knew the woman was about to bust a gasket with the effort of keeping a whole passel of nosy questions to herself. Everybody in Parable County knew Walker and Casey were friends— that was old news, like Casey being famous, and the movie stars who came and went like ducks in a carnival shooting gallery—but to Essie, this probably looked a lot like a date. Maybe even a morning-after kind of deal.

If only.

"I'll take the special," Walker ground out, willing himself not to go red behind the ears. He could feel the other diners looking on, speculating. They'd be lucky if they got out of there, he and Casey, before the buzzing commenced.

"With or without gravy?" Essie asked, going all twinkly.

Walker, who hadn't the first idea what the day's special actually was, replied simply, "With." To his way of thinking, there were very few foods that couldn't be improved with a dollop of Essie's epicurean gravy.

Casey ordered something—Walker didn't hear what—and Essie swept them both up in a knowing smile, gathered the menus with a flourish and pranced off toward the kitchen.

Spoons clattered in coffee cups all around as the clientele took up wherever they'd left off when Walker and Casey came strolling in, bold as you please, like they were a couple or something.

Casey smiled at him over the rim of her coffee cup. "It's reassuring to know I'm not the only one here who's nervous," she said.

Walker wasn't about to admit to the jitters. He was calm, perfectly calm. Not that he was going to reach for his own coffee anytime soon, since he didn't quite trust his grip.

He laced his fingers together, hands resting idly on the tabletop. Throwing in breakfast before they got down to business had seemed like a good idea at the time, but now he wasn't so sure.

Casey's green eyes widened mischievously. "Walker," she said, "you look ready to jump out of your skin." A pause. "I don't bite, you know."

This time, he couldn't resist. He raised one eyebrow and asked, "Don't you?"

Casey went as red as the vinyl bench she was sitting on. Leaning in a little, clearly flustered, she replied in a terse whisper, "Nipping and biting are *not* the same thing."

That was when the tension broke, and Walker couldn't help it—he laughed. Right out loud and with all those nosy locals there to hear.

Casey glared at him. "It isn't funny," she said.

Walker pulled himself together. "Whatever you say, Casey Jones," he replied, falsely gracious.

"Dammit," Casey shot back in a furious undertone, "I *hate* it when you do that!"

"When I do what?" Walker asked innocently. "Call you 'Casey Jones'?"

"No," Casey bit out, "when you say things like 'Whatever you say.' It's placating, it's condescending—it's a way of dismissing my feelings! 'Pay no attention to the little lady, she gets like this sometimes.'"

"Whoa," Walker said. "Hold it. It seems to me you're reading a whole lot into a few simple words."

Casey sat back, hard. If it wouldn't have meant she'd have to make a scene, she probably would have stormed out of the café right then and marched herself home to Rodeo Road without a backward glance.

"Right," she snapped. *"Whatever you say,* Walker."

"Look," Walker said, catching her gaze and holding it, "if you're trying to pick a fight so we don't have to talk about—well, what we're fixing to talk about—

give it up, because I'm not *about* to get sucked into an argument."

Casey put both of her hands up, palms out, conceding the point, or so it would seem. "Okay," she said, plainly begrudging him even that much. *"Okay."*

Nothing more was said until after Essie brought their food—a poached egg on wheat toast for Casey, biscuits, sausage and eggs swimming in gravy for Walker.

All of a sudden, he didn't have an appetite—he'd been ravenous as a bear after a long winter earlier—but leaving his food untouched would have let Casey know she'd gotten to him, and he wasn't having that. He picked up his knife and fork and got ready to eat.

Casey stared down at her meal with a kind of low-key horror, as if it was an eyeball looking back at her instead of an ordinary chicken egg riding a raft of toasted bread. "Why does this always happen?" she asked in a voice soft so that Walker barely heard it, even though the Butter Biscuit Café was unusually quiet.

Walker could have pretended he didn't know what she meant, tossed the question back at her as he had the one before it, but his personal code of honor wouldn't let him do that a second time.

Once had been pushing it.

"I'm not sure," he admitted. "But in the past, it always ended well."

Casey tried hard to look sour, but she ended up giving a little snort of laughter. "You're awful," she said. Then, in a whisper, she added, "It *ended* with a baby, and then *another* baby."

"I wondered what was causing that," Walker teased, making her laugh again.

After that, things lightened up considerably.

They finished their meal—twice interrupted by pass-ersby asking for Casey's autograph, which she cheer-fully gave. Walker paid the check, left a tip on the table for Essie and looked squarely back at everybody who looked at him as the two of them left the restaurant.

Returning to the truck, Walker transferred a very happy Doolittle to the backseat, and Casey took the critter's place up front. Push, he realized grimly, had just come to shove, because they were alone now, ex-cept for the dog, and they could talk freely.

They didn't, though.

Casey rode in silence, seemingly lost in thought, and Walker just drove. When they reached the ranch house, Brylee's rig was gone, which meant she was working, and the hands were all busy elsewhere.

This was a relief to Walker, since he had his hands full dealing with one person—Casey—and any addi-tions would have constituted a crowd.

"I don't suppose you remember how to saddle a horse," Walker ventured, getting out of the truck, going around to open Casey's door for her and then hoisting Doolittle from the backseat to the ground.

"I never knew how in the first place," Casey re-sponded nonchalantly, jumping down from the run-ning board. Walker wondered if she was scared, if it was a lamebrain idea on his part, having one of the most important discussions of their lives somewhere on the open range. Maybe they ought to go inside the house, like normal people, to have their say.

Except that, to Walker, the exchange was much too important, and too sacred, to take place anywhere but under the big sky. The house, spacious as it was, would close in around him, making it hard to breathe, let alone concentrate on the subject at hand.

"Allow me," he said with a grand gesture in the direction of the barn.

If Casey *was* scared, she wouldn't have let him know it. Chin high and shoulders back, she sashayed through the tall, open doorway of that barn like Annie Oakley about to perform a little trick riding and some fancy shooting in a Wild West show.

Whatever else a person might say about Casey Elder, Walker conceded silently, she had guts, no question about it. He saddled Smokey, the gelding Shane had ridden the day before, and then Mack, his own favorite. Casey trailed after him as he led both horses out of the barn.

Sunlight glistened on the animals' well-brushed coats, and Doolittle wandered over, curious about the goings-on.

Cussedly independent, Casey mounted up on her own—somewhat awkwardly, though Walker pretended not to notice that—and he put down an urge to show off a little and simply put one foot in the stirrup and swung sedately up into the saddle. The fact was, he and Brylee had grown up riding bareback, often using halters instead of bridles, and when it came to getting on or off a horse, they were as agile as a pair of Apaches.

"You can come along if you want to," he told Doolittle, who stood looking up at him, head tilted slightly to one side as he pondered this new development.

Instead of following, though, the dog turned away, walked slowly toward the porch, lapped up some water from Snidely's outside bowl and settled down for a nap in the shade.

"I'll be," Walker said.

"He knows you'll be back," Casey observed softly.

"So it seems," Walker agreed.

He looked back a couple of times as they headed for the road—one of his favorite trails snaked up into the foothills from the other side—but old Doolittle didn't move a muscle. Maybe he'd had enough excitement for one morning.

Casey, it turned out, was a natural in the saddle. She held the reins correctly, instead of sawing on them as most greenhorns did, and as they climbed the hill just across the road, Walker and Mack leading the way, she knew to lean forward over Smokey's neck instead of grasping the saddle horn in both hands and holding on for dear life as he'd half expected her to do.

Walker was proud of her, in a quiet and private way that had little or nothing to do with her status as a world-famous singer. He resettled his hat, pleased, and rode on, slowing his pace when he figured Casey was having trouble keeping up.

After twenty minutes or so, they reached the high, wide pasture overlooking the valley where his cattle, the ones he raised for beef, grazed on sweet grass and drank from Timber Creek, an offshoot of the Big Sky River.

Dismounting in a copse of maple and oak trees—there had been a cabin here once, though only part of the chimney remained, along with a few weathered floorboards with wildflowers growing between the cracks—Walker looked up at Casey, stricken by the sight of her. For the umpteenth time since they'd met, years before, during some down-at-the-heels rodeo where she'd been asked to sing the national anthem and he'd been entered in the bull-riding competition, he thought how impossibly beautiful she was.

Casey got down off Smokey, stretched the small of her back and looked around. "Who lived here?" she asked, still holding the reins.

"My great-great-grandparents," Walker replied, and he could almost feel roots sprouting from the soles of his feet, reaching deep into the rocky but fertile ground. "This was the original homestead, where they parked the covered wagon, unhitched the oxen, dug a well and threw together a shack just before winter hit."

Casey approached a runaway thicket of peony bushes, tall as trees and laden with red blossoms and buzzing with lazy bees. "These must have been her flowers," she said, her voice wistful. "Your great-great-grandmother's, I mean."

Walker nodded. "She brought them all the way from Kansas," he answered. "Planted them that first spring, as the story goes."

Casey turned to look at him, shading her eyes from the sun with one hand. "It's a happy sorrow," she said, "seeing them untended, in this lonely place, but growing like crazy just the same."

A happy sorrow. It was a phrase Walker wouldn't have thought up in a million years, but it sounded like poetry coming from Casey. He figured she'd eventually weave it into one of her songs. He secured the reins and left Mack to graze, and did the same for Casey's horse.

"It was a hard life," he said, remembering the small gravestone hidden in the tall grass, where his ancestors had buried their three-month-old daughter after she died of scarlet fever. "But they stuck it out, made it mean something."

Casey wandered farther afield, and bent to pluck something from the ground. It was a spear of asparagus, the stray remnant of a garden that had been gone for better than a century. "It's perfect," she said, pleased.

"Grows all over the place," Walker said, pleased himself, and a little hoarse with it. "Brylee and I used to gather asparagus by the bushel out here, take it home and boil it up for supper."

Casey stopped, gazing at him. "Is that a happy story?" she asked. "Or is it more like a tale of hard luck?"

Walker grinned, though something about her question made his throat thicken a little. "We were okay as kids," he replied. "Mom didn't take a whole lot of interest in us, but Dad was rock solid."

"I wish I'd known him."

"Me, too," Walker answered. "He'd have liked you."

Casey found a large, flat rock rising out of the grass, brushed away dirt and pine needles and sat down. "My folks died when I was a toddler," she said without a trace of self-pity. "I grew up with my paternal grandparents."

"Yes," Walker replied, joining her, since the rock was wide enough to accommodate both of them. "I think I read about that in *People* magazine."

Casey's smile was a little thin by then, but her lips quirked up at the corners for a moment. "You read *People* magazine?" she joked. "I had you pegged for a *Western Horseman* subscriber."

"I'm that, too," Walker admitted. "But when your face or your name is on the cover of a magazine—any magazine—I buy it and I read it."

That seemed to unsettle her slightly. She slid her

palms along the thighs of her jeans, as though smoothing a skirt. "You know, of course, that there's a lot of hype out there. You can't believe everything you read, and all that."

Walker nodded, removed his hat, held it loosely between his hands. "Yep," he said. Then he grinned. "I admit I was intrigued by that tabloid story about your having a secret husband tucked away somewhere."

She drew a deep breath, let it out slowly, taking in the hardy antique flowers and the ruins of the cabin and the herd, way off in the distance. "You think that was bad?" she countered lightly. "What about the one that claimed I was abducted by aliens and my children are the result?"

Walker chuckled. "I might have believed it happened once," he joked. "But twice would stretch my credulity."

She laughed, but that was quickly followed by a barely stifled sob.

"Hey," Walker said awkwardly. "Don't cry."

For God's sake, don't cry.

She turned her head to look directly at him, her beautiful eyes moist. "I can't help it," she said. "Clare and Shane are the most important people in my life, and now I have to tell them I've been lying through my teeth since day one!"

Walker set his hat aside, took her hand, interlaced his fingers with hers. "If you need more time—"

"No," Casey broke in, glumly resolved. "I should have told them a long time ago. Putting it off would only make everything harder."

Walker was quiet for a long time, still holding her hand. Then he asked, his voice husky and pitched low, "Why *didn't* you, Casey? Why didn't you tell Clare and

Shane that I'm their father? And why didn't you tell me the truth, right from the beginning?"

She swallowed hard, swiped at her eyes with the back of one hand, sat up a little straighter. Her chin wobbled, but she got the answer out, hard as it was to hear. "I thought you'd want us to get married."

"I did," Walker said, remembering. Hurting. "But I wouldn't have held a gun to your head, Casey. You could have said no."

"That's easy for *you* to say." She sniffled. "You wouldn't have needed a gun—you could have talked me into anything, including marriage, and it would have been all wrong because—because *dammit,* I wanted to sing, on a real stage, in front of a real audience. I had something to prove, and you, Walker Parrish, didn't need to prove a darn thing!"

"So you told me Clare was another man's child," Walker said evenly. After all these years, it still stuck in his craw, that memory.

"I'm sorry about that," Casey said. "I was young and I was confused and I just didn't know what else to do."

"You could have *trusted* me just a little, Case," Walker told her, sad through and through. "I might be a cowboy, and I might be a little old-fashioned, too, but I wouldn't have forced you to give up your career, move to this ranch and start ironing shirts, raising vegetables and cranking out more babies." He paused, dealing with old wounds that still hurt like hell whenever he acknowledged them, which wasn't often. "I knew how much your music meant to you, how talented you were. Knew even then, when you were singing for peanuts, that you had a big future. I would have done my level best to help you any way I could."

Casey started crying again then, in earnest. Even the horses noticed, looking up from their grass-munching as though catching the scent of trouble on the breeze.

Walker gathered Casey in his arms, not knowing what else to do. He held her close, feeling her hot tears soaking through the fabric of his shirt, propped his chin on top of her head and waited in silence for the storm to subside. Words wouldn't help now, even if he'd known what to say. He'd probably said too much as it was.

After a while, Casey recovered her composure enough to accept the clean cotton handkerchief he handed her. She swabbed her puffy cheeks and then blew her nose, foghorn-style.

"How are we going to tell Clare and Shane the truth?" she finally asked, her voice small and her shoulders drooping a little.

"I've been thinking about that," Walker said, not holding her quite so tightly but not turning her loose, either. "It'll have to be just the four of us, in a quiet place, but there's no way to make this easy, Casey. It's a hard thing to tell, and it'll be a hard thing to hear."

She nodded, sniffled again, started to hand the handkerchief back to him in a crumpled wad, decided against that and stuffed it into her bra, where it bulged comically. "I don't think I could do this alone," she said, looking away.

Walker cupped her chin lightly, turned her face toward him, looked into the Irish-green depths of her eyes. "You don't have to do it alone," he told her.

And then, without intending to, he kissed her, a mere brush of their mouths at first. Her lips felt damp against his, and tasted of salt.

She stiffened, then opened to him, sliding her arms

around his neck, drawing him closer. Need rocked him, as powerful as an earthquake deep underground, the kind that starts tsunamis, far out to sea.

The kiss deepened.

Casey moaned softly, warm against him. Curvy and pliable, the perfect fit.

Walker pulled away, got to his feet, grabbing up his hat as he moved, breathing hard and keeping his back to Casey while he fought to regain control. He felt her approach, almost flinched when she laid her hands, fingers splayed wide, on his shoulder blades. Fire raced through his system and branded his soul.

"Walker," she said. That was all, just his name, but there was a world of sorrow and regret in that one word.

"We'd better go," he said, still not turning to face her, his voice rough as gravel. "I don't know about you, but I'm on the ragged edge of doing something stupid right about now, and with our track record, you'd probably get pregnant."

She was silent for a few moments, then she slipped around in front of him, put her arms around his waist. Looking up at him with eyes full of tears, she gave a raspy chuckle. "I can see where that might be a problem for you," she confessed, "my getting pregnant, that is, but I kind of like the idea."

Of all the things Casey might have said at that moment, that was the last one he would have expected. Something inside Walker soared at the thought of Casey carrying and then bearing his child, but another part of him was downright pissed off. What part of *We're in a big fix here* did she not understand?

"I've already got two kids who are bound to think, at least for a little while, that they're mistakes we tried to cover up," he said coldly, "and I'm not about to let that happen to a third."

Casey looked startled, almost as though he'd struck her. She started to say something, then caught herself and clamped her mouth shut.

Moving stiffly, she strode over to Smokey, stuck a foot in one stirrup, grabbed the saddle horn in her right hand and hauled herself up onto the gelding's back.

Walker knew he could have stated his case in a more tactful manner, but he *also* knew he'd been speaking the God's truth, so he locked his jaws at the hinges and mounted Mack, and he and Casey rode all the way back down the hill, across the road and into the barnyard without a single word passing between them.

When they arrived, Brylee was sitting on the porch steps, Doolittle on one side of her, Snidely on the other.

Well, Walker fumed silently, that was just fine. Not only were he and Casey virtually at each other's throats—again—but there was an eyewitness to their folly.

Brylee stood, her wide smile fading as she sized up the situation. She slid her hands backward into the rear pockets of her jeans and came toward them.

The dogs, blessed with better sense, stayed where they were.

"Peace," Brylee said weakly, making the two-fingered hippie sign.

Walker dismounted, as did Casey, and the women remained behind while he led Mack and Smokey into the barn to remove their saddles and other tack and brush them both down. Doolittle kept him company, waiting sympathetically in the breezeway while Walker drew out chores he could have performed in his sleep for as long as possible.

Casey and Brylee had gone into the house; they were probably sitting in the kitchen, drinking coffee or tea, and talking about hardheaded men.

Though he would rather have avoided another encounter with Casey, however brief, that would have been an act of cowardice. He'd brought Casey to the ranch, and therefore it was his responsibility to take her back home. So he made for the porch steps, crossed to the door and stepped over the threshold, hat in hand, dog at his heels.

Sure enough, the two women were at the table, with steaming cups before them, talking in quiet voices. Naturally, they fell silent when they heard Walker's footsteps on the porch.

Casey lowered her eyes when he and Doolittle entered the kitchen, but Brylee glared at him through narrow eyes. She might as well have shouted the word *fool,* her thoughts were so obvious.

Walker suppressed a sigh and hung his hat on a peg. Then he ambled over to the sink, rolled up his sleeves and scrubbed his hands with the harsh yellow soap that was always waiting for him there.

That done, he picked up Doolittle's water bowl, rinsed it out under the faucet and filled it again.

Still, nobody said anything, though Brylee kept trying to wither him with her stare.

He scowled at her, leaned back against the counter while Doolittle lapped up water and folded his arms. "There are two sides to every story," he said, and then wished he hadn't, because now he'd given away the fact that the argument between him and Casey was still stuck under his hide like a fishhook.

"Nobody said there weren't," Brylee informed him coldly.

Casey finally met his eyes, squaring her shoulders and jutting out her chin as she did. "If you wouldn't mind," she said, "I'd like to go home now."

"That's fine with me," Walker replied without inflection. And he gestured toward the screen door. "After you."

Casey scraped back her chair and got to her feet. "Thank you for the tea," she said to Brylee, both of them rendering Walker invisible in that mysterious way women have.

"I could take you back to Parable," Brylee offered. To look at her, a person would have thought she was *Casey's* sister, not his. She knew zip about the situation, but she'd already thrown in with Casey—that much was obvious.

Casey shook her head. "Thanks, but I know you have to get back to work. Walker can drop me off."

With that, Walker opened the screen door and held it for Casey, who blew through it like a redheaded wind.

He was a little stung when Doolittle decided to stay behind, with Brylee and her German shepherd, instead of coming along for the ride. Dammit, Walker thought, even the *dog* was against him.

He and Casey were both in the truck, buckled up and rolling down the driveway, before he spoke. "What did you tell Brylee?" he rasped after unsticking his jaw-bones.

"Nothing about Clare and Shane, if that's what you're thinking," Casey said, self-righteous as a fanatical Puritan. "I just told her you were impossible." She tossed off a mockery of a smile. "Turns out, she already knew that. Go figure."

That was the end of the day's conversation.

CHAPTER SEVEN

FOR A FULL WEEK, nothing happened, nothing regarding the big reveal, at least. Walker didn't call or stop by, or even grace Casey's in-box with an email.

Clare and Shane remained clueless as far as their paternity was concerned. They swam in the community pool every afternoon, hung out with their friends, played tag with the dogs in the backyard and rarely sniped at each other. That last part was the tip-off, Casey figured. They were smart kids: they knew some kind of major change was imminent, and they'd formed an alliance, probably brief, probably tenuous, but an alliance nonetheless.

Casey was grateful for small favors.

Boone and Tara returned from their honeymoon, and Boone ran the sheriff's department again, but otherwise, both of them kept a low profile for a few days. Then, letting the local grapevine spread the word, they invited practically the whole county to a big Friday-night party at their place, complete with barbecued beef, washtubs full of potato salad, slow-roasted corn on the cob and biscuits the size of Frisbees. Those who knew Tara well, as Casey did, noticed right away that chicken wasn't on the menu, and were amused by the irony.

Tara, a former cosmetics tycoon, had been billing herself as a chicken farmer from the day she moved

to Parable, but, as far as anybody knew, not one of her
fine feathered friends had ever been beheaded, subsequently cleaned and plucked, cut to pieces and fried in
bacon grease, let alone turned up crispy and delicious
on somebody's dinner plate.

People were tolerant of this oddity—in rural areas
like Parable County, chickens weren't pets, and their
purpose was clear: give eggs and eventually wind up
in a skillet or a stewpot—reminding each other that,
after all, Tara was from *New York City,* and therefore
might be expected to have a few strange ideas rattling
around in that pretty head.

Though she'd rather have continued hibernating and
feeling sorry for herself, Casey spiffed herself up, put on
black jeans, a long-sleeve T-shirt to match, shiny boots
and a modicum of makeup and, to appease the part of
her that wanted to hide, a baseball cap. She drove, with
Doris and the kids, out to Boone and Tara's farm.

Ah, Boone and Tara, Casey reflected with a smile.

At first, they were feuding neighbors, that pair,
Boone living, with his two young sons, in a double-wide
trailer one step away from being condemned and surrounded by high grass and assorted junk—an annoying
contrast to Tara's well-kept farmhouse, just across the
little slice of river that separated their two properties.

Now the double-wide was long gone, and a beautiful barn and white-rail corral stood in its place, complete with horses. The newlyweds, along with Boone's
boys, Griffin and Fletcher, and Tara's teenage twin stepdaughters, Erin and Elle, resided in Tara's house, since
their doctor father was too busy to raise them. It was
spacious, that august Victorian structure, the kind of
place that would look perfect, with just a dusting of

snow and a holly wreath at the door, on the front of a Christmas card. They were already adding on, making room for babies.

Babies. Ouch.

As she parked the SUV in a field, amid dozens of other vehicles, Casey recalled the brazen thing she'd said to Walker, up there at his great-great-grandparents' homestead the day they'd gone horseback riding, about how a baby might be a problem for him, but she kind of liked the idea. Just remembering that made her blush, never mind that it was completely true.

After all, she was still young, only in her thirties, and she wanted another child very much. Maybe several. But she'd been a fool to say as much to Walker, after the way she'd brought Clare and Shane up—wholly loved, but lied to, nonetheless.

What had she been thinking?

She sighed, trying to dodge the inevitable riot of emotions. She hadn't been thinking at all, and that was the trouble. She'd never been able to put two sensible thoughts together when it came to Walker Parrish. If she had been, everything would have been different. She'd either be a childless loner, still pursuing her career at full throttle, or married to Walker, living on the ranch and popping out brothers and sisters for Clare and Shane.

"Mom?" Clare prompted as they walked toward the Taylors' yard, which was already bursting with laughing visitors. "This is a *party,* not a funeral. Buck up, for Pete's sake."

Casey smiled while scanning the crowd for any sign of Walker. "You're right, honey," she agreed quietly, but part of her still wanted to turn tail and run like hell.

They'd gotten into that stupid row, she and Walker, before they could agree on a time and a place for the powwow to end all powwows, and she'd been guiltily grateful for the reprieve. At the same time, the nearly unbearable dread had continued to build.

According to the kids, who kept track of him like a pair of private detectives staking out a cheating husband, Walker had been off hauling bulls and broncos to some distant rodeo over the past week or so, and, much to Shane's thinly disguised irritation, he'd taken Dawson McCullough along with him, wheelchair and all.

With any luck, Casey thought, he was still away.

She made her way through the throng of guests to Boone and Tara, who beamed like a pair of human lighthouses as people shook Boone's hand and hugged Tara and congratulated them over and over again.

When her turn came, Casey hugged both of them, first Tara, then Boone. Doris and the children, it seemed, had already been absorbed into their various circles of friends, because they were nowhere in sight.

"You look beautiful," Casey told Tara, meaning it.

Tara *did* look beautiful, glowing with happiness as Boone slipped a husbandly arm around his bride's shoulders and gave her a squeeze. "There's nothing like a honeymoon to perk a person up," Tara said, and then blushed.

Casey smiled. She couldn't have been happier for her friends, so why was her throat thick with unshed tears? Another pang of envy struck, too, shaming her. "And where did you go on this mysterious honeymoon, or is that still a secret?"

"Hawaii," Tara said with delight, stretching out her

bare arms to show off her golden tan. "We had our very own grass hut."

Boone sighed cheerfully at the memory, and Tara gave him a light poke in the ribs with one elbow.

"It's good to have you back," Casey said, kissing Tara's cheek. "Let's get together soon."

Tara nodded. "Soon," she agreed.

Since other new arrivals were waiting to speak to Tara and Boone, Casey moved on, looking for Kendra or Joslyn much the same way a shipwrecked sailor might search the horizon for land.

In the process, she crashed right into a broad, hard and all-too-familiar chest, looked up and met Walker's eyes. The impact of *that* rocked her far more than the physical collision had, and that was saying something.

Well, she thought, trying to be philosophical while her heart flailed around in her chest like a bird trying to escape a cage, that settled one question, anyway. Walker Parrish was definitely back from his travels.

"Hello, Casey," he drawled, smiling down at her.

Did he know what that smile did to her? If he did, he was an unconscionable rake, taking unfair advantage.

"Walker," Casey croaked out in reply. Why hadn't she stayed at home, camping out in her room, watching the Soap Channel in her bathrobe and eating too much ice cream?

Because Tara and Boone were her friends, that was why, she reminded herself sternly. And because, mostly, it wasn't like her to hide out.

"We didn't finish our conversation," Walker reminded her. His voice was gruff and low, but his eyes were gentle. He'd decided, in his infinite mercy, to make things easy for her, she concluded.

The arrogant bastard.

"No," she said sweetly. "You went off to some rodeo and left me to stew in my own juices, wondering what was going to happen next. Waiting for the proverbial other shoe to drop."

Walker rolled his shoulders, the only outward indication that he was tense, too. "It's my job. I had a contract. What was I supposed to do, Casey?"

"You could have called," she replied, smiling hard for the benefit of anybody who might be looking their way while she knew her eyes were shooting green fire. "Said you'd be out of town for a while. *Something.*"

He leaned in until their foreheads were almost touching. "You mean," he said, barely breathing the words, "the way *you* called *me* almost fifteen years ago and told me you were carrying my baby?"

Casey's cheeks flamed, and she was glad she hadn't been to the punch bowl yet, because she might not have been able to keep herself from flinging the contents of her cup in his handsome, self-righteous face. *That* would have been a fine how-do-you-do, with the whole of Parable County looking on.

"There's no need to be rude," she snapped rudely, folding her arms and letting the smile fall away, since it was too hard to hold on to, anyhow.

"Tomorrow," Walker said, and she couldn't tell whether that glint in his eyes was fury or amusement. "My place, at high noon. That's when the sh—mustard hits the fan, Casey Jones."

Casey, on fire moments before, went icy cold. Swallowed hard, looked away for a moment, forced herself to look back. He'd drawn a line in the sand, and she had no choice but to step over it if she wanted to make things right with her children.

"We'll be there," she said.

Walker had the gall to grin that wicked grin, the one that always made her want to either slap him silly or tear off all her clothes and jump his bones on the spot.

Obviously, the latter wasn't an option, and, for that matter, slapping was off the table, too. Casey had taught Clare and Shane that hitting was wrong, and she could hardly go against her own rule, as badly as she might want to do just that. Especially not in public.

"Noon," he repeated, like Gary Cooper scheduling a showdown on the street in front of the old saloon.

Casey fairly snarled her response. "Noon," she agreed.

Then she turned on one heel and proceeded to put as much space between herself and Walker Parrish as she could.

WALKER WATCHED HER walk away, smiling to himself and enjoying the way her shapely blue-jeaned backside swayed from side to side as she moved. She was wearing a baseball cap, pulled down low over her eyes, and her long ponytail jutted through the opening in back, swinging to the beat of her outrage.

Though nobody would have guessed it, Walker figured he was as nervous about tomorrow as Casey was—maybe more so, because Shane and Clare would probably be just as mad at him as they would be at their mother, and neither he nor the lady had a leg to stand on when it came to the right and wrong of it all.

A lie, however well-intentioned, was still a lie.

"Where's Brylee?" asked a feminine voice at his side just as Casey vanished into the mob.

Walker looked over and saw Joslyn Barlow standing next to him. She was pretty calm and collected, for somebody trying to smuggle a bowling ball under her dress.

"Why do people keep asking me that?" he asked calmly, but with a smile. He liked Joslyn, after all, liked her husband, Slade, too, and he knew she really cared about his sister.

Joslyn widened her eyes in a mockery of innocence and countered, "Because we'd like to get a straight answer?"

Walker, remembering the glass of beer he was holding for the first time since he'd nearly spilled it all over Casey in the collision, took a sip and savored it before offering a reply. "She's probably at home, or in her office or racing around on a forklift in the warehouse."

Brylee owned Décor Galore, a direct marketing company specializing mostly in home parties and online sales. She'd built it from nothing to a multimillion-dollar corporation in a few short years, and Walker worried that she'd die of overwork before she ever got a chance to enjoy the fruits of all those twelve- and sixteen-hour days.

Sipping punch, Joslyn smiled sadly. "It's only fair to warn you," she said, "that Opal's getting mighty concerned about Brylee, and she's thinking about stepping in."

Walker pretended horror. "Oh, no," he gasped, splaying his free hand on his chest, "not *that*."

Joslyn laughed. "Never underestimate the power of

Opal," she told him. "When she's on a mission, she's a force to be reckoned with."

"I thought she specialized in matchmaking," Walker said. Over the tops of people's heads, he caught a distant glimpse of Casey, talking with Kendra Carmody and none other than the great Opal herself.

For some reason, that made his shirt collar feel too tight, even though he'd left the uppermost snaps unfastened.

"That's true enough," Joslyn agreed. "Opal has uncanny instincts, particularly when it comes to romance."

"All that and a fantastic housekeeper, too," Walker said, trying to ignore Casey, especially now that Kendra had wandered away and left her alone to confer with Opal.

Joslyn smiled. "We'll be losing Opal soon," she said. "At least, as far as housekeeping goes. She's getting married."

"I heard," Walker said.

Casey and Opal seemed deep in conversation, earnest as all get-out. What the devil were those two talking about?

Joslyn said goodbye then and slipped away, and Walker remembered that he'd been on his way over to talk to Patsy McCullough about Dawson when he got sidetracked talking to Casey. *Talking?* They'd been taking potshots at each other, the way they did everywhere but in bed.

It was downright discouraging. Looking around, he spotted Patsy once again, now sitting primly on a folding chair in the shade of a maple tree, a full paper plate balanced on her lap, though she didn't look all that interested in food.

Walker had dropped Dawson off at home on his way to Boone and Tara's place—the boy had had a fine time at the rodeo, but he'd declined the invitation to go on to the party, claiming, with all justification, that he was too tired.

It wasn't the tiredness that troubled Walker, though; he could have used twelve hours of uninterrupted sleep himself, right about then. No, it was what the boy had said about Doolittle, who went along on the trip—that he thought the dog used to belong to Treat McQuillan, his mother's current boyfriend. Dawson and his sister were getting attached to the critter when he just dropped off the radar—there one day, gone the next.

Dawson, who'd been spending a lot of time alone back then, having just gotten out of the hospital after yet another surgery, had missed the dog's company, so he'd asked Treat where he was. Treat had evaded the question repeatedly, finally saying that "the mutt" had run off, and good riddance, since he'd turned out to be more trouble than he was worth.

The last thing Walker had wanted to do was give up Doolittle—they were true partners now—but what's right is right, and he'd asked Dawson if he wanted the dog back. He'd been relieved, of course, when the boy shook his head no and said Doolittle was better off staying where he was.

Now, making his way toward Patsy, who smiled at passersby but didn't make any noticeable effort to join the festivities, being famously shy by nature, Walker considered the obvious fact that Patsy had every right to date whoever she wanted, and her relationship with Treat was none of his or anybody else's business. He didn't even know what he was going to say to the woman, but he'd made up his mind to say *something*.

By his reasoning, if McQuillan would turn out a helpless dog, leaving it to fend for itself, how kind was he likely to be to Dawson and his little sister? Would *they* end up being "more trouble than they were worth," as Doolittle had been? Would Patsy?

"Hello, Patsy," Walker said, very quietly, when he reached her.

"Walker," she replied with a cordial nod. "I guess you must have left Dawson off at home."

"He was tired," Walker said, affirming her assumption.

"It was good of you to take him with you," Patsy offered. "I haven't seen my boy so happy since before— before—" She fell silent, swallowed hard.

It was no wonder that the accident was hard for her to talk about, Walker figured. Most likely, the image of her son plunging off the water tower haunted her, waking and sleeping, and how did a person deal with the knowledge that Dawson would need more surgeries in the years to come, none of which would give him back the use of his legs?

Walker crouched, reached over and took Patsy's thin, work-worn hand. Things were better for the Mc-Culloughs, at least financially—the community had been generous, Casey included—but all that trouble would have scratched the shine off just about anybody's spirit. She'd had a lifetime of it, even before Dawson got hurt.

"You holding up okay, Patsy?" he asked.

She didn't pull her hand free, but she did look a

mite uncomfortable. Was McQuillan the jealous type? Probably.

"Most of the time," she answered. "Some days are harder than others, though."

Walker let go of her hand but remained where he was, sitting on his haunches and looking up into her weary, resigned face. He'd made a sizable donation to Dawson's medical fund, and he knew Brylee had, too, as well as the Barlows, the Carmodys, Boone and Tara, and others. Even the itinerant movie stars had sent hefty checks, though they rarely took part in anything that went on in Parable or Three Trees.

"Treat's good with the kids?" Walker asked.

Patsy's eyes immediately widened. "Who says he isn't?" she immediately retorted.

"Nobody," Walker said gently. "I was just wondering."

"Why?" It was a demand. Patsy McCullough, normally so docile, so beaten down by bad husbands and hard times, was riled.

Walker let out his breath. "Dawson said there was a dog—"

"That dog ran away," Patsy snapped. "They *do* that, Walker. It isn't Treat's fault."

Walker stood up, glad he was a Montana cowboy and not an ambassador of some kind. With his talent for diplomacy, he'd likely have started World War III just by pissing somebody off at a cocktail party.

Before he could think of anything to say—anything that wouldn't make matters worse, that is—Treat showed up, in uniform and obviously on the lookout for something to raise hell about. If the pompous-ass rent-a-cop didn't find any trouble handy, Walker thought, he was likely to *make* some.

Walker would have welcomed a confrontation in any other setting, but this was Boone and Tara's home-from-the-honeymoon party, and a brawl would not only spoil it, it would become the communal memory of the occasion, overriding everything good.

Patsy immediately leaped into the breach, shooting up from her folding chair and overturning her untouched food on the ground, her voice soft but nearly frantic. "Walker was just telling me that he and Dawson had a good time at the rodeo."

Walker frowned. Was she scared of McQuillan? He couldn't help recalling that night at the Boot Scoot Tavern, when the then-deputy had essentially manhandled Brylee after she refused to dance with him. Did Treat make a *habit* of pushing smaller, weaker people around?

"Isn't that nice," Treat said acidly.

"Now, Treat, don't—" Patsy protested lamely.

"I'll be on my way," Walker put in, ignoring the chief of police and focusing on the lady. If he didn't go, things were going to get ugly. "If you ever need anything, Patsy, call me. Dawson has my numbers."

Treat's color flared, as though there were an overheated engine inside his head, fixing to throw a rod. "If Patsy *needs* anything—" he seethed "—*I'll* be the one she calls."

People were starting to notice, turning toward them. Slade, Hutch and Boone, none of them fans of Treat McQuillan, started moving in their direction.

Patsy clutched Treat's arm. "Take me home," she pleaded, her voice quiet and quick. "Right now. My boy's been gone for a while, and I want to see him."

Treat's Adam's apple raced up and down the length

of his neck like an elevator gone haywire, and his eyes bulged, but he finally gave in and, with stiff-spined dignity, squired Patsy toward the road, where his car was parked with lots of others.

Walker watched them go, troubled.

"Everything all right?" Boone asked, being the first one there. He might have been the bridegroom, but he was also the sheriff, and he took the job seriously.

"I hope so," Walker answered, finally turning to face his friend.

Slade and Hutch joined them. Slade had been the sheriff of Parable County before Boone took office, and Hutch was the type to go ahead and deputize himself whenever he thought there might be a need for reinforcements. Whatever their differences over Brylee, and the infamous wedding-that-wasn't, Walker liked Hutch Carmody.

Treat and Patsy roared off in his fancy new police car, throwing up a plume of dust behind them.

Slade shook his head, quietly disgusted, and returned to the party.

Boone went back to his bride, as any sane man would have done in his place, which left Hutch and Walker by themselves.

An awkward development, to say the least.

Hutch laid his hand briefly on Walker's shoulder, saying nothing, then turned and walked away.

Walker lingered awhile, circulated among the other guests as best he could and kept one eye on Casey Elder the rest of the evening.

CASEY COULDN'T EVEN *think* about breakfast the next morning, so she sat at the table on the sunporch, her coffee untouched and her plate empty, watching Shane and Clare as they simultaneously bickered and consumed their oatmeal and fresh fruit.

So much for the brother-sister alliance.

Doris, in uniform and miffed because she prided herself on her cooking and got cranky when everybody didn't choose to eat it, came and went from the kitchen with her carefully powdered nose in the air, her mouth tight and her eyes averted.

"I suppose you'd eat if *Lupe* had made breakfast," she said, sniffing, on one swing through with the coffeepot.

Casey smiled sadly, getting the reference. Lupe had been Casey's grandmother's housekeeper and cook, and Doris knew that Casey adored the woman. When she was younger, Lupe and Juan had been more like family than her well-heeled grandparents. Some of the happiest days of her childhood, in fact, had been spent on Lupe's father's truck farm, in the Texas hill country, where he and the rest of his gigantic family had raised various vegetables and sold them at farmers' markets and from various roadside stands throughout July and August and well into September.

Good-natured people, who spoke so little English that they always communicated with Casey through Lupe or Juan, the Garcias had taken Casey into the fold, treated her like one of their own, right down to the hoeing, weeding and harvesting.

She'd been proud to sell squash and tomatoes, lettuce and cabbage, cobs of corn still in their green husks, watermelons and asparagus and all the rest. If her grandparents, who traveled widely and chose to leave their sometimes unruly granddaughter in the care of the help, had known she was on the farm, wearing borrowed overalls and getting the knees grubby, digging potatoes and weighing produce and making change for passing strangers, they'd have had a fit.

They *hadn't* known, of course, until one day when Casey was twelve—not quite Shane's age now—and they'd returned unexpectedly from a European cruise, after an outbreak of food poisoning struck down half the ship's passengers, who had to be hospitalized in Barcelona. Her grandparents, whom no mere stomach bug would have dared afflict, had cut the trip short and flown back to the States more than a week early.

Naturally, they'd expected their granddaughter—she of the incessant *singing*—to be in the mansion, eagerly awaiting their return.

Instead, she'd been manning one of the roadside stands with Lupe, and when one of the housemaids called to say they were home, demanding to know where Casey was, Lupe and Juan had rushed her back to Dallas in their old rattletrap of a car.

Her grandmother, who would not hear any explanation, had fired Lupe and Juan on the spot, and never mind their years of dedicated service. They were traitors, never to be forgiven.

Soon after that incident, Casey had been sent away to a New England boarding school, where she was completely miserable, sustained only by encouraging letters from Lupe. When Casey's grandmother died suddenly a few months later, her grandfather had sent for her, intending to send her straight back to those hallowed halls of learning directly after the funeral.

But she'd cried and cajoled and, finally, her grandfather had agreed to let her stay and return to her old school, which, though stuffy and intolerant of red-haired girls who wanted to be country singers, was better than living among strangers far away.

That Christmas, she received her first guitar. But Lupe and Juan were still gone, and Casey was still lonely, so she threw her whole heart and soul into her music. Using a Dummies book, she taught herself to read notes, and she practiced chords on that guitar until her fingertips were raw, then, mercifully, calloused.

She sang along with her radio, alone in her room, copying the old-timers—Patsy Cline and Loretta Lynn, then Reba McEntire and Faith Hill and LeAnn Rimes and anyone else she admired, which added up to a lot of people. Then she started singing on the street, to her grandfather's mortification, collecting quarters and crumpled dollar bills—and a whole lot of pennies—in her open guitar case resting at her feet on the sidewalk.

From there, she'd gotten bookings in grange halls and old folks' homes and high school gymnasiums, and she'd known even then, with her grandfather nurturing an ever-greater disapproval, that she had something special, that she was going to *make it.*

And she had. The breaks had finally started coming, barely noticeable at first. She'd played rodeos and, having lied about her age so many times that she believed herself, bars and nightclubs.

Her grandfather had finally stopped speaking to her entirely, though she still heard from Lupe and Juan, even now.

"Mom?" Shane snapped his fingers in front of her face. "Hello? Mom?"

Casey chuckled. "Sorry," she said. "I guess I was drifting."

"How come you're not eating?" Clare wanted to know. She could be bossy at times, that child.

"Because I'm not hungry," Casey answered patiently. By the time this day ended, she thought, these children would know she'd deceived them, and they might never be together, in exactly this way, again.

Tears burned behind her eyes, but she held them back. Even smiled, which took some grit. "We're going out to Timber Creek today," she said. "All three of us."

Shane looked thrilled. "Can we take the dogs?"

"Not this time," Casey told her son with gentle regret.

Clare, not only older than Shane but female, and therefore more perceptive, studied her mother with frank concern. "What's going on?" she asked.

Casey had to swallow several times before she could answer. "You'll know soon enough," she said. "For now, let's leave it at that."

"Mom," Clare demanded, "are you sick? Are you going to tell us that you're dying of some horrible disease?"

"No," Casey was quick to reply. "It's nothing like that."

"Then, what?" Shane wanted to know. "We're moving? You're going back on the road?"

Casey almost told them the whole story then, but words failed her. She didn't like admitting that she needed anybody, but she needed Walker beside her for this one—that was for sure.

She shook her head. "We're not moving and I'm not going back on the road," she assured Shane, who was visibly relieved. "I'm calling the crew together, after Labor Day, to record some songs and block out a new video, but that's the extent of it."

She hadn't heard from Mitch by phone or email since he'd stormed off after she'd turned down his proposal, nor had she received his letter of resignation.

Hopefully, *that* mess, at least, would blow over. She liked Mitch, and he was a good manager. Besides, the thought of starting from scratch with somebody new, after all these years, was overwhelming.

Mercifully, the kids stopped asking questions after that.

Casey retreated to her room and stepped into her ridiculously large—and full—closet. She would have known what to wear if she was going to sing for a president or any level of royalty, but how did one dress to tell her children that she'd been deceiving them since birth? No harmless fib, this. Instead, it was a lie so big that it had become a lifestyle, and Casey had lived it so long and so thoroughly that she didn't know who she—or any of them—would be without it.

Black seemed too funereal and white too innocent, so she finally chose a green voile sundress that brought out the color of her eyes and complemented her red hair. Forswearing pantyhose—there was a limit to the suffering she was willing to endure, even in this situation—she slipped sandals onto her bare feet, squirted a little perfume at the hollow of her throat and called it good.

Studying her reflection in the mirrors above her vanity, Casey made a simple, motivational speech.

"Buck up, cowgirl," she said.

CHAPTER EIGHT

THE KITCHEN OF the house at Timber Creek Ranch was probably a quarter the size of her own, if that, Casey observed, sitting numbly at the large round table, with Clare seated to her left, Shane to her right and Walker straight across. Under any other circumstances, she would have enjoyed the cozy normality of the room, the pretty cotton curtains at the old-fashioned windows, the natural-rock fireplace where cheerful blazes surely snapped and crackled on winter mornings, the rustic plank floor dotted here and there with colorful hand-made rugs. At the moment, though, she was so focused on what she had to say—what she was *afraid* to say—that her surroundings barely registered.

Walker's gaze connected with hers, held. The impact reminded her of railroad cars coupling with a jolt.

The inside of Casey's head buzzed, as though her brain were a wasps' nest, and her stomach bounced continually between her pelvis and her esophagus.

"Would somebody *please* tell us what's going on?" Clare burst out, glancing from Casey to Walker and back again, speaking for her brother as well as herself, it would seem. As the older of the two, and a natural take-charge type, she often did that.

Shane remained silent, his gawky, youthful body stiff with tension. One day, Casey thought, those now-thin shoulders of his would be broad and strong, like Walker's, but, for now, they were narrow and a little stooped, making the boy look all too vulnerable.

Casey opened her mouth to reply to her daughter's question, but no sound came out. Not even a croak, though she felt a scraping sensation, as though she were trying to swallow a rusty hasp of the sort used to file horses' hooves.

Walker's grin was slight, but encouraging. "It'll be okay," he said, his voice gruff and gentle, both at once.

Casey swallowed, her hands knotted together in her lap, and nodded, but she still couldn't get her vocal cords to work.

"Mom," Clare insisted, arms folded across her beginning-to-blossom chest, eyes troubled. *"What?"*

Casey looked at her daughter, her son and then Walker.

"This is hard," she finally managed. Tears blurred her vision for a moment, and she blinked them away.

"Go on," Walker urged quietly.

Casey knew he would speak up if she couldn't, or wouldn't, but it was *her* responsibility to tell her children the truth, because she'd been the one to start that first lie rolling. And then sustain it, with many, many *other* lies.

Clare and Shane seemed on the verge of panic, though, and there was no more time left, Casey realized with a painful start. The sand had all run through the hourglass.

So she blurted it out, starkly and far too abruptly. "Walker is your father," she said.

A thunderous silence fell, filling the room, pushing

the walls outward. Casey waited for the roof to cave in, though, of course, it didn't.

She could feel her own heartbeat, pounding in the hollow of her still-sore throat, and she forced herself to look squarely at her children, each in turn. Shane was not only unfazed, he was grinning, his eyes alight with wonder.

"For real?" he asked.

"For real," Casey replied softly, shifting her gaze to Clare.

The girl's reaction was the polar opposite of Shane's—the red in her hair seemed to leach into her face, making vivid pink circles on her cheeks, and her eyes were narrowed almost to slits. Her chin wobbled, and she immediately shoved back her chair, ready to bolt.

Walker stopped her by taking hold of her hand. "Easy now, sweetheart," he told his daughter, the words thick with affection and regret. "Give your mom a chance to explain."

Clare remained seated, but her whole countenance exuded defiance. "You *lied,*" she accused, glaring at Casey. "You *knew* how much we wanted a dad, Shane and me, and you let us believe we were *freaks,* conceived in some *laboratory—*"

"Clare," Casey said miserably. "Listen to me, please—"

"I *hate* you!" Clare erupted, and this time, when she started to rise, Walker made no move to keep her at the table. She swept both parents up in a scathing sweep of a glance. "I hate you *both—*"

"No." Casey fairly whimpered the word. This was what she'd feared would happen. On some level, she'd known Shane would take the news well, but Clare would feel wounded and betrayed—by the person she'd trusted most.

Clare whirled, headed for the outside door, nearly tripping over a startled Doolittle in her hurry to escape her mother's company and, by extension, Walker's. She slammed the screen door hard and stomped across the porch, footsteps reverberating.

Casey started to rise, every instinct compelling her to go after her daughter, find a way to comfort the girl, make everything all right, but Walker put up one hand, like a traffic cop.

"Let her go," he said. "She needs a few minutes for this to sink in."

Casey, knowing Walker was right, slumped bleakly back into her chair.

Shane, still staring at Walker as though he'd just emerged from Aladdin's lamp, genie-style, remained awestruck, oblivious, evidently, to his sister's angry departure. "You're *really* our dad?" he half whispered.

"I'm really your dad," Walker confirmed.

They heard a rig come up the driveway then, a motor shutting off, ticking and clicking as it went still. A car door closed; a dog barked.

Brylee, Casey thought. The poor woman couldn't possibly know what she was walking in on.

Walker caught her eye. "I can ask her to leave for a while," he offered. "Come back later—"

But Casey shook her head. "No," she answered. "Brylee's family, and she has a right to know what's going on."

Walker gave a slight nod.

Brylee and her dog could be heard coming up the

porch steps. Her voice came gently through the screen in the door; she'd spotted Clare, probably huddled in the big wooden swing.

"Hey," Brylee said softly. "What's the trouble, honey?"

Clare's response was an angry sob, and the chains supporting the swing creaked as she started it in motion, probably with a hard kick at the floorboards.

"You can tell me," Brylee said.

"Ask *them!*" Clare cried in response. "Ask the liars!"

Casey closed her eyes for a moment, against the pain she'd caused her daughter, boomeranging back to bruise her, as well. Her stomach felt as though someone had just slammed a fist into it, hard.

Some murmuring followed, and Clare continued to cry, fury giving way to heartbreak. Neither Casey nor Walker moved or spoke, though Shane, by then out of his chair and stroking Doolittle's head and gleaming back, seemed to be lost in a happy world of his own.

He snapped out of it long enough to make a comment, though.

"I don't get it," Shane said, amazed. "We find out we're not lab experiments—that we have Walker for a dad—and Clare's bawling her eyes out like it's the end of the world or something."

Walker, leaning from his chair, laid a hand on his son's shoulder and, though he'd done that many times before, it was different this time. Casey saw pride in the way Walker touched Shane, knew he was claiming the boy, that no matter what happened after this, they would always be father and son—the bond, finally established, was unbreakable.

"Clare will be all right," Walker told Shane. Then

his gaze caught Casey's again, and he leaned back in his chair. "We all will."

The screen door opened with a slight squeal of hinges in need of oiling, and Brylee came in, the dog right behind her.

"What's going on here?" she asked bluntly, her eyes big and her cheeks pale with concern. "Did something happen—?"

Walker was still looking at Casey, and there was a question in his eyes, as clear as if he'd asked it aloud. *Should I tell her?*

Casey merely nodded.

Walker broke the news to his sister and he was a lot more diplomatic than Casey had been just minutes before. Briefly but thoroughly he outlined the circumstances that had brought them all to this moment and this place.

A slow smile spread across Brylee's wide mouth as she listened, moved up into her eyes, shining there.

"Wow," she said when Walker finished. "That's *great.*"

Great, Casey thought dismally. Except that Clare was still out there on the porch, crying her heart out, feeling cheated and furious and sold out—by her own mother, no less.

"Can I live here now, with you?" Shane asked Walker. "Can I have a horse? Does this mean my last name is really *Parrish,* instead of *Elder?*"

Walker smiled at the boy. "Whoa," he said. "You belong with your mom. As for the horse and the last name, we'll discuss all that later, after the dust settles and everybody's on the same page."

Casey tossed an appreciative glance in Walker's direction; he was letting her know he didn't plan on trying to take her children away from her, and she hadn't realized, until that moment, how afraid she'd been that he would do exactly that.

At least, she *hoped* that was his meaning.

She stood, unable to wait any longer, her knees wobbly and her head spinning a little, and moved past a sympathetic Brylee to open the screen door and step out onto the porch.

Just as she'd pictured her, Clare was crumpled up in a corner of the big swing, looking more like the little girl she had been, just a few short seasons ago, than the young woman she was so rapidly turning into.

Casey walked over and sat down beside her daughter on the plump, faded cushion padding the seat of the swing. She didn't touch Clare and she didn't speak, either. She just wanted to *be* there.

Clare, resting both forearms on the arm of the swing, shoulders shaking, eventually lifted her head. She didn't look at Casey, though. Instead, she stared off into something well beyond the rails of the porch, the nearby barn, even the distant horizon.

"Why?" she asked, after a long, long time. She sounded broken, as well as outraged.

Casey weighed the obvious answers. *It seemed like a good idea at the time,* though true, would sound flippant. *I thought it would be the best thing for all of us,* then? No, that wouldn't do, either, because while she'd wanted to believe that from the beginning, she knew now that it was just another lie. She'd wanted her career, too, and, dammit, she wasn't ashamed of that, for all her other regrets.

"No excuses," she said. "I should have told you the

truth, right from the start, and I'm really sorry I didn't, honey."

Clare turned puffy, accusing eyes on her then. *"Why?"* she repeated fiercely. "Tell me *why.*"

Casey sighed. "I'm not sure I know," she admitted, at some length. "Not the whole reason, anyhow. I was young, my career was just getting started and I wasn't expecting to get pregnant."

"So you chose your *music* over Shane and me and Walker?" The words pierced Casey's heart like a spray of porcupine quills.

"I wanted to keep singing," she said after deliberating for a while. "But it wasn't about choosing *anything*—or *anybody*—over you and your brother." Mitch, members of the band and other close friends had advised her to put her baby girl up for adoption, and she'd flatly refused, but she didn't think it would do any good to mention that just now. In fact, it might even make things worse.

"And you let it happen *twice,*" Clare marveled angrily, as though Casey hadn't spoken at all. "I'm sorry, but that's just *weird.*"

Casey smiled sadly, remembering the scared, pregnant girl with fame and fortune at her fingertips. By then, her grandparents were both dead, and when it came to kinfolks, she was alone in the world. "Maybe," she confessed presently, her voice small and soft. "But I can't imagine my life without both you and Shane."

Clare didn't answer right away, and she'd averted her eyes again, too. "What about Walker? Did he want us?"

"He didn't know," Casey replied, after biting the figurative bullet. It would have been so easy to blame

Walker, make him out to be one of those men who make babies and then skip out, fancy-free.

But she couldn't do that—it would be the worst lie of all.

"What do you mean, 'He didn't know'?" Clare shot back. "He knows *now,* so you must have clued him in at some point—*unlike Shane and me.*"

"When I found out I was expecting you," Casey said, thinking that telling the truth was overrated, "I led Walker to believe there was another man in my life. A year later, when Shane was on his way, I knew I had to tell Walker, because he was sure to guess everything if I didn't. He was madder than a bee-stung mule at first, but not because I'd gotten pregnant again—he wanted to us to be a family then, the four of us, but I wasn't ready for that."

"You weren't *ready,*" Clare echoed, scornful again. Inside the house, Walker, Brylee and Shane talked in quiet, peaceful voices, and it seemed to Casey that they were apart from her and from Clare, in some other, unreachable dimension. "You still had to win all those Grammies and CMA awards, didn't you? Make all that money?" A shuddery pause followed. "Did you even think about *us,* Mom? Did it cross your mind that maybe Shane and I would have liked to grow up in a real house, instead of airplanes and tour buses and hotels, with a mother and a father and a *regular* life?" She gestured, taking in everything around them. "We could have lived right here, gone trick-or-treating at Halloween, ridden the bus to school in town, had friends we'd known since kindergarten, put up the Christmas tree in the same part of the same room every year. We could have been *regular people*—but, no. We had to have a mother so famous she couldn't even take us to Disneyland without being mobbed!"

Where did all that come from? Casey didn't dare ask. Not yet, anyhow. All these years, she'd thought her confident, capable children were happy living unconventional lives, at least most of the time. Obviously, that had only been partially true. Her head began to ache.

"If I could go back," she said, "I'd do things differently."

"Easy to say," Clare retorted. She'd put her stubborn face on, and she meant to wear it for a while. Maybe forever.

"I love you and Shane with all my heart," Casey said. "I always have."

Clare made a contemptuous, huffy sound, barely audible. "Whatever," she replied in bitter dismissal.

After that, an invisible wall came down between the two of them, and Casey knew there would be no reaching the girl, that the time for talking was over, for now anyway.

She stood up and went back into the house, leaving Clare in the porch swing and feeling as though she'd aged twenty years in the past hour. Worse, she was literally beside herself, a step removed from her body, oddly detached, like an observer following close on her own heels.

Brylee crossed to Casey when she entered the kitchen, gave her a wordless hug.

Casey was profoundly grateful for the other woman's support, though she had no idea how long it would last, and hugged her back.

Shane remained remarkably unshaken—it was as if

he'd been told he'd won the lottery, and maybe he had. The prize was a father—just what he'd always wanted.

It hurt to know, with such certainty, that she, Casey, for all her love, for all her devotion and hands-on parenting, wasn't enough.

"I want to be Shane *Parrish* from now on," the boy announced.

Casey merely nodded, unable to look at her son or at Walker, keeping her eyes cast downward as she stood there in the middle of that plank floor, stricken all over again.

"So," Brylee said, suddenly, expansively and with a little too much enthusiasm, "suppose I take my niece and nephew out for a nice, long horseback ride? Followed by supper in town?"

"Yes!" Shane said.

"Might be a good idea," Walker agreed, standing now. Casey wondered when he'd moved, gotten up from his chair at the table. That peculiar feeling of being separated from herself remained, and the headache was getting worse, too.

"I'm not sure Clare will want to—" Casey began, but she lost momentum before she could finish the sentence. She didn't know what Clare would do next, or what she would say.

To Casey's surprise, though, Brylee easily convinced Clare to join her and Shane on an impromptu adventure, and Casey watched through the window above the sink as the three of them headed for the barn, accompanied by Brylee's dog.

Walker moved to stand behind Casey, slipping his arms loosely around her waist, giving her plenty of room, even inside his embrace. He'd always had a way about him, an ability to comfort her without making her feel cornered. "The worst part is over," he told her, his voice husky, resting his chin on the crown of her head.

The dam broke then, the one Casey had erected years ago, before she had Clare and Shane, even before she'd known Walker. A virtual torrent of emotion flooded through the barrier that had held for so long—sorrow and loss, shame and regret, loneliness and exhaustion. Casey, disoriented before, landed back in her own skin with a crash, and a cry of pain escaped her.

Walker turned her around, held her. And she sobbed into his chest, clung to his shoulders with both hands, convinced she'd collapse if she let go.

She knew that, like most men, Walker was uncomfortable with tears, but he didn't shush her, didn't tell her not to cry, didn't prattle on about how everything would turn out just fine. He merely stood there, as solid as the trunk of a venerable Ponderosa pine, holding her. It felt so right, the heat and the substance of him, the strength.

That was the trouble, of course, because it *wasn't* right. When she allowed Walker to take care of her this way, when she allowed *herself* to be a mortal woman with needs and feelings instead of a powerhouse, a star, a *success,* things happened. *Babies* happened.

For all that, she couldn't pull away from Walker.

Curving his hand under her chin, he lifted her face, kissed away her tears. "Casey," he ground out, holding her tightly.

Their lips came together naturally—inevitably—seeking at first, tentative, then demanding, fusing them together on some deeper level, where nameless forces surged and swelled, as powerful as a rain-swollen river on a downhill course.

They remained where they were for a long time, kissing, pausing to catch quick, desperate breaths, kissing again.

Vaguely, at the far periphery of her awareness, Casey heard voices—Brylee, Clare, Shane—heard the clomp of horses' hooves out in the yard, the jingle of bridle fittings, and Brylee's dog, barking with excitement.

They might have been in another world, all of them, quite apart from the one she and Walker and—somewhere nearby, Doolittle—occupied.

Her common sense, normally her north star, her personal compass, deserted her, and that wasn't even the worst part. No, the worst part was, she didn't care about practicality, about consequences, about old lessons learned the hard way and the scars they left behind.

All she wanted was to lose herself in Walker for a little while.

Need crackled between them, almost tangible.

"Are you sure?" Walker asked, reading her with perfect accuracy, the way he'd always done, at least when they were intimate.

"Yes," she said, because she'd been hungry for so long, lonely for so long, *brave* for so long. She didn't want to be her usual strong, independent self—no, instead, she yearned to give in, to let Walker's strength be enough for both of them, if only for a little while.

He lifted her easily into his arms, carried her out of the kitchen, along a corridor.

She knew she ought to stop him, right this instant, before things went any further, but she couldn't. Make that, *wouldn't*. Alarm bells should have sounded in her head—history was about to repeat itself—but they didn't. She wanted this, wanted to be swept away, wanted *Walker*.

Soon, they were in his bedroom.

Momentarily, sanity returned. What if Brylee and the kids came back?

Casey didn't realize she'd asked the question out loud until Walker answered it, his breath warm against her ear, making her skin tingle even as he eased her down onto the bed.

"They'll be gone awhile," he promised hoarsely. "Bless her, Brylee will see to that."

He was already undressing Casey, even as he spoke—or was she undressing herself? Or him? Either way, their clothes seemed to evaporate, his as well as hers, like morning dew under the light of a summer sun.

Casey murmured Walker's name, feeling the steely length of him against her side as they lay together, a breeze blowing through, cooling their flesh, if not their ardor.

His mouth fell to hers then, consuming, igniting flames within flames within flames. There was no stopping this, Casey knew—they were already lost, both of them.

Walker nibbled at her earlobe, traced the length of her neck with his warm mouth, found her breast, took her nipple with a greedy tenderness that sent hot, sweet pleasure skewering through her.

It's been so long, her body whispered—or was it the wordless language of her soul that spoke so eloquently? *Walker—Walker—it's been so long.*

Casey couldn't get close enough to him; her hands roamed up and down the muscular length of his back, urging, urging.

With a low groan, Walker parted her legs, found her most sensitive place and began plying her with his fingers. He knew just how to touch her, lightly but not *too* lightly, increasing the turmoil inside her with every skillful motion of his hand.

Casey arched her back, biting down hard on her lower lip to hold back a cry of raw, primitive surrender. "Now," she pleaded, nearly strangling on her own voice. "Please, Walker—*now*—"

But Walker would not be rushed; even in the state she was in, she should have remembered that. No, he'd take his time with her, enjoy both her breasts at his leisure, kiss her senseless, and then he would—

The memory of all those other times when they'd made love electrified her, made her gasp again in anticipation, and Walker, understanding, chuckled low in his throat.

"Hang on, cowgirl," he murmured, his lips moving against the quivering flesh of her belly now and headed slowly, inexorably south. "We're just getting started."

"I don't think—I can wait—" Casey whimpered, already wet, already expanding to receive him, take him inside her, hold him there.

"That's all right, too," Walker replied. And then he was *there,* burrowing through with his tongue, teasing her, finally taking her into his mouth.

Her entire body buckled in a spasm of frantic welcome as he shifted to his knees, slid his hands under her backside, raised her high off the sheets and went right on partaking of her, now gently, now hungrily, as though she were a honeycomb, ripe and juicy and sweet.

She buried her fingers in his hair, holding him to her even as she thought she'd surely explode into flaming fragments at any moment, like a dying star, dissolving into darkness. The pleasure was all-consuming and yet not nearly enough, a mere promise of what was still to come.

Casey rasped Walker's name, fevered, desolate, triumphant.

Walker went easy on her for a few moments, then grew more demanding again, more insistent.

Her first climax erupted like a geyser, propelling her skyward in dizzying spirals of splintered light, the force of it stopping her breath behind her throat, even as her body flexed in glorious abandon, and flexed again. Then again.

When it was over, Walker lowered her back to the mattress and Casey, though saturated with satisfaction, every muscle and bone melted, craved more. She wanted, *needed,* to feel Walker deep inside her, part of her, needed to be driven mad all over again by the friction as they moved together, in that most private, most sacred dance of all.

She could only mutter his name, though, because she'd given him all her strength, shamelessly thrown everything she had, everything she was, into that shattering, seemingly endless orgasm. For all its power, she knew it was only the first of many, each one wilder than the last, each one hurling her outside herself, outside the ordinary, everyday world, into realms of mystery and magic.

Walker shifted, and the thought flitted through Casey's mind that he was putting on a condom, and she wanted to laugh for sheer joy, though she knew she didn't have the breath for even that much effort. He'd been wearing a condom when they conceived Clare. Shane, too.

Did he remember that?

Dazed, Casey shook her head from side to side in answer to her own unspoken question. Walker was a man—was he ever—and using protection was probably a matter of habit with him. Just another responsibility.

He wasn't thinking about making babies.

"You're sure?" he rasped, poised above her now, careful not to crush her beneath his weight.

He'd always asked her that, no matter how heated the moment, and he cared about her answer. If she'd asked him to stop, he would have.

"I'm sure," she said instead.

In one powerful, earth-shattering thrust, Walker claimed her, made her his own, and she immediately climaxed again, softly, though each motion of their joined bodies aroused her more, drove her ever upward, toward another, greater release, and then still another.

Walker maintained control, even as she flailed beneath him, gave herself up to him completely, over and over again, repeated his name like a ragged litany.

Finally, though, he let go, driving deep, his whole body seizing like a single muscle as, with a long, low groan—her name—he spilled himself inside her.

Afterward, they lay in silence, too spent to talk, arms and legs entwined, skin slick with perspiration. The breeze was like a cool caress, soothing and soft. Somewhere nearby, a clock ticked, the old-fashioned kind with actual works inside, steady as a heartbeat.

Casey, flung heavenward with the last, most ferocious release, drifted slowly back to reality, floating like a feather or a snowflake. And the instant she came in for a landing, soul and body colliding with a wallop, she sat bolt upright and said, "Oh, my God, Walker— what have we done?"

He chuckled, still languid. "If I remember correctly," he murmured, "we had sex."

"Ha, ha, very funny," Casey said scathingly, though it was herself she was angry with, not Walker. After all, it wasn't as if she'd done anything to discourage him— she'd been as unstoppable as a tigress in mating season.

Now, though, she broke free of his embrace, scrambled out of bed and began snatching her discarded clothes from the floor. "I can't *believe* we let this happen!"

Walker eased himself up onto his elbows, maddeningly unperturbed, bare to the waist. Mercifully, the sheets covered him. "Simmer down," he advised, his eyes twinkling. "We're both grown-ups here."

Casey wouldn't look at him. She was struggling awkwardly into her underwear, nearly hog-tying herself in the process. "Which means we ought to know better," she sputtered.

With a chuckle, Walker got out of bed, magnificently naked, and retreated into the adjoining bathroom. Moments later, he was back, bending to retrieve his jeans from the floor, slipping them on without a hint of self-consciousness.

By then, Casey was back in her clothes and facing the mirror above Walker's antique bureau, trying to do something with her love-tangled hair. Not only had it come loose from its ponytail, it looked as though she'd been swinging upside down from a trapeze. *Bedhead* didn't begin to describe the phenomenon.

Walker sat down on the foot of the bed, the sheets

and covers so tangled that a tornado might have just passed through, and watched her, feet and chest bare, hair still mussed from her fingers delving through it. His expression was calm, amused—and a little on the smug side.

And why *wouldn't* he be smug? He'd just turned her inside out—again—and she'd let him know it, too, carrying on like that.

If she'd been the violent type, she'd have thrown something at Walker Parrish's handsome head just then.

"Don't you grin at me!" she commanded, shaking an index finger for emphasis.

"Still the same old red-hot, complicated Casey," Walker drawled, undaunted, grin firmly in place. "A she-wolf in bed, a spinster schoolmarm out of it."

"What if we did it again, Walker?" she demanded, agonized by the prospect and, at the same time, hopeful. "What if we made another baby? How would we explain *that* to Clare and Shane?"

"I used a condom," he reminded her.

"Yes," she agreed tersely. "Just as you did when we conceived Clare, and then Shane."

He looked thoughtful for a few moments, then immediately brightened. "You've got a point there," he admitted, willing, for once, to concede that she was right about something. Another pause followed, while he pondered the matter in an annoyingly unhurried way. "If you're having my baby," he finally concluded, "you're going to have me to deal with, from here on, because this time, we're doing it right."

"What does that mean?" Casey all but whispered the words.

"It means, Casey Jones, that married or not, if you're

having my child, *this time,* we're going to raise him or her together, as a team—not with you in one place and me in another."

And that, considering the note of finality in Walker's tone, was that.

CHAPTER NINE

WALKER MIGHT HAVE looked calm on the outside, but on the *inside,* a whole passel of contradictory emotions churned like the contents of a blender on high speed. Sorting all those feelings out was going to take some time, and he couldn't just sit there on the end of his bed until things fell neatly into place, now, could he, because if he did, he'd be there till his beard grew in white.

So, suppressing a sigh that would have revealed too much, he stood up, cutting a wide swath around a still-rattled Casey, made his way over to the closet, found himself a clean shirt and shrugged into it. He got the buttoning wrong on the first try and had to start over. Finally, he sat down again, to put on fresh socks and haul his boots back onto his feet.

This probably wasn't the time, he reasoned, in the privacy of his sex-addled head, to tell Casey that the condom hadn't held. She was on the verge of a melt-down as it was.

She looked a sight, though, and a fine one, as she ran a brush through her coppery hair and wrestled it back into a ponytail, as it was before they'd decided to take a roll in the hay.

Walker didn't regret what they'd done—no sane man would have, especially after a lengthy dry spell like the one he'd just been through—but he knew Casey had enough regrets for both of them. And if he was honest, the knowledge hurt a little.

"Do you want to wait for Brylee to bring the kids back here or go home?" he asked, figuring Casey might not say another word to him, ever, if he didn't make the first move.

She turned to face him, an act of pure bravado, he reckoned, placing her hands on her hips and straightening her spine until she reached her full and patently unremarkable height.

"I want to go home," she said. Not much ambiguity there.

"Okay," Walker agreed, standing up again. A part of him—a *big* part of him—wanted to lure Casey Elder right back into bed and make love to her all over again, but success seemed about as likely as a two-way conversation with his horse, so he tried to let go of the idea. For the time being, anyhow.

"That's all?" Casey sniped. "Just, 'okay'?"

"What do you *want* me to say, Casey? That we can pretend this didn't happen?"

She marched past him, out of the bedroom, along the length of the hallway, past a couple of other rooms and, finally, into the kitchen. Only then, snatching up her shoulder bag from a countertop and shoving one arm through the strap, did she deign to answer, drawing in a deep breath and then, in the next instant, deflating again.

"I'm doing it again, aren't I?" she asked, looking away from him and then, with visible determination, looking back. "Trying to pick a fight, so I can put some distance between us, give myself time to think."

Walker nodded, though he was a little surprised by

the admission. Casey was good at fooling herself, and even better at fooling other people, and she'd been living the lie for so long that he'd begun to wonder if she could no longer recognize the truth.

"Take all the time you want," he said, at some length. "But it isn't going to be business as usual, at least as far as Clare and Shane are concerned. I'm through playing the good ole dependable family friend, Case. Insofar as they'll let me, at this late date, I want to be a *father* to them both."

"Good luck with Clare," Casey said, and while she might have sounded flippant, Walker knew by the tears glinting briefly in her green eyes and the wobble of her chin that she'd meant those words, hadn't simply tossed them off in an effort to get under his skin or make him back off a step or two.

Walker wanted to put his arms around Casey then, but he didn't dare. She so rarely allowed him to comfort her that, when she did, they both lost control.

"Clare will come around, Case," he said gently, because he knew she was afraid the girl would never forgive her. And it was true enough that long-term family feuds sometimes started over a lot less, so he reckoned she had cause for concern, all right. "You're her mother, and she loves you. Plus, she's a smart kid—in time, she'll realize that everybody makes mistakes, often with the best of intentions."

Casey averted her eyes from Walker, shy all of a sudden, changeable as sunlight dancing on the surface of a creek. For just a moment, he caught a glimpse of the little girl inside her, the one who had lost her folks as a baby, grown up with stodgy if well-meaning grandparents, wealthy and past the time when child rearing might have been a realistic possibility, and probably at more of a loss, with every passing day, than pride would have allowed them to admit. He supposed they'd loved Casey, in their way, tried to make the best of a difficult situation, but she was still, for all her accomplishments, a bird with a broken wing.

"I hope you're right," she finally replied.

After that, he and Doolittle squired the lady home in the truck, and not much was said along the way.

"Do me a favor?" Walker said, when he'd seen Casey safely to the front door, waiting while she fumbled through her handbag for the keys.

"What kind of favor?" she asked, looking up at him, her expression just a touch on the wary side.

"Don't go beating yourself up over all this," he answered, his voice going husky again. "You've done what you could to make things right, and that took guts, and you don't have to fight the whole battle alone anymore. I'll help as much as I can, and I know Brylee will, too, so let's try to take things as they come." He smiled. "Play it by ear, so to speak."

Casey gave a wan little grin at the awkward pun, stuck the key in the lock and turned it. Pausing on the threshold, she looked up at him again, and broke his heart into two jagged pieces with her bravery.

"I'm going to need some time, Walker," she reminded him. "And some space. I won't stop you from seeing Clare and Shane, but—"

He touched her mouth with one finger, unable to bear hearing the rest of that sentence. "One day at a time," he said.

She nodded again, stepped inside, closed the door.

Walker waited until he heard the lock engage, then

turned to walk away, even though leaving Casey behind was about the last thing he wanted to do just then.

A WELCOMING COMMITTEE composed of three eager dogs, barely more than puppies, and two more-reserved cats awaited Casey in the cathedral-like entryway to that too-big, too-fancy house.

The place was more like one huge and soulless showcase than a home, it seemed to her, especially in comparison to Walker's spacious but functional quarters. *His* house had a history—she could picture generations of Parrishes living and loving within those solid walls, imagine simple, wholesome meals being made and shared. People had surely laughed and cried there, celebrated and mourned. In good times, they would have rejoiced, in that quiet and modest way country folks did, and when times were hard, they would have made do, and rarely, if ever, complained.

By contrast, this mansion she lived in, beautiful as it was, had an air of impermanence, of anonymity, like a grand hotel. In those reflective moments, she was more grateful than usual for the rough-and-tumble attentions of the dogs, if only because they were genuinely glad to see her.

Resolving to snap out of it, Casey stopped playing the comparison game, since the score was always zero-to-zero and nobody ever came out a winner, and wondered if she and the pets were alone in the house.

It was at moments like this that she missed the guys in the band, missed their boisterous goodwill and their willingness to make music at any hour of the day or night.

Doris, the housekeeper, was probably around somewhere, but Casey didn't go looking for her, mainly because she didn't want to answer any perceptive questions. Doris was a longtime employee and a true friend, but this fix Casey found herself in wasn't the sort of thing she could be expected to understand, being of another generation. The older woman would know at a glance, though, that something big had happened, age difference notwithstanding, and, always kindhearted, she'd try to open a dialogue—which was the last thing Casey wanted to deal with while she felt so jangled.

So she climbed the *Gone with the Wind* staircase, secretly glad when none of the pets followed, and took lonely refuge in her room.

After a quick shower, Casey put on fresh jeans, a blue silk shirt, low-heeled shoes and makeup. When Clare and Shane came home, she'd be there to greet them, on top of things, equal to any challenge, even if she had to pretend. Angry or not, Clare needed a *mother,* strong and competent and ready to engage, not some caricature of a mad housewife, disheveled and distracted.

And never mind that she felt a lot more like the latter than the former at the moment. If she'd dressed to match her present emotions, she'd have worn an old chenille bathrobe, ratty scuff slippers and a head full of foam curlers. There probably would have been a martini in her hand, too.

Alas, weakness was a luxury she couldn't afford. As soon as the kids came through the door, it would be showtime.

Having come to terms with the situation, Casey went downstairs to the kitchen, in need of a cup of tea and mindful of the fact that it was time to feed the pets. Taking care of the menagerie was normally Shane and

Clare's job, but since they weren't around to do it at the moment, she'd have to step up.

For all that, Casey might have gone right on hiding out in her room if she'd known Doris was already in the kitchen, standing in front of the eight-burner stove, stirring something in a kettle. When the other woman looked back over a shoulder and saw Casey, she started a little.

"Oh," she said, putting a hand to her heart.

"I'm sorry," Casey said quickly. "I didn't mean to scare you."

Doris tried to smile, but there was a strange, distracted glint in her eyes, and her lips moved constantly, even when she wasn't talking.

"Is everything all right?" Casey asked, forgetting her tea for a moment. Doris wasn't herself, and that alarmed her, because Doris was *always* herself.

The housekeeper looked baffled by the question, and didn't reply right away.

The dogs and cats, knowing supper was in the offing, converged on the kitchen en masse, and for the next few minutes, Casey busied herself pouring kibble rations and rinsing and refilling water bowls while she waited—for what seemed like an eternity—for Doris to say something.

"No, dear," she finally answered, shoulders drooping, unaware that whatever she'd been stirring was now dripping from the end of her wooden spoon onto the gleaming floor. "Actually—no. Everything *isn't* all right."

Casey left the pets to their meals and approached, touching Doris's arm lightly before removing the spoon from the woman's grasp and setting it aside on the stove top. "What is it? Are you ill?"

She had to resist the motherly urge to touch the housekeeper's forehead, testing for fever.

"No, I'm— I'm not sick." But Doris's nose reddened at the tip, and her eyes grew moist. "It's my sister, Evelyn," she went on. "She's fallen and broken her hip, and she's all alone over there in Seattle, with nobody to keep her company or take charge of things."

Casey took both her housekeeper's hands in her own and looked directly into her worried eyes. "Then you've got to go to her," she said softly. "Right away."

"But what will you do without me?" Doris all but wailed. "Who will cook and clean and look after the children when you're working?"

"Don't worry about us," Casey answered, biting back an automatic *We'll be fine* because it might have hurt Doris's feelings, made her think she and the kids didn't need her. She'd spoiled them all completely, over the years, but now they'd just have to buck up and do things for themselves. "Right now, Evelyn matters most. She needs you. And you need to be with her, for your own peace of mind."

"She's so scared, lying there in a hospital bed like that," Doris confirmed fitfully, nodding her head again and again, as if in answer to some other voice that Casey couldn't hear. "She's hurting something terrible, too— Evelyn never had a very high threshold for pain, you know—and she told me earlier, when she called, that the doctors and nurses aren't listening to a word she says."

"Pack your bags," Casey said firmly. "I'll charter a plane, and you'll be in Seattle, holding Evelyn's hand before you know it." Not so long ago, Casey had owned a private jet and kept a flight crew on call 24/7, but now that she wasn't doing concert tours, she wouldn't have used it enough to justify the staggering expense, so she'd sold the aircraft and canceled the service providing pilots and other staff.

Doris blinked. She was a woman with her feet firmly planted on the ground, literally and figuratively, and, unlike Shane and Clare, who'd loved flying, she'd rarely traveled with Casey and the entourage. "Are you sure I ought to go? There's so much to do around here, and Clare and Shane don't eat enough vegetables if I don't keep an eye on them, and—"

Casey chuckled, silenced her friend with a big hug. "I'll force-feed those kids spinach and broccoli, if I have to," she teased. "Go pack your bags while I make a few phone calls."

Just over an hour later, a sleek jet came in for a landing at what passed for an airport, a strip of asphalt that served both Parable and Three Trees. Casey, who had driven Doris and her suitcases there, virtually shooed the woman aboard. Doris had barely disappeared into the cabin when the copilot descended the folding stairs to stow the bags in the cargo hold and make a final flight check.

Casey was about to get back behind the wheel of her SUV, planning to head home immediately after takeoff, but at the copilot's approach, she paused. Grinning, he tipped his hat and said genially, "Hello there, Ms. Elder. Remember me?"

As many people as she'd met, Casey had a good memory for names and faces. "Joe Parker," she said, extending a hand and smiling. Back when she still owned a jet, one with her name and face splashed across the side, no less, Joe had occasionally joined the crew, which tended to rotate. "How are Shelley and the kids?"

Joe shook her hand, beaming with pride. He wasn't a player like some people who traveled more than they stayed home, and Casey had always respected him for that. "Just fine," he replied. "You and yours?"

"We're doing great," Casey lied. No point in burdening an acquaintance with a lot of unsettling and very private truths. "Clare and Shane are growing up too fast, but that's normal, I guess."

Joe nodded. "I know what you mean," he answered. "Our oldest starts college in the fall, and he's determined to go to an out-of-state school."

Casey felt a pang at that statement, reminded that it wouldn't be very long before Clare was leaving home, or Shane, either, for that matter. Clare was a gifted singer and played several instruments, but she'd made it clear from an early age that she wanted no part of the music business. *All I'd ever be, talent or no talent,* the child had decreed, with uncanny wisdom, for a ten-year-old, *is Casey Elder's daughter. I want to be a veterinarian.*

And Clare's ambition had never wavered since.

"You take good care of Doris for me," Casey said, and Joe nodded, executed a little salute and returned to the plane.

Once he was inside, the metal steps whirred their way back into the underbelly of the craft, and the door closed, sealing itself with a familiar hermetic sound, like a lid fusing itself to one of Lupe's jars of canned peaches.

Standing there on the tarmac, hands in the pockets of her lightweight jacket, even though it wasn't cold, Casey waited, smiling and waving when she saw Doris's face at one of the portholes.

After the plane lifted off, she drove home, and seeing that every light in the whole place was on, she knew Brylee must have dropped Clare and Shane off after the horseback ride and the restaurant meal.

Casey parked in the driveway—she only used the garage in bad weather—and steeled herself to go inside and face her children.

Shane was in the backyard, with the dogs, when she came around the side of the house on her way to the sunporch entrance.

Casey paused, gazing at him, trying to memorize the way he was right then, at that moment, poignantly aware that her son would be different tomorrow, and the day after that, and the day after that.

Look away from the boy, look back at the man. Her throat thickened.

"Hey, Mom," he said, as though it had been an ordinary day, with no mind-boggling revelations. Would there be a backlash at some point? Probably, Casey thought. She'd look into family counseling in the morning, though she knew both children would resist the idea.

"Hey," Casey answered when she could trust her voice.

"Where've you been?" Shane inquired. She detected a vaguely wheedling note in the question, knew he was about to make some kind of pitch—resuming the campaign to change his last name to match Walker's, most likely, or announcing that he wanted to live with his father.

"Doris's sister is in the hospital up in Seattle," she

answered, sounding normal, even if she didn't feel that way. "I drove her to the plane."

"Oh," Shane said, absorbing that. At his age, Casey figured he was still largely preoccupied with the items on his own agenda, but Doris was practically a member of the family, and he was concerned. "Will her sister be okay?"

Casey was facing him by then, and her smile, though wobbly, was genuine. "I think so," she said. "Doris says Evelyn broke her hip, though, and that can be serious for an older person."

Shane nodded thoughtfully, ignoring the trio of dogs competing like silly jesters for his attention. "Yeah," he said.

"How about you?" Casey asked carefully after waiting out a few heartbeats. "Will *you* be okay, Shane?"

He sighed, and his expression remained pensive, even solemn. "I guess," he said. Then, "Do you think Walker wants me to have his last name, Mom?"

Casey's heart ached, but she'd had a lot of practice when it came to putting on an act, whether professionally or personally, and her facade didn't waver. "I'm sure he does," she said, very quietly. "Is that what you want, Shane?"

Rhetorical question. Of course it was—he'd already made that clear.

Shane searched her face, and, as so often happened these days, she caught a glimpse of the man he was turning into. "Will you feel bad if I do, Mom?" he asked earnestly. "I mean, *Elder* is a good name, too, and it's not like I'm ashamed of it or anything."

Casey wanted to hug her son just then, fiercely, the way she'd done when he was little and still receptive to mom moves, but she restrained herself, knowing that the moment was fragile, and the boy might be, too. "I won't feel bad," she told him. "I promise."

Shane looked relieved, but not completely satisfied. Night sounds were all around them, and somewhere nearby, an owl hooted, waking up after a long day's sleep in some hidden place. "When I asked if I could go and stay with Walker—Dad—for a while, it probably sounded like I didn't want to be with you anymore—"

He fell silent, shook his head once.

Casey stepped into the breach, the way she always did. In a one-parent household, a person had to be ready be *both* father and mother at a moment's notice.

"You want to get to know your dad. That's natural, Shane." She paused, glanced up at the lighted windows lining the back of the gigantic house. Weary wistfulness overtook her for a second there, but she was quick to shake it off, because she had to be strong. "How's your sister doing?"

Shane sighed, shoved his hand through his hair in a way that was so like Walker that Casey's breath snagged in her throat. "She was okay while we were with Brylee, riding horses and eating supper at the burger place and stuff, but now she's all revved up in another major snit." He paused. "Why isn't Clare happy about this, Mom?" he asked, plaintive in his confusion. "We've always wanted a dad, and a kid couldn't have a better one than Walker, so why is Clare acting like somebody just detonated a nuclear bomb?"

Casey laid a hand on his shoulder, squeezed lightly. Maintaining her smile took more of an effort than before but, then, everything did. "I think she's confused, and maybe feeling cheated, too." That was a hard thing to get out, opening the door as it did to similar things that Shane might be feeling.

"I agree that you should have told us the truth, Mom," Shane said manfully. "But I know you must have had your reasons."

Casey stood on tiptoe and kissed her son's smooth cheek, blinking back tears. "I did have reasons, honey," she told him. "Lots of them. But I was still wrong, and I'm so sorry."

"It's okay, Mom," Shane said, awkwardly gracious. "Everybody does things they wish they hadn't."

"You know what?" Casey asked, mock-punching him in one shoulder, the way she did when she was proud of him, which was often. "You're sounding pretty grown-up, all of a sudden."

He beamed. Like most kids, few things pleased him more than being told that he was behaving like an adult. Why was that? Why were children so anxious to stop *being* children?

"Thanks, Mom," he said.

They went inside together, mother, son and dogs.

Clare wasn't in the kitchen, of course. That would have been too easy, made her too accessible to her worried mother.

"Get some rest," Casey said to her son as she locked up and set the alarm. "This has been a big day."

Shane grinned indulgently and went up the back stairway, surrounded by dogs.

Casey waited awhile before heading upstairs herself, debating whether she ought to make another attempt to talk to Clare tonight or wait until morning.

Either way, she supposed, the girl would still be furious with her, and not without reason. This wasn't a brat fit, or teenage angst, after all—Clare had a legitimate gripe.

Five minutes later, Casey rapped lightly at her daughter's bedroom door.

"Go away," Clare called immediately—and predictably.

"Sorry," Casey chimed in reply. "No can do."

She waited, by no means certain that she wouldn't have to barge in.

After a few moments and a lot of bustling around, Clare opened the door a crack and peered out, none too pleased at the interruption. "I'm serious, Mom," she said. "I have nothing to say to you."

"Well," Casey replied evenly, "it just so happens that *I* have a few things to say to *you,* Clare Elder."

"That's Clare *Parrish,* if you don't mind," Clare snapped. She wasn't giving an inch, but she didn't shut the door in Casey's face, either.

"I don't mind, actually," Casey said. "That's up to you and Walk—your father."

"*Elder* is just a made-up name anyhow," Clare pointed out, staunchly petulant even in the face of peacekeeping forces. "A *show business* name."

The girl made the phrase *show business* sound like something to be ashamed of, which nettled Casey a little, but she wasn't about to take the bait. Besides, the part about their surname was true enough; the one she'd been born with was *Eldenberry,* which was not only a mouthful, but apparently an ample reason for the other girls at boarding school to make fun of her. In retrospect, it was hard to believe such a silly thing had ever mattered to her in the first place.

But it had.

She'd been lonely and homesick back then, admittedly for Lupe and Juan rather than for her grandparents, and even one friend would have made a huge difference in her life.

"Okay," Casey responded, agreeing to nothing, easing her way forward so that Clare had to either body-slam her or step out of the way and let her pass.

Fortunately, Clare wasn't the type to get physical.

"There's nothing you can say to make this better," Clare warned. Her TV was on, though the sound was muted, and both cats lay curled in the middle of her glass-and-chrome bed, peering warily over the folds in the comforter in case they had to make a fast exit.

Casey drew back the chair at Clare's desk, sat down. "I know," she said when she was darned good and ready. "But we can't stop talking to each other, either."

Clare plunked herself on her bed, careful not to sit on the cats, and folded her legs, yogi-style. She looked like an angry goddess about to rain lightning bolts over all the earth until it burned to a cinder and, though she didn't come right out and argue with Casey's statement, her message was crystal clear: *maybe* you *can't stop talking, but* I *can.*

Casey pulled in a deep breath and ratcheted up her smile, the way she did with snarky "reporters" stringing for the tabloids, or condescending interviewers with an obvious prejudice against country music and those who sang it.

"Maybe we could look at this from the bright side," she suggested. "You've always wanted a father, Clare. Now you have one. A very good one, as it happens."

"You lied to me," Clare reminded her stubbornly. "And as for Walker, I wanted a father who wanted *me,*

not somebody who couldn't be bothered to mention that—*oh, yes*—I just happen to be his daughter."

"Walker had nothing to do with this, Clare. It was all *my* idea."

"'Nothing to do with it,' Mom? Get real. I might be fourteen, but I know how babies happen." She blushed, her brows still lowered, her lower lip protruding slightly. "Other than when some chemist starts them in test tubes, that is."

"Clare, don't be mean. Lots of very good people can only have children by turning to modern medicine for help, and those children are as precious as any other human being."

Clare seemed to pull in her horns a little then—she wasn't a hard-hearted person—but it was obvious that Casey wasn't off the hook, and wouldn't be anytime soon. "I used to wonder what my donor dad was like," she said. "You know, if he was smart, if his eyes were the same color as mine, if my laugh was just like his mother's, or his sister's—"

Casey kept her chin up, but she couldn't hide her tears, or say a single word.

"And you know what?" Clare went on, remote and withdrawn again, speaking into a space just over Casey's right shoulder. "People would say I was being silly, because anybody could see that I got my brains from you, that my eyes are like yours, and my laugh is like yours, we have the same hair and even the same *voice*. No offense, Mom, but it was almost like they thought I didn't even *need* a father, because you'd conceived me all by yourself. And that, of course, is ultraweird unless you're Jesus."

Casey laughed, sniffled, snatched a tissue from the

box on Clare's desk and dabbed at her eyes. So much for that last application of mascara, she thought. And how was a completely human and therefore imperfect mother supposed to react to a statement like the one her daughter had just made? With a sermon on the Virgin Birth?

Casey didn't have a clue, but she wanted to keep the conversation going because she sensed that if they stopped now, a door would close between them.

"Besides being angry with me," she persisted, "what are you feeling, Clare?"

Clare considered the question. "Hard to say," she replied eventually. "Mostly, I feel sad, I guess, and ripped off—like somebody gave a big party and didn't invite me."

She was taking a chance, she knew that, but Casey stood up then, walked over to Clare's bed, sat down beside her and slipped an arm around the girl's shoulders.

Clare stiffened slightly, but she didn't squirm away.

"I love you," Casey said very quietly.

"I know," Clare answered, just as quietly. "But I think I'm going to be mad for a while longer."

Casey smiled, kissed her daughter's temple. "That's okay," she said, choking up again. "We'll work through all this together, no matter how long it takes."

Clare nodded and swallowed hard, but she didn't say anything.

And that was Casey's cue to exit.

CHAPTER TEN

"WELL, BIG BROTHER," Brylee said peevishly the next morning as she set a coffee cup down on the table in front of Walker with so much force that some of the brew spilled over and burned his fingers, "you sure can keep a secret—I'll give you that."

Walker tried to smile, fell a little short of full wattage. "Why is it," he countered, "that you only wait on me when you're pissed off?"

Brylee dropped into the chair directly across from his. Decked out in her usual jeans, long-sleeved T-shirt and sneakers, with her hair twisted into a no-nonsense bun at the back of her head, she was dressed for the warehouse rather than the office, since that was where she spent most of her time. Not for her the high heels and custom-made power suits other lady CEOs probably favored.

Not that there were a whole lot of those running around Parable County, Montana, to provide him with a frame of reference.

"I wasn't 'waiting on' you," she pointed out crisply. "If you must know, my first and strongest inclination was to empty the cup over your head." The flush in her cheeks indicated that she was gathering steam. "All these years," she went on, "I've had a niece and a nephew, and you never bothered to tell me?"

Walker took a thoughtful sip of his coffee, grateful that he wasn't wearing it instead of drinking it. "Casey didn't want anybody else to know," he said reasonably. "And, anyway, I figured you'd guessed it on your own."

Brylee didn't touch her own coffee, nor was there any sign of breakfast, not that he'd expected her to cook for him or anything. Most mornings, though, she whipped up scrambled eggs or pancakes for herself, and shared them with him.

"I didn't have a clue," she said frankly, simmering down a little.

He hoped.

Walker said nothing, since excuses were all he had to offer, and he was having enough trouble with his conscience as it was.

"Why would Casey want to keep a secret like that?" Brylee asked, clearly not ready to let the subject drop, whether her brother had anything worthwhile to say or not.

A man of few words, Walker groped around inside himself for a viable reply. "She was just starting to make it as a singer at the time," he said finally. "I guess she thought I'd drag her to the altar, bring her back here to the ranch and keep her barefoot and pregnant for the rest of her life."

Brylee crooked a smile at that, but it was brief. In that getup, with no makeup on her face, she looked more like a teenager than the head of a company worth millions. "Don't try to put all the blame on Casey, Walker Parrish. You had a say in this, too. You could have spoken up at any time, with or without her blessing." She paused, and her throat worked visibly as she struggled with some private emotion. "Your daughter is devastated," she eventually went on. "And once Shane gets past the whoopee-I've-got-a-father-after-all stage, he's going to wonder why you didn't see fit to claim him and Clare a long time ago."

"I told you," Walker said, "Casey—"

But Brylee held up both palms like a referee, and blew the proverbial whistle. "Bull," she said flatly. "Since when have you ever danced to *anybody's* tune, including Casey Elder's? Nobody calls your shots but you, Walker, and *that* means that, on some level, you preferred to leave well enough alone instead of taking a stand."

"It isn't that simple," Walker said, but the words sounded lame, even to him.

Brylee didn't let up. "Isn't it?" she countered. "Face it, Walker. If you couldn't have things your own way— you and Casey married, living on this ranch, raising those kids according to some sitcom image of what a family ought to be rattling around in that hard head of yours—you were going to stand back with your arms folded and your back molars clamped together."

"That was colorful," Walker observed—once he'd unclamped his back molars so his tongue could function.

"What happens now?" Brylee demanded, cheeks pink with righteous indignation.

"Damned if I know," Walker admitted glumly.

"Well, you'd better *figure something out,* don't you think?"

Walker frowned. "Why are you all fired up about this? Aren't you even a little bit pleased to find out there's more to this family than you, me and our now-you-see-her-now-you-don't mother?"

"I'm *delighted*," Brylee snarled, pushing back her chair and standing up so suddenly that she startled her ever-present sidekick, Snidely, in the process, sending him into a brief, skittering retreat. "But my feelings are *beside* the point right now, frankly, and so are yours and Casey's. Dammit, Walker, this is about *Clare and Shane!*"

"I never said it wasn't about them," Walker pointed out, getting to his own feet because, by God, when people yelled at him, his only sister included, he didn't take it sitting down. Not even when they were 99 percent right. "What the *hell* do you want me to do, Bry?"

Tears filled her eyes. "Give your kids a home," she said. "Give them a real family."

With that, Brylee grabbed up her purse, snatched her cell phone off the charger over by the coffeemaker and stormed out of the house. Snidely followed, pausing once to look back, sadly, at Walker and Doolittle.

Give your kids a home. Give them a real family.

Walker sank back into his chair. Did Brylee think he wanted to do anything else *but* that? He loved his children, always had, even before he found out that Clare, like Shane, was his own. Not a day had gone by without his thinking of them, and Casey, too.

But when you got down to brass tacks, he had to admit that Brylee had a point. He might not have been able to persuade Casey to marry him back then, in the thick of things, but he could have asked for—and *fought for,* if necessary—some kind of joint custody arrangement. He could have played a greater part in Clare's and Shane's lives—a much greater part.

He could have told them about their ancestors, shown them pictures in the photo albums, such as they were, let his children see parts of themselves—a smile, a set of the shoulders—in the images of those who had gone before.

He could have given his son and daughter that gift, if nothing else—the sense of continuity, of belonging, of being links in a chain that went way back.

Most of all, he could have *loved them,* openly, not in secret.

Maybe, Walker thought glumly, as all this came home to him and finally got through his thick skull, he wasn't so different from his always distant, hands-off mother. Maybe, deep down, he simply hadn't wanted to be bothered.

Or was it a matter of plain old run-of-the-mill cowardice? A subconscious fear that Clare and Shane, used to private jets and the best of everything, wouldn't have wanted what he had to offer—the country life, with chores and regular school and the kind of clothes ranch kids wore?

Hell, he thought. He was never going to figure *this* one out, especially if he stood there in his kitchen stewing about it.

He had to *do* something.

Walker summoned Doolittle, grabbed his hat from its peg and plunked it down hard on his head as he strode toward the door, still not knowing what that something was.

"HEY, MOM!" SHANE yelled from the entryway. "Mrs. Dennison is here!"

Standing at the top of the front stairway, holding an armload of towels in need of washing—to her chagrin Casey hadn't been able to locate her own laundry chute, though she knew there was one, somewhere—she puzzled over the announcement for a moment, before her preoccupied brain translated *Mrs. Dennison* to *Opal*.

Being careful not to stumble, since she couldn't see her feet for the heap of towels, Casey hurried down the steps, dropped her burden nearby and stepped into the echoing foyer.

Opal stood there, grinning from ear to ear, a ratty old suitcase at her feet. She didn't seem to mind that all three dogs were sniffing at her luggage.

"I guess you must be wondering what I'm doing here, with half my worldly belongings," Opal said before Casey could manage more than a hello. The woman looked as pleased as a game show host about to award the big prize. "And the answer is, word got back to me that your Doris was called away on a family emergency, so I'm taking over for her."

In Parable, Opal Dennison was something of a legend. Wherever she went, tangled situations got *un*tangled in short order, and then there were the weddings.

Three of them, so far—that Casey knew of.

Yikes.

"Great," Shane interjected enthusiastically. "Does this mean we don't have to eat Mom's cooking?"

Opal laughed, a deep, rich sound, full of joy. "Now, I'm sure your mother is a *fine* cook, young man," she scolded affably, "but she's probably got better things to do than stand at the stove all day."

"What about Joslyn and Slade?" Casey managed to ask. After all, Opal worked for them. "Don't they need you—especially with another baby on the way?" That morning, in an email exchange with Joslyn, she'd mentioned that Doris had left town to look after her injured sister, but she certainly hadn't expected the Barlows to fork over their housekeeper. She'd been venting, that was all.

"They'll manage fine. They've got a nanny these days, and they'll have to learn to get by without me anyhow, since I'm fixing to marry the Reverend Mr. Beaumont next month." Opal slipped out of her colorful spring jacket, hung it neatly from one of the hooks on the massive coat tree opposite the grandfather clock. "Not that I'm planning to lounge around watching soap operas after the wedding," she added briskly. "Being a preacher's wife is a full-time job in itself. Now, where should I put my things?"

Casey found her voice again. Nodded to Shane to handle the suitcase. "The downstairs guest room," she said, pointing toward the opposite side of the house. The little apartment off the kitchen had once been Opal's, she knew, but now it was Doris's domain, even though she was away for the time being.

Of course, Opal was aware of the guest room in question, having worked in the mansion for years as the employee of the first owners, the Rossiters, and she marched off toward it, Shane following with the suitcase, the dogs trailing behind like members of a circus parade.

As soon as they were out of sight, Casey rushed back, gathered up the pile of towels she'd dropped at the foot of the stairs and carried them into the laundry room, stuffing half of them into the washer, then stopping, peering at the knobs and switches, momentarily baffled.

In the end, it was a matter of common sense, of course, and she got the machine going. What she needed now was a cup of tea, to settle her down a little.

Just as Opal and Shane returned to the kitchen, Clare appeared, still clad in cotton pajamas and yawning behind one hand. Tendrils of her hair stuck out around her head like a coppery halo, making her resemble an angel in a Renaissance painting.

As if.

"It's about time you got up," Shane remarked, always ready with a jibe whenever he encountered his sister.

Clare made a face at him, and then turned a sunny smile on Opal, fit to bring a field full of wildflowers into bloom. For all the notice the girl paid Casey, however, she might as well have been part of the woodwork.

Opal proceeded to open a drawer, pull out an apron and tie it around her waist. "Looks like somebody ought to haul off and make some breakfast," she said, beaming, "before wholesale starvation sets in."

"Mom tried," Shane explained tolerantly, "but the oatmeal blew up in the microwave, and even the dogs won't eat it."

Casey gave her son a look, but it bounced off him like a bullet off the big *S* on Superman's chest.

Clare, still ignoring her mother, meandered over, peered into the microwave and said, "Yuck."

The word, one of her daughter's favorites, wasn't a cheery "Hi, Mom!" nor was it directed specifically to her, but Casey figured something was better than nothing.

"I was just about to clean up the mess—" Casey faltered, embarrassed. A domestic goddess she wasn't—she'd never had to be. Growing up at her grandparents' place, Lupe and her nieces had done all the household tasks, and as soon as she'd had two nickels to rub together, Casey had hired Doris.

Opal waved her away. "I don't mind doing it," she said. "Why don't you just relax for a few minutes, go on outside and admire all those beautiful flowers in the yard? I'll give a shout when the food's ready."

Clare was rooting around in the refrigerator, looking for a carton of yogurt. "Don't make anything for me," she said brightly, still refusing to acknowledge Casey's existence. "I'm on a diet."

"Diet," Opal scoffed. "Pish-posh. You'll have a decent meal, girl, and that's the end of it."

Remarkably, Clare straightened, shut the refrigerator door and stood there empty-handed, the yogurt evidently forgotten.

"Okay," she said meekly.

Casey stared for a moment. Who was this changeling, posing as her daughter? More to the point, what magic was Opal working? Was there an instruction book?

Instead of asking, she poured a cup of coffee, carried it out through the sunporch and onto the steps and did as she'd been told. She just sat there, admiring the flower beds, where roses bloomed, fat and velvety and wildly colorful, like a convention of aging madams, clad in their best outfits and meeting to compare notes and plan better brothels. The peonies—white and red, pink and candy-striped—were at the height of their brief but spectacular glory, enjoying one last hurrah before June gave way to July, while their lilac colleagues were already gone. The Gerbera daisies and the dinner-plate dahlias and the irises and the hearty zinnias flourished, though, belonging more to summer than to spring.

The beauty and the delicious blend of fragrances all but took Casey's breath away. Up until this moment, she realized with quiet chagrin, she'd barely even *noticed* the exquisite riot of color in her own backyard. She'd been too busy, but doing what?

She heard dog feet crossing the sunporch behind her, nails clicking on the tiles and the faint squeak of Shane's sneakers.

The Labs went by, one by one, brushing against Casey's shoulder as they passed. Then Shane sat down beside her on the step, watching fondly as the critters played tag and chased butterflies and rolled in the lush green grass.

Reveling in the fact that they were alive.

In that moment, Casey knew she could have walked away from her career, if not her music, even given up this mansion and her stock portfolio, fancy equipment, buses and glittering stage clothes, and still been perfectly happy, as long as she had her children, her dogs and cats, and plenty of flowers.

She thought of Walker, of the way he'd held her and made her body sing a song all its own, wordless and fierce, the day before.

Well, okay, *almost* perfectly happy, then.

She and Walker were like a pair of dancers, both determined to lead, constantly stumbling over their own and each other's feet, always a little out of step with the tune.

Nobody had everything, did they?

Shane broke the silence, and the mood, with a chipper, "Would it be all right if I called Walk—Dad?" How long had he been working up his courage to ask her that?

"Now?" Casey stalled. Behind them, through the open door on the other side of the sunporch, Opal's and Clare's voices rose and fell, circled and finally interwove, like ribbons floating in midair, guided by a magician's wand.

"I have his cell number," Shane said, sounding mildly defensive.

Casey slipped an arm around Shane, but loosely, and was relieved when he didn't shrug her off, the way he sometimes did when there were other people around, especially kids his own age. "Go ahead and call your dad," she said with gentle humor. "You don't have to ask my permission to do that."

"I do if I want to ask him to let me go along next time he hauls stock to a rodeo," Shane said, not looking at her, but straight ahead, past the dogs and the flower gardens and the high wall at the back of the property. He was gazing, she surmised sadly, into a whole new world just opening its doors to him.

Casey set her coffee cup down beside her foot, moving with careful deliberation so she wouldn't spill the stuff. She didn't know a whole lot about what Walker actually did when he was on the road, besides hauling broncos and bulls from place to place, but she was clear on one aspect of it: he was usually gone for days at a time.

"Has he said anything about taking you with him, Shane?"

Shane shook his head. "Not recently," he admitted. "Back when Clare and I used to visit the ranch for a couple of weeks every summer, we talked about it once in a while. Walker said I'd have to wait until I was a little older." He paused, gave her a sheepish grin and spread his hands. "Well, now I'm older," he finished.

A twinge squeezed Casey's heart, and, much as she

wanted to reach out and smooth Shane's sleep-rumpled hair with a motherly hand, she refrained. If Walker refused Shane's request to follow the rodeo, the boy would be crushed. If he said yes, on the other hand, *she* would be crushed. She'd miss her son every minute of every day, and worry about him, too, and his departure, however brief the journey, would be the beginning of letting him go for good.

Her throat constricted.

"So, what's the word, Mom?" Shane asked, blithely oblivious to the fact that she was falling apart. Which, of course, was a good thing. "If Dad lets me go on the road with him, will you be cool with that?"

Hell, *no,* she wouldn't be cool with it, Casey thought. Walker worked with dangerous bucking horses and bulls bred to hurl cowboys skyward and then try to stomp them to a bloody pulp when they landed in the dirt. There was all that loading and unloading, and all those long and lonely roads.

Shane, eager to help his dad, and to prove himself, could so easily get hurt—*badly* hurt.

On the other hand, the rodeo business was as much a part of Shane's heritage as country music, wasn't it? She and Walker were like two very separate rivers, merging, and Clare and Shane were a blend of both. She'd been able to pretend for a long time that they were hers alone, but that was over.

Somehow, she had to accept that they were Walker's, too.

"Mom?" Shane prompted, determined to get an answer.

"If Walker says you can go, and he promises to make sure you stay safe," Casey forced herself to say, "then

I'll deal with it. I can't say I'll be 'cool' with it, as you put it, but I'll deal." *Somehow.*

Shane grinned. "Fair enough," he said. Then he stood up, beanstalk gangly, and sprinted over to wrestle with the dogs, using up some of their spare energy and, hopefully, some of his own, as well.

If only he'd get too tired to fall in love with rodeo, Casey thought wryly.

No such luck. He was Walker Parrish's son, and that meant the cowboy life was in his blood.

Casey sat, her coffee forgotten, and instead of Shane roughhousing with the dogs, instead of her flower gardens, she saw a dusty arena surrounded by bleachers packed with rodeo fans.

She heard the auctioneer-like drone of the announcer's voice, saw a chute gate swing open and a bull explode through the gap, with a cowboy on its back, spurring hard while the animal spun and bucked.

The rider looked like Walker, but he wasn't. He was younger and leaner, with most of the hard spills still ahead of him.

He was her Shane, but Walker's, too.

Opal yanked Casey out of the vision with a hearty "Breakfast's on the table. Come and get it!"

The next few minutes were chaotic, what with all the bounding around of one boy and three dogs, Opal fussing cheerfully that she was going to trip over one of those critters and break her neck if they kept getting underfoot like that, Clare fully dressed, with her hair brushed and caught up in a clip on top of her head, her expression civil, if not exactly mom-friendly.

Once the meal was over, and the kids had cleared

the table and loaded the dishwasher, Casey and Opal
sat alone, in the blissful quiet, collecting their thoughts.

"See what you've gotten yourself into?" Casey asked
her friend after a few moments, grinning as she lifted
her coffee cup to her lips.

Opal chuckled. "Once it's just the reverend and me,"
she observed, "without kids and dogs and some sort
of ruckus going on all the time, I'm not sure I'll know
how to act."

"You'll figure it out," Casey said, confident of that
much at least. "Did you say the wedding is scheduled
for next month?"

"We just set the date," Opal answered with a nod.
She paused to admire the respectable engagement ring
gleaming on her left hand. When she looked up again,
there was a hopeful expression in her eyes. "It'll be
July 15—that's a Saturday—and we were wondering
if you'd sing, the reverend and me. I know it's a lot to
ask, you being famous and all, but, well, we thought—"

"Opal," Casey interrupted firmly. "*Of course* I'll
sing. In fact, my feelings would have been hurt if you
hadn't asked."

The beaming smile was back. "Thank you, Casey
Elder," Opal said. A beat passed, and then the smile
faded. "Now," she said, suddenly serious, "I'm just
going to go right ahead and butt in where I've got no
business sticking my nose. What's the holdup with you
and Walker getting together?"

Casey couldn't answer for a few moments, she was so
taken aback, though she knew she shouldn't have been
surprised. Opal was famous—make that *infamous*—for
her matchmaking, after all.

This time, though, she was definitely barking up the wrong tree.

"We're friends, that's all," Casey hedged. *Friends,* mimicked a voice in her head, as every cell in her body remembered the fevered intensity of their lovemaking, *with benefits.*

"How long do you think you're going to be able to keep *that* story rolling, once word gets around that you and Walker had two kids together?" Opal challenged, firmly but not unkindly.

Casey put one hand to the base of her throat. "Where did you hear—?"

"Your Clare told me just this morning," Opal replied matter-of-factly, "while I was making breakfast. Evidently, the news came as quite a shock to the child, though I'm sure she'll manage to wrap her mind around it soon enough, smart as she is. But right now, she's mighty rattled, and I guess I'm easy to talk to, because she poured out her heart to me."

Casey propped both elbows on the table's edge and buried her face in her hands with a weary groan.

"I hope you and Walker don't think those children are going to keep this to themselves," Opal went on, "because I might be the first person one of them told, but you can bet all those gold and platinum records you've rounded up that I won't be the last."

Opal was right, of course.

And it wasn't that Casey had expected Clare and Shane to pretend nothing had changed. She'd just been in so much emotional turmoil that she hadn't thought that far ahead, hadn't even considered that the community would inevitably find out and, after that, the media. Dear God, the media.

They'd have a field day, especially the tabloids, and Clare and Shane would be at the center of the scandal—through no fault of their own. And she'd been the one to bring it down on their innocent heads.

It was going to be awful, no two ways about it, and she might as well try to plug an erupting volcano with a wine cork as attempt to avert the red-hot lava of public scrutiny.

She needed to talk to Walker—come up with some kind of plan, though damage control was all they could hope for—and it had to happen *now.*

Casey scooted back her chair and made a beeline for the wall phone, only to find that Shane was already on one of the extensions. With Walker.

She broke right into the conversation, with all the subtlety of a stunt person somersaulting through a saloon window in an old Western movie. "Walker," she said. "We have to talk. *Right now.*"

WE HAVE TO TALK. Right now.

After issuing her grand summons, Casey hadn't waited for an answer, she'd simply hung up the phone, hard.

Shane had been the first to recover from the shock. "This is bogus," he'd said angrily. "Mom *just told me* I could go to the next rodeo with you if it was okay with you, and now she's already going back on her word!"

"I don't think she was referring to the rodeo," Walker had told his son with grim resignation. "You tell her to hold on—I'll be there as soon as I can."

"Do I still get to go rodeoing with you?"

Walker had given a dry chuckle at that. The boy had plenty of stick-with-it going for him, that was for sure.

"My answer is still yes," he'd replied. "But your mother has a say, too."

After that, they'd said their goodbyes and ended the call.

Walker, who'd been tagging calves' ears all morning with some of the ranch hands, was wearing at least one layer of good Montana dirt, so, once he'd snapped his cell phone shut, he took the time to shower and change before he hoisted Doolittle into the truck and started for Parable.

Casey was pacing the driveway when he pulled in, better than half an hour later, and she looked four parts pissed off and one part scared out of her wits. If Clare and Shane were around, there was no sign of them, and the dog brigade wasn't in evidence, either.

Walker left Doolittle in the truck, got out and shut the door hard behind him.

"Where are the kids?" he asked, straight out, because, whatever Brylee or anybody else might think to the contrary, they were his first concern.

"Opal took them to the community center to swim in the pool," Casey answered, biting off the words. From her attitude, an objective observer might have gotten the impression that this powwow had been *his* idea, and she'd rather be doing something else.

Walker swept off his hat, swatted it against his right thigh and jammed it right back onto his head. "There's no need to get testy!" he growled, making an effort to keep his voice down.

Casey folded her arms. "You took the words right out of my mouth," she said acidly.

Walker leaned in until their noses were almost touching, and damn any neighbors who might be watching, fixing to carry the tale to every corner of the county. "What the *hell* is going on here?" he demanded. "If I hadn't been talking to Shane when you came on the line, I'd have thought something had happened to him or Clare!"

The green fire blazing in Casey's eyes cooled off a little. "We have to get married," she said.

Walker narrowed his eyes, thinking he must have heard wrong. *"What did you say?"*

She turned on one heel and hauled butt for the house, forcing him to follow.

"Dammit, Casey," he sputtered, furious because he had to tag after her like some schoolboy with his tongue hanging out. *"Talk to me."*

She waited until they'd reached the kitchen, then whirled on him, arms folded, feet so firmly planted that her heels might just leave dents in the floor.

"We have to get married," Casey repeated with elaborate enunciation, as though he was either deaf or didn't speak the language.

"I'll be damned," Walker muttered, taking off his hat and then, not knowing what to do with it, putting it on again. "You're pregnant? How can you know for sure, when it was only yesterday that the condom broke?"

Casey went white, then red again. *"The condom broke?"*

Walker sighed, and some of the fury seeped out of him. "I've got to change brands," he said.

That was when Casey laughed, though her eyes were still shooting green sparks and he knew he wasn't out of the figurative woods. Before he'd registered that she was amused, she turned again. "You weren't going to tell me?" she demanded.

He didn't have an answer.

And Casey didn't wait for one. "It'll be a marriage in name only, of course," she mused. "Just on paper."

Walker gaped for a moment, then rasped, *"What?"*

"We have to do this, Walker," Casey said, serious as a foreclosure notice now. "For Clare and Shane."

CHAPTER ELEVEN

STRANGE, CASEY THOUGHT WEARILY, how everything could change without anything really being *different*. Sitting alone in the same wooden swing where Clare had taken refuge, barely a week before, on the porch of the house at Timber Creek Ranch, she went over it all in her mind—again.

Walker had been understandably shocked by her proposal of marriage, but once she'd explained her reasoning, he'd grudgingly agreed. When the story broke, it would reach far beyond the borders of Parable County, and Clare and Shane would take the brunt of it, become the objects of tabloid headlines, the fodder for snide hosts on gossip TV, the prey of intrusive photographers and creeps who billed themselves as journalists.

A wedding wouldn't prevent that, of course, but both Casey and Walker were old-fashioned enough to believe that living under the same roof, as a family, would shelter their children from at least *some* of the fallout, and they couldn't live together without being legally married. Which was where the old-fashioned part came in.

So they'd quietly—*very* quietly—filed for a marriage license, not in Parable, the county seat, but in Missoula. Now the brief waiting period was over, and Opal's fiancé, the good Reverend Beaumont, had agreed to perform a simple ceremony in the ranch house living room, with Brylee, the kids and Opal in attendance. The hands and their families would be there, of course, along with very close friends.

It wouldn't be the wedding every girl dreams of, Casey reflected philosophically, sitting there in her simple blue sheath and sandals, but white lace and organ music and a fancy cake hadn't been in the cards for her and Walker anyway. Too much water under the bridge, as the old saying went, trite only because it had been true for so long. Besides, this wasn't exactly a love match—they both loved their *children,* no doubt about it, but the sad fact was, she and Walker didn't get along anywhere but in bed.

And that, by tacit agreement, was a place they'd been steering clear of since the last time.

The screen door opened just then, and Clare came out of the kitchen, looking pretty in a green sundress, with her hair tumbling around her shoulders in lovely spirals. She hadn't forgiven Casey for the deception yet, or Walker, either, for that matter, but she'd stopped pouting, slamming doors and hiding out in her room, anyway.

Sitting on the opposite end of the swing from Casey, Clare smoothed her skirt, bit her lower lip and said her piece, probably after much rehearsal.

"I know you don't really want to marry Walker, Mom. This whole thing is a sham—it's damage control."

Unlike her brother, who was thrilled about the marriage and already called Walker "Dad," Clare had shown a definite lack of enthusiasm from the first, and when she spoke to her father, which wasn't often, she still addressed him by his first name.

"We're doing what we think is best," Casey said calmly.

Clare had the good grace not to throw the big lie in her face, and Casey dared to hope she and her daughter would find common ground again soon. "What if it doesn't work?" she asked. "I mean, you'll probably throw the media off the trail, mostly anyway, but suppose you and Walker find out you can't live together and end up getting divorced? What do you think that would do to Shane?"

Casey had asked herself all the same questions. It was true enough that the scandal, just now starting to break online and in a few of the tabloids, would flare up, marriage or no marriage. And, thank heaven, it would fade into oblivion when a juicier story came along.

The deeper scars would remain, though. After the media circus moved on and set up their tents somewhere else, Clare and Shane would still be wondering what their friends thought, what it all meant. Their confidence in Casey, always rock solid before, might never be the same again.

"Whatever happens in the future," she replied carefully, "it's right now that's important. You and Shane will be legitimate, whether Walker and I stay married or not."

"'Legitimate'?" Clare echoed. She wasn't scoffing, but there was a jaded note in her voice just the same. "Please, Mom. That's so Victorian. This is the twenty-first century, and *lots* of kids' mothers aren't married to their dads."

Casey bristled a little. "Maybe so," she replied, "but that doesn't make it an ideal situation, not by any stretch. Two-parent families might not be as common as they used to be, and God knows, they're not perfect, but they're worth having, Clare. They're worth holding on to, worth fighting for."

"Why now?" Clare persisted, sounding honestly puzzled. "After all this time, I mean? In a few years, Shane and I will be grown up and away at college. What will it matter then if you and Walker are married?"

"It matters," Casey insisted quietly. "Someday, I hope you'll understand why."

And I hope I'll understand, too. Parts of the decision were still a mystery to her, and she suspected it was the same for Walker.

A short silence fell. In the near distance, horses whinnied and bulls snorted, pawing the ground and kicking up dust in their sturdy pens. There was a certain peace in the rustic ordinariness of it all, and Casey clung to that, like a blind person clutching a fragile thread that might just lead her into the light, if she could just hold on.

Clare's next remark was a humdinger.

She stood up, sighed a worldly sigh and said, without a hint of sarcasm, "I'll bet the *real* reason you and Walker are getting married is because you have to. Are you going to have a baby, Mom?"

Casey stiffened as though her daughter had just flung a bucket of cold water on her, and not just because the question caught her off guard. She might well be pregnant, given her and Walker's track record—and the broken condom. Neither of which she intended to discuss with her fourteen-year-old daughter, thank you very much, either now or in the foreseeable future.

"Your mother," Casey told the girl evenly, "is marrying your father. For now, that's all you need to know."

Clare spread her hands in a gesture of helpless resignation.

A string of cars and pickup trucks slowed down on the county road, the first of them turning in at the main gate. The wedding guests were arriving. There weren't many of them, only their closest friends.

"If there *is* a baby," Clare said, very softly, and with a note of wistfulness that bruised Casey's heart, "he or she is one lucky kid to be born with both a mom *and* a dad, and grow up here, on this ranch." With that, Clare vanished into the house.

Casey stood, but only after a few moments had passed and she was sure she could trust her wobbly knees to hold her up. At any other time, she would have caught up with Clare, tried to reach the girl with words or hugs—or something.

But, like it or not, that conversation would have to wait. There was a wedding in the offing, and the guests were here.

The various vehicles reached the top of the driveway, one by one, and people in dress clothes got out— Opal and the Reverend Walter Beaumont were the first, soon followed by Joslyn and Slade Barlow, Boone and Tara Taylor and Hutch and Kendra Carmody. Patsy McCullough brought up the rear, at the wheel of a specially equipped van, her son Dawson riding with her.

Only Hutch looked uncomfortable, and that wasn't surprising, considering that Timber Creek Ranch was Brylee's home as well as Walker's. Hutch and Brylee had come within an I-do of getting married themselves, a couple of years before, and accounts of the interrupted ceremony still surfaced occasionally, when there was a lack of fresh gossip.

Brylee was inside somewhere, probably as nervous as Hutch, but this was one wedding she wouldn't dodge, since the groom was her brother.

Casey welcomed everyone with a smile and a hug, especially Joslyn and Tara and Kendra, her closest friends, while Slade and Hutch stayed behind to help Patsy with Dawson and his wheelchair.

"When's that baby coming?" Casey asked Joslyn in a whisper after the crowd had come inside the house and moved on toward the living room, where the ceremony was to be held. Kendra lingered with them, smiling.

Joslyn sighed happily, resting her hands on her enormous belly. *"Babies,"* she corrected, sotto voce. "We're having twins. Both boys."

Casey hugged her again. "That's great!"

Joslyn nodded, beaming.

"Are you ready to get married?" Kendra asked Casey, looking as pleased as if this wedding were the real deal, instead of a public-relations move and a too-little, too-late attempt to set a few things right.

"About as ready as I'm ever going to be, I guess," Casey responded. Very few people knew the truth, but Joslyn, Kendra and Tara were among them, and not one of them had tried to talk her out of it. In fact, they actually seemed *happy* for her and Walker.

They were so certain things would work out. Casey herself, not so much. All she could do was try her hardest, dig in her heels and refuse to give up.

"What about a honeymoon?" Joslyn asked.

Casey kept her expression bland, because there were some things she wasn't ready to reveal, even to her best friends. Such as, there wasn't going to be a *wedding night,* let alone a honeymoon. "That's a secret," she said mysteriously.

Joslyn and Kendra exchanged glances, then proceeded into the living room, to seat themselves on rented folding chairs. Their husbands soon joined them.

Casey waited in the kitchen, wringing her hands a little, until Shane was beside her. Handsome in his best suit, which he was about to grow out of, he jutted out an elbow. "Showtime, Mom," he whispered, grinning. "Ready to be given away?"

A lump formed in Casey's throat. She smiled and brushed a lock of hair back from Shane's forehead, a gesture he normally wouldn't have appreciated. "Ready," she managed.

Shane escorted his mother out of the kitchen, through the formal dining area and into the wide, arched doorway leading to the living room, where they stopped.

Walker and Reverend Beaumont stood in front of the flower-festooned fireplace, Walker looking dazed, the minister all smiles.

The folding chairs were filled, and Opal had taken her place at the piano, her fingers poised to play the customary processional.

A hush fell over the gathering, and Joslyn, Kendra and Tara all turned in their seats simultaneously and gave Casey a perfectly synchronized thumbs-up.

Brylee, the only bridesmaid, stood up front, a little to the minster's right, smiling encouragement at Casey and Shane.

Careful not to look too closely at Walker—no getting around it, he was one handsome hunk of cowboy—Casey swept one last glance around the room, her heart pounding a little, looking for Clare, praying her daughter hadn't decided to hide out somewhere until the "sham" was over.

But Clare was made of better stuff than that. Whatever her misgivings, she walked, head high, into the living room through another archway, and stood next to Opal, by the baby grand piano. Tears stung the backs of Casey's eyes as she realized the implications of that.

Clare, who never sang in public, was going to sing today. It was her gift to Casey and to Walker.

Opal began to play.

Casey froze, and Shane had to give her a little tug to get her moving, between the rows of folding chairs and up to Walker's side.

Walker looked down at Casey, his eyes shining, and the smallest smile crooked the corner of his mouth.

The piano went still, then started right up again.

Casey and Walker both turned to watch as Clare began her solo, a song Casey had written long ago, as a sort of lullaby for her children. Though it was about the forever kind of love, and not about sleeping, she'd sung those words to Clare and Shane a thousand times, on buses and airplanes and in backstage dressing rooms, always at bedtime.

Now, listening to Clare's beautiful voice, Casey thought she might just burst with love and pride, and she knew, after a sidelong glance his way, that Walker was feeling pretty much the same.

When the song ended, Clare took her place up front, next to Brylee, and Brylee wrapped an arm around her niece, gave her a squeeze and whispered something to her.

Casey felt an achy surge of love for both of them.

Everything after that seemed to happen in slow motion, in the midst of a silvery haze.

Reverend Beaumont made a little speech laced with Bible references but otherwise a blur, as far as Casey was concerned.

The usual questions were asked.

The usual vows were exchanged.

It never crossed Casey's mind to say anything but the expected "I wills" and "I dos," and Walker didn't hesitate, either. They slid matching gold bands onto each other's ring fingers when prompted.

And then the minister pronounced them man and wife, and Walker, eyes twinkling, pulled Casey close and kissed her soundly—so soundly that, if he hadn't been holding her firmly by the waist, her knees might have buckled.

The guests cheered, and Shane, in a momentary lapse of preteen dignity, jumped high in the air, jamming one fist toward the ceiling, and yelled, "Yes!"

That made everybody laugh, including Casey, though she still felt like an actress, playing a part in a made-for-TV movie. Nothing seemed real—except for the echo of Walker's kiss, that is. Her mouth tingled at the recollection, and for a very long time afterward, even as the time-honored rituals continued.

Casey and Walker posed for photographs, endlessly, it seemed to her.

They cut the impressive cake Brylee had stayed up half the night to bake and decorate, and congratulations came from all sides. There was a group phone call from the guys in the band, all of them talking at once and finally coming together to sing a rowdy song that made Casey laugh and cry at the same time.

Even Mitch, who hadn't been in contact since he'd left Casey's place in a huff after she'd turned down his proposal, sent a short video, via Shane's cell, wishing the newlyweds well.

Casey was both pleased and touched, knowing Mitch's pride would have made the gesture difficult for him, to say the least. In a few days, she'd call her manager back and try to smooth things over. They'd been over bumpy ground before—Mitch periodically threatened to resign and then changed his mind later—and Casey genuinely hoped this time would be no different from the others.

After the refreshments, the hugs and handshakes and digital photos, guests began to leave, a few at a time.

Dawson McCullough, dressed up in a suit, wheeled over to Casey and Walker and, with a big smile, congratulated them. Patsy, hovering behind his chair, said nothing, but added a shy nod of agreement. Walker and Shane followed them out, to help Dawson into the van and stow the wheelchair in back.

Glancing around, still trying to come to terms with the incomprehensible fact that she and Walker were really and truly *married,* Casey spotted Hutch and Brylee standing near the piano, talking earnestly.

Kendra appeared at Casey's side, watching the exchange with quiet approval.

"What's that about?" Casey asked, worried. When it came to Hutch Carmody, her otherwise amenable sister-in-law was notoriously stubborn and prone to making scenes.

Kendra took a sip of punch from the crystal glass she held in her right hand. Swallowed. "Some fence mending, I hope," she replied. "Hutch never wanted to hurt Brylee, and we've all been worried about her." A pause, during which Kendra's perfect eyebrows drew closer together for a moment in apparent consternation. "Plus, it's awkward. You and Joslyn and Tara and I are all friends, and now you're married to Walker, which means we'll all be running into each other even more often than before. Unless we all want to walk on eggshells forever, somebody had to do something."

"You know what?" Casey said, touching her friend's arm. "You're amazing. A lot of women in your place wouldn't be so open-minded. Some of them might even be jealous."

Kendra smiled, serene as a Christmas-card Madonna. "There are a lot of uncertainties in this world," she responded, "but there's one thing I'm definitely sure of. Hutch Carmody loves me as much as I love him, and that isn't going to change."

Casey swallowed as, once again, the backs of her eyes stung with tears she wasn't about to shed. What would it be like, she wondered, to love a man like that, and be loved the same way in return? Kendra knew. So did Tara and Joslyn. Would it ever be that way for her?

Presently, Hutch left Brylee's side and came to collect Kendra. He kissed Casey's cheek, congratulated her one more time, and they left.

Casey waited a few beats, then made her way through the dwindling crowd to Brylee's side.

She was standing with her back to the room by then, gazing out the picture window toward the green hills, and Casey, looking at her sister-in-law in profile, saw a single tear slip down Brylee's cheek.

"I'm here," Casey said gently. Sometimes, that was all one person could offer another, just their presence.

"Thank you," Brylee answered with a sniffle. "I've been such a fool," she added softly, a few moments later.

"What do you mean?" Casey asked, frowning a little. Love was love, and even when it didn't end with happily-ever-after, it was nothing to be ashamed of.

Brylee surprised her then, turning her head to bestow a wide, watery smile. She seemed illuminated from the inside. "Hutch always said I was in love with love, not with him, and, finally, I believe him."

"He must have said something pretty special just now," Casey speculated.

Brylee laughed. "Not really," she replied happily. "He told me to grow up, stop feeling sorry for myself and get a life."

Casey's mouth fell open, just briefly. "And you didn't slap his face?"

Brylee was actually glowing. "No," she said. "Because I realized he was right on all counts. I also realized that, while he might be *Kendra's* Prince Charming, he's all wrong for me. Not exactly a frog, since there's no denying the man's easy on the eyes, but we'd have gone bust sooner or later, for sure, and we'd both have had a few warts and wounds to show for it."

Casey didn't know what to say, but she was stricken with admiration, and she supposed it showed, because Brylee gave her a quick hug and laughed again.

"Time to round up the kids and head for town," she said. "That menagerie of yours will be waiting at the ole mansion."

Brylee had offered to spend a few days at Casey's house, looking after Clare and Shane and the dogs and cats, so the bride and groom could be alone together, in lieu of a honeymoon.

Since the marriage was a matter of convenience, rather than mad, passionate love, a part of Casey dreaded the moment when she and Walker were the last men standing—so to speak—but another part of her was intrigued, even eager.

"Give me a second with Clare first," she told Brylee, who nodded and went off to speak with the last of the departing guests.

Casey found her daughter sitting on the piano bench, idly plunking out the bare-bones version of "Heart and Soul" with one index finger. Considering that she could play Chopin without sheet music, not to mention a rendition of "Great Balls of Fire" that would have impressed Jerry Lee Lewis himself, Clare was playing for herself, not for anyone's entertainment.

Casey slid onto the bench beside her daughter and played the other half of the time-honored duet.

Clare glanced at her, smiled shyly and showed what she could do.

When the song ended, Walker, Brylee and Shane, standing in a semicircle behind Clare and Casey, applauded.

Casey leaned over, rested her forehead against Clare's and whispered, "No matter what, sweetheart, you'll always be my baby girl. Please don't forget that."

Clare's eyes filled with tears, and her smile dazzled. "I'm still pretty mad at you," she responded softly. "Will you still love me when I finally get over it?"

Casey kissed the girl's cheek with the kind of smack only a mom can get away with. "You can take it to the bank," she promised. "I will love you forever and ever."

Clare chuckled. "Amen," she said.

After that, Casey hugged Shane goodbye and reminded him to behave himself, and then Brylee herded her niece and nephew out of the house and into her SUV.

Only Casey and Walker remained once the door closed behind those three.

And, of course, Doolittle, who seemed relieved that things might be returning to normal.

With an audible sigh, the dog curled up in front of the cold fireplace, settled his bones and drifted off to sleep.

Walker chuckled, took Casey's hand and led her through the house to the kitchen, where she collapsed into a chair and kicked off her dress shoes.

"We did it," she said with a sigh comparable to Doolittle's.

Walker grinned, arched one eyebrow and undid his tie, then the top buttons of his dress shirt. "Champagne, Mrs. Parrish?" he asked, lifting one of the half-filled bottles off the counter and holding it up for her inspection.

"Don't mind if I do, Mr. Parrish," Casey answered. She was accustomed to wearing either sneakers or boots, and those shoes had been pinching like crazy ever since she'd put them on.

He filled champagne flutes—plastic ones, from the supermarket—for both of them, carried them to the table.

After setting the glasses down, Walker sat, lifted one of Casey's feet onto his lap and began to massage away the ache.

Casey groaned with pleasure. If the man was trying to seduce her, he was on the right track.

Walker chuckled, enjoying her reaction. "So what do we do now?" he asked lightly. "Play checkers? Watch TV? Build on a couple of bedrooms for the kids?"

Casey moaned again, but the sound was part laugh. Dear God, Walker's fingers were magic, and not just in bed. She'd forgotten how he could melt her simply by rubbing her feet. "For now," she replied in a near croon, eyes closed, "let's just keep doing this."

"I'm doing all the work," Walker complained with a smile in his voice. "You're just sitting there, shamelessly enjoying my husbandly attentions."

"Mmm," Casey agreed, almost floating.

After Walker had turned that foot into a quivering heap of jelly, he started in on the other one.

"Our daughter has quite a singing voice," he said. "Is she planning to follow in your illustrious footsteps?"

Casey chortled without opening her eyes, even as she felt a mild pang of sadness. Clare was Walker's child, as much as her own, and there was so much he didn't know about her, or Shane, for that matter.

"No way," she answered. "Clare wants to be a veterinarian. She's had all the show business she wants for one lifetime."

"How about you?" Walker asked, with a deceptive note of nonchalance. "Where do you stand on the issue of show business, Casey Jones?"

Casey opened her eyes, studied him. She might be tired of the road, tired of waking up in one city and going to sleep in another, never quite sure which town was which, but she knew she'd never completely retire. Music was in her blood, and there were times when she needed to be onstage, needed to engage with an audience.

"Is it a deal breaker?" she asked. Her lifestyle, after all, was night-and-day different from Walker's. He liked ranch life, with the occasional rodeo thrown in for spice.

And she liked singing, sometimes in church, sometimes in the shower and sometimes onstage in a sold-out arena.

"I'm not trying to close any doors in your face, Casey," Walker assured her quietly. "I'm just wondering how we're going to proceed from here, that's all. We haven't talked about that much."

"No," Casey agreed. "There's a lot we haven't talked about."

One corner of Walker's very inviting mouth quirked upward. "We're a pretty unconventional pair, I'll say that for us."

Casey nodded. "We are indeed," she agreed. "Any regrets, cowboy?"

"Only that we didn't do this sooner," he answered. He sighed. "Get married, I mean. Shane's all right with having an instant dad, at least on the surface, but Clare isn't planning on letting bygones be bygones anytime soon, as far as I can make out."

"You're right about that," Casey answered.

He raised an eyebrow, his expression wry. "Wait a minute," he joked. "Did I just hear you say I'm *right* about something?"

She laughed, which was ironic, since she was close to tears. "What if some woman comes along," she began, unable, for some reason, to keep from poking at her own sore places, "and you fall head-over-bootheels for her, and here you are, tied down with me?"

Walker's expression turned solemn, but a sparkle soon leaped into his eyes. "I don't foresee that happening," he drawled.

Casey's heart picked up a little speed. It wasn't an "I love you," but she was reassured anyway. Mustn't get too comfortable, though.

"We're not having sex," she said.

Walker chuckled, shook his head. "Hell, woman," he said, "we're married, aren't we? Shouldn't some part of this crazy situation be fun?"

She pulled her foot from his lap, reached for her champagne flute and downed the lukewarm contents in a couple of gulps. Suddenly, she was all too conscious of the fact that they were alone in the house, and Walker was hot, and they were wearing each other's wedding bands.

Not to mention that his bed was just a few rooms away.

"*Now* what's gotten under your hide?" Walker asked, frowning.

"It's still light out," Casey said, ignoring his question. "If it's fun you want, let's saddle up a couple of horses and ride."

Maybe on horseback, she could behave herself. Outrun the temptation she was feeling now.

Why not just go to bed with Walker?

Because when Walker made love to her, she lost complete control, and that terrified her. She was all about living up to the image of Casey Elder she held in her mind, about standing strong, marching to her own drumbeat, setting goals and meeting them, making decisions and abiding by them. When she was in Walker's arms, she became another person entirely, a stranger, willing to bare her soul, show her deepest needs and emotions.

And that scared her half to death.

She waited for Walker's answer, knew that if he held her, or kissed her, or even started rubbing her feet again, for pity's sake, she'd be lost.

Finally, he sighed, shoved back his chair and stood.

"All right," he said, with more resignation than enthusiasm. "Let's change clothes and go saddle ourselves some horses."

The few things Casey had brought along were in a nearby guest room, still packed away in a small suitcase.

She went off to swap her wedding dress and pantyhose for jeans and a long-sleeved T-shirt, and when she got back to the kitchen, Walker was already back from his own room, clad in regular clothes. He'd even had time to brew a cup of coffee, and he smiled over the rim before setting it aside on the counter.

His gaze glided over her, leaving fire in its wake.

"You sure do fill out a pair of jeans just right, Mrs. Parrish," he said.

Casey made a face, though she was secretly pleased by the compliment, as casual and offhand as it had been.

Leaving Doolittle behind to recover from the festivities, they left the house together, heading for the barn.

No one was around—even the ranch hands were elsewhere, though they'd been present for the wedding—and yet there was a feeling in the air that made Casey uneasy. Stopping in the yard, she turned in a full circle, very slowly, looking for the source of her discomfort.

Sunlight flashed off something in one of the nearby oak trees, a silvery glint, and that was when Casey spotted the reporter, lurking in the high branches. She muttered a very unladylike word and headed in that direction, fists clenched.

Rapid clicks sounded as the sneak took pictures.

Walker, keeping pace, tilted his head back, adjusted his hat and grinned. "I'll be damned," he said.

This kind of intrusion was new to him, but Casey was anything but amused. "Get down from there before you break your darn fool neck!" she ordered, looking around again as the branches rustled and shook overhead. Where there was one photographer, in her experience, there were a dozen.

Worse, that particular tree was situated close enough to the house to provide a clear view of the living room, where the ceremony had taken place.

"This is a free country," the tree man argued, sounding braver than he probably was. "There's the First Amendment—and freedom of speech—"

"Don't you lecture me on the Bill of Rights, you jackass," Casey shot back. "It just so happens that I have a few rights of my own!"

Walker chuckled again. He was loving this, which only made Casey more furious.

"You carrying a gun, cowboy?" the spy asked warily. A round, bespectacled face peered down at Walker through the foliage.

"No," Walker answered affably, "but I could lay my hands on one in short order, if I were so inclined." He paused. "If I were you, buddy, I'd get the hell out of here before this redhead decides to climb right up there after you and smash that camera of yours over your head."

More branches shifted and creaked, and the photographer, a portly sort who had, in Casey's view, defied gravity as well as good manners by hauling himself up into that tree in the first place, made his way down.

Backing away quickly, he huffed, "Don't let her get me!"

And then he turned and ran for his life.

CHAPTER TWELVE

WALKER WAS PRACTICALLY doubled over laughing as he watched the pudgy, tree-climbing reporter making an awkward dash for the tall timbers, but Casey was *not* amused. While she understood that tabloid stringers and photographers had a right to earn a living like everybody else, she'd had so many private moments interrupted or flat-out ruined over the course of her career that she'd run out of patience a long time ago.

It only made matters worse that, since settling in Parable, she and the kids had enjoyed a certain slackening of media attention, though they'd never been entirely free of it, and now, as she'd expected and feared, the semihiatus was obviously at an end. Game on.

Time to shift emotional gears from neutral to overdrive. *Again.*

Folding her arms, Casey sighed and watched balefully as the reporter finally disappeared into a stand of brush down by the main road. Moments later, a car engine started up with a roar, soon followed by the screech of tires as he tore out of there.

Walker, quiet now, slipped an arm around Casey's shoulders—which, she realized with a stab of annoyance, were trembling. She'd better buck the heck up, she thought, because the die was cast and, by God, *her children* weren't going to come out on the losing end.

"Case," her new husband said, very quietly and with a gentleness that was very nearly her undoing, "it's *all right*. He's gone."

"For now," Casey conceded grudgingly. She did let Walker hold her close against his side, though, and it felt good not to be alone, not to have to be strong, if only for a few moments. *Too good.*

"Let's go for that ride," Walker said, steering her toward the barn.

Casey looked around, but she knew they were by themselves, at least in terms of sneaky reporters. It was small comfort, because there *had* been others, of course. They'd simply been faster than Tarzan of the Oak Tree—by now, they were probably in Three Trees, behind the doors of their cheap motel rooms, swilling beer and congratulating themselves, anticipating the fat checks they'd soon be banking. Thanks to modern technology, they'd probably already zipped very personal photos and wildly speculative stories about Casey, Walker, the children and the wedding itself off to waiting editors.

"What if we're followed?" Casey fretted. Secretly, she'd entertained a fantasy that she and Walker might consummate their marriage after all, somewhere out there under the big sky, sheltered by venerable trees and high grass, with their horses grazing peacefully nearby.

Now, of course, sex in the tall grass was out of the question. The thought of their being seen making love, let alone *photographed,* chilled her blood.

"Don't be paranoid, Casey Jones," Walker counseled with an easy grin. His arm was still around her shoulders, strong and sure, and they had almost reached the barn door. "If that guy was an example of his breed, they won't be following us on horseback, and we'd hear anything with a motor from a long way off."

Casey nodded, biting her lower lip, but she was still thinking that such things were easy enough for *Walker* to say, because he'd never been stalked, never had to console disappointed children after an innocent and entirely ordinary outing—a birthday party, an afternoon movie, a visit to a zoo or a theme park—had been spoiled, cut short by obnoxious photographers and pseudojournalists.

He'd probably never had to watch Fourth of July fireworks or the New Year's Eve countdown on a hotel TV, instead of celebrating in person, or attend weddings and christenings and even funerals in the company of several bodyguards, because there had been a rash of death threats.

While she pondered these recollections, Walker saddled a gelding named Smokey for her and then Mack, the buckskin, for himself.

Back outside, in the afternoon sunshine, he gave Casey a leg up into the saddle. She'd been too preoccupied to prove that she could damn well mount a horse on her own, whatever he thought of her riding skills.

Walker swung onto Mack's sturdy back and they were on their way, passing between the horse pasture and the bull pens and on into an open field, rippling with sweet-scented grass. The sun was warm on their backs, and the sturdiness of horse flesh and the creak of leather began to calm Casey's nerves, degree by degree.

"Tell me what life's been like for you," Walker said quietly, resettling his hat as he spoke, and reining Mack in a little to keep pace with the more sedate Smokey. "Not the visits to the White House, or being named Entertainer of the Year all those times, stuff like that—but the nitty-gritty, day-to-day things."

The response that leaped to Casey's mind was "lonely," interestingly enough, but she didn't say it. For one thing, she was too proud, too attached to her independence and the strength she made it a point to project, even when she didn't feel it.

For another, she knew Walker was still thinking about the reporters and photographers, not the good ones, the courteous professionals, of whom there were many, but the intrusive, obnoxious types who apparently lived to invade her privacy and that of her children. *Those* people, mostly men, though there were a few women in the mix, could put a scurrilous spin on something as simple as a picnic in the park or a routine stint in the hospital.

Outdoor meals with the band members and their families became cult meetings, and a bad case of strep throat, complicated by exhaustion brought on by weeks on the road and requiring IVs and medical observation, could be twisted into a secret abortion. Casey could handle being the target of that kind of gossip, but it wasn't always directed at her alone—sometimes Clare was dragged into it, and even Shane had been credited with a serious drug problem.

Casey told Walker those stories, and a few others, as they rode, and difficult though some of it was, she felt relieved just to vent to this quiet, nonjudgmental man, listening attentively to every word she said.

That was a new experience, mostly. She'd discussed such things with Mitch, and with the guys in the band, but only because they'd usually witnessed the incidents for themselves, so there was no hiding it from them. The bodyguards and members of law enforcement encountered in the course of her travels were *paid* to care what happened to Casey Elder and her children, though they were unlikely to have any real emotional investment in possible outcomes.

Joslyn, Kendra and Tara, new friends and yet among the best she'd ever had, would have sympathized, of course, but burdening them with problems brought on by her own public persona seemed unfair. After all, prying eyes and wagging tongues were part of the deal— by choosing fame, riding tall in the figurative saddle, she'd made herself a lightning rod.

All of which meant that Casey had always carried most of the load herself, and tried not to complain about the effort, even in the sanctuary of her stubborn soul.

By the time she'd finished the tale, she and Walker had reached the tumbled-down cabin in the hills, the site of his forebears' nineteenth-century homestead, via a different route than before.

Only then, when he'd dismounted and reached up to help Casey down off Smokey's wide back, did Walker offer a comment on the long and complicated diatribe.

"Things are going to be different now," he said, facing her, the reins still in their hands, their bodies not quite touching as they stood there in all that quietness, surrounded by the singular gifts of a big sky summer— the cloudless, overarching canopy of watercolor blue in a shade so tender it bruised the heart to look up at it; warm, soft breezes, caressing the flesh like the touch of an angel's fingertips; the faint, perfect fragrances of wildflowers and old-fashioned peonies; the occasional chirp of an unseen bird, guarding its nest in one of the trees.

Casey must have looked a little skeptical at Walker's words, because, seeing her expression, he gave a low chuckle and planted a light, swift kiss on her forehead.

"Things are going to be different," he reiterated without a trace of male arrogance, "because I'll be around. I figure if one of those guys gets out of line, all I have to do is make an example of him, and the others will get the message."

Casey opened her eyes wide. "You don't mean you'd *punch* one of them or something like that?"

"I mean," Walker clarified, in all sincerity, "that I'll do whatever is necessary to keep my wife and my children safe."

"Oh," Casey said. While she didn't believe that violence, the bare-fisted cowboy kind or any other, was an acceptable solution, a part of her definitely *liked* the idea that anybody who meant her or the kids harm would have to get by Walker Parrish first.

Only a fool would even make the attempt.

But, then, fools had never been in short supply, now, had they?

"There's something else I've made up my mind about, Case," Walker added, cupping her chin in his hand. The spark remained in his eyes, but it was one of passion now, of quiet but unshakable conviction, not amusement. "We got married for Clare's and Shane's sakes—I understand that. But if you're sleeping in one room and I'm in another, well, that sort of defeats the whole purpose, mostly because of the message it sends—that we're together but separate. We might as well have skipped the whole process of getting hitched, if that's how it's going to be."

Casey's heart picked up speed until it was racing. She

knew Walker was right, but sharing his bed every night was a huge risk in itself—she'd be vulnerable, and not just sexually, because her mind and soul would be laid bare to him, as well as her body.

The spirit might be willing, but the flesh was weak. Hell, the flesh—*her* flesh—wasn't just weak, it was flagrantly *wanton*. Given a voice, every part of her would have been shouting a hallelujah chorus of "Bring it on, cowboy!"

"Sex wasn't part of the deal," she reminded him, somewhat lamely.

He kissed her, not in the way he did when he fully intended to seduce her, on the spot, but with reassuring affection. "True enough," he said. Then, after an agreeable pause, he asked, "When was the last time I forced myself on you, Casey Jones?"

She straightened her spine, set her hands on her hips. She knew a full-court press when she was the object of one. "That's just the trouble," she retorted. "You don't *have* to drag me off into your cave by the hair. All *you* ever have to do, Walker Parrish, is *touch* me in the right places—and, dammit, you know just where those places are!"

He laughed, pushed his hat to the back of his head and countered, "Doesn't that tell you something?"

"It tells me," Casey answered, going on pure bravado, "that when you turn on the charm, my clothes tend to fall off. It's all bliss—until I come to my senses again."

"That," Walker responded affably, "sounds like a personal problem."

"How do you figure that?" Casey snapped. More

bravado. Things were melting inside her, expanding, getting ready.

"I'm your husband," he reminded her, not in a demanding way, but as a person stating a simple fact. "Therefore, it's my prerogative to 'turn on the charm,' as you put it, but all it would take to put the brakes on is a simple *no* from you, and you know it. I might be about as cordial as a wounded bear for a while, but I'm not going to barge in—so to speak—where I'm not wanted."

Casey merely stared at him, at a loss for words, furious because every single thing he'd said was true. Saying *no* was *her* responsibility, when push came to shove, not his.

And she was no damn good at saying *no* to Walker Parrish. She had two children, a skittish heart and a twitch in the pit of her stomach to prove it.

"I'll sleep with you," she finally said. "But you have to promise not to touch me."

"Sorry, lady," Walker answered, clearly enjoying her discomfort, "but that's a promise I can't make."

"Whatever happened to win-win negotiations?" Casey demanded, flustered, thinking she'd faint if her heartbeat didn't slow down soon.

Walker smiled, but his eyes and the set of his jaw remained serious. "I've done things your way for a long time," he told her after mulling the words over silently for a few moments. "But the way I see it, marriage is a partnership, and that means you're going to have to do some things *my* way, Mrs. Parrish. And sharing my bed is one of them."

"What about my right to say *no?*"

"You can refuse," Walker said easily, "but you'll have to pack up your stuff and move back to the mansion if you do. Either we're husband and wife or we're not. Make a choice."

Casey felt her face flush with heat. She was in that storied place—between a rock and a hard place. And she was stuck.

"Is this an ultimatum?" she challenged, though she felt anything but tough-minded at the moment.

Walker considered the question for longer than she would have liked. Then he adjusted his hat, crooked a grin at her and said, "Not exactly. I'm definitely hoping you'll decide to stay right here on the ranch with me, but if you insist on celibacy, well, then, I guess we've got a standoff."

She huffed out a breath, folded her arms again, glared up at her hardheaded husband. She wouldn't have chosen to marry Walker, since they didn't get along most of the time, now being a case in point, but she couldn't begin to imagine being anybody *else's* wife, either. Never had imagined it, actually, for all that she'd longed for a real home and an old-fashioned family setup.

And that was a big part of her problem, the main reason she had a string of go-nowhere flirtations behind her, but not much else. As far as she was concerned, there might as well have been only one man in the world: this one.

When it came to Walker, she was damned if she did, and damned if she didn't.

Forget win-win.

So she finally caved. "All right," she said. "You win." A pause. "This once."

At that, Walker threw back his head and gave a shout of laughter. Then he lifted Casey by the waist, spun her around until she was dizzy and, finally, set her back on her wobbly feet and kissed her senseless.

WHEN IT WAS finally time to turn in for the night—as in, when Casey ran out of stall tactics like folding the rented chairs, taking down wedding decorations, wrapping and freezing what was left of the cake and, in the end, whipping up a supper that proved inedible—Walker breathed a silent sigh of relief.

While he collected Casey's suitcase from the guest quarters and carried it to their room, she locked herself in the master bath and took what must have been the longest shower on record. When she finally came out, looking shy as a novice nun recently released from her vows and sent home from the convent, she was swaddled in his ancient flannel bathrobe—more like *lost* in it, since it all but went around her twice.

Walker rarely used the robe, preferring, except in the dead of winter, to simply let himself air-dry after a shower, since, for all intents and purposes, he'd lived alone for most of his adult life. Plus, it saved on towels.

How things had changed, he thought now, with an inner grin. He was already in bed, with the covers resting roughly at his waistline and a couple of pillows fluffed up behind his back, and hoped he didn't seem half as eager for Casey to join him as he was.

If this had been a real wedding night, of course, she'd have on some sexy wisp of lingerie instead of his ugly bathrobe, he mused, but there was always an upside. Since she'd been in the shower when he brought up her suitcase, she was probably bare-ass naked under all that faded flannel.

He smiled and, catching him at it, Casey planted her

feet and folded her arms, waxing stubborn. Not that that was any big stretch, when you considered how wide her streak of cussedness probably was.

"What?" she demanded. She was flushed, either from the heat of the shower or from embarrassment, and her red hair had steamed itself into limp spirals.

"I was just thinking about wedding nights in general and ours in particular," Walker drawled, cupping his hands behind his head and settling in for whatever fate had in store for the two of them.

"I'm here under duress," Casey protested. "In this room, I mean."

Walker chuckled and shook his head. If he hadn't been enjoying this so much, he'd have been riled, he supposed. She seemed to be forgetting, conveniently, that this marriage had been *her* idea.

"No," he argued, amused, "you're here because you chose to stay instead of going back to town."

"Semantics," she said dismissively, marching over to the mirror above his bureau and studying her reflection closely, as though she'd expected to see somebody else's face looking back at her. Maybe she *was* wondering who that woman in the bathrobe was, and what she'd done with the indomitable Casey Elder.

"Are you planning on wearing that robe to bed?" Walker asked mildly.

"You just never mind what I'm wearing to bed," she told him peevishly. Then she marched herself over to the bench next to the fireplace, where he'd placed her suitcase, opened the lid and rummaged through the contents until she came up with plaid flannel boxer shorts and a T-shirt that had seen better days, if not better decades.

"You're not serious," he said, referring to her choice

of nightwear. He'd have preferred the robe, by a country mile.

She gave him a look calculated to quell any stirring that might be going on under the sheets, retreated into the bathroom again and came out five minutes later, looking young enough to be jailbait.

The shorts had a placket in front, and the T-shirt was downright disreputable, with a hole under one arm and a sprinkling of bleach stains across the front.

Casey whirled slowly for his benefit, like a runway model showing off the latest fashion, fairly exuding irony.

Walker frowned. "Whose shorts are those?" he asked.

Suddenly, Casey's green eyes twinkled and, though she was still careful to keep her distance, she actually smiled. "Jealous?" she retorted.

"Hardly," Walker replied, still frowning. Whoever had owned them was a scrawny dude, obviously.

"They used to be Shane's," Casey generously informed him, all in her own good time. "He decided they were geeky and gave them a toss."

Relieved to learn that the boxers hadn't been left behind by some lover of Casey's, scrawny or not, and willing to die before he'd let on that he'd been the least bit worried, Walker smirked a little. "I'm with Shane," he said. "They're definitely geeky."

"Get used to it," Casey replied, saucy as all get-out. "I have half a dozen other pairs and I always sleep in one of them."

Walker locked his gaze with hers and tossed back the covers on her side of the bed with a smooth motion of one arm. "There are some things a man can't be expected to get used to," he answered, grinning now. "And sleeping with somebody in boxers definitely falls into that category."

Casey hesitated, then hotfooted it over to the bed and jumped in beside him. Most likely, Walker thought, she was afraid somebody was hiding outside in the shrubbery with a camera, ready to record her wedding-night attire for posterity.

Fortunately, none of the windows lined up with the bed—he'd made double-sure of that earlier. Besides, the blinds were all pulled.

She huddled on her side of the mattress, sheets and lightweight blankets drawn up almost to her chin. Her eyes were huge.

Walker became exasperated. "Will you please stop acting like a scared virgin?" he asked, tossing aside one of the two pillows he'd been propped up on and lying down flat. "It's only been about a week, in case you've forgotten, since the last time you were in this bed, clawing at my back with your fingernails and begging for more."

Color washed up from her neck to her cheekbones to her forehead. Her temper was rising, which, as far as Walker was concerned, was a good sign. He'd been starting to think she really *was* afraid of him.

"I hope you bought better-quality condoms since then," she said. Then, after a regretful pause, "Not that we're going to need any of those."

Walker rolled onto his side, propped his head on one elbow and regarded her steadily. "You're right about one thing, Mrs. Parrish," he said, in a low rumble. "We're not going to need condoms."

Again, her eyes widened. "What do you mean by that?" she asked.

As if she didn't know.

"I mean," Walker murmured, his mouth very close to hers now, "that that particular horse is not only already out of the barn, but halfway across the county by now. And you and I have never had much luck with condoms anyway, have we?"

She blinked. "You're not planning on kissing me, are you?" she asked.

"I'm planning on doing one hell of a lot more than that," Walker replied. "But if you want me to stop at any time, all you have to do is say so."

Her mouth opened, and her throat worked, but no sound came out.

Walker chuckled, covered her mouth with his and, at the same time, hauled those boxer shorts down over her knees and then her ankles.

With a groan, the kiss having turned into a sparring match between their two tongues by then, Casey kicked free of the boxers and wrapped her arms around Walker's neck.

He dealt with the T-shirt next, pushing it up until not only her silky belly but her luscious breasts were bared to him, felt a soaring triumph when she broke the kiss just long enough to pull the garment off over her head and hurl it away. An instant later, she was burying her fingers in his hair, initiating the next kiss herself, her perfect body already inviting him into her depths.

There was no foreplay that first time, because neither one of them could wait that long. Their bodies, in full mutiny, remembered the glorious fire of their last encounter viscerally, at the cellular level, and would not be denied the fusing they craved so fiercely.

Casey spread her legs wide, and Walker positioned himself between them, found the velvety entrance to all the heaven he needed at the moment and took her in a single thrust of his hips.

She crooned and arched her back as she received him, and she gasped his name. Again, their mouths sought and found each other, and their tongues did sweet battle, and Walker deliberately slowed his pace.

It wasn't easy, especially with Casey doing everything she could to drive him over the edge, but Walker called on every ounce of self-control he possessed, determined to make this ecstasy last.

Casey's hips flew, and she was warm and soft, everywhere, inside and out. Her palms roamed over his back, his shoulders, his buttocks, urging, taunting, claiming.

Walker nearly lost his mind, but he didn't surrender.

Slowly—very slowly—he moved, sheathing and unsheathing himself in Casey, breathing her name, pausing now and then to nibble at an earlobe or suckle one of her hard and waiting nipples.

She grew more and more desperate, whimpering and writhing, gasping out his name in ragged bursts.

When at last she began to climax, he knew it by her cries and the way she tightened around him, seized him, held him captive inside her. With one last thrust and a low, raspy shout of nearly unbearable pleasure, Walker let go.

It seemed like forever before their mutual releases finally subsided and they collapsed onto the mattress, landing hard, like a pair of skydivers whose parachutes had failed to open.

Because bolting out of bed on a surge of moral regret was Casey's usual M.O., Walker was ready for it. He pinned her beneath him, gently clasping her wrists and pressing them into the pillow on either side of her head.

"Say it," he challenged, getting hard again, letting her feel him pressing against her thigh. "Say *no*."

Casey made a sighing sound instead, closing her eyes.

I love you, Casey Elder, Walker thought with soul-sundering clarity, but he knew better than to say those words out loud. She'd either throw them back in his face or pretend she hadn't heard, and there was no telling which of those reactions would have hurt more.

They remained as they were for long moments, skin on skin, breath on breath, heartbeat on heartbeat, savoring those things, neither of them moving a muscle.

Walker, having admitted the truth, if only to himself, might have seemed still, but inside he was busy grappling with wild surges of emotion. He'd probably loved Casey from the instant he laid eyes on her, but the realization had taken a long time to surface, like a seed planted too deep in the ground.

Presently, she opened her eyes again, and they shone like molten emeralds, casting the kind of spell that lasts forever.

Did she know what she was doing to him?

Walker doubted it. There was a certain confounding innocence, a sort of reckless naïveté, about the woman—fame, fortune and two children born out of wedlock notwithstanding. She was part firebrand and part angel, and he liked her that way.

Casey might be infuriating at times, but she was

never dull. There was too much rip-roaring, pepper-and-vinegar, go-for-broke *life* in her.

They searched each other's eyes, and Walker finally ground out a rusty "Well?"

She smiled a little, nodded, welcomed him inside her.

WALKER SLEPT SOUNDLY, like the thoroughly satisfied man he was, and Casey, sitting up in bed, watched him, loving the way a lock of his hair fell across his forehead, loving the sweep of his unfairly thick eyelashes, the rise and fall of his muscular chest. She rested her palm over his heart, lightly, so she wouldn't wake him, and delighted in the smattering of silken furriness.

I love you, Walker Parrish, she vowed silently.

When had she fallen for him, exactly?

Hard to tell. Maybe it was that first night, when they met in a run-down cowboy bar after a rodeo held on the back acre of nowhere, and slow-danced to the jukebox. The next day, with her heart wedged into her throat and her eyes scalding with inexplicable tears, she watched him ride a bull named Say Your Prayers.

Watched him win.

When the weekend was over, they'd parted ways—Casey had some bookings coming up, and he was headed back to Montana—but running into each other became something of a habit in the months to come.

They'd taken their time becoming lovers—Casey, while not a virgin, was inexperienced, and Walker—well, suffice it to say, he'd had a reputation for knowing his way around a woman's body—but when it finally happened, in a motel room in Cheyenne, Wyoming, the skies split open and the angels sang. At least, that's how it was for Casey.

She'd been astounded by the things Walker made her feel, taking her outside herself the way he did, curling her toes with a simple kiss, causing her heart to take wing and soar, like some great bird glorying in its wildness.

And she'd been terrified. Friends warned her that Walker Parrish was the love-'em-and-leave-'em type, and she could believe it. Women swarmed around him, in bars, behind the chutes at the rodeo, even in parking lots.

Still, their paths continued to cross—Casey couldn't deny that she'd booked herself and the band at as many rodeos as possible—and each time they made love, she became more determined to guard her heart. And each time, that was harder to do.

Then Clare was conceived. Casey's career was just starting to take off by then—she was opening for some of the biggest acts in country music, and she'd just signed a recording contract. To say that pregnancy was inconvenient would have been the understatement of the modern era, and Casey knew the advice she was receiving—put the baby up for adoption—made sense, from a practical standpoint.

But her heart wouldn't hear of it.

Word had gotten back to Walker, and he'd shown up at the stage door one night, determined and bristly.

And she'd lied to him, having convinced herself that she couldn't have done otherwise, swearing that another man had fathered her child.

Walker hadn't believed her at first, but she'd kept on insisting, and, finally, she'd seen something fracture behind his eyes.

Watching him walk away was one of the hardest

things she'd ever had to do, and she'd had to fight to keep herself from calling him back, telling him the truth, letting fate take over from there.

Now, she thought, with a bittersweet pang crowding her throat, things had come full circle. She was married to Walker, for better or for worse. They didn't get along any better than they ever had, except when they were having sex, and what were they supposed to do the *other* twenty-some hours of the day?

On top of that, she'd bet her first guitar that she was pregnant—for the third time. Which only went to show that some people never learned their lesson.

CHAPTER THIRTEEN

CASEY SAT AT the kitchen table, her feet tucked behind the rung of her wooden chair, studying a dog-eared cookbook she'd found in a drawer, its margins crowded with handwritten comments from way back, judging by the faded ink and formal penmanship. There were also sticky notes jutting out from many of the pages, different, more recent observations, written in a loopy scrawl and plentiful as the feathers in a bird's wing.

The finer points of food preparation still eluded her. What did it mean, for instance, to "braise" a cut of beef? What happened when a batch of fudge "sugared"?

She eyed her smartphone, the source of easy answers—run a quick search and the mysteries of braising and sugaring would be revealed, she figured.

Too bad about the *hard* answers, though, replies to questions like *How do I love Walker Parrish without losing myself in him completely?* and *Besides Casey Elder, superstar, who am I? Is there more to me than my singing voice?*

The landline rang then, startling her out of her musings.

Since Walker was outside, conferring with his foreman, Al Pickens, Casey got up, crossed to the nearby counter and picked up the cordless receiver. Still distracted, she practically croaked, "Hello?"

"Good," a female voice said on a sigh. "It's you."

"Who is this?" Casey asked, frowning, back to the cookbook again, riffling through it, determined to find a recipe she could conceivably follow well enough to make something Walker might actually *eat*.

Unlike last night's effort at spaghetti, which wound up as one big clump of half-done noodle-substance and would have had to be cut into slices, if served in the first place, instead of spooned out in lovely, steaming dollops.

"It's Brylee," came the answer, patient but a little breathless. "Your sister-in-law?"

"Oh," Casey said, closing the cookbook, which was roughly the size of a classroom dictionary. Now that she was tracking the conversation, her first question was, as always, "Are the kids okay?"

"So far," Brylee said, causing a little trapdoor to swing open in the pit of Casey's stomach, one she might just fall through if she didn't hold on. "We're at the supermarket in Parable, and we're *surrounded*."

"By what?" Casey asked, nerves jangling like a pocket full of small change.

"By reporters," Brylee answered, almost in a whisper. "There are all these—these *people* out in the parking lot, with cameras and microphones. Even vans with satellite dishes on top. Evidently, they've been keeping out of sight, waiting for us to come out of your house, so they could follow us. They keep calling out Clare's and Shane's names, and the manager locked the doors, but he's worried about keeping customers out, too. And *in,* of course. It's like being under siege."

Casey paced, too agitated to sit or even stand still

in one place. She strode over to the back door, opened it and yelled, "Walker!"

"Oww," Brylee complained, probably wincing and holding her cell away from her ear.

"Sorry," Casey threw out.

Walker immediately broke off the discussion he'd been having with Al and several of the ranch hands, looking worried, and hurried in her direction.

"Stay put," Casey said to Brylee. "Tell the manager not to open those doors until Walker and I get there—"

"Wait," Brylee broke in, calmer now. "The manager just called the sheriff's office—Boone Taylor is on his way over here right now, with a couple of deputies for backup. He'll get us to the ranch okay, so there's nothing to fret about."

Nothing to fret about. Casey fought down a swell of exasperation; this was no time to lecture Brylee on mob psychology.

Walker burst in from the porch just then, almost tearing the screen door off its hinges in the process. His face was stony with concern, his eyes narrowed. "What is it?" he demanded, shuffling to one side so he wouldn't step on Doolittle, squeezing past him through the slim gap.

"Put Clare on for a moment, will you, Brylee?" Casey asked, and mouthed *Stay calm* at Walker while she waited to hear her daughter's voice.

"Mom," Clare said, moments later, a note of panic in her voice. "The tabloids came out early—special editions, evidently—and we're *all over* them, you and Walker and Shane and me. The headlines—they're all about us being your guilty secrets, and they're calling you a liar—"

"Clare," Casey broke in, "never mind the headlines for now. We can talk about all of that later, when you and Shane are back here, with us, where you belong."

Walker was glowering by then. He looked like an old-time gunslinger facing a showdown and more than ready to draw and fire. "I don't read lips," he informed Casey in a scratchy whisper.

Casey waved her hand, tried to ignore him. Not easy, since he seemed to fill that kitchen from wall to wall and ceiling to floor, he was so—*present*.

"Do we, Mom?" Clare's voice was small, shaky. She was used to living in the limelight, but this latest development was clearly getting to her. "Do we belong anyplace, Shane and me? What's real and what isn't?"

Those questions pierced Casey like the tip of a poisoned spear. "Listen to me, sweetheart. Boone—Sheriff Taylor—will be there any minute. He'll bring you home and we'll deal with the situation then, when we're all together."

"Okay," Clare whispered uncertainly.

Once, she'd believed Casey would keep her and her brother safe, no matter what. Now, her faith had been shaken, maybe toppled, and little wonder. She'd been lied to, by her own mother, repeatedly.

Casey felt sick, pressed her free hand to her stomach.

Brylee came back on the phone. "Boone's here," she said with obvious relief. "We'll be on our way shortly."

Casey nodded, opened her mouth to answer, but the dial tone was already buzzing in her ear.

Numbly, she turned to Walker, explained that the press had effectively cornered Brylee, Clare and Shane inside a supermarket.

Walker shoved a hand through his hair as he listened,

his jawline so tight that a white pallor pulsed under his tan. He'd caught the reference to Boone, though, or he might have been even more upset than he was.

Casey finished the account as it had been relayed to her, and then swallowed hard, willing herself not to cry. She'd had run-ins with the tabloid press before, of course, but never like this, with her children trapped inside a public building, and never in Parable or Three Trees. She felt violated, helpless and scalded all over with fury, all at once.

Walker took her firmly by the shoulders, probably afraid her knees would give out and she'd crumple to the floor if he didn't hold her up. The rage in his eyes softened to a kind of bleak comprehension.

Casey knew he was realizing what it could really mean, being married to someone like her, and in another moment or two, he'd be wishing he'd never *heard* of Casey Elder, let alone fathered two of her children, brought them all here to Timber Creek and effectively blown the lid off his otherwise ideal life.

"I'm sorry," she whispered.

Walker drew Casey close, just when she would have expected him to push her away, cupped the back of her head in one hand, squashing her ponytail. "Don't apologize," he said hoarsely. "This isn't your fault."

She tilted her head back, looked up at him, astonished. "Of *course* it is, Walker," she argued. "And I wouldn't mind if I was the only one who might get hurt in all this, but I'm not. Shane and Clare are directly in the line of fire, and so are you."

He kissed her forehead, gave her ponytail a light, teasing tug. "The kids are safe, Casey," he reminded her. "Brylee, too. Right now, that's what matters. And you saw this coming, remember?" His mouth twitched at one corner. "It's the main reason you got down on one knee and asked for my hand in marriage, as I recall."

Casey gave a raw little rasp of laughter, in spite of herself, and thumped Walker's chest with the side of her right fist. "I *didn't* get down on one knee," she said. "Let's get that straight."

The twitch became a full-fledged grin. "But you *did* propose," he insisted.

"I *suggested*." Even as she spoke, Casey wondered what was wrong with her. Why was her first response to Walker always an urge to argue?

Just then, a rap sounded, rattling the screen door, and Al Pickens stuck his head partway inside. "Boss? Is there a problem?"

Walker turned to look at his most faithful employee and longtime friend, and smiled. "It might be time to circle the wagons, all right," he said.

Briefly, Walker explained the situation.

Casey frowned, puzzled. *Do what?*

Al clearly understood, which was more than she could have claimed. He nodded and said, "I'll put a couple of men at the main gate, and the rest can beat the brush for any of them sneaky reporters, make sure they don't get close to the house again."

Walker nodded. "No rough stuff," he specified mildly.

"Darn." Al grinned, showing a few missing teeth, and tugged once at the brim of his battered hat. His face was round and weather-worn, his eyes small and twinkly. "I was kinda looking forward to going all John Wayne on at least one of those yahoos."

Walker chuckled, waved Al off with a motion of one hand and focused his attention on Casey again.

She felt as though the floor had turned to rubber under her feet, and she thought she might throw up.

Walker eased her back into the chair she'd been sitting on before the phone rang, lost in the arcane realm of home cooking, and related what Brylee had told her about the supermarket siege. He walked over to one of the cupboards, got out a glass, moved to the sink, filled it to the brim with cold water and brought it to Casey.

She took the glass in both hands, sipped slowly, in hopes that the stuff would stay down.

Walker took the chair nearest hers and waited with her, lightly massaging her nape, where the muscles had clenched up tight, like a knot in a length of steel cable.

Slowly, Casey began to feel a little better, though she knew she wouldn't relax completely until Shane and Clare got there, until she could see both her children with her own eyes and touch them and know for sure that they hadn't been hurt.

"Has this happened before?" Walker asked gently, after she'd stopped trembling and begun rolling her head from side to side in response to the massage. The release of tension was almost sexual.

"I've tangled with the so-called press a few times in the past," Casey responded, "and they've made up some pretty nasty stories about Clare and Shane along the way, too. Especially Shane. They claimed he was on drugs and I sued them for that one, but this is the most aggressive they've ever gotten." She remembered what her daughter had said about the early editions of the weekly tabloids, headlines and photos blazing with manufactured scandals. *Extra! Extra! Read all about it!*

Thoughtfully, Walker sorted through her answer in his head. Then he pushed back his chair, crossed to the desktop computer on a counter against the far wall and logged on.

Even before she saw his back stiffen, Casey knew it was bad. Maybe worse than bad.

Walker swore under his breath, clicking from one site to another.

When he turned around to face her again, his face was like a storm cloud. He looked as though he might be about to go find Al and the other cowboys and form a posse, vigilante-style, forgetting the "No rough stuff" decree he'd issued earlier.

Casey went to him, slipped her arms around his waist. This time, *she* was the voice of reason. "This will pass, Walker," she said gently. "It always does."

He looked grim, even harried. Again, he raked his fingers through his hair. "Greaseball reporters are one thing," he ground out, "and the crazies who take everything they write as gospel are *another,* dammit. Suppose some freak job hears voices telling him to kidnap Clare and Shane and actually follows through? Have you ever thought of that?"

She touched his cheek, felt the stubble of a new beard bristling against her palm, even though she'd watched him shave less than two hours before. "Only about a million times," she answered softly. "Walker, I'm truly sorry for dragging you into this—"

Walker's nostrils flared, and his eyes flashed, bull angry. "'Dragging me into this'?" he retorted through his teeth. "These are my *children* we're talking about here, Casey. I should have been in the loop a long time ago, don't you think? I'm Clare and Shane's *father,* remember? What if something had happened to them because I wasn't around to protect them?"

Casey had never seen Walker, or anybody else, so furious. "Nothing *did* happen, though," she said, very carefully and very quietly. "I was never, *ever* careless about their safety, Walker. When I thought there was a need for extra security, I notified the police, in whatever city we happened to be in, or I hired bodyguards—"

His nose was practically touching hers, and his eyes continued to shoot fire. She was half expecting him to paw at the ground with one foot, sprout horns and lower his head to charge. *"I'm their father,"* he said. "You kept me from them, all this time." A pause, one of those dangerous moments when everything can change. "How am I supposed to forgive you?"

There it was, the elephant in the room, the thing they hadn't really talked about.

If Walker couldn't forgive her, Casey reasoned dizzily, he certainly couldn't *love* her, either. The honeymoon, such as it had been, was definitely and permanently over, and last night's lovemaking, as powerful, as transformative, as *sacred* as it had seemed, hadn't been *love*making at all. It had been garden-variety sex, the cheap, meaningless kind that belonged in the backseats of cars or in trashy rooms rented by the hour.

If Walker had drawn back his fist and punched Casey in the stomach, he couldn't have hurt her any more deeply. She reeled away from him, shrugged him off when he tried to lay his hands on her shoulders, stared blindly out one of the windows until she saw Boone's squad car turn in the gate, lights whirling.

Two other official cars followed close behind the sheriff's, while news vans and less impressive rigs of all sorts trailed behind, at a cautious distance, but advancing just the same.

Casey got to the door before Walker did, even though he was closer, elbowed her way past him and dashed across the porch, down the steps, out into the yard.

Boone brought his cruiser to a stop nearby, and, through the windshield and the blinding blue-and-white swirl of light, Casey spotted Brylee's face on the passenger side, pale moon rising. Clare and Shane rode in back, behind the grill, and as soon as Boone put on the brakes, they spilled out on either side of the vehicle, dashing toward her.

Casey wrapped one arm around each of them.

Clare cried, while Shane, almost gleeful, seemed to see the experience as an adventure.

Walker stood at a little distance, painfully separate, while Brylee rounded the car from the other side, heading toward her brother, and Boone climbed from behind the wheel, his expression sober.

"It was so awesome, Mom!" Shane crowed. "Like one of those action-adventure movies, where Bruce Willis goes after the bad guys, even when he has to walk barefoot over broken glass—"

Casey winced at the image, but it was Clare who spoke.

"Oh, shut up!" she broke in tearfully, glaring at her brother. "It *wasn't* awesome! It was *terrible!* And this *isn't* one of your stupid *Die Hard* movies!"

Shane rolled his eyes, looking disgusted by this display of emotion. "Whatever," he said in a dismissive drawl. Then, under his breath, he added, "Hormones."

Casey gave her son a warning look and he shrugged and ambled off toward Walker.

She took Clare's face between her hands. "Honey," she said, "I know this was scary, but those guys wouldn't have hurt you—they just wanted a story."

Clare pulled free, glared at her. "Oh, yeah?" she challenged furiously. "Then how come the *sheriff* had to bring us home in a *police* car, with a bunch of deputies to run interference?"

How could Casey answer that? Maybe the *reporters* presented no physical danger, they were just pesky, but Walker had been right—the "freak jobs" who obsessed over every aspect of a celebrity's life definitely did pose a threat. And they tended to follow the newshounds wherever they went, getting some kind of sick satisfaction out of hanging around on the fringes, watching and hoping to get involved in some way.

Clare, evidently tired of waiting for an answer her mother didn't have to offer, pulled away and hurried into the house, slamming the screen door hard behind her.

Casey, feeling that odd sense of dissociation again, as though she'd split into two people, one concerned, one impassive, walked over to Boone, who tried to smile and failed.

"Thank you," Casey told him, putting out her hand.

Boone took it, gave her fingers a squeeze, nodded ever so slightly. "I can post a couple of deputies at your gate if you'd like," he said, inclining his head in that direction, "but it looks like the ranch hands have things under control, for the moment, anyhow."

Casey swallowed, nodded back. "We'll be all right," she assured the sheriff. "Once the excitement dies down a little, anyway."

We'll be all right.

She and the children? They'd be fine, because a *new*

story would come along any minute, and the stringers would be off chasing some other celebrity, climbing the trees in their yard, harassing *their* children, peeking through their windows and generally complicating every other aspect of their lives. No matter how juicy the current scandal, there was always another, better, one, waiting in the wings.

But would she and *Walker* be all right? As a couple?

Not likely. Walker was a regular person, those spectacular looks aside, and things like this didn't *happen* to people like him. Try though he might to understand, intelligent as he was, he had no frame of reference for the downside of fame. How could he?

To him, fame meant bright lights, glamorous photo shoots, designer clothes, star-studded parties, limos and private jets and packed arenas all over the world. Thousands of unseen hands holding up their lighters, creating a flickering backdrop of flame.

To Casey and, by extension, to her children, it meant those things, all right, but there was a whole heck of a lot more to the celebrity lifestyle. It meant taking extreme security precautions, even in places where normal people felt safe. It meant keeping her eyes wide-open, no matter how tired she was, staying alert, even when there were bodyguards on all sides. It meant avoiding malls, popular restaurants and movie theaters, never personally answering a knock at a hotel room door, even when room service was expected. It meant flinching when someone raised a camera or shoved a pen at her, when all they wanted was a snapshot or an autograph.

Usually, that was all it was. And then there were the other times.

Had John Lennon expected to be shot dead by a

fan, right out in front of his own apartment building? Of course not—the possibility probably hadn't even crossed his mind. Why should it? He'd been going about his business, that was all. Living his life. Meeting someone for drinks or dinner, expecting to be home before bedtime.

Except that none of that happened.

Stop it, Casey told herself. *Get a grip.*

Shane and Clare were already inside the house by then, and Brylee was close behind. Casey followed, while Walker remained where he was, talking solemnly with Boone and the deputies.

In the kitchen, Brylee tossed a fistful of undersize "newspapers" onto the table, while Clare fled to her appointed bedroom and Shane crouched to greet a waggy-tailed Doolittle with an ear-ruffling and a tummy rub.

"If we had a parrot, we could use these," Brylee said of the tabloids, "to line the cage."

Casey reached for a copy, her hand trembling slightly, and, though she'd thought she was prepared, the sight of Clare, photographed standing beside the piano the day before in her pretty, modest dress, singing the song that was her wedding gift to her parents, struck Casey like a freight train going downhill.

Clare was fully clad, of course, unlike certain movie stars who'd been captured for posterity sunbathing nude on the deck of some yacht, or British royalty indulging in hanky-panky beside a swimming pool, but there was something too intimate about the shot just the same. It was, Casey decided, the sense of close proximity; the picture might have been taken by someone attending the ceremony, instead of through a window.

Love child turns songbird, the caption read and, beneath that, in smaller print, *But will she fly the coop, now that her famous mama and cowboy daddy have finally tied the knot?*

"Love child," Casey murmured, shaking her head. She supposed the term was apt enough, if ridiculously outdated. She and Walker *hadn't* been married when it counted, that was true, but there had never been any doubt that Clare was loved, and Shane, too.

Brylee busied herself at the counter, brewing coffee. "Snidely's still in town," she fretted. "I thought we'd be going back to your place after we picked up the stuff to make tacos, but—"

Snidely, Casey recalled distractedly, was Brylee's faithful German shepherd, and, according to Walker, they went everywhere together.

"Dad and I will go get him for you," Shane assured her manfully, getting to his feet and heading for the refrigerator. Growing as fast as he was, he was forever taking on fuel. "Maybe we can bring our dogs out here, too. The cats will probably be okay where they are for a while—"

Brylee, moving deftly, stepped between Shane and the fridge. "Wash your hands first," she said.

"Good call," Casey agreed, distracted, still leafing through the other "special editions." There were pictures of her and Walker exchanging vows, then, later, laughing as they fed each other wedding cake, an image of Shane loading Dawson's wheelchair into the back of Patsy's van while Walker lifted Dawson himself onto the passenger seat. None of it was offensive, but *all* of it was too personal, too private.

The headlines, however, grew progressively worse. One rag featured a picture of Walker, crouching beside Dawson's wheelchair on the ranch house porch, talking earnestly, faces solemn.

Another of the cowboy's love children? screeched the inch-high, boldfaced line beneath the photo.

Shane, meanwhile, washed his hands, as ordered by his aunt, then rooted through the fridge in earnest, coming away with an armload of cellophane-covered refreshments left over from the wedding.

He and Brylee discussed the plan for dog retrieval in quiet voices, somewhere at the periphery of Casey's awareness.

When she thought enough time had elapsed, Casey headed for Clare's room—once Brylee's—and tapped at the door, resting her forehead against the panel while she waited.

"Go away," Clare said predictably.

"You know I'm not going to do that," Casey responded, keeping her tone light. She turned the glass knob, realized that she was locked out. Got her hackles up just a smidge. "Let me in, Clare."

"There's nothing you can say to make this better," Clare retorted.

"Let me in," Casey repeated. When it came to stubbornness, her daughter would find her a worthy opponent. Besides, Brylee could probably come up with a spare key to the room in no time.

Clare's sigh was loud enough to come right through the thick wood of that sturdy door. There was a scraping sound as she worked the lock, and then she was peeking out, the crack so narrow that only one of her eyes was visible.

Casey eased the door the rest of the way open, careful not to push too hard and stub one of Clare's toes, which were probably bare, since, like her mom, the girl never wore shoes if she could avoid it.

The room was spacious, though not as big as its counterpart on Rodeo Road, with a window seat and built-in bookshelves and even a small Franklin stove. The closet ran the length of one wall, and the furniture was obviously antique: four-poster bed, matching bureau, chest of drawers and nightstands. A pair of delicate chairs, slipcovered in a muted pink floral fabric, faced the stove.

A few of Clare's belongings were scattered around, here and there—the tiny chiming clock she treasured, a stack of books, a framed photo of the three of them—Casey, Clare and Shane—with a remarkably authentic Santa Claus, back when the lie was still working.

Casey picked up the photograph and smiled, remembering the Nashville party where it had been taken, four or five years before. Was it really that long ago? It seemed like yesterday.

"That was quite a night," she reflected somewhat wistfully, setting the photo back on the shelf where she'd found it.

The bed creaked as Clare leaped into the middle of it and sat cross-legged, the way she liked to do, but her expression was snarky, not nostalgic. "Yes," she said. "Everybody there was either famous or *related* to somebody famous, and doesn't *every* Santa Claus wear a real velvet suit, trimmed in the best fake fur available, and pass out state-of-the-art iPads instead of candy canes?"

Casey sighed, let the gibe pass. She saw herself in Clare, recognized the trick of picking a fight in order to establish boundaries. "What, exactly," she began wearily, "do you hope to accomplish by being so difficult?"

"I'm letting you know that I'm unhappy," Clare said pertly. "We're having a dialogue."

"You've been watching too many *Oprah* reruns," Casey answered, perching on the edge of the bed, not too close, but not too far away, either.

"You might want to take in one or two episodes when you get the chance," Clare answered airily. "Oprah was always big on telling the truth."

Zing. Shot through the heart. Casey knotted her fingers together in her lap and silently counted to ten.

"What do you want, Clare?" she asked evenly when she was relatively sure she wouldn't lose it.

Clare rolled deftly onto her stomach, cupping her chin in her hands and bending her knees to swing her feet back and forth. She was wearing cut-off jeans and a skimpy top that ended a good eight inches above her waist. Casey didn't recognize the outfit, and was about to say as much when she spotted the tattoo.

It was just a tiny rosebud, nestled in the graceful curve at the base of Clare's spine—not a skull and crossbones, not a gang symbol or a four-letter word—and yet the sight of it stunned Casey.

"When did you get *that?*" she asked very quietly.

Clare looked back over one shapely shoulder, acknowledging the tattoo's presence with a nonchalant glance, and shrugged slightly. "Last year, in Vegas," she said blithely. "When you were doing that one-night charity gig at Caesar's, with Brad and Trace and everybody."

"You were *thirteen* at the time," Casey reminded her daughter. "Who signed the permission slip?" Even in Glitter Gulch, where practically anything went, minors couldn't get tattoos without the signature of a qualified adult. In short, a parent or guardian.

"You'll be mad," Clare warned.

"I'm *already* mad," Casey replied. *"Who was it?"*

"It was some reporter guy," Clare said. "I got bored hanging out in the suite while you were rehearsing, so I gave the bodyguards and Uncle Mitch the slip and went out for a walk. This man with a camera came up to me on one of the sky bridges and asked me if I was your daughter. I figured he already knew I was, or he wouldn't have asked me in the first place, and he looked nice enough, so I said yes. He told me he wrote for a real newspaper, not a tabloid, and we ended up striking a deal. He wanted an interview, and I wanted a tattoo. So we went into this shopping center, where there was one of those places where you can get body piercings and stuff—it was *nice,* Mom, and very clean, and there were *loads* of people around, so nothing was going to happen. They had these computers, and all you had to do was scroll through the different designs until you found the perfect tattoo."

Casey closed her eyes for a moment, imagining her thirteen-year-old daughter wandering around Las Vegas by herself, talking to strangers, finagling a tattoo. A shudder went through her. Not only had this *happened,* but she hadn't known a thing about it—until now.

Clare, apparently uncomfortable with the silence, launched back into the story. "Anyway, the reporter guy pretended to be my dad. I paid for the tattoo myself, of course—out of my allowance—and *it hurt like anything*—the tattoo, I mean, not forking over the cash. He asked me a couple of questions and that was that. No big deal. *Plus,* I was back in the suite before anybody even noticed I was gone."

"Excuse me," Casey said, standing up suddenly. Clare's new room came with an adjoining bath, cramped but blessedly nearby and, at the moment, it was a good thing.

"Mom?" Clare asked, sounding mildly alarmed. "Mom, what—?"

Casey hurried into the bathroom, lifted the lid of the toilet and threw up everything but her socks.

CHAPTER FOURTEEN

WALKER WAS PRYING a pebble out of Mack's right front foot with a hoof pick when he heard his daughter's voice behind him. He glanced up, saw her standing in the breezeway, arms braced atop the stall gate, watching him.

"Walker?" she queried. Shane called him "Dad" these days, but Clare was holding out, unwilling to give so much as an inch of ground. It was as if she believed he and Casey could turn back the clock and set everything right, if only they weren't so all fired determined to make her life as miserable as possible.

Teenage girls. He hadn't had to deal with that particular species since Brylee was Clare's age, but now it was all coming back to him, and the prospect was discouraging. His sister hadn't even *begun* to snap out of it until she started college, which meant the snit-storms weren't likely to let up anytime soon—in fact, they were bound to get worse.

He sighed inwardly, straightened, lowered Mack's foot and turned in her direction. He couldn't blame the kid for being angry, of course—probably would have been pretty damn furious himself, in Clare's place. Fit to be tied, as his dad used to say.

"What's up, shortstop?" He opened the stall gate, and Clare stepped back so he could pass. His little girl was turning into a *big* girl and, though it would take a while, he knew it was out there, waiting, the time when she'd no longer need him, or even Casey, in any real way.

It made him feel, well, *optional*. And he had nobody to blame but himself—and Casey.

"Mom just threw up." Clare looked genuinely worried, and somewhat guilty, too. Her color was high and her mouth was a mite wobbly, as though she wanted to cry and was doing her darnedest not to. "And it's my fault."

Walker frowned. "Your mom's had a hard day," he said, trying not to show his own concern. "Lots of stress—the media blitz, getting married, moving to the ranch." He paused, studying Clare's face. "How do you figure any of that's your fault?"

Clare swallowed, gnawed at her lower lip for a moment. A sheen of tears glistened in her eyes. "I got a tattoo," she said meekly. "It was a long time ago, but Mom just found out and—"

"And that tattoo is such an awful sight that your poor mama took one look at it and lost her lunch?" Walker asked lightly. He had his own theory as to why Casey might be feeling a little green around the gills, but it might be wishful thinking.

A third child. Wouldn't that be something?

Clare flushed, but a little grin tugged at the corners of her mouth, and she blinked away the tears. "Mom thinks I'm too young for a tattoo, and that's just plain hypocritical if you ask me, because she's got this tiny guitar on one ankle—"

"You *are* too young," Walker said after his daughter's voice trailed off into an uncertain, shaky-chinned silence. He knew about the little guitar, of course, and the butterfly, too, though that was on a less obvious part of Casey's anatomy, a place he particularly liked to kiss. "Your mother, on the other hand, is an adult, legally entitled to make her own decisions. How is that 'hypocritical'?"

Clare's expression turned stubborn, but she backed down quickly enough. She knew how to push Casey's buttons, Walker figured, but he was another matter. "Aren't you going to check on her?" she asked petulantly. "I just told you she was feeling sick, after all."

"I'm headed her way," Walker replied, resting his hands on his hips and regarding his daughter solemnly, "but I've got a few things to say to you first."

Clare's green eyes, so like her mother's, widened, and the thick lashes fluttered a couple of times. "What?"

"I realize that finding out that you're mine must have come as a shock, and you'll need a while to sort through all of it, but, mistakes or no mistakes, your mom has had your best interests at heart all along, yours *and* your brother's. Sooner or later, you're going to have to make a decision, Clare. You can rebel and make an all-around fool of yourself, like the poor, abused children of other celebrities we could both name, or you can make her proud. You can try to get back at her, or you can *stand by* her, the way she's always stood by you. So, which is it, cowgirl? In the long run, are you going to be an asset or a liability?"

"Wow," Clare breathed after a few moments, looking amazed. "Coming from you, that was practically the Gettysburg Address. I'm used to cowboy-speak, like *yep* and *nope* and *howdy* and *so long.*"

"Get used to *dad*-speak," Walker advised, firmly but not unkindly. "You can be as mad at me as you want to. You can yell and throw things and call me by my first name until we're both old and gray. But you *will not* make life harder for your mother, punishing her for whatever sins you think she's committed—not on my watch. Understood?"

Clare sighed, and she didn't answer for a long time.

"Understood," she said, conceding that round.

Walker returned to the house then, Clare and Doolittle following, and found Brylee and Shane in the kitchen, playing Parcheesi at the table.

"We need to go get the dogs, Dad," Shane said.

Walker gave a crisp nod. "In a little while," he replied, his gaze sliding to meet Brylee's. "Is Casey in our room?"

Brylee nodded.

Walker made his way past the dining and living rooms and into the corridor. After rapping lightly at the bedroom door, he stepped inside.

Casey lay in the middle of the bed, almost in a fetal position, fully dressed and shivering a little.

She looked so small and so alone that Walker's heart turned over, a slow, bruising process. Casey Elder might be world famous, and one of the strongest, most courageous women he'd ever known, but she'd been fighting her own battles for so long that she'd worn herself out.

Gently, he covered her with a quilt his grandmother had made before he was even born, and sat down on the edge of the bed, wanting to touch her but not sure he ought to.

"I hear you're feeling a little under the weather," he ventured when Casey didn't say anything.

"I'll be fine," she said, her voice so small he barely heard her. "Eventually."

"You don't *sound* fine, Casey Jones," Walker pointed out. "And you don't *look* all that terrific, either."

"Gee," she murmured with flimsy irony, *"thanks."*

Walker chuckled, laid a hand lightly on her shoulder, squeezed. "Anything I can do?"

"Shoot me," Casey groaned, then gave a strangled little chortling sound that might have been part sob.

"Not an option," Walker replied. "I'm a law-abiding man."

Pulling the quilt up over her head, Casey started to cry.

Walker sighed, methodically kicked off one boot, then the other, and stretched out beside her, gathering her quilt-bundled self into his arms, careful not to hold her too tightly. The moment was fragile, and so was his wife.

"Talk to me," he said.

Her voice was muffled and croaky. "I'm pregnant."

Walker waited out a swell of pure jubilation. "Isn't it a little early to know that?" he asked gruffly. "It's only been—"

"I *know* when I'm pregnant, Walker Parrish," she said.

"And you figure this is a bad thing?" he prompted carefully. There wasn't much he was afraid of, but the thought that Casey might not want this baby scared the hell out of him.

"Of course not!" she wailed, sounding for all the world as though she was still hoping he'd shoot her. How the devil was he supposed to know how she really felt when she acted one way and talked another?

Walker uncovered her face, which was tear-streaked and puffy around the eyes, kissed her red-tipped nose.

"If it's a boy," he teased in a mischievous drawl, "can I raise him to be a bull rider?"

Casey laughed and freed one hand from the quilt long enough to slug him in the arm. "No," she said with reassuring spirit. "He's going to be president."

Walker grinned. "And if this little stranger turns out to be a girl?"

"President," Casey reiterated firmly, finally snuggling up a little closer.

After that, the conversation lapsed into an easy silence.

Walker held Casey, stroked her hair and waited. He'd had a whole lot of practice at waiting for Casey Elder, he thought, and, most likely, he'd have plenty more of it in his future. He propped his chin on top of her head. No matter what the future might bring, he was in this for the duration.

He was just about to tell Casey that, straight out, when he realized she'd drifted off to sleep.

WHEN CASEY WOKE UP, afternoon was fading into evening, and she was still wrapped up snug in that time-softened, lavender-scented quilt Walker had spread over her earlier. When had anyone done that for her, seen to her comfort in that simple, homey way?

It had been years before, she realized, when she'd had a bad case of stomach flu and Lupe—dear Lupe—had looked after her. Slowly, things came into sharper focus.

Walker was gone now, and she wondered how long he'd stayed with her, holding her, letting her feel what she was feeling without any apparent need to hurry her through the crying jag. Walker's head had left an indentation in the pillow, and his fresh-air, meadow-grass scent lingered, too.

With a smile, Casey touched the crumpled covers next to her, where he'd lain, and even though the warmth of Walker's body was long gone, she got a sense of him, a physical vibration, just the same. She rolled onto her back, waited to see if her stomach would rebel and, when it didn't, she stretched out luxuriously, peeled away the quilt and got up.

The ranch house, while not huge, was good-sized, and she heard voices from the distant kitchen, laughter and the intermittent, happy barking of the dogs.

Casey padded into the bathroom she now shared with Walker, brushed her teeth, splashed cool water on her face, fluffed out her hair. Her T-shirt was wrinkled, but her jeans looked okay, so she didn't bother changing clothes.

When she reached the kitchen, brightly lit and ranchhouse cheery, Brylee and Clare were there, with the three chocolate Labs and Snidely keeping them company. Shane and Walker were absent, and Doolittle must have been with them.

Casey greeted her dogs with head pats and the nonsense words that meant "I love you," at least to those of the canine persuasion.

"I see the rescue mission was successful," she said with a smile.

"Went off without a hitch." Brylee grinned. "And we didn't see a single reporter, either. They must have crawled back into their holes."

Casey chuckled. "Good," she said.

Clare's expression was more subdued, a combination

of sadness and stubborn pride. What was going on in that complicated adolescent brain of hers?

"The cats are here, too," she offered. "I put them in my room."

Casey smiled. Could this child possibly know how much her mother loved her? Probably not, though that would change when Clare was grown-up and married, with children of her own.

Don't go there. She's still your girl.

"They'll feel safe there," she said of the cats. "In your room, I mean."

Clare nodded slowly. For a moment, she looked as though she might say something more but, in the end, she cast a brief glance at Brylee and went back to what she'd been doing when Casey came in—which was peeling potatoes.

Amazing.

"Are you feeling better?" Brylee asked Casey. Her tone was light, nonintrusive, but her eyes betrayed quiet concern.

"I just needed to rest for a little while," Casey said with a nod. "Are Walker and Shane around?"

"They're doing chores," Brylee replied. "Walker sent the ranch hands home early, since they've been guarding gates and patrolling the property lines on horseback most of the day."

Casey winced inwardly—nothing could prepare hardworking, down-to-earth people like Walker and Brylee for the kind of onslaught they'd experienced that day, and yet Walker was out doing chores and Brylee was making supper, which was probably business as usual.

"Can I do something to help?" Casey asked, mindful

of her sad lack of cooking skills but still optimistic that she could at least learn the basics, given half a chance. She'd taught herself to read music, after all, along with a number of other useful things.

Brylee started to say no, caught herself, smiled warmly and scooted aside to make room for Casey at the counter, where she was dipping plump pieces of chicken in beaten egg, then rolling them in seasoned flour. An electric frying pan stood nearby, the grease inside it hot enough to bubble.

Casey, normally a stickler for good nutrition, grinned. *Good old-fashioned country food,* she thought appreciatively. *Just what the doctor ordered.*

Pretty soon, she was taking over for Brylee, who stood virtually at her elbow to supervise. The chicken went into the waiting pan, piece by piece, each time raising a loud sizzling sound, and the aroma was heavenly, even at that early stage.

"Bacon grease," Brylee explained with wicked glee. "I usually bake chicken, and eat it without the skin, but once in a while, a person's got to pull out all the stops and go for broke."

"Amen." Casey laughed. "What do we do now?" she asked when all the chicken pieces were in the frying pan and the noise had abated a little.

"We brown the bird on one side," Brylee answered, happy to be helpful, "and then we brown it on the other. Then we put on the lid and turn down the heat and wait."

The side door opened then, and Walker and Shane came in, fresh from doing chores. Shane was walking tall, his face flushed with pride, his eyes shining. He washed up at the kitchen sink, following Walker's lead, and then sniffed the air.

"Mom." He beamed. "You're *cooking.*"

Casey grinned. "With a lot of help from your aunt," she said, but she was as pleased as if her son had just given her a big compliment.

"I'm cooking, *too,* dweeb," Clare put in, glowering at Shane.

"Peeling potatoes," Shane said. "Anybody can do that."

Clare stuck her tongue out at him, but there was no venom in the response. It was, Casey figured, sibling lingo, habitual and, in an odd way, nice.

"I'll keep an eye on the chicken," Brylee told Casey, raising her eyebrows comically, widening her eyes and inclining her head toward Walker.

Casey got the message—only a lighted billboard could have conveyed it more clearly—and approached Walker, taking his outstretched hand.

He led her out onto the side porch, and the two of them sat down in the swing.

The sky was a pale shade of purple by then, and the stars were popping out everywhere. The moon, full and brilliant, seeming almost close enough to touch, loomed over the western foothills.

Casey pictured the remains of that old homestead, where Walker's people had settled so long ago, imagined how it would look in the twilight, surrounded by tangled mobs of flowers, and felt soothed, connected, somehow. She could fall in love with Timber Creek Ranch, she thought, if she let herself.

They rocked slowly back and forth, she and Walker, content with saying nothing at all. Lights glistened on the far side of the river, and distant laughter rode over on the breeze—children playing games, dogs barking with glee, screen doors creaking on their hinges, grown-ups calling out that supper was ready.

Ordinary sounds, Casey supposed, but they brought back precious memories—not of her life in her grand-parents' stately mansion, but of the times she'd spent with Lupe and Juan in the country, running free with their legions of nieces and nephews, playing softball and hide-and-seek until it was too dark to continue.

Rare and precious as those interludes had been, they were more than Clare and Shane had had when they were small, their other advantages aside.

Just be, Casey told herself. *Let now be now.*

Walker didn't release her hand, and she allowed her-self to enjoy the sensation as he stroked her knuck-les lightly with the calloused pad of one thumb. There was nothing sexual about his touch, but Casey knew that would change once they were alone in their bed-room later that night, and she felt a racy little thrill at the prospect.

"I guess I was a little overemotional this afternoon," she said, for his ears alone. "Thanks for riding out the storm."

Walker let go of her hand then, but only so he could slip his arm around her shoulders. She allowed herself to lean into him, rested her head against his strong upper arm. "Anytime," he finally replied.

She felt a need to warn him, like an honest person selling a used car with a few hitches in its get-along. "I'm like that when I'm—stressed out."

"It happens," Walker said easily. "You're allowed, Casey Jones."

Casey was willing to lose herself in *this* Walker, the gentleman rancher, the easygoing cowboy, the expert

lover, at least for a little while, but that didn't mean
she'd forgotten the *other* one, the man who wasn't sure
he'd ever be able to forgive her for keeping him from
his children for so long. *That* Walker was just as real
as the one who'd covered her in a quilt a few hours before, held her while she cried, made her feel safer than
safe and finally led her out here to sit in a porch swing
and admire the moon and the stars.

"This is good," she told him.

"And it'll get better," he promised with a grin.

Sure enough, after supper was over and the dishes
were cleared away, after Brylee had retreated into her
apartment, taking both kids and four out of five dogs
right along with her to watch the current crop of reality
shows on her big-screen TV, after Walker and Casey
had shared a bath in his long, deep tub, things *did* get
better, and then better still.

MONTANA SPRAWLED ALL around Walker, blessedly normal, as he and Shane rode out to look for strays, accompanied by all three of the boy's dogs.

The uproar in the media had gone on for the better
part of a week, but then, after a catastrophic earthquake
in South America, Casey and Walker and their "love
children" became old news.

Hell of a way to escape the limelight, though. Relief agencies from all over the world had their opera-
tions up and running at the scene of the disaster, and
the situation was dire.

Deliberately turning his mind back to his usual
concerns, since there was nothing he could do for the
earthquake victims besides making a donation, Walker
readjusted his hat and shifted a little in the saddle,

wondering how Casey had managed to raise Clare and Shane to be reasonably grounded human beings when practically everything she did or said seemed to be a matter for public scrutiny. Granted, this last round had been unusual, even for them, but Walker wouldn't be forgetting it anytime soon.

Beside him, riding Smokey, Shane mimicked the hat-shifting gesture the way he mimicked just about everything Walker did. The kid seemed to be trying out different mannerisms, picking the ones he liked.

Walker was both amused and touched.

"So the Parable County Rodeo is coming up," Shane said. It was an intro, of course, a preamble, an opening riff.

Walker grinned to himself. Let the kid think he was being subtle. Where was the harm in that?

"Yep," he agreed. Remembering what Clare had said about his one-word sentences, he grinned again. "It's always the weekend right before the Fourth of July."

"And we'll be providing the bucking stock?"

"Always do," Walker said. Two words now. Why, he was turning downright loquacious! He didn't ask the boy where the conversation was headed, because he already knew.

Sure enough, Shane finally came out with it. "Do you think I could enter one of the junior events?"

Walker didn't smile, but he wanted to. "You mean, like the mutton busting?" he teased. The younger kids rode sheep in that particular event, and it was a lot harder than it looked—Walker had done it himself, back when he was knee-high to the proverbial grasshopper. So had Brylee.

Shane colored up, glaring out from under the brim

of the hat he'd found in the tack room a few days before and immediately appropriated. It didn't quite fit him, and he kept having to push it back off the bridge of his freckled nose, where a red welt was forming. "Riding *sheep?*" he marveled furiously. "That's for little kids!"

Walker was unruffled. He cast a sidelong glance in his son's direction and drawled, "You're too easy to rile, boy. If you don't get over that, and quick, you'll get nothing else done but defending your honor."

Shane gulped and scowled into the distance, ostensibly looking for strays.

"As for the rodeo," Walker went on idly when Shane didn't reply, "you're gonna have to consult your mother on that one."

"You're my dad," Shane pointed out, still testy but leaking steam instead of spouting it, as before. "Your permission should be enough."

Walker chuckled. "That theory might have held water once upon a time," he said, "but 'once upon a time' was quite a while ago."

"So you're saying Mom is the boss and you'll do whatever she says?"

He sighed. "Watch it," he warned pleasantly. "What I'm *saying* is, your mother has raised you and Clare this far, with no help from me, and I can't see my way clear to step in now and start overriding her decisions."

Shane grumbled under his breath for a few moments, riding along beside Walker in silence, but it soon became clear that he hadn't been retreating, he'd been reloading. "You'd *never* go against anything Mom said?" he challenged.

"I didn't say that," Walker answered. "But I'd have to feel pretty strongly to raise an objection, because she's a smart woman, and it just so happens that she's right about most things."

A long, throbbing silence fell.

Then Shane asked evenly, "Do you think she was right to lie to Clare and me since we were babies?"

He'd been expecting this for a while, but it still unsettled him a little.

"No," Walker replied reasonably, "but sometimes people do the wrong thing for the right reasons. Things aren't as cut-and-dried as they seem from your perspective, son—a lot of decisions are shots in the dark, judgment calls, essentially, and it's *real* easy to make a mistake."

Shane mulled that over for a while. They spotted half a dozen strays on the other side of a thicket of brush and rounded them up, with considerable help from the dogs, heading them toward the main herd.

They bawled and kicked up dust, those cows, too stupid to know they were on their way back to good water and safety in numbers. Walker cussed them a little out of sheer habit, calling them sorry-looking, lop-eared knotheads, much to Shane's amusement.

"You got something against cows, Dad?" the boy asked.

"Facts are facts," Walker replied with a grin. "Dogs are smart. Horses are smarter yet. But there's only one domestic animal dumber than these critters, and that's a sheep."

The remark brought them right back around to the subject of the upcoming junior rodeo, albeit indirectly.

"I'm too old for mutton busting," Shane said.

"Tell that to your mother," Walker answered.

An hour later, when they got back to the barn, Shane

did a creditable job of unsaddling Smokey, leading him into his stall, checking his hooves and giving him a good brushing down.

Casey came out of the house as they were approaching, looking four kinds of good in trim jeans and a white suntop with a few strategically placed ruffles. Walker drank in the sight of her, thinking they'd get through life just fine, the pair of them, if they made love every night and took care not to say more than two words to each other in the daylight.

They had their tender moments, Walker was willing to admit that much, but they still disagreed on just about every subject known to civilization.

She favored one political party, he supported the other.

She wanted to keep Clare and Shane close to home, so they wouldn't be kidnapped, develop drug habits or give interviews to scumball reporters.

Walker believed in giving kids as much freedom as they could handle. How else would they learn to stand on their own?

Casey insisted on going to church as a family, while Walker thought he was more likely to make God's acquaintance on the open range than inside some building with a belfry and pews.

It seemed to Walker that they both had one foot in the marriage, and one foot out, and either one of them might bolt at any time.

Oh, but the sex was better than good.

And Casey was all but certain she was carrying their baby.

Count your blessings, cowboy, Walker thought.

"Mom," Shane began, "I was wondering—"

"Not now," Casey broke in. She tried to smile at her son, but something was wrong and Walker knew it. "Go on inside so I can talk to your dad."

Shane jerked off his hat, slapped it against his thigh and stalked off toward the house.

Walker and Casey remained where they were—just outside the barn door, in the last blaze of afternoon sunshine.

Walker tensed, knowing something—God only knew what—was coming.

"Might as well just come right out and say it," he said, adjusting his hat.

"Mitch called," she said. "Some artists are putting together a benefit concert—for the earthquake victims."

In his mind, Walker saw instant replays of some of the news clips out of South America. Children separated, perhaps permanently, from their parents. Bad water and broken roads, houses and buildings toppled, tents serving as temporary hospitals, doctors and nurses working shifts that were measured in days, rather than hours.

"And you want to be part of it," Walker said. He understood her desire to help, and shared it, but he saw this as the beginning of a tug-of-war that might last for the rest of their lives. Work pulling against home and family, and vice versa. Eventually, the rope would break.

Casey swallowed, nodded. "Yes."

"Where?" Walker asked, turning his hat brim in his hands, in slow, thoughtful revolutions.

"L.A.," Casey answered, watching him closely. "The concert will be shown live all over the world, next Saturday night. There's some setting up to do, though, and of course I'll want to rehearse with the band—"

"Of course," Walker agreed, thinking he'd sounded snappish, when he hadn't meant to, but not ready to backpedal and make it right.

"I know that's the weekend of the rodeo over in Parable, and I was supposed to sing the national anthem, but—"

"Folks will understand," Walker put in.

"Will you?" Casey asked.

The question stung. She knew he'd seen the devastation left by that earthquake; did she think his heart was made of concrete?

"Do what you have to do, Casey," he said gruffly. "I'll look after the kids and the critters and we'll all be just fine."

She slipped her arms around him, laid her cheek against his chest. "I thought you'd try to talk me out of this," she confessed. "Because of—everything."

He curled a finger under her chin, lifted her face so he could look directly into her now-misty green eyes. "I'd rather you stayed," he said, in all honesty, "mainly because there might be a baby on the way, and for a few other reasons, too."

Casey's whole being twinkled as she gazed back at him, casting her spell. "Will you miss me?"

"You, yes. The sex, yes. The bickering—not so much."

She pretended indignation. At least, Walker *hoped* she was pretending.

"You know that old phrase *honest to a fault?*" she asked.

"I know it," Walker said.

"It describes you to perfection."

He laughed and then, because he couldn't help it, because he could already feel her slipping away into that other life, where he was a foreigner, he kissed her.

CHAPTER FIFTEEN

CASEY TOOK A commercial flight out of Missoula the next morning, changed planes in Seattle and landed in Los Angeles after several delays, to be met outside security by a smiling Mitch, the guys in her band, her technical crew and other important members of the entourage.

While they waited for her luggage near one of the baggage carousels, autograph seekers and a few representatives of the tabloid press crowded in close.

Casey had always thrived on this kind of attention—hell, she'd *loved* it, would have felt invisible without it, even just a few months before—but something had changed. All she could think about was Walker and the kids and the peaceful grandeur of Timber Creek Ranch, with its canopy of sky and miles of open space, that sacred sense of being tucked into the heart of God.

Nothing if not professional, though, she smiled and signed her name and posed for cell-phone snapshots, even answered a few questions from the "reporters," but part of her simply wasn't present.

Mike Reynolds, her lead guitar player and longtime friend, must have seen through the act, because once they'd collected her bags, made their way to one of several waiting limos and ducked inside, he looked her straight in the eye and said, "I've seen sadder brides, but I can't remember when."

Mitch and two assistants rode with them, but, mercifully, they had their heads together, busily conferring over various schedules—rehearsals, radio and TV interviews, a few public appearances in random places like shopping malls, and photo ops with politicians and other celebrities.

Casey tried to smile at Mike, but she'd used up most of her wattage back there in the baggage area. Her comeback—"How many of those sad brides were yours?"—fell a little flat.

Mike merely grinned, used to being kidded about his overactive love life, but his eyes were solemn as he looked at her, seeing too much. "Case," he said patiently, "this is me. Mike. Next best thing to a brother. Please don't tell me things are going wrong between you and the cowboy already."

"'The cowboy,'" she reminded him gently, "has a name. It's Walker. And, no, it isn't that. I'm just a little—"

I'm just a little pregnant.

Maybe.

Please, God.

"Worn-out?" Sweet Mike, prodding for answers and then trying to throw her a conversational lifeline.

She shook her head. *I'm not sure I even want this crazy, wonderful gypsy life anymore,* she thought to herself. *And if I'm not Casey Elder, country-music hotshot, then who* am *I?*

This was an identity crisis.

"I miss Clare and Shane, and Walker, of course," she replied. That was purest truth, but it wasn't the *whole* truth. Not that she owed an explanation to Mike or anybody else. Would have been nice to understand it *herself,* though. "It's been great, spending so much time together. Not being on the road, rushing from place to place, setting up gear and taking it down again."

As if she'd set up or taken down equipment since the earliest days of her career, but still.

Mike ducked his shaggy head slightly and looked at her even more closely than before. "Really? You really don't miss the road? Because I've been climbing the walls—itching to hit the concert circuit and soak up some bright lights and unbridled adoration."

Casey chuckled, but deep down, she felt an ache of guilt. She couldn't expect Mike or the others in the group to cool their vocational heels indefinitely, waiting for her to take up where she'd left off. They were talented musicians— some of the best in the business—and they were still in the prime of their lives, working and otherwise.

They had plans and dreams of their own, naturally, and even though money wasn't an issue for any of them, the occasional recording and video session at her house in Parable, Montana, wasn't going to be enough to sat- isfy their creative drive, not forever, anyhow.

"You getting restless, Mike?" she asked finally.

Beyond the tinted windows of the limo, palm trees and looping tangles of freeway zipped by. Cars were ev- erywhere, taking people somewhere else, always some- where else. Why wasn't it okay to just *be* in one place, even for a little while?

Mike took her hand and patted the back of it. "It's not that," he said. "I just miss the music we made to- gether. So do the other guys."

"Me, too," she said. "Sometimes."

Mike smiled. "And other times?"

"Other times, I just want to learn to cook comfort

food, ride horses and sit in the porch swing, watching that big Montana sky change. The kids are growing up so fast it makes my head spin—I can't stop thinking about the way time slips by." She paused for a deep, slow breath, knowing her talk of home and family probably sounded pretty prosaic to Mike, a man used to traveling in the fast lane, always at full throttle. "I like my life." *And I love Walker Parrish, even if I am scared to tell him so.*

"Okay," Mike said, musing, gazing out the car window now.

Clearly the conversation was over, for the time being at least, and if nothing had been settled, well, Casey was getting used to that. She'd always been so certain, so focused. Now, she was totally uncertain.

Clare was still angry and confused, and Shane, though he put a good face on things, surely had some issues of his own.

And then there was Walker, the man she loved. The man she'd basically cheated out of his son's and daughter's childhoods. At times, she could almost believe that Walker cared for her, cared deeply, especially when they made love. *Other* times, like now, she wondered if he'd ever be able to forgive her completely, as hard as he might try.

Battling despair, she settled deeper into the cushy seat of that limo and silently reminded herself that, problems or no problems, the Casey Elder show must go on. She knew all her lines, and why wouldn't she? She'd had years of practice, built herself a successful persona. But was there a real person behind the polished image?

Hard to say.

BRYLEE COULDN'T HELP with the kids while Casey was away because she had her annual "motivational retreat" scheduled for that week, and several hundred of her salespeople would be converging on the campgrounds near her company headquarters to stay in cabins, sit around campfires, receive awards and be inundated with workshops and speeches.

She was taking Snidely with her, and she'd invited Clare to go along, but it seemed to Walker that the girl had developed mildly antisocial tendencies since Casey's departure for L.A. She mostly hid out in her room, where, according to Shane Parrish, Master Spy, she kept company with her cats, changed the polish on her fingernails and toes roughly every ten minutes, read books, surfed the internet and picked out mournful ballads on an old guitar.

Once or twice, Walker got as far as her closed door, fist raised to knock companionably, but each time, something had stopped him. She'd been singing, and her voice was so like Casey's that it haunted him, as did the few lyrics he could make out. The theme was clear enough, though—loneliness, deception, betrayal.

Was this regulation teen angst, Walker wondered helplessly, or genuine sorrow?

Back in the day, when he'd been the guy who came to dinner now and then, he'd have known how to reach Clare. Ironically, now that he'd assumed the role of father, he didn't seem to have a clue.

No, what he had, apparently, was a gift for saying the wrong thing.

Relating to Shane was easier, since they had more in common, both being male for starters. They shared a love of horses and wide-open spaces and rodeo, too, and their outlooks and basic thought processes were remarkably similar. Though the boy did show flashes of resentment now and then, he also tried hard to make the best of whatever came his way.

The same could not be said of Clare, though, and it worried Walker, not just because her attitude hurt Casey, but because she seemed to be drifting away from all of them, becoming someone else, closing the book on their efforts to forge the framework of a family.

Life went on, though, and there were chores to be done, meals to be cooked and eaten, plans to be made, with the rodeo coming up so soon. Walker put one foot in front of the other, mostly, missing Casey with an ache that ground inside him 24/7.

"I forgot to ask Mom if I could enter the rodeo," Shane said on the third night Casey had been gone, after they'd eaten supper and done the dishes. The two of them were alone in the kitchen, except for the dogs; Clare had eaten a few bites and helped clear the table after the meal, but she hadn't said more than two words the whole time, and she'd retreated to her room at the first opportunity.

Walker refrained from pointing out that the boy had had plenty of chances to make his pitch, since Casey called regularly and texted even more often than she dialed the home number.

"So text her," he said.

"She's rehearsing," Shane reminded him. "And then she's having dinner with a bunch of VIPs. The vice president is going to be there."

Walker knew all that—he'd spoken often with Casey, though always briefly and in a sort of awkward, out-of-step way. "She'll read the text and answer when she gets a chance," he told his son. "As she always does."

Shane rolled his eyes. "She'll say *no,*" he said. "Without even thinking about it. Because that's what she does when she's busy, which is all the time. She just says *no* and goes right on doing whatever she's doing."

"That being the reason you haven't asked her," Walker observed mildly.

"All I want to do is enter one stupid rodeo event," Shane persisted. "What's the big, huge, hairy deal?"

Walker, sitting at the table now, with one last cup of coffee going cold in front of him, stifled a smile. "Which 'stupid event' do you have in mind?" he asked, in his own good time.

Shane's whole face lit up. "Bareback riding," he answered. "Broncs."

Oh, hell, Walker thought. He knew what bucking horses could do, because he bred them to do it. "That's a rugged game," he said. "Even in the junior category."

"They're *all* rugged," Shane argued spiritedly. "That's the whole point. It's *rodeo*."

"Have you ever been bucked off a horse?" Walker asked calmly.

Color flared in the boy's earnest face. Tanned and freckled from all the time he'd been spending outdoors, helping Walker and the hands with ranch work, he was beginning to look more like a real, rough-and-tumble country kid than the sheltered son of a famous singer. Casey had done a good job raising him, and his sister, too, despite the present rocky road they were all traveling, but she wasn't big on letting either one of her children take chances.

It went without saying that taking foolish ones, like hitchhiking or messing with drugs or alcohol, would never lead to anything but trouble and heartache. But calculated risks? That was another thing, an important part of growing up and learning to hold your own in a tough world.

"Did *you* enter the junior rodeo when you were a kid?" Shane wanted to know.

He'd make a damn good lawyer, Walker thought, or even a politician, though he sincerely hoped the boy wouldn't take that route. Most politicians ranked pretty low on Walker's list.

"Yes," Walker replied wearily. "But I'd ridden horses all my life, Shane, and my dad believed a few hard knocks were good for a person." *My mother, on the other hand, far from being overprotective like yours, just didn't give a damn what I did, one way or the other.*

"How am I supposed to grow up to be just like you if you won't let me *do* anything?" Shane pressed.

Walker, ridiculously pleased that the boy even *wanted* to be like him, now or at any time in the future, thought the kid had a point. Risk was part of life, and not much could be accomplished without it.

"Here's the deal," he said at some length. "I'll ask your mother if you can ride in the rodeo—do my best to talk her into it, too—but if she says *no,* then *no* it is. Agreed?"

Shane put out his hand to shake on the agreement, beaming again. "Agreed," he said.

Obviously, the boy had more faith in his dad's influence over Casey than history justified, but there was no harm in trying.

Shane took the dogs outside, Doolittle included, waited while they did what dogs do outside and then merrily retreated to his room to play video games on his computer, his feet barely touching the floor as he walked out of the kitchen, trailed by a trio of loyal canines.

Doolittle stayed behind, resting his muzzle on Walker's knee and gazing soulfully up into his eyes.

Walker laughed and patted the mutt's head. "You're a good old dog," he said.

He sat there awhile, wondering if he'd be interrupting something important if he called Casey on her cell, then took the advice he'd given Shane and texted her instead. Call me when you get a chance, he wrote. Nothing to worry about on this end, but I've got a question to ask.

Five minutes later, his phone rang, and he felt a little leap of anticipation when he saw Casey's number in the caller ID panel.

"Hey," she said, sounding shy and slightly breathless.

"Hey," he said back.

"So what's the question?" she prompted after waiting a few beats.

When are you coming home? was certainly a contender, and so was *Do teenage girls speak a language all their own and, if so, can you clue me in on some of the basic vocabulary?*

Walker cleared his throat. Best stick to the point. "Shane wants to enter the rodeo."

"No way," Casey said immediately.

"Not the regular rodeo—the one for kids."

A silence.

"Are you still there?" Walker prodded.

"Riding sheep or something like that?" Casey asked. He could practically feel the wheels and gears turning in her head.

"Not exactly."

"Then, what?"

"Bronc busting," Walker said, feeling much as he had as a kid, when the river froze over and he took the first, cautious step onto the ice, hoping it would hold his weight.

"Bronc busting?" Casey echoed. "Not just no, but *hell,* no."

"Casey, this isn't bull riding at the National Finals. It's kid rodeo, in Parable, Montana. I provide the horses myself and, trust me, the ones for the junior events are not the kind you're probably picturing right now."

"Shane is thirteen," Casey reminded him. "The only time he's done any horseback riding at all was when he visited you on the ranch. Walker, *he could get killed.*"

"Or he could just get a mouthful of dirt, feel real good because he tried and be ready the next time he faces a challenge."

"You want to let him ride," Casey accused. She might have used the same tone to say, *You told him to jump off a bridge.*

"Yes," Walker said. "He's good on a horse, Case— a natural."

He didn't need to see her face to know she was biting her lower lip, torn between the knowledge that Walker was right about Shane's abilities and the rigors of growing up and a natural desire to protect her child from unnecessary dangers.

"I'm his mother," Casey said, rhetorically, of course. "It's my job to make sure my son doesn't break his neck in some rodeo arena."

"And I'm his father," Walker pointed out quietly. "So he's *our* son."

"Is this some kind of macho thing?" Casey asked after another silence. "Is it some rite of passage?"

Walker chuckled. "Neither," he said. "Shane doesn't have to prove himself to me or anybody else, Casey, but he wants this. A lot."

"It's genetic," Casey spouted. To hear her tell it, a person would have thought Walker had passed down a penchant for robbing banks through his DNA, instead of a love for all things Western, including rodeo.

"Maybe," Walker allowed. "But this isn't about me, Casey, and it isn't about you. It's about Shane, pure and simple, and the man he'll be some day."

"If anything happens to him, Walker Parrish—"

Inwardly, Walker sighed with relief and no little amazement. *I'll be damned,* he thought, *she's caving.*

"Nothing's going to happen to Shane," he said when she left the last part of her sentence dangling. "Most likely, he'll take a spill, but that's one hell of a lot better than hanging back because he's afraid. Trying will net him some bruises for sure, but *not trying* will hurt his soul."

"I hate it when you're philosophical."

"No, you hate it when I'm right."

Another pause. "If he's afraid, why does he want to enter the rodeo?" Casey asked, sounding resigned now, but also confounded.

"Courage isn't about not being scared," Walker explained gently. "It's about being frightened out of your mind and going ahead with whatever it is you want to do, in spite of the fear." He paused for a second or two. "Kind of like stepping out onto a stage that first time, and singing for an arena packed with people who might or might not like what they hear."

"That's different," Casey said, but weakly.

"Is it? Weren't you scared the first time you opened

for some big-name act, thinking you might get booed off the stage if only because you weren't the performer the audience came to see?"

"Heck," Casey answered, "I *still* get scared."

Walker smiled. That was a big admission, for one of the queens of country music. "I miss you," he said.

"Me, too," she answered. "I mean, I miss you and the kids, not that I miss myself."

"I figured that was what you meant," Walker teased. He wanted to say he loved her, right then and there, but he didn't, because there were over a thousand miles between them and things like that had to be said face-to-face, if only the first time. "Come home soon."

"Sunday morning," she said with a little sigh that raised Walker's spirits considerably. "In the meantime, it's interviews, and fancy dinners with speeches, and plenty of rehearsals and sound checks."

"Speaking of fancy dinners," Walker said, wondering if he was detaining her, keeping her from rejoining the VIPs, "Shane says you're eating with the vice president."

"Yes," Casey confirmed in a whisper, "and the man is a dweeb."

Walker laughed. "I voted for that guy's running mate," he said. "And, therefore, indirectly, for him."

"There is no accounting for taste," Casey replied succinctly. "How's Clare doing?"

"Well," Walker joked, "she hasn't been arrested or run off to join the circus or anything drastic like that."

"Gee, that's comforting," Casey responded.

"Clare's acting like what she is," Walker said, seriously now, "a fourteen-year-old girl whose life was just turned upside down, trying to figure out what the heck hit her." They were all dealing with some variation of the same theme, he supposed.

"Keep them safe, Walker," Casey said. It was a request, not a command—almost a plea.

"Count on it," Walker replied.

"See you Sunday," she said. "We'll probably talk before then, but…" Again, her voice trailed off.

"See you Sunday," Walker affirmed gruffly.

Sunday, it seemed to him, was a long way off.

THE JUNIOR RODEO opened on Friday afternoon, and Shane strutted around with his number pinned to the back of his shirt, sporting the new hat Walker had bought him and brimming with confidence. He was eager to ride, and bone-certain he'd wind up in the money when the final scores were tallied. Stranger things had happened.

Walker hoped the boy would place, of course, but he knew most of the other kids entered in the competition, and they were good. The horses and bulls, while tamer than some, were appropriate for the sport, which meant they were flat-out ornery and guaranteed to do their best to unseat a cowboy long before the buzzer sounded.

Clare, who had come along only because Walker refused to leave her home alone, shook her head as she watched her younger brother conferring with other cowboys his age. "He's such an idiot," she said.

Walker, just back from taking a look at the day's stock, all of which belonged to him, adjusted his hat. "Harsh words," he replied easily. "If I thought you really believed that, I'd be mighty discouraged."

Clare sighed heavily. She was wearing jeans, sneakers and one of Walker's old shirts, and she carried a backpack, a fact he didn't register as unusual. Not at the time, anyhow.

"What if Shane gets hurt?" she fretted.

Walker grinned down at her. "Chances are, he won't," he said.

"Mom will *kill* you if Shane breaks a bone or gets a concussion or something," the girl warned. "He's her favorite, you know."

Walker hid his surprise. "She will indeed be four kinds of furious if anything like that happens," he agreed, "but what makes you think your mom favors either one of you over the other?"

"Parents always have a favorite," Clare said wisely, still watching her brother. "They just won't admit it, but kids know anyway."

"Well," Walker replied slowly, "I'm a parent, it just so happens, and I love you just as much as I love Shane."

Clare made a sputtering sound with her lips, a sort of modified raspberry, adequate to convey her skepticism. "He's a *boy.* Dads always like boys better than girls."

"Not true," Walker said, wondering why important conversations like this one always seemed to start up in public places, when there was little or no time to pursue the matter. On impulse, he plopped his hat onto his daughter's head and tugged the brim down over her eyes.

Much to Walker's relief, Clare laughed. "Really?" she asked, pushing back the hat and looking up at him with the first hint of a sparkle he'd seen in her in days.

"Really," he confirmed, choked up and trying not to show it.

She took off his hat, handed it to him. That quick, the father-daughter moment was over.

"Some of my friends from school are here," she said, not bothering with a segue. "Mind if I go find them?"

Walker nodded his permission, but qualified it with "Stay on the rodeo grounds, and check in, either by cell phone or in person, every hour or so."

She sighed dramatically but Walker thought, by the look in her eyes, that she was glad he was looking out for her. Later, he'd wonder if he was any better at predicting teenage behavior than he was at saying the right words at the right time, but at the moment, he was a sucker for a pretty girl—especially when that pretty girl was his daughter.

"All right," she agreed, and disappeared into the growing crowds.

Walker immediately had second thoughts. There were a lot of spectators on hand for the big weekend, out-of-towners as well as locals. Had he done the right thing, letting Clare go off looking for her friends? Casey, given her tendency to hire bodyguards and avail herself and her children of police escorts, probably wouldn't approve.

The trouble was, it was too late to call Clare back— she was already out of sight and, unless he missed his guess, she wouldn't answer if he called her cell.

This is Parable County, Montana, he reminded himself. *Not the mean streets of some big city.*

The opening ceremony was impressive, with flags and firecrackers and a six-jet flyover, courtesy of the United States Air Force. The kids in the high school chorus group sang "The Star-Spangled Banner," and every hat was off as men, women and children joined in.

When that part was over, Walker made his way behind the chutes, looking for Shane but trying not to be too obvious about it.

The calf roping was just starting, soon to be followed by steer wrestling—also known as bull dogging, in rodeo lingo. After that would come the barrel racing, an all-girl competition, and a show of skill on the part of both the rider and the horse that never failed to rouse Walker's admiration.

Shane appeared as quickly as his sister had vanished, standing beside Walker at the fence. He'd probably been hanging out with his buddies from school, but none of them were around at the moment.

"Does that hurt the calves?" the boy asked quietly, watching the competition over the top rail of the fence. Clearly, this wasn't a concern he wanted broadcast all over the rodeo grounds. "Being roped like that, then jerked off their feet and tied up?"

"No," Walker said. "It's not like roping a human being or a dog and throwing them down. Calves are sturdy little devils, but if they look at all fragile for any reason, we pull them before the competition gets started." He paused, watching the proceedings for a few moments. Shane hadn't said anything in reply, which might mean he had his doubts. "Roping calves is part of ranching," Walker went on. "It's usually the only way to give them their shots or treat them for disease or any kind of injury."

Shane nodded. "I guess calves don't come when you call them, the way dogs do," he observed.

Walker laughed and slapped his son on the shoulder. "Nope," he said. "They surely don't come when you call them."

They watched another competitor and then another,

in companionable silence, as did lots of other fathers and sons. Both calves evaded the rope entirely, to the discouragement of the youthful and very earnest cowboys attempting to lasso them from the back of their trained horses.

"I drew a bronc called Backflip," Shane said as the announcer chatted up the audience while another calf and mounted rider prepared to make their run.

Walker knew Backflip, of course—knew all the horses, because he owned them. This particular animal was a fair-to-middling bucker, but he didn't have the juice for the main event, so he'd wound up in the junior category. "He's a good ride," Walker said, studying the boy out of the corner of one eye. He seemed nervous, which only showed he had good sense, but wasn't out-and-out scared.

"I guess eight seconds probably seems like a long time, when you're out there trying to stay on some bronc or bull."

"It can be an eternity," Walker said, speaking from experience. He'd given up rodeo a long time ago, except for some fooling around out on the ranch, when he and Al and the hands were winnowing out the duds, broncos and bulls who weren't athletically inclined, and there were times when he missed it a lot.

What he *didn't* miss was eating dirt, hitting the ground hard and running like hell for the fence when a bull came after him instead of just trotting off across the arena, the way they usually did, proudly showing themselves to be cowboy-free.

"If you don't feel ready to tackle this, Shane," he added quietly when the boy didn't say more, "that's okay. Nobody will think any less of you for it, including me."

Shane beamed at him. "I'm gonna do this," he said, and that was the end of that particular discussion.

Clare checked in by cell phone, as agreed, some forty-five minutes later. She was hanging out with some of her friends from school, and they were all headed for the carnival, set up right there on the fairgrounds, to try out some of the rides.

Walker, reassured, told her to have fun and call back in an hour.

By then, Shane had wandered off with a few of his pals, and Walker, thinking this fathering business wasn't as hard as folks made it out to be—folks like Casey, for instance—didn't give the matter another thought.

When the bareback event finally got underway, Walker kept some distance between himself and the chutes, knowing it would embarrass Shane if he hovered too close.

Shane was the third rider in the lineup, as it turned out, and Backflip proved himself worthy of his name by shaking the kid off at the three-second mark.

Shane landed hard, sprawled on his back, while the pickup men herded Backflip out of the arena without incident.

"A good try for a first-timer!" the announcer boomed as Shane got his wind back, rolled to his feet and stooped to retrieve his hat. "That's Shane Parrish, ladies and gentlemen, from over in Three Trees. Let's give him a hand!"

The crowd cheered.

Using his phone, Walker snapped a quick picture of his son, dented and dust-covered as he ambled toward the fence, grinning from ear to ear. He texted the shot to Casey, so she'd know Shane was alive and well in spite of entering the rodeo, snapped the device shut and dropped it back into his shirt pocket.

Shane scrambled deftly over the fence to stand beside Walker, with that grin still splitting his face.

"I did it," he said.

"You sure did," Walker agreed, resting a hand on the boy's shoulder, his voice a mite gruff.

In the next moment, his phone rang, and Walker plucked it out of his pocket, expecting the caller to be Casey.

Instead, it was Treat McQuillan.

"One of my officers just arrested your daughter on a charge of shoplifting," the chief of police said, not even trying to hide his satisfaction over this turn of events. "We're holding her here, at the station."

CHAPTER SIXTEEN

CASEY, TAKING A break in her dressing room between rehearsals, smiled at the snapshot Walker had sent, showing a recently thrown Shane sauntering across the rodeo arena back in Parable, covered in dust and grinning as widely as if he'd just been named All-Around Cowboy for that year.

She was about to respond with a digital thumbs-up when the second message came in. Expecting another installment in the Shane saga, Casey opened it.

This new image brought her up short, made her breath catch in her throat and her heart lurch, then go into free fall. The picture showed a sullen Clare, hands cuffed behind her back, being placed in the back of a police car.

Fresh shock jolted through Casey before the first rush had entirely abated, swamping her whole system with adrenaline. She paced, shaking, and Mitch, who had been chatting with the hair and makeup people, noticed her distress, came over to her and silently took the phone from her hands.

She watched, helpless with panic, as her manager took in the shot of Clare, and though his color changed a little, he stayed cool. Expertly, Mitch thumbed from that screen to another, searching for the sender's name.

Casey could have told him not to bother, that he

wouldn't find it. People who took pictures like that, delighting in the havoc it would wreak, normally crawled right back under their favorite rock as soon as the deed was done.

"No information," Mitch said with a sigh. "I can get in touch with your service provider, have them do some checking—"

"Forget it," Casey said. "Even if we found the sender, it wouldn't help." She drew in a breath, thought of all the good people who were depending on her and the other performers to make the benefit concert a big success. A *lifesaving* success, for some of the victims of that South American earthquake. "I've got to get back to Parable, Mitch. As soon as possible."

"Your show is tomorrow night," Mitch reminded her gently. "And it's live, Casey."

"We could record our performance—"

"Casey. Get a grip. It looks as though Clare's in some trouble, all right. But she's not injured or sick. If this turns out to be an emergency, fine, Godspeed, catch the first plane home, do whatever you need to do and I'll cover for you on this end. But we don't know that it *is* an emergency, do we?"

Knowing Mitch was right didn't do one thing to calm Casey down. Concerned raged in her like a fever. "That's my *daughter* in that picture, Mitch," Casey replied in a ragged whisper.

"And she has a father," Mitch replied reasonably. This was the old Mitch, the one she knew so well, not the one who had proposed to her, and that was reassuring. "Walker's right there, isn't he? Anyway, the situation probably isn't as bad as it looks. Kids do stupid things, Casey. It *happens*."

All well and good, but this wasn't some nameless stranger, some statistic—this was *Clare*. Her firstborn, her baby, and she felt 100 percent responsible.

It made sense to call Walker, though. She shooed Mitch and the others out of her dressing room and speed-dialed her husband's cell number.

Walker's voice was taut when he answered, an immediate giveaway that he already knew Clare was in trouble, and he probably knew why. Instead of *hello,* he said, "Take a breath, Casey. I'll handle this."

Casey thought the crown of her head might just shoot skyward, like a dinner plate spinning atop an erupting geyser. "You'll handle it? Walker, *what happened?* Why did I just receive a picture of my daughter in handcuffs from some—some *onlooker?*"

"I'm on my way to the police station right now," Walker replied calmly, though his voice was as rough and rocky as the bottom of a dry creek bed. "All I know is Clare's been charged with shoplifting. One of Treat McQuillan's officers arrested her, somewhere on the rodeo grounds."

Somewhere on the rodeo grounds?

He'd let Clare go wandering off, unattended? Didn't he realize how many things could have happened to her?

She didn't dare go there, not now, anyway.

"Shoplifting? Clare?" Casey stopped pacing and collapsed into the chair in front of her dressing-room mirror. Seeing herself in triplicate was hardly comforting, so she wheeled the seat around backward. "It must be a mistake."

Walker took a beat too long to answer. "We'll see," he said, measuring out his words in a sparing way that put an invisible wall between them. "Casey, I'll call you as soon as I know exactly where things stand—I promise. In the meantime, try to be calm."

So much for good intentions. "Calm? *Calm?* I leave home for a few days—*less than a week,* Walker—and something like this happens?" While she didn't actually accuse him outright of neglecting their daughter, the implication was there just the same. *I trusted you.*

"I'll call you, Casey," Walker reiterated flatly, drawing the words out, leaving wide spaces between them.

Casey nodded, overcome, remembered Walker couldn't see her and said, "Do that, please."

The call ended there.

Since there was nothing Casey could do but wait, she practiced deep breathing until her shoulders lowered, no longer pressing against her ears, and the muscles in her neck, though still tight, began to relax a little. If she hadn't had reason to believe she was pregnant, she probably would have sent out for a drink—a double shot of whatever, on the rocks. Moonshine, maybe. Did they sell moonshine in L.A.?

It didn't matter.

Clare mattered and she, Casey, was two plane rides away.

THE SPIFFY NEW Parable Municipal Police Station occupied the spot where the town's "historic" water tower had stood, until a few concerned citizens tore it down the day Dawson McCullough fell fifty feet and did permanent damage to his spine.

Walker parked his truck in one of three spots marked Visitor, shut off the engine and shoved open the door. "Wait here," he told Shane, who was sitting, pale and wide-eyed, in the passenger seat.

The station house was small, with a reception area in front, composed of a counterlike desk, a computer, a multiline phone and not much else. The chairs were plastic, and there were a few outdated magazines scattered around, in case somebody wanted to do a little light reading while they waited to see a prisoner, evidently.

There were a grand total of two cells in back, behind Treat McQuillan's cubicle-size office, giving the place a distinctly Mayberry feel. That was where the similarities ended, though, because McQuillan was nothing like the genial Sheriff Andy Taylor. No, he was a puffed-up, self-important little pit bull of a man, and he had to be enjoying *this* situation, big-time.

Walker didn't recognize the receptionist, a woman in her mid-forties who, going by the insignia on her starched blue uniform, doubled as a crossing guard or maybe a meter maid. Since the whole town of Parable only boasted a dozen parking meters and school was out for the summer, she must have worked the desk during the intervals between nothing-much and nothing-much.

"I'm here to see Clare Elder," he told the woman after giving his name.

The woman picked up a clipboard and made a production out of scanning several pages of official documents. Serious business, this. She and the Parable Police Department had a dangerous criminal on their hands, and they couldn't be too careful.

"I have a Clare *Parrish* listed," she said.

Walker unclamped his back molars. "That would be my daughter," he replied.

She gave him a look, as though she might have expected him to get the prisoner's name right in the first place, if he was Clare's father.

"I'll have to check with Chief McQuillan," the woman said after pursing her lips for a while, turning to open a door behind the counter, whisking through and shutting it with a click that struck Walker as faintly authoritarian.

Almost immediately, the chief popped out of his office, looking very pleased with himself, and when he spoke, his tone was gratingly cordial.

"Well," he said, "you certainly got here quickly."

"I want to see my daughter," Walker said evenly.

McQuillan opened the door wide and gestured grandly for Walker to precede him. The meter maid ducked out, looking smug.

Inside, Clare sat miserably at a small round table, head lowered. She wasn't handcuffed, at least, and she wasn't wearing an orange jumpsuit with a number stenciled on it, but Walker took small consolation from those observations.

"I'm sorry," she said without looking up at Walker.

Walker scraped back a chair, sat down across from her. He glared at McQuillan in silence until the chief stepped out, leaving them alone.

"Clare," Walker began, as the girl began to cry without making a sound, "tell me what happened."

She spent a couple of moments gathering her composure, but she still wouldn't look at him. "I stole some earrings, from one of the vendors at the fairgrounds," she answered. A tear zigzagged down her right cheek, and she seemed to be folding in on herself, trying to disappear, shoulders stooped, head down, spine curved forward.

"Now, why would you do a thing like that?" Walker asked calmly. He would have expected to be angry as hell. As it turned out, he was heartbroken instead. No need to ask where he'd gone wrong—he knew that already.

"I don't know," Clare said, very softly.

"I think you do," Walker replied, his tone mild.

She raised her eyes then, and he saw shame in them, along with naked, hopeless truth. "I was going to give the earrings back," she said, "or pay for them, honest. I just wanted to see if I could get away with it."

"Now you know," Walker said. "I've heard stupider ideas in my time, but not many of them. What were you thinking?"

Clare's shoulders rose and fell in a semblance of a shrug, and that was answer enough. She *hadn't* been thinking—and that was the problem.

"I tried to explain when the vendor caught me, but she was really pi—really *mad*—and she called the police right away. I guess it was technically the sheriff's jurisdiction, since the rodeo grounds are outside the city limits, but maybe some wires got crossed. Anyway, when the cop got there, he must have recognized me, because he sort of sneered and said celebrities' kids think they're above the law, and he hoped some judge would make an example out of me." She paused, and the look on her face made Walker ache inside. She was only fourteen and, as far as he knew, she'd never been in this kind of trouble before. Throwing her mom's fame in her face seemed unfair, but that was the way of the world.

"Can we go home now?" she finished meekly.

She was young—too young to be tossed into a jail cell—but that didn't mean the situation wasn't serious. Walker wondered if his head was going soft, right along with his heart, but his instincts told him Clare was telling the truth—thus far, anyway.

He didn't answer her question right away. "So what was the purpose of the backpack?" Walker asked, having spotted the one she'd been carrying earlier on a table behind her.

Clare's chin wobbled, and tears brimmed in her Casey-green eyes. "I was going to run away," she admitted. "But then I got to thinking about how it was a dumb plan, about kidnappers and perverts and all the stuff they warn you about, and I changed my mind." She studied him closely. "Really, Walker. That's how it was."

He figured if she'd been trying to snow him, she'd have called him "Dad," not 'Walker," but there was no way to know for sure. He was going to have to trust Clare, at least for now. He'd give her a chance to prove she wasn't a bad kid; he owed her that much. He simply watched her, arms folded, saying nothing.

Clare sniffled. "Does Mom know?"

"She knows you've been arrested. We'll fill her in on the details in a little while."

Fifteen minutes later, acting as though he were turning Bonnie Parker loose on an unsuspecting society, McQuillan released Clare into Walker's custody, taking care to point out that, if the vendor followed through and pressed charges, a date would be set for her to appear in juvenile court.

Walker couldn't bring himself to thank the chief or shake his hand, either, but he made one concession. After signing the papers, he waited until he was outside to put his hat back on.

Clare, backpack slung by one strap over her right shoulder, opened the back door of the extended cab and climbed inside.

Shane, sitting in front, glanced back at her once, but

a warning look from Walker stopped him from making any comments on his sister's budding criminal career.

Walker started the engine, got out his cell phone, keyed in Casey's number and handed the device back to Clare without a word.

The girl said, "Hi, Mom," and then broke into wrenching sobs. If this contrition was an act, Walker thought, it was a darn good one.

While he drove toward home, Clare sputtered out the story.

Walker stayed silent, and so did Shane.

They were almost at the turn-in at the ranch when Clare thrust the phone back at Walker, over his right shoulder. "Mom wants to talk to you," she said.

Walker drew the truck to a stop at the gate, and Shane jumped out to swing it open. "Hello, Casey," Walker said stiffly, pressing the phone hard against his ear.

"Thanks," Casey said, and it sounded as though she wasn't in much better emotional shape than her daughter was. "Thanks for picking Clare up and taking her home, Walker."

What had she *thought* he'd do? Leave their fourteen-year-old in police custody? Suggest that Clare be remanded to some juvenile detention center to ponder the error of her ways?

Walker's voice was ice-cold when he replied. "You're welcome."

"I'll be home Saturday night—tomorrow—right after our gig is over," Casey said. "We can decide what to do then."

"We will definitely be deciding some things," Walker answered. He was madder than a scalded cat all of a sudden, but he couldn't have said if that anger was directed at himself, at Casey or at Clare. All he really knew was that some changes had to be made, and the sooner the better.

Casey drew a breath, but whatever she'd been about to say, she held it in. "I'll see you tomorrow night."

"Good," Walker answered.

And they both hung up.

"Mom's disappointed in me," Clare said, very quietly, as they drove through the open gate. Shane shut and latched it behind them, but instead of getting back inside the truck, he rode on the running board, holding his hat in place with his free hand.

"She'll have to take a number," Walker replied.

Doolittle and the three chocolate Labs—Walker still couldn't keep their names straight, so he called them all "Dog"—were waiting at the kitchen door when he stepped over the threshold, and it cheered him up a little, their eager, uncomplicated welcome.

Clare lit out for her room right away, and Walker made no move to stop her.

While Shane fussed over the dogs and subsequently took them outside for a much-needed yard break, Walker washed his hands at the sink, as he'd done about a million times before, and opened the freezer side of the refrigerator, looking for supper possibilities.

Brylee, bless her practical and somewhat compulsive soul, cooked often, and he found a covered casserole dish, marked "Lasagna," wedged in behind a pork roast and a bag of green beans.

Lifting the lid, he noted that the food hadn't sprouted a coating of ice-fur or shrunk away from the sides of the dish, and thought, *Good enough*.

There were no instructions, but since Brylee's culinary concoctions always seemed to call for thirty minutes at 350 degrees, he turned the oven to that setting and waited for it to heat up.

Shane came back inside with the dogs, and hung his hat carefully beside Walker's on one of the pegs next to the door. After that, he rolled up his sleeves, washed his hands and face and the back of his neck at the sink, and used paper towels to dry off.

That last part, an improvisation, made Walker smile to himself.

"Clare's never been in trouble before," Shane announced very quietly.

Since the boy rarely if ever defended his sister, Walker was struck by that statement. He glanced over at Shane and said, "All right."

"You believe me?"

"Why wouldn't I?'

The boy flushed with conviction and maybe pleasure because Walker was taking him at his word. "I think Clare did what she did to get attention. Things have been kind of confusing lately. I mean, one day you're Mom's friend, a sort of uncle, and the next, you're our dad, and Mom's husband—"

"I know that, son," Walker said. The timer buzzed and he opened the oven, slid the dish of lasagna inside.

"I guess you'll probably just wash your hands of us now," Shane went on. "Clare and me, I mean. Because we're too much trouble."

Walker turned slowly to face the boy. "Son," he said, "I'm not going anywhere, and neither are you or your sister. We're a family now, and we're going to stick together, the four of us, and figure things out. It'll take gumption and elbow grease, but we can do it."

The relief in Shane's face was so profound that Walker came as close to crying in that moment as he ever had in his adult life. Reaching out with one arm, he pulled the boy to him, gave him a quick but firm hug.

Shane clung to him for a moment, before remembering that he wasn't a little kid anymore and stepping back.

They finished throwing supper together, and Shane took a plate to Clare, along with a glass of milk and a wad of paper towels to serve as dinner napkins.

Later, Shane got out his cell phone and showed Walker a jerky video of that day's ride, taken by a friend of his.

"Not even three seconds," the boy commented, sounding unfazed.

"Three is better than nothing. I once got thrown while they were still opening the chute."

Shane looked pleased. "Really?"

"Gospel truth," Walker answered, holding up one hand to underscore the oath.

IT WAS AFTER midnight when Casey's chartered plane landed at the small airstrip midway between Parable and Three Trees, and she was exhausted. Mitch had promised to have a car waiting to take her home to the ranch, but when she peered out of one of the oval-shaped windows, she saw a pickup truck instead.

Walker. Her heartbeat sped up a little, the way it always did when the two of them entered the same airspace. This proximity usually resulted in something more like a collision than an embrace, but she was glad he was there, nonetheless.

He got out of the truck as she came down the steps from the airplane, hatless in the thin moonlight, but he didn't approach. No, he just stood there, straight-spined and broad-shouldered, unsmiling.

Casey forced herself to move slowly, though she wanted nothing more than to run to Walker and leap into his arms. She stopped about three feet away from him, heart pounding.

"Clare's fine," he said at some length. "And so is Shane."

Casey swallowed hard, nodded. Behind her, the small private plane taxied for takeoff. She hadn't even brought her luggage along, she'd been in such a hurry to leave L.A.

"Do we have a chance, Walker?" she heard her own voice ask.

He frowned, and neither of them moved. "What do you mean, 'Do we have a chance?'" he asked.

"After all that's happened," Casey choked out, watching him. "Two babies, all that time apart, all the mistakes and the lies—" She couldn't go on.

Walker took her gently by the shoulders and said the words she'd thought he'd never say. "I love you, Casey. And the mistakes and lies belong to both of us, so why don't we just let them go and move on?"

"Did you just say you love me?" Casey all but whispered. Her voice was almost gone, and not just because she'd sung her heart out on live TV a few hours before.

The slightest smile lifted one corner of Walker's mouth. "That's what I said, all right. Am I in this all alone, or what?"

She gave a sob of laughter then, and threw her arms around his neck. "I love you now, and I always have, Walker Parrish," she blurted out, clinging to him, reveling in the hard, warm substance of him.

"You might have said as much," he told her gruffly, his breath warm at her ear, his arms tight and strong around her.

"Back at you, cowboy," Casey said, happier than she'd ever thought she could be. "I didn't hear 'I love you' coming from your direction, either."

He chuckled, and then he kissed her, so deeply and so thoroughly that her last doubts gave way.

At home, the kids and the dogs were all asleep, which was a good thing because Casey and Walker had had a heck of a time even getting that far before they started making love.

Walker picked Casey up in the kitchen and carried her to their room, his strides long.

There was a lot to settle—the problems with Clare, for starters, and where things would go from here—but this time, this shining strand of moments and minutes and hours, belonged only to the two of them.

Behind closed doors, they undressed each other, stepped into the shower stall together, kissing even as the warm spray of water drenched them both, slickening their fevered bodies, spiking their eyelashes, soothing away everything but the desperate drive to be joined, two beings melded into one.

They took things slowly, though, savoring every kiss, every caress, every whispered word. All the unsaid "I love yous," stored up for years, came rushing to the surface now, as unstoppable as lava from a volcano.

They lathered each other with soap, rinsed away the suds, and Casey marveled at the pitch of her arousal. Lovemaking wasn't new to them, but that night, it *seemed* new, a first in the history of Creation.

Presently, Walker knelt, his hands stroking Casey's

thighs before he parted her, ever so gently, with a motion of his thumbs.

When he took her into his mouth, her whole body convulsed with primitive pleasure, and she bit down hard on her lower lip to keep from shouting his name in welcome, in need, in love. Not the paper roses and Valentines kind of love, but the real thing, a sacred equation of one man and one woman.

Satisfaction came quickly for Casey, consuming her like a fire. She flexed and flexed again as Walker continued to enjoy her, her hands locked behind his head to hold him there.

But once was never enough, and when the violent shudders of release had finally ceased, Walker draped her legs over his shoulders—they wouldn't hold her any longer—and nuzzled in for an encore.

The water turned lukewarm, but neither of them cared; they might have been making love under a summer rainfall, or anywhere. The place didn't matter, nothing did, beyond the simple fact that they were together. *Really* together, for the first time ever.

Somehow—Casey was in too much of a daze to recall the mechanics later—they wound up on top of their bed, still slippery-wet, hair dripping, bodies frantic, and she saw their whole future in Walker's eyes as he looked down at her, silently asking her permission, the way he always did.

She saw them raising Clare and Shane together, with all their combined love and determination.

She saw them bringing home the new baby, the one growing inside her, nurtured not only by her body, but by her soul.

She saw more children, and grandchildren, too. All

of them as much a part of the ranch as the land and the creeks, the river and the sky.

Most of all, she saw love, the tough, durable kind that knows no endings, but only beginnings, only a shared freedom, and the gift to grow in all directions, like those flowers rioting around the ruins of the homestead cabin up on the hill.

She nodded, said it again. "I love you."

Walker was inside her in a single stroke, going deep, commanding, conquering, and yet with a tenderness so poignant that Casey's spirit soared, even before her body did.

Their releases were simultaneous, a fusion of two lightning bolts into one cataclysmic flash, and achieved only after much sweet striving. They were locked in a kiss all the while, their cries echoing between them.

The descent was long, slow and delicious.

In between skirmishes, the lovers slept, arms and legs entwined, Walker's chin resting atop Casey's head. Each time they awakened, they made love again, sometimes sleepily, sometimes desperately, and when dawn finally broke, they were joined, and the sunrise became Casey's climax, blinding and beautiful, all pink and gold dazzle, a sky full of fire.

July 15

OPAL STOOD AT the front of the little church, head high and shoulders squared, beside her bridegroom, the Reverend Walter Beaumont. One of the reverend's colleagues had come to Parable especially to perform the ceremony, and every pew was packed.

Standing in the choir loft, Casey scanned the congregation, found Walker and Clare and Shane, and she was glad she wouldn't have to sing for a few more minutes, because just then, her heart was filling her throat.

A family—*her* family, with all the attendant challenges and triumphs, all the ups and downs. How did she get so lucky?

Walker looked up at her then, as if he'd heard her thoughts. His expression was completely solemn—until he winked.

Casey smiled, blushed a little and looked away.

She spotted Joslyn and Slade Barlow, their firstborn squirming between them on the pew, as toddlers will, each of them holding a blue-wrapped bundle in loving arms. Shea, Slade's stepdaughter, was there, too, beaming proudly at one of the week-old twins, then the other.

She found Hutch and Kendra Carmody next, sitting with their shoulders touching and their gazes on the bride and groom. Their little girl, Madison, sat beside them, fussing over her baby sister, kicking and cooing in her infant seat.

Boone and Tara Taylor, with four children between them, took up most of one pew. Tara's arm was looped through Boone's, Casey noticed, and her head rested against his shoulder.

Casey brought her gaze back around to Walker and Clare and Shane, and happy tears filled her eyes, because there sat Brylee, big as life, her face glowing with joy as Opal and Walter exchanged their vows.

Walter's kiss was Casey's cue to sing, and sing she did.

The song was a special one, a collaboration between herself and Clare, about love finding its own way, in its own time, and enduring.

Clare turned to look up at Casey midsong, mouthing the words they'd written together at the piano in the ranch house living room, and Casey's heart swelled again, with love for her daughter, her good husband, her fine son, and the wings of her gratitude carried her voice to the heights.

When the song ended, there was a stirring silence, almost palpable.

Then Opal and Walter broke with tradition and turned, smiling up at Casey and clapping their hands. The rest of the congregation joined in, and Casey stepped back, out of view, and descended the stairs from the small loft.

The celebration, held at the house on Rodeo Road, which Casey used as headquarters and a place to record with the band, went on for hours. She still wasn't doing concert tours, but singing itself wasn't optional for her—she had to have music, had to *make* music—and Walker not only understood, he was proud of her.

Except for a brief flurry of media attention centered around Clare's brush with the law—the shoplifting charges had been dropped, but Walker and Casey had insisted she perform some kind of community service just the same—the tabloids and other "news" outlets had backed off. Clare helped Marti Wren out three afternoons a week at the animal shelter, and once remarked that if this was punishment, she should have gotten into trouble sooner.

Shane, a cowboy through and through, rode the range with his dad as often as possible, and did his chores without complaint—mostly. He was bound and determined to last longer than three seconds the next time he entered a rodeo, and that seemed like a reasonable goal to Casey.

She still hated the idea of her son on the back of a bucking bronco, of course, but she kept that to herself—*mostly*.

While the band played, Opal and her new husband danced on the floor specially constructed for the occasion, smiling into each other's eyes, surrounded by friends and family, immersed in the glow of their love.

Walker stepped up behind Casey, slipped his arms around her and rested his chin on top of her head. "Pretty romantic," he said, turning her gently around to face him, handing her a small velvet box.

Casey, not expecting a gift, was taken aback. "What's this?"

"Open it and see," Walker said.

She lifted the lid, peered inside the box and saw a beautiful heart-shaped pendant in tones of gold and silver, with two tiny charms suspended in the center—two Western hats, one to represent each of them. "Thank you," she murmured, overwhelmed with love for this man she'd married.

Fingers trembling a little, she removed the necklace from its case and handed it to Walker, so he could drape it around her neck and fasten it.

He did that, squeezed her shoulders lightly. "I think we ought to go straight home and celebrate."

Casey laughed, turned in Walker's embrace and smiled up at him. "That's not a bad idea, cowboy," she said. "Not a bad idea at all."

* * * * *

COWBOY'S REDEMPTION

B.J. Daniels

This one is for Stelly, who even at four loves stories where the heroine gets to help save herself.

CHAPTER ONE

RUNNING BLINDLY THROUGH the darkness, Lola didn't see the tree limb until it struck her in the face. It clawed at her cheek, digging into a spot under her right eye as she flung it away with her arm. She had to stifle the cry of pain that rose in her throat for fear she would be heard. As she ran, she felt warm blood run down to the corner of her lips. The taste of it mingled with the salt of her tears, but she didn't slow, couldn't. She could hear them behind her.

She pushed harder, knowing that, being men, they had the advantage, especially the way she was dressed. Her long skirt caught on something. She heard the fabric rend, not for the first time. She felt as if it was her heart being ripped out with it.

Her only choice was to escape. But at what price? She'd been forced to leave behind the one person who mattered most. Her thundering heart ached at the thought, but she knew that this was the only way. If she could get help...

"She's over here!" came a cry from behind her. "This way!"

She wiped away the warm blood as she crashed through the brush and trees. Her legs ached and she didn't know how much longer she could keep going. Fatigue was draining her. If they caught her this time...

She tripped on a tree root, stumbled and almost plunged headlong down the mountainside. Her shoulder slammed into a tree trunk. She veered off it like a pinball, but she kept pushing herself forward because the alternative was worse than death.

They were closer now. She could feel one of them breathing down her neck. She didn't dare look back. To look back would be to admit defeat. If she could just reach the road before they caught up to her…

Suddenly the trees opened up. She burst out of the darkness of the pines onto the blacktop of a narrow two-lane highway. The glare of headlights blinded her an instant before the shriek of rubber on the dark pavement filled the night air.

CHAPTER TWO

M<small>AJOR</small> C<small>OLT</small> M<small>C</small>C<small>LOUD</small> felt the big bird shake as he brought the helicopter low over the bleak landscape. He was back in Afghanistan behind the controls of a UH-60 Black Hawk. The throb of the rotating blades was drowned out by the sound of mortar fire. It grew louder and louder, taking on a consistent pounding that warned him something was very wrong.

He dragged himself awake, but the dream followed him. Blinking in the darkness, he didn't know where he was for a moment. Everything looked alien and surreal. As the dream began to fade, he recognized his bedroom at the ranch.

He'd left behind the sound of the chopper and the mortar fire, but the pounding had intensified. With a start, he realized what he was hearing.

Someone was at the door.

He glanced at the clock on his bedside table. It was after three in the morning. Throwing his legs over the side of the bed, he grabbed his jeans, pulling them on as he fought to put the dream behind him and hurry to the door.

A half dozen possibilities flashed in his mind as he moved quickly through the house. It still felt strange to be back here after years of traveling the world as an Army helicopter pilot. After his fiancée dumped him, he'd planned to make a career out of the military, but then his father had died, leaving him a working ranch that either had to be run or sold.

He'd taken a hundred-and-twenty-day leave in between assignments so he could come home to take care of the ranch. His father had been the one who'd loved ranching, not Colt. That's why there was a for-sale sign out on the road into the ranch.

Colt reached the front door and, frowning at the incessant knocking at this hour of the morning, threw it open.

He blinked at the disheveled woman standing there before she turned to motion to the driver of the car idling nearby. The engine roared and a car full of what appeared to be partying teenagers took off in a cloud of dust.

Colt flipped on the porch light as the woman turned back to him and he got his first good look at her and her scratched, blood-streaked face. For a moment he didn't recognize her, and then it all came back in a rush. Standing there was a woman he'd never thought he'd see again.

"Lola?" He couldn't even be sure that was her real name. But somehow it fit her, so maybe at least that part of her story had been true. "What happened to you?"

"I had nowhere else to go." Her words came out in a rush. "I was so worried that you wouldn't be here." She burst into tears and slumped as if physically exhausted.

He caught her, swung her up into his arms and carried her into the house, kicking the door closed behind him. His mind raced as he tried to imagine what could have happened to bring her to his door in Gilt

Edge, Montana, in the middle of the night and in this condition.

"Sit here," he said as he carried her in and set her down in a kitchen chair before going for the first-aid kit. When he returned, he was momentarily taken aback by the memory of this woman the first time he'd met her. She wasn't beautiful in the classic sense. But she was striking, from her wide violet eyes fringed with pale lashes to the silk of her long blond hair. She had looked like an angel, especially in the long white dress she'd been wearing that night.

That was over a year ago and he hadn't seen her since. Nor had he expected to since they'd met initially several hundred miles from the ranch. But whatever had struck him about her hadn't faded. There was something flawless about her—even as scraped up and bruised as she was. It made him furious at whoever was responsible for this.

"Can you tell me what happened?" he asked as he began to clean the cuts.

"I… I…" Her throat seemed to close on a sob.

"It's okay, don't try to talk." He felt her trembling and could see that she was fighting tears. "This cut under your eye is deep."

She said nothing, looking as if it was all she could do to keep her eyes open. He took in her torn and filthy dress. It was long, like the white one he'd first seen her in, but faded. It reminded him of something his grandmother might have worn to do housework in. She was also thinner than he remembered.

As he gently cleaned her wounds, he could see dark circles under her eyes, and her long braided hair was in disarray with bits of twigs and leaves stuck in it.

The night he'd met her, her plaited hair had been pinned up at the nape of her neck—until he'd released it, the blond silk dropping to the center of her back.

He finished his doctoring, put away the first-aid kit, and wondered how far she'd come to find him and what she had been through to get here. When he returned to the kitchen, he found her standing at the back window, staring out. As she turned, he saw the fear in her eyes—and the exhaustion.

Colt desperately wanted to know what had happened to her and how she'd ended up on his doorstep. He hadn't even thought that she'd known his name. "Have you had anything to eat?"

"Not in the past forty-eight hours or so," she said, squinting at the clock on the wall as if not sure what day it was. "And not all that much before that."

He'd been meaning to get into Gilt Edge and buy some groceries. "Sit and I'll see what I can scare up," he said as he opened the refrigerator. Seeing only one egg left, he said, "How do you feel about pancakes? I have chokecherry syrup."

She nodded and attempted a smile. She looked skittish as a newborn calf. Worse, he sensed that she was having second thoughts about coming here.

She licked her cracked lips. "I have to tell you. I have to explain—"

"It's okay. You're safe here." But safe from what, he wondered? "There's no hurry. Let's get you taken care of first." He'd feed her and get her settled down.

He motioned her into a chair at the kitchen table. He could tell that she must hurt all over by the way she moved. As much as he wanted to know what had happened, he thought she needed food more than anything else at this moment.

"While I make the pancakes, would you like a hot shower? The guest room is down the hall to the left. I can find you some clothes. They'll be too large for you, but maybe they will be more comfortable."

Tears welled in her eyes. He saw her swallow before she nodded. As she started to get to her feet, he noticed her grimace in pain.

"Wait."

She froze.

"I don't know how to say this delicately, but if someone assaulted you—"

"I wasn't raped."

He nodded, hoping that was true, because a shower would destroy important evidence. "Okay, so the injuries were…"

"From running for my life." With that she limped out of the kitchen.

He had the pancake batter made and the griddle heating when he heard the shower come on. He stopped to listen to the running water, remembering this woman in a hotel shower with him months ago.

That night he'd bumped into her coming out of the hotel bar. He'd seen that she was upset. She'd told him that she needed his help, that there was someone after her. She'd given him the impression she was running from an old boyfriend. He'd been happy to help. Now he wondered if that was still the case. She said she was running for her life—just as she had the first time they'd met.

But that had been in Billings. This was Gilt Edge, Montana, hundreds of miles away. Didn't seem likely she would still be running from the same boyfriend. But whoever was chasing her, she'd come to him for help.

He couldn't turn her away any more than he'd been able to in that hotel hallway in Billings last year.

LOLA PULLED OUT her braid, discarding the debris stuck in it, then climbed into the steaming shower. She stood under the hot spray, leaned against the smooth, cool tile wall of the shower and closed her eyes. She felt weak from hunger, lack of sleep and constant fear. She couldn't remember the last time she'd slept through the night.

Exhaustion pulled at her. It took all of her energy to wash herself. Her body felt alien to her, her skin chafed from the rough fabric of the long dresses she'd been wearing for months. Stumbling from the shower, she wrapped her hair in one of the guest towels. It felt good to free her hair from the braid that had been wound at the nape of her neck.

As she pulled down another clean towel from the bathroom rack, she put it to her face and sniffed its freshness. Tears burned her eyes. It had been so long since she'd had even the smallest creature comforts like good soap, shampoo and clean towels that smelled like this, let alone unlimited hot water.

When she opened the bathroom door, she saw that Colt had left her a sweatshirt and sweatpants on the guest-room bed. She dried and tugged them on, pulling the drawstring tight around her waist. He was right, the clothes were too big, but they felt heavenly.

She took the towels back to the bathroom to hang them and considered her dirty clothing on the floor. The hem of the worn ankle-length coarse cotton dress was torn and filthy with dirt and grime. The long sleeves were just as bad except they were soiled with her blood. The black utilitarian shoes were scuffed, the heels worn unevenly since she'd inherited them well used.

She wadded up the dress and shoved it into the bathroom wastebasket before putting the shoes on top of it, all the time feeling as if she was committing a sin. Then again, she'd already done that, hadn't she.

Downstairs, she stepped into the kitchen to see Colt slip three more pancakes onto the stack he already had on the plate.

He turned as if sensing her in the doorway and she was reminded of the first time she'd seen him. All she'd noticed that night was his Army uniform—before he'd turned and she'd seen his face.

That he was handsome hadn't even registered. What she'd seen was a kind face. She'd been desperate and Colt McCloud had suddenly appeared as if it had been meant to be. Just as he'd been here tonight, she thought.

"Last time I saw you, you were on leave and talking about staying in the military," she said as he pulled out a kitchen chair for her and she sat down. "I was afraid that you had and that—" her voice broke as she met his gaze "—you wouldn't be here."

"I'm on leave now. My father died."

"I'm sorry."

He set down the plate of pancakes. "Dig in."

Always the gentleman, she thought as he joined her at the table. "I made a bunch. There's fresh sweet butter. If you don't like chokecherry syrup—"

"I love it." She slid several of the lightly browned cakes onto her plate. The aroma that rose from them made her stomach growl loudly. She slathered them with butter and covered them with syrup. The first bite was so delicious that she actually moaned, making him smile.

"I was going to ask how they are," he said with a laugh, "but I guess I don't have to."

She devoured the pancakes before helping herself to more. They ate in a companionable silence that didn't surprise her any more than Colt making her pancakes in the middle of the night or opening his door to her, no questions asked. It was as if it was something he did all the time. Maybe it was, she thought, remembering the first night they'd met.

He hadn't hesitated when she'd told him she needed his help. She'd looked into his blue eyes and known she could trust him. He'd been so sweet and caring that she'd almost told him the truth. But she'd stopped herself. Because she didn't think he would believe her? Or because she didn't want to involve him? Or because, at that point, she thought she could still handle things on her own?

Unfortunately, she no longer had the option of keeping the truth from him.

"I'm sure you have a lot of questions," she said, after swallowing her last bite of pancake and wiping her mouth with her napkin. The food had helped, but her body ached all over and fatigue had weakened her. "You had to be surprised to see me again, especially with me showing up at your door in the middle of the night looking like I do."

"I didn't even know you knew my last name."

"After that night in Billings… Before I left your hotel room, while you were still sleeping, I looked in your wallet."

"You planned to take my money?" He'd had over four hundred dollars in there. He'd been headed home to his fiancée, he'd told her. But the fiancée, who was supposed to pick him up at the airport, had called instead with crushing news. Not only was she not picking him up, she was in love with one of his best friends, someone he'd known since grade school.

He'd been thinking he just might rent a car and drive home to confront the two of them, he'd told Lola later. But, ultimately, he'd booked a flight for the next morning to where he was stationed and, with time to kill, had taken a taxi to a hotel, paid for a room and headed for the hotel bar. Two drinks later, he'd run into Lola as he'd headed from the bar to the men's room. Lola had saved him from getting stinking drunk that night. Also from driving to Gilt Edge to confront his ex-fiancée and his ex-friend.

"I hate to admit that I thought about taking your money," she said. "I could have used it."

"You should have taken it then."

She smiled at him and shook her head. "You were so kind to me, so tender…" Her cheeks heated as she held his gaze and remembered being naked in his arms. "I'm sure I gave you the wrong impression of me that night. It wasn't like me to…with a complete stranger." She bit her lower lip and felt tears well in her eyes again.

"There is nothing wrong with the impression you left with me. As a matter of fact, I've thought of you often." He smiled. It was a great smile. "Every time I heard one of those songs that we'd danced to in my hotel room that night—" his gaze warmed to a Caribbean blue "—I thought of you."

She looked away to swallow the lump that had formed in her throat before she could speak again. "It wasn't an old boyfriend I was running from that night. I let you believe that because I doubted you'd have believed the truth. I did need your help, though, because right before I collided with you in that hallway, I'd seen one of them in the hotel. I knew it was just a matter of time before they found me and took me back."

"Took you back?"

"I wasn't a fugitive from the law or some mental institution," she said quickly. "It's worse than that."

He narrowed his gaze with concern. "What could be worse than that?"

"The Society of Lasting Serenity."

CHAPTER THREE

"THE FRINGE RELIGIOUS cult that relocated to the mountains about five years ago?" Colt asked, unable to keep the shock from his voice.

She nodded.

He couldn't have been more stunned if she'd said she had escaped from prison. "When did you join that?"

"I didn't. My parents were some of the founding members when the group began in California. I was in Europe at university when they joined. I'd heard from my father that SLS had relocated to Montana. A few years after that, I received word that the leader, Jonas Emanuel, needed to see me. My mother was ill." Her voice broke. "Before I could get back here, my mother and father both died, within hours of each other, and had been buried on the compound. According to Jonas, they had one dying wish." Her laugh could have cut glass. "They wanted to see me married. Once I was on the SLS compound, I learned that, according to Jonas, they had promised me to him."

"That's crazy." He still couldn't get his head around this.

"Jonas is delusional but also dangerous."

"So you were running from him that night I met you?"

She nodded. "But, unfortunately, when I left the hotel

the next morning, two of the 'sisters' were waiting for me and forced me to go back to the compound."

"And tonight?" he asked as he pushed his plate away.

Lola met his gaze. "I escaped. I'd been locked up there since I last saw you within miles of here at the Montana SLS compound."

Colt let out a curse. "You've been held there all this time against your will? Why didn't you—"

"Escape sooner?" She sounded near tears as she held his gaze.

He saw something in those beautiful eyes that made his stomach drop.

Her voice caught as she said, "I had originally gone there to get my parents' remains because I don't believe they died of natural causes. I'd gotten a letter from my father right before I heard from Jonas. He wanted out of SLS, but my mother refused. My father said he feared the hold Jonas had on her and needed my help because she wasn't well."

"What are you saying?"

"I think they were murdered, but I can't prove it without their bodies, and Jonas has refused to release them. Legally, there isn't much I can do since my parents had signed over everything to him—even their daughter."

Murder? He'd heard about the fifty-two-year-old charismatic leader of the cult living in the mountains outside of town, but he couldn't imagine the things Lola was telling him. "He can't expect you to marry him."

"Jonas was convinced that I would fall for him if I spent enough time at the compound, so he kept me there. At first, he told me it would take time to have my parents' remains exhumed and moved. Later I realized there was no way he was letting their remains go anywhere even if he could convince me to marry him, which was never going to happen."

Maybe it was the late hour, but he was having trouble making sense of this. "So after you met me…"

"I was more determined to free both my parents and myself from Jonas forever. I wasn't back at the compound long though, when I realized I was pregnant. Jonas realized it, too. I became a prisoner of SLS until the birth. Then Jonas had the baby taken away and had me locked up. I had to escape to get help for my daughter."

"Your daughter?"

She met his gaze. "That's why I'm here… She's *our* daughter," she said, her voice suddenly choked with tears. "Jonas took the baby girl that you and I made the first night we met."

COLT STARED AT HER, too shocked to speak for a moment. *What the hell?* "Are you trying to tell me—"

"I had your child but I couldn't contact you. Jonas kept me under guard, locked away. I had no way to get a message out. If any of the sisters tried to help me, they were severely punished."

He couldn't believe what he was hearing. "Wait. You had the baby at the compound?"

She nodded. "One of the members is a midwife. She delivered a healthy girl, but then Jonas had the child taken away almost at once. I got to hold her only for a few moments and only because Sister Amelia let me. She was harshly reprimanded for it. I got to look into her precious face. She has this adorable tiny heart-shaped birthmark on her left thigh and my blond hair. Just fuzz really." Tears filled her eyes again.

Colt ran a hand over his face before he looked at her again. "I'm having a hard time believing any of this."

"I know. If Jonas had let me leave with my daughter, I wouldn't have ever troubled you with any of this," she said.

"You would never have told me about the baby?" He hadn't meant to make it sound like an accusation. He'd expected her to be offended.

Instead, when she spoke, he saw only sympathy in her gaze. "When I met you, you were on leave and going back the next day. You were talking about staying in the Army. Your fiancée had just broken up with you."

"You don't have to remind me."

"What you and I shared that night…" She met his gaze. "I'll never forget it, but I wasn't fool enough to think that it might lead to anything. The only reason I'm here now is that I need help to get our daughter away from that…man."

"Don't I have a right to know if I have a child?"

"Of course. But I wouldn't be asking anything of you—if Jonas hadn't taken our daughter. I'm more than capable of taking care of her and myself."

"What I don't understand is why Jonas wants to keep a baby that isn't his."

She didn't seem surprised by his skepticism, but when he looked into her eyes, he saw pain darken all that beautiful blue. "I can understand why you wouldn't believe she's yours."

"I didn't say that."

"You didn't have to." She got to her feet, grabbing the table to steady herself. "I shouldn't have come here, but I didn't know where else to go."

"Hold on," he said, pushing back his chair and coming around the table to take her shoulders in his hands. She felt small, fragile, and yet he saw a strength in her that belied her slim frame. "You have to admit this is quite the story."

"That's why I didn't tell you the night we met about the cult or the problems I was having getting my parents' remains out. I still thought I could handle it myself. Also I doubt you would have believed it." Her smile hurt him soul deep. "I wouldn't have believed it and I've lived through all of this."

He was doing his best to keep an open mind. He wasn't a man who jumped to quick conclusions. He took his time to make decisions based on the knowledge he was able to acquire. It had kept him alive all these years as an Army helicopter pilot.

"So what you're telling me is that the leader of SLS has taken your baby to force you to marry him? If he's so dangerous, why wouldn't he have just—"

"Forced me? He tried to…join with me, as he put it. He's still limping from the attempt. And equally determined that I will come to him. Now that I've shamed him…he will never let me have my baby unless I completely surrender to him in front of the whole congregation."

"Don't you mean *our* baby?"

Lola gave him an impatient look. Tears filled her eyes as she swayed a little as if having trouble staying upright after everything she'd been through.

He felt a stab of guilt. He'd been putting her through an interrogation when clearly she was exhausted. It was bad enough that she was scraped, cut and bruised, but he could see that her real injuries were more than skin deep.

"You're dead on your feet," he said. "There isn't anything we can do tonight. Get some rest. Tomorrow…"

A tear broke loose and cascaded down her cheek. He caught it with his thumb and gently wiped it away before she let him lead her to the guest bedroom where she'd showered earlier. His mind was racing. If any of this was true…

"Don't worry. We'll figure this out," Colt said as he pulled back the covers. "Just get some sleep." He knew he wouldn't be able to sleep a wink.

Could he really have a daughter? A daughter now being held by a crackpot cult leader? A man who, according to Lola, was much more dangerous than anyone knew?

Lola climbed into the bed, still wearing his too-large sweats. He tucked her in, seeing that she could barely keep her eyes open.

"Dayton." At his puzzled look, she added, "That's my last name." They'd shared only first names the night they met. But that night neither of them had been themselves. She'd been running scared, and he'd been wallowing in self-pity over losing the woman he'd thought he was going to marry and live with the rest of his life.

"Lola Dayton," he repeated, and smiled down at her. "Pretty name."

He moved to the door and switched off the light.

"I named our daughter Grace," she said from out of the darkness. "Do you remember telling me that you always loved that name?"

He turned in the doorway to look back at her, too choked up to speak for a moment. "It was my grandmother's name."

LOLA THOUGHT SHE wouldn't be able to sleep. Her body felt leaden as she'd sunk under the covers. She could still feel the rough skin of Colt's thumb pad against her cheek and reached up to touch the spot. She hadn't been wrong about him. Not that first night. Not tonight.

She closed her eyes and felt herself careening off that mountain, running for her life, running for Grace's life. She was safe, she reminded herself. But Grace…

The sisters were taking good care of Grace, she told herself. Jonas wouldn't let anything happen to the baby. At least she prayed that he wouldn't hurt Grace to punish her even more.

The thought had her heart pounding until she realized the only power Jonas had over her was the baby. He wouldn't hurt Grace. He needed that child if he ever hoped to get what he wanted. And what he wanted was Lola. She'd seen it in his eyes. A voracious need that he thought only she could fill.

If he ever got his hands on her again… Well, she knew there would be no saving herself from him.

COLT KICKED OFF his boots and lay down on the bed fully dressed. Sleep was out of the question. If half of what Lola had told him was true… Was it possible they'd made a baby that night? They hadn't used protection. He hadn't had anything. Nor had she. It wasn't like him to take a chance like that.

But there was something so wholesome, so innocent, so guileless…

Rolling to his side, he closed his eyes. The memory was almost painful. The sweet scent of her body as she lay with her back to him naked on the bed. The warmth of his palm as he slowly ran it from her side down into the saddle of her slim waist to the rise of her hip and her perfectly rounded buttocks. The catch of her breath as he pulled her into him and cupped one full breast. The tender moan from her lips as he rolled her over to look into those violet eyes.

Groaning, Colt shifted to his back again to stare up at the dark ceiling. That night he'd lost himself in that delectable woman. He'd buried all feelings for his former fiancée into her. He'd found salvation in her body, in her arms, in her tentative touch, in her soft, sweet kisses.

He closed his eyes, again remembering the feel of her in his arms as they'd danced in his hotel room. The slow sway, their bodies joined, their movements more sensuous than even the act of love. He'd given her a little piece of his heart that night and had not even realized it.

Swinging his legs over the bed, he knew he'd never get any rest until he checked on her. Earlier, he'd gotten the feeling that she wanted to run—rather than tell him what had brought her to his door. She hadn't wanted to involve him, wouldn't have if Jonas didn't have her baby.

That much he believed. But why hadn't she told him what she was running from the night they'd first met? Maybe he could have helped her.

He moved quietly down the hallway, half-afraid he would open the bedroom door only to find her gone and all of this like his dream about being back in Afghanistan.

After easing open the door, he waited for his eyes to adjust to the blackness in the room. Her blond hair lay like a fan across her pillow. Her peaceful face made her appear angelic. He found himself smiling as he stared down at the sleeping Lola. He couldn't help wondering about their daughter. She would be three months old now. Did she resemble her mother? He hoped so.

The thought shook him because he realized how much he wanted to believe her. A daughter. He really could have a daughter? A baby with Lola? He shook his head. What were the chances that their union would bring a child into this world? And yet he and Lola had done more than make love that night. They'd connected in a way he and Julia never had.

The thought of Julia, though, made him recoil. Look how wrong he'd been about her. How wrong he'd been about his own mother. Could he trust his judgment when it came to women? Doubtful.

He stepped out of the room, closing the door softly behind him. Tomorrow, he told himself, he would know the truth. He'd get the sheriff to go with them up to the compound and settle this once and for all.

Colt walked out onto the porch to stare up at the starry sky. The air was crisp and cold, snow still capping the highest peaks around town. He knew this all could be true. Normally, he would never have had intercourse with a woman he didn't know without protection. But that night, he and Lola hadn't just had sex. They'd made love, two lost souls who'd given each other comfort in a world that had hurt them.

He'd been heartbroken over Julia and his friend Wyatt. Being in Lola's arms had saved him. If their lovemaking had resulted in a baby…a little girl…

Yes, what was he going to do? Besides go up to that compound and get the baby for Lola? He tried to imagine himself as a father to an infant. What a joke. He couldn't have been in a worse place in his life to take on a wife and a child.

He looked across the ranch. All his life he'd felt tied down to this land. That his father had tried to chain him to it still infuriated him—and at the same time made him feel guilty. His father had had such a connection to the land, one that Colt had never felt. He'd loved being a cowboy, but ranching was more about trying to make a living off the land. He'd watched his father struggle for years. Why would the old man think he would want this? Why hadn't his father sold the place, done something fun with the money before he'd died?

Instead, he'd left it all to Colt—lock, stock and barrel, making the place feel like a noose around his neck.

"It's yours," the probate attorney had said. "Do whatever you want with the ranch."

"You mean I can sell it?"

"After three months. That's all your father stipulated. That you live on the ranch for three months full-time, and then if you still don't want to ranch, you can liquidate all of your father's holdings."

Colt took a deep breath and let it out. "Sorry, Dad. If you think even three *years* on this land is going to change anything, you are dead wrong." He'd put in his three months and more waiting for an offer on the place.

When his leave was up, he was heading back to the Army and his real job. At least that had been the plan before he'd found Lola standing on his doorstep. Now he didn't know what to think. All he knew was that he had to fly. He didn't want to ranch. Once the place sold, there would be nothing holding him here.

He thought about Lola asleep back in the house. If this baby was his, he'd take responsibility, but he couldn't make any promises—not when he didn't even know where he would be living when he came home on leave.

Up by the road, he could see the for-sale sign by the gate into the ranch. With luck, the ranch would sell soon. In the meantime, he had to get Lola's baby back for her. His baby.

He pushed open the door and headed for his bedroom. Everything was going to work out. Once Lola understood what he needed to do, what he had to do...

He lay down on the bed fully clothed again and closed his eyes, knowing there was no chance of sleep. But hours later, he woke with a start, surprised to find sunlight streaming in through the window. As he rose, still dressed, he worried that he would find Lola gone, just as she had been that morning in Billings.

The thought had his heart pounding as he padded down to the guest room. The door was partially ajar. What if none of it had been true? What if she'd realized he would see through all of it and had taken off?

He pressed his fingertips against the warm wood and pushed gently until he could see into the dim light of the room. She lay wrapped in one of his mother's quilts, her long blond hair splayed across the pillow. He eased the door closed, surprised how relieved he was. Maybe he wasn't a good judge of character when it came in women—Julia a case in point—but he wanted to believe Lola was different. It surprised him how *much* he wanted to believe it.

LOLA WOKE TO the smell of frying bacon. Her stomach growled. She sat up with a start, momentarily confused as to where she was. Not on the hard cot at the compound. Not locked in the claustrophobia-inducing tiny cabin with little heat. And certainly not waking to the wonderful scent of frying bacon at that awful prison.

Her memory of the events came back to her in a rush. What surprised her the most was that she'd slept. It had been so long that she hadn't been allowed to sleep through the night without being awakened as part of the brainwashing treatment. Or when the sisters had come to take her breast milk for the baby. She knew the only reason, other than exhaustion, she'd slept last night was knowing that she was safe. If Colt hadn't been there, though...

She refused to think about that as she got up. Her escape had cost her. She hurt all over. The scratches on her face and the sore muscles were painful. But far worse was the ache in her heart. She'd had to leave Grace behind.

Still dressed in the sweatshirt and sweatpants and barefoot, she followed the smell of frying bacon to the kitchen. Colt had music playing and was singing softly to a country music song. She had to smile, remembering how much he'd liked to dance.

That memory brought a rush of heat to her cheeks. She'd told herself that she hadn't been in her right mind that night, but seeing Colt again, she knew that was a lie. He'd liberated that woman from the darkness she'd been living in. He'd brought out a part of her she hadn't known existed.

He seemed to sense her in the doorway and turned, instantly smiling. "I hope you don't mind pancakes again. There was batter left over. I haven't been to the store. But I did find some bacon in the freezer."

"It's making my stomach growl. Is there anything I can do to help?"

"Nope, just bring your appetite." He motioned for her to take a seat. "I made a lot. I don't know about you, but I'm hungry."

She sat down at the table and watched him expertly flip pancakes and load up a plate with bacon.

As he set everything on the table and took a chair, he met her gaze. "How are you feeling?"

"Better. I slept well." For that he couldn't imagine how thankful she was. "On the compound, they would wake me every few hours to chant over me."

"Sounds like brainwashing," Colt said, his jaw tightening.

"Jonas calls it rehabilitation."

He pushed the bacon and pancakes toward her. "Eat while it's hot. We'll deal with everything else once we've eaten."

She looked into his handsome face, remembered being in his arms and felt a flood of guilt. If there was any other way of saving Grace, she wouldn't have involved him in this. But he had been involved since that night in Billings when she'd asked for his help and he hadn't hesitated. He just hadn't known then that what he was getting involved in was more than dangerous.

Once Jonas knew that Colt was the father of her baby... She shuddered at the thought of what she was about to do to this wonderful man.

CHAPTER FOUR

COLT PICKED AT his food. He'd lied about being hungry. Just the smell of it turned his stomach. But he watched Lola wolf down hers as if she hadn't eaten in months. He suspected she hadn't eaten much. She was definitely thinner than she'd been that night in Billings a year ago.

But if anything, she was even more striking, with her pale skin and those incredible eyes. He was glad to see her hair down. It fell in a waterfall of gold down her back. He was reminded again how she'd looked the first time he'd seen her—and when he'd opened the door last night.

"I've been thinking about what we should do first," Colt said as he moved his food around the plate. "We need to start by getting you some clothing that fits," he said as if all they had to worry about was a shopping trip. "Then I think we should go by the sheriff's office."

"There is somewhere we have to go first," she said, looking up from cutting off a bite of pancake dripping with the red syrup. "I know you don't trust me. It's all right. I wouldn't trust me, either. But don't worry, you will." She smiled. She had a slight gap between her two front teeth that made her smile adorable. That and the innocence in her lightly freckled face had sucked him in from the first.

He'd been vulnerable that night. He'd been a broken man and Lola had been more than a temptation. The fact that she'd sworn he was saving her that night hadn't hurt, either.

He thought about the way she'd looked last night when he'd found her on his doorstep. She still had a scratch across one cheek and a cut under her right eye. It made her look like a tomboy.

"You have to admit, the story you told me last night was a little hard to believe."

"I know. That's why you have to let me prove it to you."

He eyed her suspiciously. "And how do you plan to do that?"

"Do you know a doctor in town who can examine me?"

His pulse jumped. "I thought you said—"

"Not for that. Or for my mental proficiency." Her gaze locked with his. "I need you to know that I had a baby three months ago. A doctor should be able to tell." He started to argue, but she stopped him. "This is where we need to start before we go to the sheriff."

He wanted to argue that this wasn't necessary, but they both knew it was. If a doctor said she'd never given birth and none of this was real, then it would be over. No harm done. Except the idea of him and Lola having a baby together would always linger, he realized.

"I used to go to a family doctor here in town. If he's still practicing…"

Dr. Hubert Gray was a large man with a drooping gray mustache and matching bushy eyebrows over piercing blue eyes.

Colt explained what they wanted.

Dr. Gray narrowed his gaze for a moment, taking them both in. "Well, then, why don't you step into the examination room with my nurse, Sara. She'll get you ready while I visit with Colt here."

The moment Lola and Sara left the room, the doctor leaned back in his office chair. "Let me get this straight. You aren't even sure there is a child?"

"Lola says there is. Unfortunately, the baby isn't here."

The doctor nodded. "You realize this won't prove that the child is yours—just that she has given birth before."

Colt nodded. "I know this is unusual."

"Nothing surprises me. By the way, I was sorry to hear about your father. Damn cancer. Only thing that could stop him from ranching."

"Yes, he loved it."

"Tell me about flying helicopters. You know I have my pilot's license, but I've never flown a chopper."

Colt told him what he loved about it. "There is nothing like being able to hover in the air, being able to put it down in places—" he shook his head "—that seem impossible."

"I can tell that you love what you do, but did I hear you're ranching again?"

"Temporarily."

A buzz sounded and Dr. Gray rose. "This shouldn't take long. Sit tight."

True to his word, the doctor returned minutes later. Colt looked up expectantly. "Well?" he asked as Dr. Gray took his seat again behind his desk. Colt realized that his emotions were all over the place. He didn't know what he was hoping to hear.

Did he really want to believe that Lola had given

birth to their child to have it stolen by some crazy cult leader? Wouldn't it be better if Lola had lied for whatever reason after becoming obsessed with him following their one-night stand?

"You wanted to know if she has recently given birth?" the doctor asked.

"Has she?" He held his breath, telling himself even if she had, it didn't mean that any of the rest of it was true.

"Since she gave me permission to provide you with this information, I'd say she gave birth in the past three months."

Just as she'd said. He glanced at the floor, not sure if he was relieved or not. He felt like a heel for having even a glimmer of doubt. But Lola was right. He'd had to know before he went any further with this. It wasn't like he really knew this woman. He'd simply shared one night of intimacy all those months ago.

There was a tap at the door. The nurse stuck her head in to say that the doctor had another patient waiting. Behind the nurse, he saw Lola in the hallway. She looked as if she'd been crying. He quickly rose. "Thank you, Doc," he said over his shoulder as he hurried to Lola, taking both of her hands in his. "I'm sorry. I'm so sorry. You didn't have to do this."

Her smile was sad but sweet as she shook her head. "I just got upset because Dr. Gray is so kind. I wish he'd delivered Grace instead of…" She shook her head. "Not that any of that matters now."

"It's time we went to the sheriff," he said as he led her out of the building. She seemed to hesitate, though, as they reached his pickup. "What?"

"Just that the sheriff isn't going to be able to do anything—and that's if he believes you."

"He'll believe me. I know him," he said as he opened the pickup door for her. "I went to school with his sister Lillie and her twin brother, Darby. Darby's a good friend. Both Lillie and Darby are new parents. As for the sheriff—Flint Cahill is as down-to-earth as anyone I know and I'm sure he's familiar with The Society of Lasting Serenity. Sheriff Cahill is also the only way we can get on church property—and off—without any trouble."

She still looked worried. "You don't know Jonas. He'll be furious that I went to the law. He'll also deny everything."

"We'll see about that." He went around the truck and slid behind the wheel. As he started the engine, he looked over at her and saw how anxious she was. "Lola, the man has taken our daughter, right?" She nodded. "Then I don't give a damn how furious he is, okay?"

"You don't know how he is."

"No, but I'm going to find out. Don't worry. I'm going to get to the bottom of this, one way or the other."

She looked scared, but said, "I trust you with my life. And Grace's."

Grace. Their child. He still couldn't imagine them having a baby together—let alone that some cult leader had her and refused to give her up to her own mother.

Common sense told him there had to be more to the story—and that's what worried him as he drove to the sheriff's department. Sheriff Cahill would sort it out, he told himself. As he'd said, he liked and trusted Flint. Going up to the compound with the levelheaded sheriff made the most sense.

Because if what Lola was telling him was true, they weren't leaving there without Grace.

SHERIFF FLINT CAHILL was a nice-looking man with thick dark hair and gray eyes. He ushered them right into his office, offered them a chair and something to drink. They took chairs, but declined a beverage.

"So what is this about?" the sheriff asked after they were all seated, the office door closed behind them.

Colt could see that Lola liked the sheriff from the moment she met him. There was something about him that exuded confidence, as well as honesty and integrity. She told him everything she had Colt. When she finished, though, Colt couldn't tell from Flint's expression what he was thinking.

The sheriff looked at him, his gray eyes narrowing. "I'm assuming you wouldn't have brought Ms. Dayton here if you didn't believe her story."

"I know this is unusual." He glanced over at her. Her scrapes and scratches were healing, and she looked good in the clothes they'd bought her. Still, he saw that she kept rubbing her hand on her thighs as if not believing she was back in denim.

At the store, he'd wanted to buy her more clothing, but she'd insisted she didn't need more than a couple pairs of jeans, two shirts, several undergarments and hiking shoes and socks. She'd promised to pay him back once she could get to her own money. Jonas had taken her purse with her cash and credit cards. Her money was in a California bank account. Once she had Grace, she said she would see about getting money wired up to her so she could pay him back.

Colt wasn't about to take her money, but he hadn't argued. The one thing he'd learned quickly about Lola was that she didn't expect or want anything from him—except help getting her baby from Jonas. That, she'd said, would be more than enough since it could get them both killed.

At the time, he'd thought she was exaggerating. Now he wasn't so sure.

"I believe her," Colt told the sheriff. "What do you know about The Society of Lasting Serenity?"

"Just that they were California based but moved up here about five years ago. They keep to themselves. I believe their numbers have dropped some. Probably our Montana winters."

"You're having trouble believing that Jonas Emanuel would steal Lola's child," Colt said.

Flint sighed. "No offense but, yes, I am." He turned to Lola. "You say your only connection to the group was through your parents before their deaths and your return to the States?"

"Yes, they became involved after I left for college. I thought it was a passing phase, a sign of them not being able to accept their only child had left the nest."

"You never visited them at the California compound?" the sheriff asked.

"No, I got a teaching job right out of college in the Virgin Islands."

Flint frowned. "You didn't visit your parents before you left?"

Lola looked away. "By then we were…estranged. I didn't agree with some of the things they were being taught in what I felt was a fringe cult."

"So why would your parents promise you to Jonas Emanuel?" the sheriff asked.

She let out a bitter laugh. "To *save* me. My mother believed that I needed Jonas's teaching. Otherwise, I was doomed to live a wasted life chasing foolish dreams and, of course, ending up with the wrong man."

"They wanted you to marry Jonas." Flint frowned. "Isn't he a little old for you?"

"He's fifty-two. I'm thirty-two. So it's not unheard-of."

The sheriff looked over at Colt, who was going to be thirty-three soon. Young for a major in the Army, he knew.

"I doubt my parents took age into consideration," Lola said. "One of the teachings at the SLS is that everyone is ageless. My parents, like the other members, were brainwashed."

"So you went to the compound after you were notified that your parents had died," the sheriff said.

"I questioned them both dying especially since earlier I'd received a letter from my father saying he wanted out but was having a hard time convincing my mother to leave SLS," she said. "Also I wanted to have them buried together in California, next to my older sister, who was stillborn. My parents were both in their forties when they had me. By then, they didn't believe they would ever conceive again."

"So you had their bodies—"

"Jonas refused to release them. He said they would be buried as they had wished—on the side of the mountain at the compound. I went up there determined to find out how it was that they had died within hours of each other. I also wanted to make him understand that I would get a lawyer if I had to—or go to the authorities."

"That's when you learned that you'd been promised to him?" the sheriff asked.

"Yes, as ridiculous as it sounds. When I refused, I

was held there against my will until I managed to get away. I'd stolen aboard a van driven by two of the sisters, as they call them. That's when I met Colt."

"Why didn't you go to the police then?" Flint asked.

"I planned to the next morning. I'd gone into the back of the hotel when I saw one of the sisters coming in the front. I ducked down a hallway and literally collided with Colt. I asked for his help and he sneaked me up to his room."

The sheriff looked at Colt. "And the two of you hit it off. She didn't tell you what she was running from?"

"No, but it was clear she was scared. I thought it was an old boyfriend."

Flint nodded and looked to Lola again. "You didn't trust him enough to ask for his help the next morning?"

"I didn't want to involve him. By then I knew what Jonas was capable of. This flock does whatever he tells them. The few who disobey are punished. One woman brought me extra food. I heard her being beaten the next morning by her own so-called sisters. When I had my daughter, they took her away almost at once. I could hear her crying, but I didn't get to see her again. The women would come in and take my breast milk, but they said she was now Jonas's child. He called her his angel. I knew I had only one choice. Escape and try to find Colt. I couldn't fight Jonas and his followers alone. And Jonas made it clear. The only way I could see my baby and be with her was if I married him and gave my life to The Society of Lasting Serenity."

Flint pushed back his chair and rose to his feet. "I think it's time I visited the compound and met this Jonas Emanuel."

CHAPTER FIVE

COLT FOLLOWED THE sheriff's SUV out of town toward the Judith Mountains. The mountains began just east of town and rose to the northeast for twenty miles. In most places they were only about ten miles wide with low peaks broken by stream drainages. But there were a number of peaks including the highest one, Judith Peak, at more than six thousand feet.

It was rugged country. Back in the 1950s the US Air Force had operated a radar station on top of the peak. The SLS had bought state land on an adjacent mountaintop in an isolated area with few roads in or out. Because it was considered a church, the SLS had rights that even the sheriff couldn't do anything about.

So Colt was nervous enough, but nothing compared to Lola. In the pickup seat next to him, he could feel her getting more agitated the closer they got to the SLS compound. He reached over to take her hand. It was ice-cold.

"It's going to be all right," he tried to assure her—and himself. If what she'd told him was true, then Jonas would have to hand over the baby. "Jonas will cooperate with a lawman."

She didn't look any more convinced than he felt. He'd dealt with religious fanatics for a while now and knew that nothing could stop them if they thought they were in the right.

"Jonas seems so nice, so truthful, so caring," she said. "He's fooled so many people. My parents weren't stupid. He caught them in his web with his talk of a better world." She shook her head. "But he is pure evil. I hate to even think what he might have done to my parents."

"You really think he killed them."

"Or convinced my mother to kill herself and my father."

Colt knew that wouldn't be a first when it came to cult mania.

"Clearly the sheriff wasn't called when they died. Jonas runs SLS like it's his own private country. He told me that his religious philosophy requires the bodies to be untouched and put into the ground quickly. Apparently in Montana, a religious group can bury a body on their property without embalming if it is done within so many hours."

The road climbed higher up the mountain. Ahead, the sheriff slowed. Colt could see that an iron gate blocked them from going any farther. Flint stopped, put down his window and pushed a button on what appeared to be an intercom next to the gate. Colt whirred down his window. He heard a tinny-sounding voice tell him that someone would be right down to let them in.

A few minutes later, an older man drove up in a Jeep. He spoke for a few moments with the sheriff before opening the gate. As Colt drove through, he felt the man's steely gaze on him. Clearly the SLS didn't like visitors. The man who'd opened the gate was wearing a gun under his jacket. Colt had caught sight of the butt end of it when the man got out of his rig to open the gate.

As they passed, he noticed something else interesting. The man recognized Lola. Just the sight of her made the man nervous.

LOLA FELT HER body begin to vibrate inside. She thought she might throw up. The memories of being imprisoned here for so long made her itch. She fought the need to claw her skin, remembering the horrible feel of the cheap cloth dresses she was forced to wear, the taste of the tea the sisters forced down her throat, the horrible chanting that nearly drove her insane. That wasn't all they'd forced on her once they'd quit coming for her breast milk. There'd been the pills that Sister Rebecca had forced down her throat.

She felt a shiver and hugged herself against the memories, telling herself she was safe with Colt and the sheriff. But the closer they got to the compound, the more plagued she was with fear. She doubted either Colt or the sheriff knew who they were dealing with. Jonas had gotten this far in life by fooling people. He was an expert at it. At the thought of what lies he would tell, her blood ran cold even though the pickup cab felt unbearably hot.

"Are you all right?" Colt asked, sounding worried as he glanced over at her.

She nodded and felt a bead of perspiration run down between her shoulder blades. She wanted to scratch her arm, feeling as if something was crawling across it, but feared once she started she wouldn't be able to stop.

Just driving up here brought everything back, as if all the crazy they'd been feeding her might finally sink in and she'd be a zombie like the other "sisters." Isn't that what Jonas had hoped? Wasn't that why he was just waiting for her return? He knew she'd be back for Grace. She couldn't bear to think what he had planned for her.

By the time they reached the headquarters and main building of the SLS, there was a welcome group waiting for them. Lola recognized Sister Rebecca, the woman Jonas got to do most of his dirty work. Sister Amelia was there, as well, but she kept her head down as if unable to look at her.

Lola felt bad that she'd gotten the woman in trouble. She could still hear Amelia's cries from the beating she'd received for giving her extra food. She could well imagine what had happened to the guards after she'd escaped. Jonas would know that she hadn't been taking her pills with the tea. Sister Amelia would be blamed, but there had been nothing Lola could do about that.

Flint parked his patrol SUV in front of the main building. Colt parked next to him. Lola felt her body refuse to move as Colt opened his door. She stared at the two women standing like sentinels in front of them and fought to take her next breath.

"Would you feel better staying out here in the truck?" Colt asked.

She wiped perspiration from her lip with the back of her hand. How could she possibly explain what it was like being back here, knowing what they had done to her, what they might do again if Colt didn't believe her and help her?

Terrified of facing Jonas again, she thought of her baby girl and reached for her door handle.

COLT WONDERED IF bringing Lola back here wasn't a mistake. She looked terrified one moment and like a sleepwalker the next. What had they done to her? He couldn't even imagine, given what she'd told him about her treatment. They'd taken her baby, kept her locked up, hadn't let her sleep. He worried that was just the tip of the iceberg, though.

One of the two women, who were dressed in long simple white sheaths with their hair in braided buns, stepped forward to greet them.

"I'm Sister Rebecca. How may we help you?" Appearing to be the older of the two, the woman's face had a blankness to it that some might have taken for serenity. But there was something else in the eyes. A wariness. A hardness.

"We're here to see Jonas Emanuel," the sheriff said.

"Let me see if he's available," she said, and turned to go back inside.

Colt started to say something about Jonas making himself available, but Flint stopped him. "Let's keep this as civilized as we can—at least to start."

The second woman stood at the foot of the porch steps, her fingers entwined and her face down, clearly standing guard.

A few moments later, Sister Rebecca came out again. "Brother Emanuel will see you now." She motioned them up the porch steps as the other woman drifted off toward a building in the pines where some women were washing clothes and hanging them on a string of clotheslines.

"Seems awfully cold to be hanging wash outside this time of year," Colt commented. Spring in Montana often meant the temperature never rose over forty in the mountains.

Sister Rebecca smiled as if amused. "We believe

in hard work. It toughens a person up so a little cold weather doesn't bother us."

He thought about saying something about how she wasn't the one hanging clothes today in the cool weather on the mountaintop, but he followed the sheriff's lead and kept his mouth shut.

As Sister Rebecca led them toward the back of the huge building, Colt noticed the layout. In this communal living part of the structure, straight-backed wooden chairs were lined up like soldiers at long wooden tables. Behind the dining area, he could hear kitchen workers and the banging of pots and pans. An aroma arose that reminded him of school cafeterias.

What struck him was the lack of conversation coming from the kitchen, let alone any music. There was a utilitarian feeling about the building and everything in it—the workers included. They could have been robots for the lack of liveliness in the place.

Sister Rebecca tapped at a large wooden door. A cheerful voice on the other side said, "Come in." She opened the door and stood back to let them enter a room that was warm and cozy compared to the other part of the building.

A sandy-haired man, who Colt knew was fifty-two, had been sitting behind a large oak desk. But now he pushed back his office chair and rose, surprising Colt by not just his size, but how fit he was. He had boyish good looks, lively pale blue eyes and a wide, straight-toothed smile. He looked much younger than his age.

The leader came around his desk to shake hands with the sheriff and Colt. "Jonas Emanuel," he said. "Welcome." His gaze slid to Lola. When he spoke her name it was with obvious affection. "Lola," Jonas said, looking pained to see her scratched face before returning his gaze to Colt and the sheriff.

"We need to ask you a few questions," Sheriff Cahill said, introducing himself and Colt. "You already know Ms. Dayton."

"Please have a seat," Jonas said graciously, offering them one of the chairs circled around the warm blaze going in the rock fireplace to one side of the office area. Colt thought again of the women hanging wet clothes outside. "Can I get you anything to drink?"

They all declined. Jonas took a chair so he was facing them and crossed his legs to hold one knee in his hands. Colt noticed that he was limping before he sat down.

"How long have you known Ms. Dayton?" Flint asked.

"Her parents were founding members. Lola's been a member for the past couple of years," Jonas said.

"That's not true," she cried. "You know I'm not a member, would never be a member."

Colt could see that she was even more agitated than she'd been in the truck on the way up. She sat on the edge of her chair and looked ready to run again. "Just give me my baby," she said, her voice breaking. "I want to see my baby." She turned in her chair. Sister Rebecca stood at the door, fingers entwined, head down, standing sentry. "My baby. Tell her to get my baby."

Colt reached over and took her hand. Jonas noticed but said nothing.

"As you can see, Ms. Dayton is quite upset. She claims that you are holding her child here on the property," the sheriff said.

Jonas nodded without looking at Lola. "Perhaps we

should speak in private. Lola? Why don't you go with Sister Rebecca? She can make you some tea."

"I don't want any of your so-called tea," Lola snapped. "I want my child."

"It's all right," Flint said. "Go ahead and leave with her. We need to talk to Jonas. We won't be long."

Lola looked as if she might argue, but when her gaze fell on Colt, he nodded, indicating that she should leave. "I'll be right here if you need me." Again he could feel Jonas's gaze on him.

After Sister Rebecca left with Lola, the leader sighed deeply. "I'm afraid Lola is a very troubled woman. I'm not sure what she's told you—"

"That you're keeping her baby from her," Colt said.

He nodded sadly. "Lola came to us after her parents died. She'd lost her teaching job, been fired. That loss and the loss of her parents… We tried to help her since she had no one else. I'm sure she's told you that her parents were important members of our community here. On her mother's death bed, she made me promise that I would look after Lola."

"She didn't promise Lola to you as your wife?" Colt asked, and got a disapproving look from the sheriff.

"Of course not." Jonas looked shocked by the accusation. "I had hoped Lola would stay with us. Her parents took so much peace in living among us, but Lola left."

"I understand she ran away some months ago," Flint said.

"A year ago," Colt added.

Again Jonas looked surprised. "Is that what she told you?" He shook his head. "I foolishly suggested that maybe time away from the compound would be good for her. Several of the sisters were making a trip to Billings for supplies. I talked Lola into going along. Once there, though, she apparently became turned around while shopping and got lost. In her state of mind, that was very traumatic. Fortunately, the sisters found her, but not until the next morning. She was confused and hysterical. They brought her back here where we nursed her back to health and discovered that while she'd been lost in Billings, she'd been assaulted."

Colt started to object, but the sheriff cut him off. "She was pregnant? Did she say who the father was?"

Jonas shook his head. "She didn't seem to know." The man looked right at Colt, his blue eyes giving nothing away.

"Where is the baby now?" Flint asked.

"I'm afraid the infant was stillborn. A little boy. Which made it all the more traumatic and heartbreaking for her since we all knew that she had her heart set on having a baby girl. I'm not sure if you know this, but her mother had a daughter before Lola who was stillborn. I'm sure that could have played a part in what happened. When Lola was told that her own child had been stillborn, she had a complete breakdown and became convinced that we had stolen her daughter."

"Then you won't mind if we have a look around," the sheriff said.

"Not at all." He rose to his feet, and the sheriff and Colt followed. "I'm so glad Lola's been found. We've been taking care of her since her breakdown. Unfortunately, the other night she overpowered one of her sisters and, hysterical again, took off running into the woods. We looked for her for hours. I was going to call your office if we didn't hear from her by this afternoon. When she left, she forgot her pills. I was afraid she'd have another psychotic event with no one there to help her."

"Don't you mean when Lola *escaped* here?" Colt asked.

Jonas shook his head as if trying to be patient. "Escaped?" He chuckled. "Do you see razor wire fences around the compound? Why would she need to escape? We believe in free will here at Serenity. Lola can come and go as she pleases. She knows that. But when she's in one of her states…"

"What kind of medication is she on?" the sheriff asked.

"I have it right here," Jonas reached into his pocket. "I had Sister Rebecca bring it to me when I heard that you were at the gate. I was so glad that she had come back for it. I believe Dr. Reese said it's what they give patients with schizophrenia. I suppose she didn't mention to you that she'd been taking the medication. It helps with the anxiety attacks, as well as the hallucinations."

"Dr. Reese?" Flint asked.

"Ben Reese. He's our local physician, one of the best in the country and one of our members," Jonas said.

"I'd like to see where the baby was buried," Colt said.

"Of course. But let's start with the tour the sheriff requested."

Colt memorized the layout of the buildings as Jonas led them from building to building. Everywhere they went, there were people working, both men and women, but definitely there were more women on the compound than men. He saw no women with babies as most of the women were older.

"Our cemetery is just down here," Jonas said. Colt followed Jonas and the sheriff down a narrow dirt path that wound through the trees to open in a meadow. Wooden crosses marked the few graves, the names of the deceased printed on metal plaques.

He spotted a relatively fresh grave and felt his heart drop. It was a small plot of dark earth. What if Jonas was telling the truth? What if Lola had had a son? *His* son? And the infant was buried under that cold ground?

"It is always so difficult to lose a child," Jonas was saying. "We buried him next to Lola's parents. We thought that would give her comfort. If not now, later when she's…better. We're waiting for her to name him before we put up the cross."

"I think I've seen enough," Sheriff Cahill said, and looked at Colt.

Colt didn't know what to think. On the surface, it all seemed so…reasonable.

"Sister Rebecca took Lola to the kitchen," Jonas said. "Lunch will be ready soon. I believe we're having a nice vegetable soup today. You're welcome to join us. Some of the sisters are better cooks than others. I can attest that the ones cooking today are our best."

"Thank you, but I need to get back to Gilt Edge," Flint said. "What about you, Colt?"

He knew the sheriff wasn't asking just about lunch or returning to town. "I'll see what Lola wants to do," he said, after taking a last look at the small unmarked grave before heading back toward the main building.

"If Lola is determined not to stay with us, I just hope she'll get the help she needs," Colt heard Jonas tell the sheriff. "I'm worried about her, especially after your visit. Clearly she isn't herself."

LOLA SHOVED AWAY the cup of tea Sister Rebecca had tried to get her to drink. She'd seen Colt and the sheriff go out to search the complex with Jonas. "I know you hid her the moment the sheriff punched the intercom at the gate. Please…" Her voice broke. "I just want to see her so I know she's all right."

Sister Rebecca reached over to pat her hand—and shove the tea closer with her other hand.

Lola jerked her hand back. "You can't keep her. She's mine." Tears burned her eyes. "Keeping a baby from her mother…"

"You aren't taking your medication, are you? It makes you like this. You really should take it so you're more calm."

"Brain-dead, you mean. Half-comatose, so I'm easy to manipulate. If you keep me drugged up, I won't cause any trouble, right?"

"You wouldn't have left here if you'd been taking your medication." Sister Rebecca shook her head. "You know we were only trying to help you. I should have been the one giving you your medication instead of Sister Amelia. She let you get away with not taking it and look what's happened to you, you poor dear."

Lola scoffed. "As if you care. And Sister Amelia didn't know anything about what I was doing," she said quickly, fearing that the next beating Amelia got could kill her. "I was hiding them under my tongue until she turned away."

The woman nodded. "Well, should you end up staying here, we won't let that happen again, will we."

"I'm not staying here."

Sister Rebecca said nothing as the front door opened and Colt came in. Through the open doorway, Lola could see Jonas and the sheriff standing out by the patrol SUV. She could tell that Jonas had convinced the sheriff that she was crazy.

Standing up too quickly, Lola knocked over her chair. It clattered to the floor. Dizzy, she had to hang on to the table for a moment. When the light-headedness passed and she could let go, she started for the door. But not before she realized Colt had seen her having trouble standing.

She swept past him, determined not to let the sheriff leave. Her baby was hidden somewhere in the complex. Jonas had had one of his followers hide her. The sheriff had to find her. Lola had to convince him—

At the sound of a baby crying, she stumbled to an abrupt stop. "Do you hear that?" she called down to the sheriff from the top of the porch steps. "It's my baby crying." He looked up in surprise. So did Jonas. Both seemed to stop to listen.

For a moment, Lola thought that she had imagined it. Fear curdled her stomach. She felt Colt's hand on her shoulder as he reached for her. She could see that they believed Jonas. Her eyes filled with tears of frustration and pain.

And then she heard it again. A baby began to squall loudly. The sound was coming from the laundry. She shrugged off Colt's hand and ran down the steps. Jonas reached for her, but she managed to sweep past him. Grace. It was her baby crying for her. She knew that cry. She'd heard it in the middle of the night when the sisters had come for her breast milk. Somehow Grace had known she was here.

"Lola, don't," Jonas called after her. "Sister Rebecca, help Lola. She's going to hurt herself."

She could hear running footsteps behind her, but she was almost to the laundry-room door. Sister Rebecca had set off an alarm. As Lola burst into the room, a half dozen women were already looking in her direction. Lola paid them no mind. She ran toward the woman holding the baby.

Inside this room with the washers and dryers going, though she could barely hear the baby crying, all Lola could think about was getting to the woman before they hid Grace away again. Reaching the woman, she heard the infant let out a fresh squall as if the mother had pinched the poor thing.

Lola grabbed for the baby, but the woman swung around so all she got was a handful of dress cloth from the woman's shoulder.

"Lola, stop." It was the sheriff's voice as he stepped between her and the woman with the child. "May I see your baby?" he said to the woman.

CHAPTER SIX

COLT WATCHED THE woman with the infant look at Jonas standing in the doorway. The leader nodded that she should let the sheriff look. Colt held his breath as the woman turned so they could see the baby she held. The infant had stopped crying and now looked at them with big blue eyes fringed with tear-jeweled lashes.

"Grace?" Lola whispered as she tried to see the baby.

"May I?" the sheriff asked, and held out his arms.

After getting Jonas's permission, the woman released the baby to Flint. He carefully pulled back the knitted blanket the infant was wrapped in. Colt found himself holding his breath.

The sheriff peeked under the gown the baby wore. Colt knew he was looking for the small heart-shaped birthmark that Lola had told him about. He checked under the baby's diaper. His shoulders fell a little as he looked up at Lola and shook his head. "It's a little boy."

"No," Lola cried. "I heard my baby. This isn't the baby I heard crying. It can't be. Sister Rebecca pulled the alarm. She warned them to hide my baby." She looked from the sheriff to Colt and back again before bursting into tears.

Colt stepped to her and pulled her into his arms. She cried against his chest as he looked past her to the sheriff. He'd watched the whole thing play out, holding his breath. The baby the sheriff had taken from the woman was adorable and about the right age. Was it possible Lola was wrong about the sex of the infant she'd given birth to? Maybe the baby hadn't died.

But Lola had been so sure it was a little girl. She'd convinced him. And there was the tiny heart birthmark that Lola had seen on their daughter. But what if she was wrong and Jonas was telling the truth about all of it?

Now he felt sick. He thought of the small grave next to Lola's parents'. He felt such a sense of loss that it made him ache inside. He pulled Lola tighter to him, feeling her heart breaking along with his own.

As the sheriff spoke again with Jonas, Colt led Lola out of the laundry and down the path toward his pickup.

"I heard her," she said between sobs. "The first baby I heard. It was Grace. I know her cry. A mother knows her baby's cry. Sister Rebecca pulled the alarm to warn them so they could hide her again." She began to cry again as he led her to the truck and opened the passenger-side door for her. "Please, Colt, we can't leave without our baby."

He tried to think of what to say, but his throat had closed with all the emotions he was feeling, an incredible sense of loss and regret. It broke his heart to see Lola like this.

Lola met his gaze with a look that felt like an arrow to his chest before she climbed into the pickup. As he closed the passenger-side door, the sheriff walked over. "You all right?" Flint asked.

All Colt could do was nod. He wasn't sure he would ever be all right.

"I think we're done here," the sheriff said. "If you want to take it further..."

He shook his head. "Thanks for your help," he managed to get out before walking around to the driver's side of his pickup. As he slid behind the wheel, he saw that Lola had dried her tears and was now sitting ramrod straight in her seat with that same look of surrender that tore at him.

He started the engine, unable to look at her.

"You don't believe me. You believe…" She stopped and he looked over at her. She was staring straight ahead. He followed her gaze to where Jonas was standing on the porch of the main building. There was both sympathy and pity in the man's gaze. "He's lying." But Lola said it with little conviction as Colt started the pickup and headed off the compound.

LOLA CLOSED HER eyes and leaned back against the pickup as they headed down the mountain road. What had she expected? That Jonas would just hand over Grace? She'd been such a fool. Worse, she feared that they'd made things worse for Grace—not to mention the way Colt had looked at her. Leaving them alone with Jonas had been the wrong thing to do. She knew what that man was like. Of course the sheriff would believe anything the leader told him. But Colt?

"What did Jonas tell you?" She had to ask as she squeezed her eyes shut tighter, unable to look at him. "That I'm crazy?"

"He said your baby died. That it was a little boy. He showed me the grave."

She let out a muffled cry and opened her eyes. Staring straight ahead at the narrow dirt road that wound down the mountain, she said, "Is that what convinced you I was lying?"

"Why didn't you tell me you were on prescription medication?" Colt asked.

She let out a bark of a laugh. "Of course, my *medication*. What did he tell you it was for?"

"He hinted it was for schizophrenia and that after your breakdown—"

"Right—my breakdown. What else?"

He glanced over at her. "He said you were fired from your teaching job."

Tears blurred her eyes. She bit her lower lip and drew blood. "That at least is true. I resisted the advances of the school principal. When some materials in my classroom went missing, I was fired. Three days later, I heard that my parents had died. Perfect timing," she said sarcastically. "I'm not a thief. I wouldn't give in, so she did what she said she would, she fired me, claiming I stole the materials. It was my word against hers—even though it wasn't the first time something like that had happened involving her. I had planned to fight it once I took care of getting my parents remains returned to the California cemetery. So what else did Jonas tell you about me?"

"That you're a troubled young woman."

"I am that," she agreed. "Given everything that has been done to me, I think that is understandable." Ahead she could see Brother Elmer waiting at the gate for them. Elmer was her father's age. When she'd first arrived at the compound, she'd asked him what had happened to her parents and Elmer had been too terrified to talk to her. She'd only had that one opportunity. Since then Elmer had kept his distance—just like the rest of them.

"Stop up here, please," Lola said, even though the gate was standing open.

Colt said nothing and did as she asked.

She put down the truck window as Colt pulled alongside the man. Elmer met her gaze for a moment before he dropped his head and stared at his feet. "Elmer, you know I'm not crazy. Help me, please," she pleaded. "You were my father's friend. Tell this man the truth about what really goes on back there in the compound."

Elmer continued to focus on the ground.

"Okay, just tell me this," she said, her voice cracking with emotion. "Is Grace all right? Are they taking good care of her?" She didn't expect an answer. She knew the cost of going against Jonas. Everyone did. If she was right and Jonas had had her parents killed…

Elmer raised his head slowly. As he did, he grabbed hold of the side of the truck, curling his fingers over the open window frame. His fingers brushed her arm. His gaze rose to meet hers. He gave one quick nod and removed his hands.

"You should move on now so I can close this gate, Sister Lola."

COLT BLINKED, TELLING himself he hadn't just seen that. His heart beat like a war drum. He swore under his breath. He'd seen the man's short, quick nod. He'd seen the compassion in Elmer's eyes.

Jonas Emanuel was a liar.

Colt wasn't sure who he was more angry with, Jonas or himself. He'd bought into the man's bull. He'd *believed* him. But the man had been damned convincing. The grave. The pills. The crying baby that wasn't Grace.

Shifting the pickup into gear, he felt as if he'd been punched in the gut numerous times. He kept seeing that tiny grave, kept imagining his son, their son, lying in a homemade coffin under it—just as he kept seeing Lola sobbing hysterically in his arms after hearing what she thought was her baby crying.

"Lola."

"Please, just leave me alone," she said as she closed her window and tucked herself into the corner of the pickup seat as he pulled away, the gate closing behind him. When he looked over at her a few miles down the road, he saw that anger and frustration had given way to emotional exhaustion. With the sun streaming in the window, she'd fallen asleep.

Colt was thankful for the time alone. He replayed everything Lola had said, along with what Jonas had told him. He hadn't known what to believe because the man was that persuasive. Jonas had convinced the sheriff—and Flint Cahill was a shrewd lawman.

But as he looked over at the woman sleeping in his pickup, he felt his heart ache in ways he'd never experienced before. He would slay dragons for this woman. He wanted to turn around and go back and...

He couldn't let his emotions get the best of him. He never had before. But this woman had drawn him from the moment he'd met her. He thought about the fear he'd seen in her eyes that first night. There'd been no confusion, though. If anything, they'd both wanted to escape from the world that night and lose themselves in each other. And they had. He remembered her naked in his arms and felt a pull stronger than gravity.

Would he have believed her if she'd told him on that first night what was going on? Probably not. Look how easily he'd let Jonas fool him. Colt was still furious with himself. He would never again question anything she told him.

Glancing in the rearview mirror, he wasn't surprised

to see that they were being followed. Everything she'd told him had been true.

So where was the child he and Lola had conceived? He couldn't bear the thought of Grace being in Jonas's hands. But he also knew that they couldn't go back there until they had a plan.

As he slowed on the outskirts of Gilt Edge, Lola stirred. She shot him a glance as she sat up.

"Before we go back to the ranch, I thought we'd get something to eat," he said, keeping his eye on the large dark SUV a couple of car lengths behind them.

"There is no reason to take me back to the ranch. You can just pull over anywhere and let me out."

"I'm not going to do that."

"I can understand why you don't want to help me, but I'm not leaving town until—"

"You get Grace back."

She stared at him. "Are you mocking me?"

"Not at all," he said, and looked over at her. "I'm sorry. I should have believed you. But I do now."

Tears welled in her eyes and spilled down her cheeks. "You believe me about Grace?"

"I do. I saw that armed guard who let us through the gate. I saw him nod when you asked him about Grace."

She wiped at her tears. "Is that what changed your mind?"

"That and a lot of other things, once I had time to think about it. That first night, you were scared and running from something, but you weren't confused. Nor do I think you were confused the next morning. You checked my wallet to see who I was. You considered taking the four hundred dollars in it, but decided not to.

Those were not the actions of a troubled, mentally unstable woman. Also, we're being followed."

Lola glanced in her side mirror. "How long has that
vehicle been back there?"

"Since we left the compound."

She seemed to consider that. "Why follow us? If they
wanted to know where you lived…"

"I think they are more interested in you than me,
but I guess we'll find out soon enough. That's the other
thing that made me believe you once I was away from
Jonas's hocus-pocus disappearing-baby act. I saw guards
armed with concealed weapons around the perimeter of
the compound. While there might not be any razor wire
and a high fence, that place is secure as Fort Knox."

"So how are we going to find Grace and get her out
of there?"

"I don't know. I haven't worked that out yet."

She looked at him as if afraid of this change in his
attitude. "The sheriff believes Jonas."

"I don't blame Flint. Jonas is quite convincing. He
certainly had me going."

Lola let out a bitter laugh. "How do you think he got
so many people to follow him to Montana? To give him
all their money, to convince them that to find peace,
they needed to give up everything—especially their
minds and free will."

"Why wasn't he able to brainwash you?" he asked as
he glanced in the rearview mirror. Their tail was still
back there.

"I don't know. The meditation, the chanting, the af-
firmations on the path to peace and happiness? I blocked
them out, thinking about anything else. Also, I didn't
buy into any of it. I was surprised my father did. It's

one reason I didn't see them for so many years. My father wrote me and I spoke with my mother some on the phone, but there was no way I was going to visit them on the compound and they never left except to move to Montana with SLS."

"How was it your father was one of the founding members if it wasn't like him to buy into Jonas's propaganda?"

"My father would have done anything to make my mother happy. That's why he didn't leave after he quit believing in Jonas. He wouldn't have left her there alone. I'm sure he finally saw what my mother couldn't. That Jonas was a fraud. I feel terrible for those lost years."

"The man at the gate…"

"Elmer? He and my father were friends. It's possible that, like my father, he has doubts about SLS and Jonas. Also, not everyone is easily brainwashed into believing everything Jonas says. They might believe he has a right to my child because he says so. But that doesn't mean some aren't sympathetic to a mother losing her baby, our baby, to Jonas."

"I still don't understand how Jonas thinks he can get away with this."

"Because he has."

He glanced over at her, seeing that she was right. Jonas did rule that compound like it was his own country, and because his society was considered a church, he was protected.

"He has Grace," she said. "He knows I can't live without her. Except he's wrong if he thinks I'll let him keep my child, let alone that I would ever be his wife."

Colt glanced over at her. "So he knows we'll be back."

CHAPTER SEVEN

LOLA LOOKED OUT the side window as the road skirted Gilt Edge. Her heart beat so loudly that she thought for sure Colt would be able to hear it. Tears stung her eyes, but this time they were tears of relief.

Colt believed her.

The liberation made her weak. She'd seen his face earlier in the laundry when the baby had turned out not to be hers. She'd seen the heart-wrenching sympathy in his gaze, as well as the pain. He'd been so sure at the moment that she was everything Jonas had told him. A mentally unstable woman who couldn't accept the death of the baby she'd carried for nine months. *His* baby.

But Colt had seen the truth. He'd seen Elmer's slight nod, and when he looked at everything, he knew she was telling the truth.

She wiped at her tears, determined not to give in to the need to cry her heart out. They still didn't have Grace. Her stomach ached with a need to hold her baby. Jonas had Grace and that alone terrified her. Would he hurt the baby to get back at her?

No. He'd fooled the sheriff. He would feel safe and superior. He would simply wait, knowing, as Colt said, that they'd be back. Or at least she would. Jonas thought he'd fooled Colt, too.

She tried to assure herself that Jonas wouldn't hurt

Grace just to spite her. The baby was his only hope of getting Lola back to the compound. She'd looked into Jonas's eyes as they'd left. He hadn't given up on her being his wife. He would need Grace if he had any hope of making that happen.

At least that must be his thinking, she told herself. It would be a cold day in hell before she would ever succumb to the man. And only then so she could get close enough to kill him.

"Do you think Jonas knows I'm Grace's father?" Colt asked, dragging her out of her dark thoughts. "He looked me right in the eye and told me that you swore you didn't know who the father was."

"I did. I was afraid he'd come after you. Or send some of his men to hurt you—if not kill you. He was quite upset to realize I was pregnant. I told him I didn't know your name. You were just someone who'd helped me."

"Helped himself to you. Isn't that what Jonas thought?"

She shrugged. "He was so angry with me. I'm not sure when he decided he wanted my baby. Our baby."

"Well, he can't have her."

"We will get her back, won't we?"

He reached over and took her hand.

"I mean, if you dig up the grave and prove that—"

"Lola, that would take time and be very iffy. First off, that is probably what Jonas is expecting us to do. Second, even if we had proof that your baby didn't die, I'm not sure we could get a judge to send up an army to search the place for Grace."

"Then what do we do?" She felt close to tears again.

"The problem is that it is hard for the authorities to get involved in these types of pseudo-religious groups,

especially when, according to Jonas, you're a member—
and so were your parents. It's your word against Jonas's.
So I'm afraid we're on our own. But that's not a bad
thing." He smiled at her. "I'll do everything in my power
and then some to bring Grace home to you."

She smiled and squeezed his hand, knowing that she
could depend on Colt.

COLT PULLED UP in front of the Stagecoach Saloon on
the outskirts of Gilt Edge. The large dark SUV that
had been following them drove on past. He tried to see
the driver, but the windows were tinted too dark. The
license plate was covered with mud, no accident either,
he figured.

But it didn't matter. He knew exactly where it had
come from.

"The sheriff's brother and sister own this place," Colt
said as he parked and turned off the engine. "They serve
some of the best food in the area. I thought we'd have
something to eat and talk. It shouldn't be that busy this
time of the day."

Lola's stomach growled in answer, making him smile.
"I thought I would never eat after Grace was taken from
me. But soon I realized that I needed my strength if I
had any hope of getting her back. Not that I was given
much food on the compound."

They got out, Lola slowing to admire the place. "I
love this stone building."

"It was one of the original stagecoach stops along
here. Lillie Cahill bought it with her brother Darby, to
preserve it." He pushed open the door and Lola stepped
in.

"Something smells wonderful," she whispered to Colt

as they made their way to an out-of-the-way table by the window. All this time eating nothing but the swill that had come out of the compound kitchen had left her ravenous.

There were a few regulars at the bar but other than that, the place was empty. A man who resembled the sheriff came over to take their orders. He had Flint's dark hair and gray eyes and was equally good-looking. "Major McCloud," the young man said, grinning at Colt.

"Just Colt, thank you."

"I heard you were back. Welcome home. Again, so sorry about your father."

"Thanks, Darby." All of the Cahills had been at the funeral. Colt's father would have liked that. He'd always respected their father, Ely Cahill, even though a lot of people in this town considered him a nut. "This is my friend Lola."

Darby turned to Lola and said, "Nice to meet you."

"Congrats on the marriage and fatherhood. How's your family?" Colt asked, since that's what small-town people did. Everyone knew everyone else. He was sure Darby had heard about Julia and Wyatt since they'd all gone to school together.

"Fine. Lillie's married and now has a son, TC. She married Trask Beaumont. If you're sticking around for a while, you'll have to meet Mariah and my son, Daniel. Don't know if Flint mentioned it, but his wife, Maggie… Yep. Expecting."

Colt laughed. "Must be somethin' in the water. Which reminds me. Ely still kickin'?"

Darby laughed. "Hasn't changed a bit. Still spends most of his time up in the mountains when he's not hanging around the missile silo." He sighed. "So what can I get you?"

"What's cooking today? Something smells delicious."

"Our cook, Billie Dee, whipped up one of her down-home Texas recipes. Today it's shrimp gumbo. Gotta warn ya, she's determined to add some spice in our lives and convert us Montanans."

"I'll have that," Lola and Colt said in unison, making Darby chuckle.

"Two coming up. What can I get you to drink?"

Colt looked at Lola. "Two colas?" She nodded and Darby went off to place their order.

"What was that about... Ely?"

"The Cahill patriarch. Famous in these parts because back in 1967, he swore he was abducted by aliens next to the missile silo on their ranch." Colt explained how the government had asked for two-acre plots around the area for defense back in the 1950s. "You might have seen that metal fence out in one of my pastures? There might be a live missile in it. No one but the government knows for sure."

"The missile silos on your property would be scary enough, but aliens?"

He laughed and nodded. "What makes Ely's story interesting to me is that night in 1967 the Air Force detected a flying-saucer type aircraft in the area. Lots of people saw it, including my father."

"So it's possible Ely is telling he truth as he knows it," she said, wide-eyed.

He shrugged. "I guess we'll never know for certain, but Ely swears it's true."

Darby brought their colas, and they sat in companionable silence for a few minutes.

"It feels so strange to be in a place like this," Lola said. "It's so...normal. I haven't had normal in way too long."

"How long had you been held at the compound before I met you in Billings?"

"Almost a month. The first week or so I was trying to get my parents' remains released to a mortuary in Gilt Edge. Jonas had been kind enough to offer me a place to stay until I could make arrangements. I didn't realize that he was lying to me until I tried to leave and realized there were armed guards keeping me there. At least I wasn't locked up in a cabin that time. I had the run of the place, or I would never have gotten away in the back of the van when the sisters drove to Billings."

And Colt would never have met her. They would never have made love and conceived Grace, Colt thought. Funny how things worked out.

Darby put some background music on the jukebox. The sun coming in the window gave the place a golden glow. Colt had been here a few times when he was home on leave. He was happy for Lillie and Darby for making a go of the place.

"How did you manage to get away this last time?" he asked.

"I'd been hiding my pills under my tongue until Sister Amelia left my cabin. I would spit them out and poke them into a hole I'd found in the cabin wall. The night I escaped, I pretended to be sick and managed to distract Sister Rebecca. When she wasn't looking, I hid the fork that was on my tray. She didn't notice that it was missing when she took my tray and left. I used the fork to pick the lock on the window and went out that way."

Darby returned a few moments later, accompanied by a large woman with a Southern accent carrying two steaming bowls of shrimp gumbo.

"Billie Dee, meet Colt McCloud," Darby said as he joined them. "Colt and I go way back. He's an Army helicopter pilot who's finally returned home—at least for a while, and this is his friend Lola."

"Pleased to meet you," the woman with the Texas accent said. "Hope you like my gumbo."

"I know we will," Colt said, and took a bite.

"Not too spicy for you?" the cook asked with a laugh.

"As long as it doesn't melt the spoon, it's not too spicy for me," Colt said, and looked to Lola.

She had tasted the gumbo and was smiling. "It's perfect."

Billie Dee looked pleased. "Enjoy."

Darby refilled their colas and gave them pieces of Billie Dee's Texas chocolate sheet cake to convey both "welcome home" and "glad to meet you."

Left alone again, Colt asked, "How are you doing?"

Lola realized that she felt better than she had in a long time. Just having food in her stomach made her feel stronger and more able to hold off the fear and frustration. She needed her baby.

But Colt believed her, and that made all the difference in the world. That felt like a huge hurdle given how convincing Jonas could be. Even more so, she was glad that she hadn't been wrong about Colt. They'd only been together that one night, but she hadn't forgotten his kindness, his tenderness, his protectiveness. Just having someone she could depend on... Her heart swelled as she looked over at him. "We're going to get Grace back, aren't we?"

Jonas stood at the window of his cabin. He'd had his cabin built on the side of the mountain so he could look down on the compound. For a man who'd started with nothing, he'd done all right. He often wished his father was still alive to see it.

"Look, you sanctimonious old son of a bitch. You, who so lacked faith that I would accomplish anything in my life. You, who died so poor that your congregation had to scrape up money to have you buried behind the church you'd served all those years. You, who always managed to cut me down as if you couldn't stand it that I might do better than you. Well, I did!"

Thinking about his father made his pulse rise dangerously. He had to be careful not to get upset. Stress made his condition worse. So much worse that some of his followers had started to notice.

He stepped over to the small table where he kept his medication. He swallowed a pill and waited for it to work. He tried not to think about the father who had kicked him out at sixteen. But it wasn't his old man who was causing the problem this time. It was Lola.

"Lola." Just saying her name churned up a warring mix of emotions that had been raging inside him for some time. Over the years, a variety of willing women had come to his bed in the night. He'd turned none of them away, but nor had he wanted any of them to keep for himself. Until Lola.

Her mother had shown him a photograph of her daughter back when Maxine and her husband, Ted, had joined SLS. The Society was just getting on its feet in those days. The Daytons' money had gone a long way to start things rolling.

Jonas had especially liked Maxine, since he knew

she was the one calling the shots. Ted would do anything for his wife. And had. All Jonas had to do was steer Maxine in whatever direction he wanted her to go and Ted would come along as a willing participant. If only they were all that easy to manage, he thought now with a sigh.

The photo of Lola had caught him off guard. There was a sweetness, a purity in that young face, but it was what he saw in her eyes. A fire. A passion banked in those mesmerizing violet eyes that had made him want to be the one to release it.

He'd done everything he could to get the Daytons to bring Lola to the California ranch. But the foolish girl had taken off right after high school to attend a college abroad. She'd wanted to become a teacher. Jonas had groaned when Maxine told him, and he'd conveyed his thoughts.

I think she could be anything she wants to be with my help. I really want to help her meet her potential. Lola is destined to do so much more than teach. She and I could lead the world to a better place. She might be the one person who could bring peace to the world.

Maxine had loved it, but Lola hadn't been having any of it. Right after college she'd headed for the Virgin Islands to teach sixth-grade geography at a private school down there. What a waste, he'd thought, not just for Lola but for himself. He had imagined what he could do with a woman like that warming his bed at night. They could run SLS together. Lola would bring in the men. He'd bring in the women. They could build an empire and live like royalty.

He'd known that Ted wasn't happy after the move to Montana. Jonas had heard him trying to get Maxine to leave. That was the first time that Jonas had realized that Ted had held out on him. Ted hadn't bought into SLS either mentally or financially. He hadn't turned over all his money. He'd set some aside for Lola, and no small amount, either.

Ted's dissatisfaction and attempts to get Maxine to leave hadn't fitted into Jonas's plan. He suddenly realized there was only one way to get Lola to come to him. Maxine and Ted would have to die—and soon.

Getting Maxine to sign a paper of her intentions to persuade Lola to marry him had taken only one private session with her. Maxine had bought into SLS hook, line and sinker. If she wanted to save her daughter... He'd promised to give Lola the kind of life her mother had only dreamed of. Then he'd had Ted and Maxine disposed of and, just as he'd planned, Lola flew to Montana, bringing all that fire inside her.

But he'd underestimated her. She was nothing like her mother. He'd thought that his charm, his wit, his sincerity would work on the daughter the way it had on her mother. That was where he'd made his first mistake, he thought now as he watched dusk settle over the compound.

There'd been a series of other mistakes that had led to her getting pregnant by another man. That was a blow he still reeled from. But it hadn't changed his determination to have Lola, one way or another. Not even some Army pilot/rancher could stop him. No, he had the one thing that Lola wanted more than life.

She would be back. And this time, she wouldn't be leaving here again.

CHAPTER EIGHT

AFTER SHRIMP GUMBO at the Stagecoach Saloon, Colt took them to the grocery store. He and Lola grabbed a cart and began to fill it with food. He loved her enthusiasm. After being locked up and nearly starved for so long, she was like a kid in a candy store.

"Do you like this?" she would ask as she picked up one item after another.

"Get whatever sounds good to you."

She scampered around, quickly filling the cart with food she obviously hadn't had for a while as he grabbed the basics: milk, bread, eggs, butter, bacon and syrup.

"I suspect you can live on pancakes," she said, eyeing what he'd added to the cart.

He'd only grinned, realizing that he'd never enjoyed grocery shopping as much as he had with her today. They felt almost like an old married couple as they left the store. He found himself smiling at Lola as she tore into a bag of potato chips before they even reached the pickup. He unloaded their haul and had started to replace the cart in the rack when he heard someone call his name.

"Colt?"

He froze at the sound of Julia's voice. Somehow he'd managed not to cross paths with her since he'd been back in town, but only because he'd shopped either very early or very late. He'd picked a bad day to run out of groceries, he thought now with a grimace.

"Colt?"

Lola set her potato chip bag in the back of the pickup bed and walked over to join him. He could feel her looking from him to Julia, wondering why he wasn't responding. With a silent curse, he turned to face the woman he'd been ready to marry a year ago.

Julia looked exactly the same. Her dark hair was shorter, making her brown eyes seem even darker. She looked good, slim and perfect in a dress and heels. Julia always liked to dress up—even to go to the grocery store. Gold glittered at her ears, her neck and, of course, on her ring finger, along with the sizable diamond resting there. The one he'd bought hadn't been nearly as large.

He swore under his breath. As many times as he'd imagined what it would be like running into her again, he'd never imaged this. Lola was watching the two of them as if enjoying a tennis match.

Colt had hoped that he wouldn't feel anything, given what Julia had done to him. But he'd believed in this woman, believed they would share the rest of their lives; otherwise, he would never have asked her to marry him. It had taken him almost three years to pop the question. He'd wanted to be sure. What a fool he'd been.

"I heard you were back," Julia said, and glanced from him to Lola beside him. "I was so sorry to hear about your father. I was at the funeral…"

He'd seen her and managed to avoid her.

"How are you?" she asked, sounding as if she cared. As if sensing who this woman was and what she'd meant to him, Lola reached over and took his hand, squeezing it gently.

"I'm good," he said, squeezing back. "And you?"

"Fine." She looked again at his companion, her gaze going to their clasped hands.

"I heard you've put the ranch up for sale." Julia hesitated. She brushed a lock of her hair back from her forehead, looking not quite as confident. "Does this mean you're going back into the military?" His joining the Army's flight program had been a bone of contention between them.

He shook his head, as if what he planned to do was any of her business.

"I was just wondering," she said, no doubt seeing him clenching his teeth. "I was hoping that if you were staying around Gilt Edge we could…" Again she hesitated. "Maybe we could have a cup of coffee sometime and just talk."

Just talk the way they had before she'd had an affair with Wyatt? Or talk the way they had when she hadn't shown up at the airport to give him a ride home?

"Our last conversation…" Julia looked again at Lola for a moment. "It went so badly. I'd left you messages. I had no way of knowing you hadn't gotten them or the letter I sent."

"You were clear enough on the phone the last time we talked," he said, wishing she would just say whatever it was she needed to say so he didn't have to keep standing there. He could tell that she was waiting for him to introduce her to Lola, but his heart was beating too hard. Julia and Wyatt had hurt him badly. Her and one of his friends? Equal amounts of anger and regret had him shaking inside.

But he didn't want to get into an argument here in the grocery store parking lot in front of Lola. He didn't want Julia to know just how much she and Wyatt had hurt him. And he feared that if he started in on her, he wouldn't be able to stop until all of his grief and rage and hurt came pouring out.

"I'm glad you're home." Julia looked from him to Lola again and forced a weak smile. "It was good to see you. If you change your mind about that cup of coffee…" She stood for a moment, looking awkward and unsure, something new for Julia, he thought. And he realized that she needed him to tell her it was okay, what she'd done. That he forgave her. That he wanted her and Wyatt to be happy. Julia was struggling with the guilt.

That alone should have made him feel better, he thought as she turned and left them standing there. Instead, he felt as if he'd been ambushed by a speeding freight train.

"I'm sorry," Lola said as she let go of his hand.

He couldn't speak so merely nodded as he took the cart to the rack and quickly returned to the pickup. Lola grabbed her potato chips out of the back and joined him in the cab. He'd expected her to be full of questions.

Instead, she buckled up, holding the bag of potato chips as if she'd lost her appetite, and quietly let him process what had just happened. He was thankful to her for that. And for taking his hand back there.

"Thanks," he said, after he got the truck going and drove out of the parking lot.

"It was the first time you've seen her since…since the breakup." It wasn't a question, but he answered it anyway.

"I've managed to avoid her. Just my luck…" He shook his head.

"I can see how painful it is."

"I'm more angry than hurt."

Lola looked out the side window. "Betrayal is always painful." She hugged herself.

He glanced over at her, thinking what a strong, determined woman she was. Not the kind who would give up when things got a little tough.

"Julia turned out not to be the woman I thought she was," he said. "I'm better off without her."

Lola said nothing, no doubt sensing that no matter what he said, he wasn't completely over his former fiancée or what she had put him through.

It made him angry that his heart hadn't let go of the hurt. The anger he didn't mind living with for a while.

WHAT WOULD LOLA do now? That was the question Jonas knew he should be asking himself as he stepped back inside his warm, elegantly furnished cabin.

She must think him a complete fool. Her great escape. He let out a bark of a laugh. Did she really think she could have gotten away unless he'd let her? Sure, he'd had his men chase her with instructions to make sure that she got away.

He'd known she would run straight to the father of her baby. As if he hadn't known she was lying about not knowing who she'd lain with. He scoffed at the idea. Sister Rebecca had seen her with a man near the hotel bar that night. Unfortunately, Lola and the man had disappeared on the elevator too quickly.

But Rebecca had managed to get the information. Major Colt McCloud. An Army helicopter pilot. Jonas would ask what she could see in a man like that, but he wasn't that stupid. The man was good-looking, part cowboy, part flight jockey. He had just inherited a large ranch.

Not that Jonas had been certain Colt McCloud was the man who'd knocked Lola up. No, he hadn't known that until today when the man had shown up with Lola and the sheriff.

Lola was too bound up from her conservative upbringing to go to bed with just anyone. So she'd seen something beyond Colt McCloud's good looks. Jonas swore under his breath as he moved to the fireplace to throw on another log. Just the thought of the cowboy pilot made his blood boil. How dare the man come up here making demands.

Jonas thought he might have convinced Colt that Lola was unstable and not to be believed. She'd certainly played into his plan perfectly when she'd lost it in the laundry room. But he couldn't be sure about Colt. The man was probably smitten with Lola and would want to believe her.

At least the sheriff wouldn't be returning. He'd been sufficiently convinced. Law enforcement always backed off when it came to churches. Just like the government did. He smiled at the thought of how he'd been able to build The Society of Lasting Serenity without anyone looking over his shoulder.

Until now.

"You could return the baby," Sister Rebecca had dared to say to him before the dust had even settled earlier today. "You know she'll be back if you don't."

"Mind your place," he'd snapped. He'd seen how jealous the older woman was of Lola. He suspected she'd been mean to her, cutting her rations, possibly even being physically abusive to her. He hadn't stopped it, wanting Sister Rebecca's loyalty.

But now he wondered how much longer he might be able to count on Rebecca. Once Lola was back—and she would be back—Sister Rebecca might have to be taken down a notch or two. Then again, maybe it was time to retire her. Not that she would ever be allowed to leave. She knew too much.

Strange how a valuable asset could so quickly become a liability.

As soon as he had Lola… Yes, he would dispose of Sister Rebecca. It would be almost like a wedding gift for his new wife. Not that he would tell Lola what had really happened to the older woman. Let her believe he'd given Rebecca a golden parachute and sent her off to some island to bask in the sun for the rest of her days.

He stared into the flames as the log he'd added began to crackle and spark. If he was Colt McCloud, what would he do? Jonas smiled to himself, then picked up the phone. "We're going to need more guards tonight, especially around the cemetery."

AFTER RUNNING INTO JULIA, Colt had known it was just a matter of time before he and Wyatt crossed paths. He'd promised himself that when it happened, when he finally did see his traitorous, former good friend, he would keep his cool. He wasn't going to lose his temper. If Wyatt wanted Julia, a woman who would betray her fiancé while he was fighting a war oceans away, then she was all his.

He'd visualized seeing both of them, but even in his imagination, he hadn't known what he would do. He'd told himself that he would tell them both off, make them feel even more guilty, if possible, hurt them the way they had hurt him.

But look what had happened when he'd seen Julia. He'd been boiling inside, his heart pounding, anger and hurt a potent mixture. And he'd said none of what he'd planned. Instead, he hadn't wanted them to know how much they'd hurt him. Or even how angry he still was.

After seeing Julia, it made him wonder when it could happen with Wyatt. How would Wyatt react? He just hoped Lola wouldn't have to witness it again. Colt thought that Wyatt must be dreading the day when they would come face-to-face again as much as he was. Colt hoped he'd given Wyatt a few sleepless nights worrying about it. Because, in a town the size of Gilt Edge, a meeting had to happen.

But Colt was sorry that it had to happen at this moment as he stopped to get gas on the way out of town. Lola had gone inside the convenience mart to use the ladies' room.

As he stood filling the pickup with gas, Wyatt drove up, pulling to a pump two away from him.

Colt froze, his heart in this throat, as he watched Wyatt get out of his pickup and step to the fuel pump. He thought about staying where he was, pretending he never saw him. But that was way too cowardly. Anyway, he wanted to get this over with.

He finished fueling his truck and walked down the line of gas pumps. Wyatt looked up and saw him and seemed to freeze. They'd grown up together, hung out with many of the same friends since grade school. It was only after college that Colt, needing to do something more with his life, had enlisted in the Army helicopter program.

Wyatt had tried to talk him out of it. "Why do you need to go so far away? You're going to get yourself killed and for what?"

Colt hadn't been able to explain it to him. So he'd left to fly and fight while Wyatt had stayed on his family ranch and stolen Julia.

He took a step toward the man he'd thought he'd known better than himself. As he did, he wondered what he would come out of his mouth or if he would be able to speak. His pulse thundered in his ears as he advanced on his former friend.

"Colt." Wyatt was a big, strong cowboy. He put up both hands in surrender but held his ground. "Colt, whatever you're thinking—"

Colt hit him hard enough to drive him back a couple of steps. Wyatt banged into the side of his pickup.

"I don't want to fight you," Wyatt said as one large hand went to his bleeding nose.

"That's good," Colt said. "Since you'd probably take me." He knew that might be true since Wyatt had a few inches on him and a good twenty pounds, but as angry as he was, he'd fight like hell.

His hands were balled into fists, but he didn't hit him again. Wyatt's bleeding nose looked broken. Colt was reminded of the time Wyatt had taken on the school bully, a kid twice his size back then. His former friend was tough and had never backed down from a fight in all the time Colt had known him.

He took a step back, hating that he was remembering the years of their friendship. His eyes burned with tears, but damned if he was going to cry. Looking at Wyatt, he realized that losing Julia had hurt; losing someone he'd considered a close friend, though, had ripped out his heart.

He turned on his heel and walked back to his pickup before he made a complete fool of himself. His knuckles hurt, but nothing like his heart as he listened to Wyatt get into his truck and drive away.

LOLA HAD SEEN everything from the front window of the convenience store when she'd come back from the restroom. The "fight" had ended quickly enough.

She didn't have to ask who the man had been.

Wyatt Enderlin. When she'd asked Colt about him, he'd said they'd been friends. "It's a small town. We make friends for life here." She could imagine how much Wyatt's betrayal hurt Colt.

She pushed open the door and walked out to Colt's truck, climbing in without a word. Out of the corner of her eye, Lola saw him rub his skinned and swollen knuckles before he climbed behind the wheel.

It wasn't until they were in the pickup headed toward the ranch that Colt said, "You saw?"

She hesitated, forcing him to look over at her. "I wanted you to hit him again."

He smiled sadly at that. "I hadn't planned to even hit him once."

"Do you feel better or worse?"

Chuckling, he said, "Better and worse."

"Well, you got that out of the way."

"Right, I got to see them both on the same day. Lucky me." He drove in silence for a few minutes. "Wyatt and I were like brothers at one point growing up. I'd always wanted a brother…" He shook his head.

"He was your friend."

"*Was* being the key word here. My other friends like Darby Cahill never would have done that."

"Which hurts worse?" she finally asked.

Colt shot her a glance before turning back to his driving. "Wyatt."

"Maybe one day—"

"I don't think so. Being in the military you learn which men you can trust in battle. Those are the men you want watching your back. Wyatt, as it turned out, isn't one of them."

"I'm sorry." She let the words hang in the air for a moment. "Do you believe in fate?"

They were almost at the turnoff to the ranch. Ahead she could see the for-sale sign. They hadn't talked about it. She doubted they would because she already knew from the first time they'd met how Colt felt about flying the big birds in the military.

"Fate?" he asked, glancing at her for a moment before he slowed for the turn.

"Maybe it was fate that has brought us all to this point in our lives."

FATE? LOLA COULDN'T be serious. If his fate was having his fiancée hook up with his good friend behind his back, then he'd say he was one unlucky bastard. He said as much to Lola.

"I was thinking more about the way we met."

Instantly he hated having rained on her parade like that.

"If Julia hadn't broken up with you and had met you at the airport like she was supposed to, then you wouldn't have been in that hotel that night and I wouldn't have…"

Would some other man have saved her? Or taken advantage of a young woman who was obviously inexperienced and desperate? The thought made him sick to his stomach, but he wouldn't have known because he would never have laid eyes on Lola Dayton.

Nor would he be worrying about how to get their baby away from a madman at an armed and dangerous cult compound at the top of a mountain, he thought as he parked in front of the house at the ranch and shut off the engine.

But as he looked over at Lola, the anger he'd been feeling ebbed away. "You're right," he said, softening his tone as he reached over and squeezed her hand. "It definitely was fate that brought us together." Damn fickle fate, he thought, realizing with growing concern how much Lola was getting to him.

He put Julia, Wyatt and the past out of his mind and concentrated on what to do next. He knew what he was going to have to do. It went against his military training. A man didn't go in alone with no backup. Nor did he take matters into his own hands. He went through proper channels.

But there was no way the sheriff was going to be able to get a warrant to have whatever was buried on the church grounds exhumed—even if Colt could talk Flint into doing it. Jonas would fight it and drag out the process. Meanwhile, that madman had their baby. Baby Grace, the daughter he had yet to lay eyes on.

After helping put the groceries away, he went into the ranch office. The maps were in a file—right where his father had kept them. He found the one he needed and spread it out on the desk.

"We need proof that Jonas is lying," Lola said from the open doorway.

"Proof won't do us any good. We need to find Grace and get her out of there."

"But that grave. If you dig it up—"

Colt shuddered at the thought. "That's exactly what Jonas will expect me to do." He recalled a shortage of manpower on the compound. But a woman could be just as deadly with a gun, he reminded himself. "While they're busy guarding the cemetery, I'll find Grace."

"I'm going with you," she said, stepping into the small office.

He shook his head, hating how intimate it felt with her in here. "It's going to be hard enough for me to get onto the grounds—and away again—without being caught."

"Exactly. They will expect you and will have doubled the guards. You're going to need me."

He started to argue, but she cut him off. "I have lived there all this time. I know the weakest spots along the perimeter. I also know the guards. And, maybe more important, I know where to look for Grace."

Admittedly, she made a good argument. "Lola, if we are both caught, no one will know we're up there. If Jonas is as dangerous as you think he is, we'll end up in the cemetery."

"If one of us is caught, then the other can distract them while whoever has Grace gets away."

He hated that her argument made sense, more sense than him trying to find Grace on his own. "Can you draw a map of the place?"

She nodded.

"Good. We leave at midnight."

LOLA HADN'T DARED HOPE, but as she watched Colt studying the web of old logging roads around the mountain compound on the map, she let herself believe they could succeed. They would get in, find Grace and slip back out with her. Once she had Grace in her arms, no way would she let anyone rip her out again. Especially Jonas.

"I'll need paper and a pen," she said as she leaned over the desk. Their gazes met for a moment, his gaze deepening. She felt goose bumps ripple over her skin. Heat rushed to her center. Then he quickly looked away and began searching for what she needed.

She drew a map of the compound buildings, marking those that were used for housing. "I know you got a tour, but I thought this would help. As you can see there are two women's dorms, one for the women with babies. There is only the one men's dorm on the opposite side the main building."

"What's this?" Colt asked as he moved to her side to point at a large cabin away from the others and at the top of her diagram.

"Jonas's. He likes to look down on his followers."

"And this one at the bottom right?" His fingers brushed hers.

A shiver ran the length of her spine. She felt her nipples harden to pebbles under her top. "That's the storage room, shop and health center." Her voice cracked with emotion.

"And this one bottom left?" There was no doubt. He'd purposely brushed against her as he pointed to the only other structure. The bare skin of his arm was warm.

His touch sent more shivers rippling through her. Her nipples ached inside her bra.

"Laundry." She turned enough to meet his eyes. What she saw made her molten inside. His gaze was dark with desire as his fingers trailed up her arm to brush against the side of her breast.

WHAT THE HELL are you doing? As if he could stop himself. He looked into Lola's beautiful violet gaze and knew he was lost. He wanted her. Needed her. Thought he would die if he didn't have her right now. This had been building inside him all day, he realized. Maybe since the first time he'd met her.

"Colt?" she breathed, and shuddered as his fingers brushed over the hard tip of her nipple. She moaned softly, her head going back to expose her slim silken neck.

He bent to kiss her throat, nipping at the pale skin, and felt her shiver before trailing kisses down into the hollow between her breasts. "Yes, Lola?" he asked, his muffled voice as filled with emotion as hers had been.

When she didn't answer, he raised his head to look into her eyes. He held her gaze, seeing the answer in all that lovely blue.

Cupping her other breast, he backed her up against the office wall and dropped his mouth to hers. Her lips parted and he took the invitation to let his tongue explore her as his free hand found the waistband of her jeans and slipped inside.

She let out a gasp as he found the sweet cleft between her legs. "Colt." This time it was a plea. She was wet. He began to stroke her, drawing back to look into her eyes. Her head was back and her mouth open. Tiny sounds escaped her lips as he slowly stroked, until he could feel her quiver against his fingers and finally cry out.

Withdrawing his hand, he swung her up into his arms and strode to his bedroom. He didn't want to think about later tonight when they would go up the mountain. Nor did he want to think about the future or even why he was doing this right now.

All he knew was that he wanted her more than his next breath. The only thing on his mind was making love to this woman who had captivated him from the first time he'd laid eyes on her.

CHAPTER NINE

JUST BEFORE MIDNIGHT, Lola and Colt loaded into his pickup and headed toward the SLS encampment. Colt had programmed his phone with the latest GPS information and had mapped out their best route up the mountain.

They'd both dressed in dark clothing. Lola had borrowed one of his black T-shirts. Her blond hair was pulled up under one of his black caps.

Earlier, after making love several times, they'd showered together, then sat down again with the map. His plan was to approach this like a battle.

Lola had showed him on her diagram what she thought was the best way in—and out again. The layout of the compound was star shaped, with the large main building at its center. It was where everyone ate, met for church and meetings, and where Jonas had his office.

From it, the other buildings formed the points of a star. At the top was Jonas's cabin, on the left center were the women's two dorms and on the right, the men's dorm. At the bottom was the laundry to the left and the health center, shop and storage building to the right.

"Once we grab Grace, someone will sound the alarm. Everyone will get a weapon and go to the edge of the property."

"The SLS is sounding less and less like a church by the moment," Colt had said.

"If the intruder or escapee is caught, a second signal will sound announcing the all clear," she'd said.

Colt had studied her for a moment. He couldn't help thinking of her earlier, naked in his arms. He wondered if he could ever get enough of this woman. "You're sure about this?"

She'd smiled, nodding. She really did have an amazing smile. "Whichever one of us has Grace gets out if the alarm goes off. Whoever doesn't have her distracts the guards to give them a chance to escape."

"Who will have Grace?" he'd asked.

"I guess it will depend on who finds her first. Once we approach the housing part, someone is bound to see us."

Colt would have preferred a more comprehensive plan. "You must have some idea where they are keeping Grace."

"Normally, she would be in the second women's dorm where the other babies are kept," she'd said. "But Jonas will know that I haven't given up. He might have ordered that Grace be kept in the other women's dorm."

"Where were they keeping you before you escaped?"

She'd drawn in a tiny box. "That's the cabin. It serves as the jail."

"And you could hear Grace crying when they came to pump your breast milk?" She'd nodded. "You're thinking they had our baby in this dorm, the farthest one to the west and closest to the cabin where you were being kept. I'll take that one, then head east to the second women's dorm if I don't see you. They won't expect us to come in from different directions."

"We'll meet up there. Or if the alarm goes off, just try to meet back at the pickup"

Now, as the road climbed up the mountain, he looked over at Lola. She appeared calm. Her expression was one of determination. She was going after her baby. *Their* baby. Her last thought was her own safety.

His heart ached at the thought of their lovemaking. He couldn't let anything happen to this woman. Grace needed her. He needed her, he thought and pushed the thought away. What he needed was to get himself, Lola and their baby out of that compound alive tonight. Later he'd think about what he needed, what he wanted, what the hell he was going to do once Lola and Grace were safe.

The night was thankfully dark. Low clouds hunkered just over the tops of the tall ebony pines. No stars, let alone the moon, shone through. Colt thought they couldn't have picked a better night.

Still, he was anxious. So much was riding on this and he felt they were going in blind. What he did know had him both worried and scared. If Jonas or any of his followers caught them…

He couldn't let himself go down that trail of thought. If they wanted to get Grace out of there, they had no choice but to sneak in like thieves, find her and take her. Isn't that what Jonas had done?

LOLA HAD BEEN lost in thought when Colt pulled the pickup over, cut the engine and doused the lights. She'd been thinking about the ocean and the time she'd almost drowned.

Her father had saved her, plucking her from the depths and carrying her to the beach. She remembered lying on the warm sand staring up at the sky and gasping for breath as her father wept in relief over her.

She had no idea why that particular memory had surfaced now. Anything to keep her mind off what was about to happen once they reached the compound. She'd learned to let her mind wander during Jonas's attempts to brainwash her. She would think of anything but what was happening—just like now.

With the headlights off, they were pitched into blackness. She listened to the tick, tick, tick of the cooling engine, her heart a hammer in her chest.

"You ready?" he asked, his voice low and soft.

She nodded and locked gazes with him. Colt looked as if there was something he wanted to say. She'd seen that same look earlier after they'd made love.

Earlier, she'd put a finger to his lips. She hadn't wanted him to say the words that he thought he needed to say. Colt was an honorable man, but she couldn't let him say things that he'd later regret. Nor had she been able to bear the thought of him pouring his soul out to her at that moment. Just as now.

There was too much riding on what they were about to do. Emotions were high and had been since she'd appeared at his door in the middle of the night. There was no need to say anything then or now, though she understood his need. She too wanted to open her heart to him because both of them knew how dangerous this mission was. Neither of them might get out of this alive.

Just as he started to speak, she opened her door and stepped into the darkness. She gulped the cold spring-night air and fought her fear for Colt and their daughter, a gut-wrenching fear that made her eyes burn with tears.

COLT SAT FOR a moment alone in the cab of the dark pickup. What had he been about to say? He shook his head. Lola had cut him off—just as she had earlier.

He sighed, wondering at this woman.

Then he got out, and the two of them headed through the dark pines for the hike to the compound.

They moved as silently as they could once their eyes adjusted to the darkness under the towering pines. A breeze stirred the boughs high above them, making the pines sigh.

Colt led the way until they were almost to the SLS property. The whole time, he'd been acutely aware of Lola behind him.

Now he stopped and motioned her forward. They stood inches apart for a long moment, listening.

Lola had suggested entering the property on the opposite side of the cemetery and the farthest away from any main road up to the mountaintop.

The main road was gated, so Jonas wouldn't be expecting them to come that way. That was also the most visible, so they'd opted for this approach.

But now it was time to separate. Colt could feel the tension in the air, as well as the tension between them. Lola had made it clear that she didn't want any words of undying love. But, after everything they'd shared, he felt the need to say something, do something.

He drew her close, looked into her violet eyes and kissed her.

"What was that?" she demanded in a whisper. "It felt like a goodbye kiss."

He shook his head and leaned close to whisper, "A promise to see you soon." As he drew back, he saw her smile. "Good luck," he whispered, and turned and headed in the opposite direction, his heart in his throat. If things didn't go well, he didn't want his last memory to be of her standing in the darkness, looking up at him with those big blue eyes and him not doing a damned thing.

Now he thought of her slightly gap-toothed smile and held it close to his heart for luck. Ahead he saw the no-trespassing sign and knew a guard wasn't far away.

LOLA TOUCHED HER tongue to her lower lip as she made her way through the pines. Just the thought of Colt's kiss made her heart beat a little faster. If she'd been falling for him before that moment, well, she'd just fallen a little further. She warned herself that this wasn't any way to go into a relationship.

Her mother would have called it "going in the back door." Maxine would not have approved of Lola having a baby out of wedlock when she could have married Jonas and given Grace a father.

But Grace did have a father. A fine father. Lola just didn't see them becoming a family. She shook the thought from her head and tried to concentrate. Getting Grace back, that was all that mattered.

She hadn't gone far when she saw a faint light bobbing through the trees ahead of her.

Ducking down, she watched as Elmer made his way along the edge of the property. She waited until he was well past her before she rose and sneaked onto the compound. The only lights were the ones outside the buildings that illuminated parts of the grounds.

Lola edged along the pines until she reached the edge of the men's dorm. Only one light shone at the front. She moved cautiously along the back, keeping to the dark shadows next to the building and being careful not to step on anything that might make a sound.

She had no desire to wake anyone, though she thought the men's dorm was probably fairly empty. All of the men would be on guard duty tonight and maybe even some of the women.

Elmer would be turning back soon on his guard circuit. If she hurried, she should be able to reach the closest women's dorm and slip inside the nursery before he started back this way.

Before the first time she'd escaped, she'd had the run of the place, including the one women's dorm, where she'd stayed with the sisters. She'd even helped with the babies a few times. Because of that, she knew where to find the main nursery.

"If I find her first, how will I know her?" Colt had asked.

She'd smiled and said, "You'll know her and she'll know you."

"No, seriously."

"There were two babies born in the past six months that I know of. The boy we saw in the laundry and Grace."

At the end of the men's dorm, Lola stopped to listen. She heard nothing on the breeze. The distance between her and the women's dorms was a good dozen yards— all of them in the glow of the men's dorm light.

She looked for any movement in the darkness beyond. Seeing none, she sprinted the distance and dropped back into the shadows. Her heart pounded as she waited to see if she'd been spotted by one of the guards. The only one she'd seen was Elmer, but she knew there were others stationed around the compound, more than usual, just as she'd told Colt.

As she caught her breath, she thought of Colt and wondered where he was. Saying a silent prayer for his safety, she crept along the edge of the building to the door to the main nursery and grasping the knob, turned it.

COLT RECOGNIZED THE guard as one he'd seen here yesterday. The man looked tired and bored as he moved along the edge of the property and fiddled with the handgun holstered at his hip.

The guard had only gone a few feet when he stepped into the shadows and suddenly drew his weapon like an Old West gunfighter. He took the stance for a moment, pointing the gun into the darkness ahead of him and then holstered his weapon again as he moved on to practice his fast draw a few yards later.

Colt had been startled for a moment when the guard had suddenly drawn his weapon. He'd been more than a little relieved to see that the man's gun was pointing only at some imaginary person in the dark.

He slipped behind the man, closing the distance from the dense pines to the edge of the closest women's dorm. Stopping to listen, he heard a sound that froze him in place.

A low growl followed by another. This part of the country had its share of bear from black bear to grizzly. But the low growling sound he'd just heard wasn't coming from the darkness, he realized. Instead, it floated out of the open window on the back side of the women's dorm. Someone was snoring loudly.

It gave him good cover as he moved cautiously along

the dark side of the building. Only a dim light shone inside. Staying as far back as possible, he peered in. The large room was filled with bunk beds like a military barrack. He recognized the woman in the closest lower bunk. Sister Alexa, a woman Colt had met in passing the day Jonas gave him the tour.

She let out a snort and stirred. He saw her eyes flicker and he froze. She blinked for a moment before her eyes fluttered shut and her snoring resumed.

Colt ducked away from the window and made his way down to the end that Lola said could house a second nursery. The outside light high over the front door of the main building cast a circle of golden light.

He watched from the dark shadows at the edge of the light. He'd only seen two guards so far, one on the way in and another crossing the complex, before he'd made his way to the far end of the building where he would find the nursery.

From where he stood, he could see toward the cemetery where Lola's parents were buried. He wondered about the small mound of fresh dirt next to them. Was something buried under there?

Jonas seemed like a man who didn't take chances. At the very least, he would have buried a small wooden casket. Colt remembered seeing the shop on his tour of the complex. Followers made wooden crosses in the shop that they sold when they went into town to raise money for the poor, Lola had told him. She said she doubted the poor ever saw a dime of it.

"I think it's Jonas's way of keeping them busy and making a little extra cash. The crosses are crude, but I think people feel sorry for the followers and give them money."

He thought now about the small casket he'd seen in one corner of the shop during his tour and swallowed hard. What if Jonas had filled the casket under that mound of dirt since their visit?

The thought made his stomach roil. He pressed his back against the side of the women's dorm and waited for the guard he'd seen earlier to cross again.

From inside the women's dorm, he heard a baby begin to cry. His heart lodged in his throat. Grace?

LOLA TURNED THE knob slowly. The door creaked open an inch, then another. A small night-light shone from one corner of the room, illuminating four small cribs. In one of the cribs, a baby whimpered.

She looked toward the doorway into the sleeping room with its bunk beds. She could hear someone snoring softly, heard the rustle of covers and then silence.

Her heart pounded as she slipped through the door and into the nursery. The first two cribs were empty. She moved to the third one. The baby in it was small. A newborn. Sister Caroline's baby, she realized. Caroline had been due when Lola had run away from the compound that night.

She stepped to the last crib, looked down at the sleeping baby and felt her heart begin to pound.

COLT STOOD AGAINST the wall in the darkness outside the nursery. Inside, he heard the sound of footfalls as someone awakened in the dorm and headed for the nursery.

A few moments later, he heard a woman talking soothingly. The baby quit crying. He could hear the woman humming a tune to the child, but he didn't recognize the song.

Then again, he knew no children's songs. He tried to imagine himself getting up in the middle of the night to calm his crying infant and couldn't. It was so far from what he'd been doing for the last eleven years.

What kind of father would he make when he didn't even know a song he could sing a child? Or could even imagine himself doing something like that? In all his years he'd never held a baby. He'd be afraid he would drop it with his big clumsy hands.

He could see the woman's shadow as she'd come into the room and now watched her swaying with the infant in her arms, singing softly, willing the baby back to sleep. Was the baby Grace?

He waited, staying to the dark shadow of the building as, in the distance, he saw the guard come back from making his rounds. The man was headed for the men's dorm. Change of shift? He hadn't anticipated that and realized he should have.

Where he was standing, the man would have to pass right by him. Colt had no chance of going undetected. Nor could he move away from the building without being seen.

Inside the nursery, he saw the shadow of the woman move. The singing continued as she seemed to lay the infant back into its crib. The man was getting closer now. His head was down. He looked tired, bored, ready to call it a night.

Where was his replacement? For all Colt knew, there could be another guard headed from the opposite direction.

He realized the music had stopped inside the nursery. Reaching over, he tried the door. The knob turned in his hand.

He had no choice. He could stay where he was and be seen by the guard, or he could chance slipping into the nursery and coming face-to-face with the woman tending the baby.

He slipped into the nursery to find it empty except for four cribs lined up against one wall. As the door closed behind him, he heard voices outside. Two men. And then silence.

Colt waited a few more seconds before he approached the cribs and saw that all but one of the cribs was empty.

He moved quietly to the crib being used and looked down at the sleeping baby. The infant lay on its back, eyes closed. He carefully reached in and pulled up the homemade shift the baby wore.

FOR A MOMENT, Lola couldn't move or breathe. Her heart swelled to bursting as she looked down at the precious sleeping baby. She would have recognized her baby anywhere, but still, with trembling fingers, she lifted the hem of the infant's gown.

There on Grace's chubby little left thigh was the tiny heart-shaped birthmark. A sob rose in her throat. She desperately wanted to lift her daughter from the crib. For so long she'd yearned to hold her baby in her arms.

She tried to get control of her emotions, knowing that once she picked up Grace, she would have to move fast. With luck, Grace wouldn't cry. But being startled out of sleep she might, and it would set off an alarm that would awaken the women in the dorm, if not the whole complex.

Lola wiped at the warm tears on her cheeks as she stared at her daughter. Grace was beautiful, from her tiny bow-shaped mouth to her chubby cheeks. As if sensing her standing over the crib, Grace's eyes fluttered and she kicked with both legs.

Lola grabbed two of the baby blankets stacked next to the cribs. Reaching down, she hurriedly lifted her daughter. Grace started, her eyes coming wide-open in alarm.

Quickly wrapping her infant in the blankets, Lola turned toward the door and felt a hand drop to her shoulder.

CHAPTER TEN

LOLA HAD BEEN in midstep when the hand dropped to her shoulder. The fingers tightened, forcing her to stop. She turned, terrified of who she would find standing behind her.

Sister Amelia put a finger to her lips before Lola could speak. Their gazes locked for what seemed an eternity. Neither looked away until Grace stirred in Lola's arms.

"Go," Amelia whispered, and pushed her toward the door. From back in the dorm came the sound of foot-falls. "Go!"

Lola stumbled out the door, Grace wrapped in a blanket and clutched to her chest. Behind her, she heard Sister Amelia say something to the woman who'd awakened. Then the door closed behind her and she was standing out in the dark of the building.

Run! The thought rippled through her, igniting her fight-or-flight impulse. She had Grace. If she could get her off the compound…

From the dark, she heard a sound. A whisper of movement. A dark shadow emerged and she saw it was one of the guards. She recognized him by the arrogant way he moved. Brother Zack. She'd seen the way the former military man looked at her when he thought no one was watching. She'd heard that he'd been drummed out of the service but could only guess for what. He'd struck fear in her the nights when she knew he was the guard working outside the cabin where she was being held.

If Sister Rebecca hadn't been in charge of her "re-habilitation" and had sisters coming every hour or so to chant over her, Lola feared what Brother Zack might have done.

Now she watched him move through the darkness, her heart in her throat. Had he seen her? He appeared to be headed right for her. From inside the baby blankets, Grace whimpered.

COLT CHECKED THE BABY. No heart-shaped birthmark on either chubby leg. The moment he lifted the thin gown, the baby began to kick. Its eyes came open. Colt froze, afraid to breathe. The baby's gaze became more unfo-cused. Its eyes slowly closed.

He took a breath and let it out slowly. Grace wasn't here. He stepped toward the door. The floor creaked under his boot. He froze again, listening. With a glance over his shoulder, he stepped to the door, pushed it open a few inches and slipped outside.

The dark night felt like a shroud over the complex. Only circles of golden light from the outside lamps illu-minated a few spots around the complex. He waited for his eyes to adjust, keeping himself tucked back against the shadow of the building. Nothing seemed to move but the pine boughs in the breeze.

Off in the distance, an owl hooted, then the night fell silent again. He had no idea how long he'd been inside the nursery or where the guards might be now.

On the way in, he'd thought they'd been changing shifts. That meant the new ones might be more alert, having just started. He thought of Lola. She'd gone to the other women's dorm. Had she found Grace?

His fear was that Jonas would want the baby closer to him, knowing Lola wouldn't give up. But wouldn't he want one of the sisters watching over her? Jonas didn't seem like a hands-on father figure. Colt wondered if he, himself, was. He could only hope that Lola had already found Grace.

He looked around, but saw no one. It appeared that most of the guards were out by the cemetery. Jonas had thought Lola would try to get evidence to take to the sheriff. He had thought no one believed her—not even Colt. Maybe especially Colt.

He spotted one of the guards moving slowly through the pines out on the perimeter. He wanted desperately to go look for Lola, but they'd agreed that the best plan would be for them to meet at the pickup. That way if one of them was caught, the other could go for help rather than walk into a trap that would snare them both.

As soon as the guard was out of sight, Colt crossed between the buildings and worked his way along the dark side of the second women's dorm.

He reached the end of the building and looked to the expanse of open land he would have to cross to reach the dark safety of the pines.

As he started to take a step, he heard a sound behind him and spun around to come face-to-face with Lola. One glance at her expression told him that the bundle in her arms was Grace.

She took a step toward him, smiling, tears in her eyes, and suddenly the night came alive with the shrill scream of an alarm.

LOLA FELT GRACE start at the horrible sound. From inside the blankets, the baby began to cry. Lola tore the blankets from the crying baby and thrust Grace's wriggling small body at Colt. "Take her and go!" she cried. "Go! I'll distract them." She could see that he wanted to argue. "Please."

He grabbed the now-screaming baby and, turning toward the pines, ran.

Lola felt a fist close on her heart as she looked down at the empty blanket in her hand. She didn't have time for regrets. She'd gotten to see her daughter, hold her for a few priceless minutes, but now she had to move, and she knew the best way to make the alarm stop.

Grabbing up several large stones lying along the side of the building's foundation, she quickly wrapped them in the baby blankets, then hugged the bundle against her chest. It wouldn't fool anyone who got too close, but it might work long enough to get her where she needed to go.

Turning, she hurried back toward the center of the compound. She desperately needed to distract the guards and give Colt a chance to escape with Grace.

SLS members poured out of the dorms in their nightwear. She half ran toward Jonas's cabin, screaming at the top of her lungs. Guards came running from all directions.

Zack saw her and charged her. He would have taken her down, but Jonas had come out of his cabin. Seeing what was happening, he shut off the alarm with his cell phone.

"Leave her alone, Brother Zack!" he yelled down. "Don't hurt the baby."

Zack stopped just inches from her. She could see his

disappointment. He hadn't cared if he hurt the baby. He had been looking forward to getting his hands on her.

"Bring her to me," Jonas ordered.

Zack reached for her, but she jerked back her arm. One of the rocks shifted and she had to grip her bundle harder.

"Never mind, Brother Zack," Jonas called down. "Lola, I know you don't want to hurt the baby. Come up to my cabin. I promise I won't hurt you or the child."

As if she believed a word out of his mouth. But she walked slowly up the hill, holding the bundle of rocks protectively against her breast.

She listened to make sure that none of the guards had stumbled across Colt and Grace. But there'd been no more activity at the edge of the complex, no shouts, no gunshots. Jonas had sounded the all clear siren. His followers were slowly wandering back to either their beds or their guard duty.

Before she reached the steps to the cabin, Jonas told Zack to leave only a few guards on duty. The rest, he said, could go to bed for what was left of the night.

Clearly he thought that the danger was over and that Lola had acted alone.

She stopped at the bottom of the porch steps and looked up at Jonas. He had a self-satisfied look on his face. He thought he'd won. He thought he had her and he had Grace.

"How did you get here?" Jonas asked suddenly, looking past her.

"I stole his pickup."

"Colt McCloud's? I thought he was your hero?" he mocked.

"Some hero," she said. "But that doesn't surprise you, does it? You knew he'd believe you and not me."

Jonas almost looked sorry for her. "The man's a fool."

She hugged the bundle tighter.

"You should come in. It's cold out here," he said. "Is the baby all right?"

She knew he had to be wondering how Grace had been able to sleep through all of the racket. He had to be getting suspicious.

"She is so sweet," Lola said, glancing down for a moment to peel back of the edge of the blanket so only she could see what was inside. She smiled down at the rock. "She really is an angel." She wanted to give Colt as much time as possible to get away with Grace, but she knew she couldn't keep standing out here or Jonas was going to become suspicious.

"As I've said all along," he agreed as she mounted the steps. He reached for the baby, but she turned to the side, holding the bundle away from him.

"Please, let me hold her just a little longer." Tears filled her eyes at just the thought of the few minutes she'd had Grace in her arms and the thought that they might be all she was going to get.

Jonas relented. "Of course, hold her all you want. There is no reason you should be separated from your child. If you stay here, you will have her all the time. Imagine what your life could be like here with me."

"I have." She hoped she kept the sarcasm out of the voice as she moved to the middle of the room, giving herself a little elbow room.

"We could travel. Europe, the Caribbean, anywhere your heart desired. We could take Angel with us."

"Her name is Grace."

He ignored that as he started to close the door. He froze and cocked his head, taking in the bundle in her arms again. "It really is amazing she slept through all of that noise," he said again.

"She knows she's with her mother now. She knows she's safe."

Jonas looked out the still-open doorway as if suddenly not so sure about being alone with her. She saw Zack watching them.

Lola knew she had no choice. Zack was watching, expecting trouble, and Jonas was getting suspicious. She had no choice.

"Europe? I love Europe," she said, and saw Jonas relax a little. He waved Zack away and closed the door. She looked around, remembering the last time she'd been brought here. Jonas had told her that he would make her his wife—one way or another. He'd tried to kiss her and she'd kicked him hard enough in the shin to get away and, apparently, given him a permanent limp.

Behind her, she heard him lock the door and limp toward her.

CHAPTER ELEVEN

COLT REACHED THE PICKUP. All the way, he'd hoped that he would find Lola waiting for him even though he knew there was little chance of that.

Still, he was disappointed when he got there to find he was alone. Grace had quit crying not long after they'd left the compound. He was grateful for that since he was sure it had helped him get away.

He opened the passenger-side door, the dome light coming on as he laid the bundle Lola had given him on the seat to get his first look at his daughter.

A pair of big blue eyes stared up at him. He lost his heart in that moment. He touched the perfect little cheek, soft as downy feathers. She did resemble Lola, but he thought he could see himself a little in her, too.

"Hi, Grace," he whispered, his voice breaking. Tears welled in his eyes. He swallowed the lump in this throat. He had the baby, but what now?

He turned off the dome light, realizing that if someone had followed him, they would be able to see him through the pines. He stared into the darkness, willing Lola to appear.

He had to assume that Jonas had her by now. He'd heard the alarm go off and then another signal, which he'd assumed must be the all clear. Why would Jonas sound it unless he'd thought there was nothing more to fear?

Which meant he had Lola. She'd sacrificed herself to save her daughter. Their daughter.

He looked toward the dark trees, silently pleading for that not to be the case. He needed her. Grace needed her.

They had Lola. He couldn't leave without her. But he couldn't go back for her with the baby for fear of getting caught.

Nor could he stay there much longer. If Jonas suspected she hadn't come alone...

"What are we going to do, Grace?" he asked as he wrapped her in his coat and watched her fall back to sleep.

WITH HER BACK to Jonas, Lola reached into the baby blanket with her free hand and slowly turned to face him.

"What really happened to my parents?"

He had been moving toward her but stopped. "They were getting old, confused toward the end. Your mother came down with the flu. It turned into pneumonia. Your father stayed by her side. She was getting better and then she just...died."

She nodded, knowing that it happened at her mother's age, and not believing a word of it. "And my father?"

"I think he died of grief. You had to know how he was with your mother. I don't think he could live without her."

That too happened with people her parents' age who had been married as long as they had. "You didn't have them killed?" She said it softly so he wouldn't think it was an accusation. It wasn't like she expected the truth.

"Lola." There was that disappointing sound in his

voice again. He took a step toward her. "Why must you always think the worst of me? Your parents believed in me."

Well, at least her mother had—until he'd had her killed, Lola thought. She wondered if he'd done it himself and realized how silly that was. Of course, he hadn't. Her heart went out to her parents. She couldn't bear thinking about their last moments.

"I took care of your baby for you. I wouldn't hurt a hair on that sweet thing's head. Or on yours. Let me see her." He was close now, and she feared he would make a grab for the baby.

She loosened her hold on the baby blanket bundle a little and faced him, her hand closing tightly around the rock inside.

"Thank you for taking care of her," she said, letting her voice fill with emotion.

"I will take care of you, too—if you give me a chance." He was getting too near—within reaching distance.

She took a step toward him, closing the distance between them as she pretended to hold out the baby for him to take. She had to be close. She had to make it count. It was her only hope of getting out of here and being with Grace.

As Jonas opened his arms for the baby, she pulled out the rock and swung it at his head. He managed to deflect the blow partially with his hand—just enough to knock the rock from her hold.

But she'd swung hard enough that the rock kept going. It caught him in the temple. He stumbled back. She pulled out the second rock, dropping the baby blankets, as she swung again.

This time, he didn't get a chance to raise an arm.

The rock connected with the side of his head. His blood splattered on the rock, on her hand. He stood for a moment, looking stunned, then he went down hard on the wood floor.

Lola didn't waste any time. For all she knew he could be out cold—or only momentarily stunned and soon sounding the alarm so the whole cult would be on her heels.

She ran just as she had before. Only this time, she wasn't leaving her baby behind.

COLT HAD NEVER had trouble making a decision under duress. He'd been forced to make quick ones flying a chopper in Afghanistan. But one thing he'd never done was leave a man behind.

He couldn't this time, either. He'd purposely not taken a weapon into the compound earlier. They'd needed to get Grace out clean, and that meant not killing anyone— even if it meant getting themselves killed.

Now he took the weapons he would need. He was changing the rules—just as he was sure Jonas was. Wrapped in his coat, he laid Grace down on the floorboard of the pickup. She would be plenty warm enough— as long as he came back in a reasonable amount of time.

Locking the pickup door, he turned back toward the woods and the SLS compound. He wasn't leaving without Lola. And this time, he was armed and ready to fight his way in and out of the place if he had to.

LOLA FELT A sense of déjà vu as she ran through the woods. Her pulse hammered in her ears, her breath coming out in gasps. And yet she listened for the sound of the alarm that would alert the SLS members to fill the woods. Jonas would not let her get away if he had to run her to ground himself.

If he was able.

She had no idea how badly he'd been hurt. Or if he was already hot on her heels.

She crashed through the darkness, shoving away pine boughs that whipped her face and body. Colt had said how important it was for them get in and out of the compound without causing any more harm than was necessary.

"We're the trespassers," he'd told her. "We're the ones who will get thrown in jail if we fail tonight. We need to get in there and out as clean as possible."

She thought about the blood on the rock and could see something staining her right hand as she ran. Jonas's blood. She hadn't gotten out clean. She might have killed him. A cry escaped her lips as her ankle turned under her and she fell hard.

She struggled to get up as she hurriedly wiped the blood on the dried pine needles she'd fallen into. But the moment she put pressure on her ankle, she knew she wasn't going far. She didn't think it was broken, but she also couldn't put any weight on it without excruciating pain.

Grace. Colt. She had to get to them. They would have left by now, but she couldn't stay here. She couldn't let Jonas or one of his sheep find her. If Jonas was still alive. The thought that she might have killed him made her shudder. It had been one thing to wish him dead, to think she could kill him to save her daughter, but to actually know that she might have killed the man...

She crawled over to a pine tree and used the trunk to

get to her feet. As she started to take a step, she saw a figure suddenly appear out of the blackness of the trees.

Lola felt a sob rise in her throat. She'd never been so glad to see anyone in her life. Colt. He seemed just as overwhelmed with joy to see her. She'd thought he would have left—as per their plan. But he couldn't leave her.

Another sob rose as he ran to her, grabbed her and pulled her to him, holding her so tightly she could hardly breath. "Lola," he kept saying against her hair. "Lola."

She couldn't speak. Her throat had closed as she fought to hold back the tears of relief. As he let go, she stepped down on her bad ankle and let out a cry of pain.

"You're hurt. What is it?" he asked, his voice filled with concern.

"My ankle. I'm not sure I can walk."

He swung her up in his arms and carried her through the trees to the truck. She hadn't realized how close she was to where they'd parked it earlier.

She looked around, suddenly scared. "Grace? Where's Grace?"

He unlocked the passenger side of the pickup, opened the door and picked up a bundle wrapped in his coat. She heard a sound come from within the bundle as Colt helped her into the pickup and put Grace into her arms. The tears came now, a floodgate opening. No longer could she hold back.

Tears streaming down her face, she turned back the edge of Colt's coat, which was wrapped around the infant. "Grace," she said as Colt slid behind the wheel, started the truck and headed off the mountain.

Lola held her baby, watching her daughter's sweet face in the faint light as Grace fell back asleep. She thought she could stare into that face forever. For so long she'd feared she'd never see her again, never hold her. She wiped at her tears and looked over at Colt. He smiled and she could see the emotion in his face.

"Have you met your daughter?" she asked.

"I have," he said, his voice sounding rough. "We got acquainted while we were waiting for you, until I couldn't wait any longer and had to come looking for you."

"I'm so thankful you did."

"Let's go home," he said, his voice breaking.

Tears filled her eyes again as she looked from him to their daughter. She pulled Grace close as they left the mountain and headed toward the ranch. Home.

CHAPTER TWELVE

JONAS CAME TO, lying on his back in a pool of his own blood. His hand went to the side of his head and came away sticky. He stared for a few moments at his fingers, the tips bright red, before he tried to sit up.

His head swam, forcing him to remain where he was. He couldn't remember what had happened. Had he fallen? He'd been meaning to have one of the brothers fix that rug to keep the corner from turning up.

But from where he lay, he could see that the rug wasn't to blame. Not twelve inches from him sat a rock the size of a cantaloupe. A dark stain covered one side of it. Nearby was a baby blanket and another rock of similar size.

Memory flooded him along with a cold, deadly rage. The pain in his skull was nothing compared to the open wound of Lola's betrayal. His heart felt as if it had been ripped out of his chest.

He thought of those moments when she'd been holding what he thought was her infant in her arms. They'd been talking and she had made it sound as if she was weakening toward him. His heart had soared with hope that she was finally coming around. He had so much to offer her. Had she finally realized that she'd be a fool to turn him down?

He'd been so happy for those moments when he'd

thought things were going to work out with her and even the baby. That other man's baby, but a baby Jonas was willing to raise as his own as long as Lola became his wife and submitted to him.

The shock when she'd pulled the rock from the baby blankets was still painfully fresh. It had taken him a moment, his arms outstretched as he'd reached to take her and the infant to his bosom. The shock, the disappointment, the disbelief had slowed his movements, letting the rock get past his defenses and stun him just long enough that she was able to pull out the second rock and hit him much harder.

He closed his eyes now. He was in so much pain, but a thought wriggled its way through. His eyelids flew open. His mind felt perfectly clear, making him aware of the quiet. He recalled the alert alarm going off. When Lola had come to him with the baby... Yes, he recalled. He'd sounded the all clear signal.

Why hadn't there been another alert? He had to assume that Lola had gotten away. Gotten away with the baby. If she'd been caught, she would have been brought to him by now. And if Sister Rebecca had checked the crib and found the baby missing...

For a moment, he thought the alarm must have sounded while he'd been unconscious. But if that was true, then Brother Zack would have come to check on him and found him lying here, bleeding to death.

Two things suddenly became crystal clear. Even through the excruciating pain, he saw now that Lola couldn't have acted alone. She would have had help to get the baby off the compound. And her showing up at his door with what he thought was the baby was only a diversion.

He let out a bitter laugh. As persuasive as he'd been, it was just as he'd feared. He hadn't convinced Colt Mc-Cloud that the woman was unbalanced, that their baby boy had died, that he should leave Lola while he could.

Apparently, she'd been more convincing than he had been. He grimaced at the thought. Admittedly, he had to give her credit—her plan had worked. Or had it been Colt McCloud's plan? He closed his eyes, cursing the man to hell. Colt was a dead man.

But so was he, he realized, if he didn't get help. He was still bleeding and even more light-headed. He felt around for his cell phone to activate the alarm.

He had to turn his head to find it. The pain was so intense that he almost passed out. He closed his hand around the phone and, leaving bloody fingerprints, hit the button to activate the alarm.

His hand holding the phone dropped to his side as the air filled with the shrill cry of the alert. Any moment Brother Zack would come bursting through the door. He could always depend on Zack.

Unlike someone else, he thought, remembering his second realization. If he was right, Colt had taken the baby while Lola had pretended to be acting alone. The alarm had sounded and she had known that she couldn't get away. So she'd come up to Jonas's cabin with the rocks in the baby blankets.

But wouldn't someone have checked the baby's crib? And then wouldn't Sister Rebecca, who was responsible for the infant, have realized the baby was gone and summoned help? Pulled the alarm again?

As Brother Zack burst through the front door and rushed to him, Jonas felt the steel blade of betrayal cut even deeper. One of his flock had betrayed him.

CHAPTER THIRTEEN

COLT WOKE TO find Lola and the baby sleeping peacefully next to him. He felt his heart do a bump in his chest. The sight filled him with a sense of joy. A sense that all was right in the world.

Last night on the way down the mountain he'd felt like they were a family. It was a strange feeling for a man who'd been so independent for so long. They'd been exhausted, Lola barely able to walk on her ankle. He'd gotten them both inside the house and safe as quickly as he could.

With Grace sleeping in the middle of his big bed, he'd taken a look at Lola's ankle. Not broken, but definitely sprained badly. He'd wrapped it, both of them simply looking at each other and smiling. They'd done it. They'd gotten Grace back.

He had questions, but they could wait. Or maybe he never had to know what had happened back at the compound. He told himself it was over. They had Grace. That was all the proof they needed against Jonas should he try to take either the baby or Lola back.

They'd gone to bed, Grace curled between them, and fallen asleep instantly.

At the sound of a vehicle, Colt wondered who would be coming by so early in the morning as he slipped out of bed and quickly dressed.

Someone was knocking at his front door by the time he reached it. He peered out, worried for a moment that he'd find Jonas Emanuel standing on his front step.

"Sheriff," Colt said as he opened the door.

"A moment of your time," Flint said.

Colt stepped back to let the sheriff enter the house. Flint glanced around, clearly looking for something.

He'd been wondering how Jonas was going to handle this. He'd thought Jonas wouldn't call in the sheriff about the events of last night. He still didn't think he would. But this was definitely not a social call.

"What can I help you with, Sheriff?"

Flint turned to give him his full attention. "Jonas reported a break-in at the SLS compound last night. I was wondering if you knew anything about that."

"Was anything taken?"

Flint smiled. "Apparently not. But Jonas was injured when he tried to apprehend one of the intruders."

That was news. Colt thought of Lola just down the hall still in bed with Grace. Last night when he was wrapping her ankle, he'd seen what looked like blood on her sleeve. But he hadn't want to ask what she'd had to go through to get away.

"He see who did it?" Colt asked.

"Apparently not," Flint said again.

Just then the sound of a baby crying could be heard down the hall toward the bedroom.

Flint froze.

"So nothing was taken," Colt said. "Jonas's injuries…"

"Aren't life-threatening at this point," Flint said as Lola limped down the hall from the bedroom, the baby in her arms.

Lola spotted the sheriff and stopped, her gaze flying to Colt. She looked worried until Colt said, "You remember Lola. And this is our daughter, Grace."

Colt moved to her to take the baby. He stepped to the sheriff, turning back the blanket his daughter was nestled in.

Every time he saw her sweet face his heart swelled to overflowing. She was so precious. Having never changed a diaper in his life, he'd learned quickly last night.

Now he lifted the cotton gown she'd been wearing when Lola had taken her from the crib last night at SLS to expose the tiny heart-shaped birthmark.

"Our baby girl," Colt said. "We'll be going to the doctor later today to have her checked over—and a DNA test done, in case you were wondering."

Flint nodded solemnly, and Colt handed Grace back to Lola. As she limped into the kitchen with the baby, the sheriff said, "I'm not going to ask, but I hope you know what you're doing."

"That little girl belongs with her mother."

The sheriff met his gaze. "And her father?"

"I'm her father."

Flint sighed. "I was at the hospital this morning taking Jonas's statement. He isn't filing assault charges because he says he doesn't know who attacked him. I see Lola is limping."

Colt said nothing.

"You sure this is over?" the sheriff asked.

"It is as far as I'm concerned."

Flint nodded. "Not sure Jonas feels that way. Got the impression he's a man who is used to getting what he wants."

Colt couldn't have agreed more. "He can't have Lola and Grace, but I don't want any trouble."

The sheriff shook his head at that. "I'm afraid it won't be your choice."

He knew a warning when he heard one. Not that he had to be told that Jonas was dangerous. "He's brainwashed those people, taken their money and keeps them up on that mountain like prisoners."

Flint nodded. "A choice each of them made."

"Except for the children up there."

"You think I like any of what I saw on that mountain?" Flint swore. "But you also know there is nothing I can do about it. That's private property up there. Jonas has every right to keep trespassers off. Not to mention it is church property, holy ground under the law."

"I have no intention of going up there."

"I wish I thought it was that simple." The sheriff had taken off his Stetson when he'd come into the house, and now he settled his hat back on his head. Turning, he started for the door. "You know my number," he said over his shoulder. "I'll come as quickly as I can. But I fear even that could be too late."

"Thanks for stopping by, Sheriff."

At the door, Flint turned to look back at him. Lola had come out of the kitchen carrying the baby. She was smiling down at Grace, cooing softly.

Flint's expression softened and Colt remembered that Darby had mentioned the sheriff's wife was pregnant. "Have a good day," Flint said, and left.

JONAS LISTENED TO the doctor tell him how lucky he was. He had a monster headache and hated being flat on his back in the hospital when he had things that needed to be done—and quickly.

"You lost a lot of blood," the doctor was saying. "If your…friend hadn't gotten you here when he did…"

"Yes, it is fortunate that Brother Zack found me when he did," Jonas said. He didn't need the doctor telling him how lucky he was. He was very aware. But a man made his own luck. He'd learned that when he'd left home to find his own way in life.

Not that he discounted what nature had given him—a handsome, honest-looking face, mesmerizing blue eyes and snake-oil-salesman charm. But he was the one who'd taken those gifts and used them to the best of his ability. Not that they always worked. Lola, a case in point. They'd worked enough, though, that he was a very rich man and, until recently, he would have said he had very loyal followers who saw to his every need. What more could a man ask for?

"You're going to have a headache for a while, but fortunately, you suffered only a minor concussion. A fall like that could have killed a man half your age. Like I said, lucky."

"Lucky," Jonas repeated. "Yes, Doctor, I was. So when can I be released?"

"Your laceration is healing quite nicely, but that bandage needs to be changed regularly so I'd prefer you stay in the hospital at least another day, maybe longer."

That was not what he wanted to hear. "One of the sisters could change my bandage for me. Really, I would be much more comfortable in my own home. I have plenty of people to look after me."

The doctor wavered. Jonas knew that the hospital staff would be much more comfortable with him gone, as well. A half dozen of the brothers and some of the SLS sisters had been coming and going since his "accident." He'd seen the way the hospital staff looked at them, the men in their black pants and white shirts, the woman in their long shapeless white dresses.

"I'd prefer you stay another day at least. I'll give instructions to one of your…sisters for after that. We'll see how you're doing tomorrow."

"I'm feeling so much better. I promise that when you release me, I will rest and take care of myself." His head ached more than he had let the doctor know. He didn't want any medication that would make his brain fuzzy. He needed his wits about him now more than ever.

"Like I said, we'll see how you are tomorrow," the doctor said, eyeing him suspiciously. The man knew Jonas couldn't be feeling that good, not with his head almost bashed in. He also knew the doctor had to be questioning how he could have hurt himself like this in a fall.

Jonas just wished he would go away and leave him alone.

"I need to ask you about these pills you've been taking," the doctor said, clearly not leaving yet. "One of your church members told me they were for a bad heart, but that's not the medication you're taking."

"No, it's not for a heart ailment," Jonas had to admit. "I'd prefer my flock not worry about my health, Doctor."

"If you're suffering from memory loss at your age, then we need to run some tests and see—"

"I have early-onset Alzheimer's," Jonas interrupted. The doctor blinked.

"It is in the beginning stages, thus the pills I'm taking. I can assure you that I'm being well taken care of."

The doctor seemed at a loss for words.

"I believe Brother Zack is waiting in the hall," Jonas said to the doctor. "Would you ask him to step in here? I need to talk to him."

Realizing he was excused, the doctor left. A few moments later, Zack stuck his head in the door.

Jonas motioned him in. "Close the door. Have you seen Sister Rebecca?"

"Not since last night."

"Who was on duty at the second nursery last night?" he asked.

Zack frowned. "Sister Alexa." His eyes widened as he realized what the leader was really asking. "Sister Rebecca was taking care of the…special baby."

The angel. That's what Jonas had told his flock. That he'd had a vision and Lola's baby was a chosen one.

"Sister Rebecca." Jonas nodded and closed his eyes for a moment. He'd known it, but had needed Zack to verify his suspicions. Rebecca had been with him since the beginning. If there was anyone he knew he could trust, could depend on, it was her. He slowly opened his eyes and stared up at the pale green ceiling.

Zack stood at the end of the bed, waiting. Rebecca and Zack had never gotten along. Jonas blamed it on simple jealousy. Both were in the top positions at SLS. He knew how much Zack was going to enjoy the task he was about to give him.

"Go back to the complex," Jonas told him. "I want Sister Rebecca—" if she was still there "—restrained. Use the cabin where Sister Lola stayed. Guard it yourself." He finally looked at Zack, who nodded, a malicious glint in his gaze even as he fought not to smile.

"I'll take care of it."

AFTER THE SHERIFF LEFT, Colt stepped to Lola and Grace
and pulled them close. He knew the sheriff was worried and with good reason. Jonas was an egomaniac
who enjoyed having power over other people. He ran
his "church" like a fiefdom. He would be incensed to
have lost Lola and the baby, but there was really nothing he could do. At least not legally. Once the DNA results came back, once they had proof that Grace was
Colt's daughter...

He tried to put it out of his head. Jonas was in the
hospital. He'd lied to the sheriff. It was over. Hopefully,
the man would move on with some other obsession.

Colt cooked them breakfast while Lola fed Grace.
He loved watching them together. It made his heart ex-
pand to near bursting.

Their day was quickly planned. First the DNA tests,
then shopping for baby things. Never in his life had
Colt thought about buying baby things, but now he realized he was excited. He wanted Grace to have whatever she needed.

At the doctor's office DNA samples were taken, then
Colt took Lola and Grace to the small-box store on the
edge of town. He was amazed at all the things a baby
needed. Not just clothing and a car seat, but bottles and
formula, baby food, diapers and wipes.

"How did babies survive before all of these things
were on the market?" he joked, then insisted they get
a changing table.

"It's too much," Lola said at one point.

"It's all good," he'd said, wanting only the best for
his daughter. At the back of his mind, like a tiny devil
perched on his shoulder, a voice was saying, "What are
you doing? You are going back on assignment soon."

He shoved the thought aside, telling himself that he'd cross that bridge when he got there. He still had time. But time for what? There hadn't been any offers on the ranch. It was another thought that he pushed aside. Instead, he concentrated on Lola and Grace, enjoying being with them. Enjoying pretending at least for a while that they were a family.

He didn't even need the DNA test. That was all Lola. "We need it for Jonas should he ever try to take Grace again," she'd said. "Also, I don't want you to have doubts."

"I don't have any doubts."

She'd given him a dubious look. "I want it settled. Not that I will ever ask anything of you. And I will pay you back for all the baby things you bought. I called this morning and am having some money wired to me."

"That isn't necessary."

But she said nothing, a stubborn tilt to her chin. He hadn't argued.

Instead, he took them back to the Stagecoach Saloon where, the moment they walked in, he knew that Billie Dee was cooking up her famous Texas chili.

Lillie Cahill Beaumont just happened to be there visiting her brother, along with Darby and his wife, Mariah. They oohed and aahed over Grace and Lola did the same with their babies.

By the time they got home, Colt was ready for a nap, too. After Lola put Grace down, she came into the bedroom and curled up against him. He held her close, breathing in the scent of her. He'd never been more happy.

CHAPTER FOURTEEN

THE NEXT DAY, Jonas couldn't wait for the doctor to stop by so he could hopefully get out of the hospital. He knew that Zack was taking care of things on the complex, but he worried. He still couldn't believe that Rebecca would betray him. It shook the stable foundation that he'd built this life on. Never would he have suspected her of deceiving him.

When the doctor finally came by, he hadn't wanted to send Jonas home yet. It took a lot of lying to get the doctor to finally release him. It was late in the day before he finally got his discharge papers.

Elmer picked him up at the hospital and drove him to the compound. He liked Elmer, though he'd seen the man's faith in their work here fading. He and Lola's father had been friends. Jonas suspected Elmer only stayed because he had nowhere else to go. But that was all right. Jonas still thought that when the chips were down, he could depend on Elmer.

Once at the compound, Zack was waiting, Excusing Elmer, Jonas let Zack help him inside. He was weak and his head ached, but he was home. He had things that needed to be taken care of and had been going crazy in the hospital.

Three of the sisters entered his cabin, fussed over him until he couldn't take it any longer and sent them scurrying. The pain in his head was better. It was another pain that was riding him like a dark cloak on his shoulders.

As soon as he was settled, Jonas asked Zack to bring him Sister Rebecca. "She's still detained in the small cabin, right?"

"She is," Zack said.

"How is her…attitude?"

"Subdued."

Jonas almost laughed since it didn't seem like a word Zack would ever have used. "Subdued? Is she on anything?"

"No, but I've had the sisters chanting over her every few hours. I thought it was something you would have done yourself had you been here."

He was both touched and annoyed by Zack taking this step without his permission. But he needed Zack more than ever now so he let it go. "You did well. Thank you."

Zack beamed and Jonas saw something in the man's eyes that gave him pause. Zack wanted to lead SLS. The man actually thought he had what it took to do it. The realization was almost laughable.

"Bring Sister Rebecca to me," he said, and closed his eyes, his head pounding like a bass drum. He wondered if he shouldn't have put this off until he was feeling better.

Zack hurried out, leaving him peacefully alone with his thoughts. Lola had made a fool out of him by sleeping with Colt McCloud. To add to his embarrassment, she'd gotten pregnant. That child should have been his.

Instead, he'd put aside his hurt, his fury, his embarrassment and offered to raise the baby as his own. Still, she'd turned him down. How could she have humiliated him even more?

He let out a bark of a laugh. What had she done? She'd almost killed him—after giving him hope that she was weakening. The latter hurt the most. Offering hope was a poisonous pill that he'd swallowed in one big gulp. And now even his flock was turning against him.

Was he losing his mind faster than he'd thought? Could he trust his judgment?

He started at the knock on the door, forgetting for a moment that he'd been expecting it. "Come in."

The moment Rebecca walked through the door, he could see the guilt written all over her face. Brother Zack stood directly behind her. He started to step into the cabin, and Jonas could tell Zack thought he was going to get to watch this.

"That will be all, Zack."

The man looked surprised and then disappointed. But it was the flicker of anger he saw in Zack's eyes that caused concern.

Jonas watched his right-hand man slowly close the door, but he could tell he'd be standing outside hoping to hear whatever was going on. Was Zack now becoming a problem, too?

He saw Sister Rebecca quickly take him in. In her gaze shone concern and something even more disturbing— sympathy, if not pity. His head was still bandaged, dark stitches under the dressing, but his headaches were getting better. Stuck in the hospital, he'd had plenty of time to think over the past two days.

It was bad enough to be betrayed by Lola, even worse by Sister Rebecca, because he'd come to depend on her. She had to have known that Lola's baby had gone missing. It would have been the first thing she would have checked. Seeing the baby missing, she should have come to him.

He was anxious to talk to her, but as he looked at her standing there, he felt a loss of words for a moment. He kept telling himself that he was wrong. Sister Rebecca had been with him for years. She wouldn't betray him. Couldn't. He'd always thought she was half in love with him.

Which was probably why she hadn't come to him to let him know the baby wasn't in her crib. Even if she'd seen Lola with that bundle in her arms entering his cabin, she should have come to him. If she had, his head wouldn't be killing him right now. But he suspected Rebecca had wanted to be shed of Lola and the baby he was so determined to make his.

Since Zack had locked up Rebecca, she would know she was in trouble. He wondered what story she would tell him and how much of it he could believe?

Colt almost changed his mind. Things had been going so well that he didn't want or need the interruption. He enjoyed being with Lola and Grace. If he said so himself, he'd become proficient at diaper changes and getting chubby little limbs into onesies. He liked the middle-of-the-night feedings, holding Grace and watching her take her bottle. Her bright blue eyes watched him equally.

"I'm your daddy," he'd whispered last night, and felt a lump rise in his throat.

So when Julia had called and said it was important that they meet and talk, he hadn't been interested.

"If this is about you needing me to forgive you—"

"No. It's not that," she'd said quickly. "I doubt you can ever forgive me. I know how badly I hurt you."

Did she? The news had blindsided him. Hell, he'd been expecting her to pick him up at the airport—not break up with him to be with one of his friends. He still couldn't get his head around how that had gone down. No warning at all. He'd thought Wyatt hadn't even liked Julia. He knew that Darby didn't think she was right for him. Not that Darby had ever said anything. But Colt had been able to tell.

He could laugh now. He used to think that Darby just had his expectations set too high. But then Colt had met Mariah and realized that his friend had just been holding out for the real thing. Darby had done well.

"Julia, I can't see what meeting you for coffee could possibly—" It had been Lola who'd insisted he meet with Julia. She'd walked in while he was on the phone. As if gifted with ESP, she'd motioned to him that he should go.

"Fine," he'd said into the phone. "When and where?" He had just wanted to get it over with.

Now he drove past the coffee shop, telling himself that there was nothing Julia could say that would change anything. But she'd sounded…strange on the phone. He suspected something was up. Did he care, though?

He circled the block, saw a parking space and pulled his pickup in to it. For a moment he sat behind the wheel debating what he was about to do. And why had Lola been all for him seeing his ex? Was she worried that he wasn't over Julia? Or was she hoping to hook the two of them up again?

He'd heard her on the phone calling a car dealership

to order a vehicle. "You don't have to do that. You can use my pickup whenever you want."

"I need my own car, but thank you," she'd said.

He thought of the discussion they'd had after he'd hung up from Julia.

"I knew that was Julia on the phone," Lola had said. "I wasn't eavesdropping. You talk to her in a certain way." She'd shrugged.

"A certain way?"

"I can't describe it, but you owe her nothing."

"Then why should I meet with her?"

"Because it won't be over until you tell her how you feel," Lola had said.

He had laughed. She made life seem so simple, and yet could her life have been any more complicated when he'd met her? "Okay, I'll meet with her with your blessing."

"You don't need my blessing."

He stepped to her and, taking her shoulders in his hands, pulled her close. "All I care about is you and Grace. You have to know that."

"So you'll talk to her. You'll be honest. You'll see if there is anything there that you might have missed. Or that you want back."

He'd wanted to argue the point, but she'd put a finger to his lips.

"You should go. She'll be waiting."

Let her wait, he thought now as he glanced at his watch. Let her think he wasn't coming—look how she'd treated him at the Billings airport.

Then, just wanting to be done with this, he climbed out and walked down to the coffee shop. It was mid-afternoon. Only a few tables were taken. Julia had chosen one at the back. Where no one would see the two of them together and report back to Wyatt?

As he pushed open the door, he saw her frowning down at her phone. Checking the time? Or reading a text from Wyatt?

She looked up as if sensing him and motioned him over. "I got you a coffee—just the way you like it."

Except he'd never liked his coffee that way. Julia had come out to the ranch when they'd first started dating with some caramel-mocha concoction. When he'd taken a sip, he'd had to force a smile and pretend he'd liked it. His mistake.

"It's good, huh. I thought you'd like it. You always have the same boring coffee. I thought we'd shake things up a bit," she'd said. And from then on, she'd decided that was the way he liked his coffee.

"Thanks," he said now, without sitting down, "But I never liked my coffee that way. I'll get my own." He moved to the counter and ordered a cup of black coffee before returning to the table.

She looked sullen, pouting like she used to when he'd displeased her—which was often enough that he knew this look too well.

"So what is it you want?" he asked as he sat down but didn't settle in. He didn't plan to stay long and was regretting coming here, no matter what Lola had said. He couldn't see how this could help anything.

Julia let out a nervous laugh. "This is not the way I saw this going."

"Oh?"

She seemed to regroup, drawing in a long breath, sitting up a little straighter. He was suddenly aware that she'd dressed up. He caught a hint of the perfume she used to wear when they were together because he'd commented one time that he liked it. He frowned as he realized she hadn't been wearing it the day they'd accidentally run into each other.

"What's going on, Julia?"

She looked away for a moment, biting down on the corner of her lower lip as if nervous. He used to think it was cute.

"I've made a terrible mistake. I didn't mean to blurt it out like that, but I can tell you're still angry and have no patience with me. Otherwise, you wouldn't have been so late, you would have drunk the coffee I ordered you and you wouldn't be looking at me as if you hated me."

He wasn't going to try to straighten her up on any of that. "Mistake?"

Julia looked at him as if she thought no one would be that daft. "Wyatt. I was just so lonely, and it looked as if you were never going to quit the military and come home…"

"How did you two get together? I always thought Wyatt didn't like you."

She mugged a face at him. "You don't need to be cruel."

"I'm serious. He never had a good word to say about you. Or was he just trying to keep his feelings for you from me?"

"I have no idea. And I don't care. He probably didn't like me. Maybe that's why we aren't together anymore."

Colt realized he wasn't surprised. Julia hadn't gotten him to the altar. He remembered that had been the case with an earlier boyfriend, too. Looked like there was a pattern there, he thought but kept it to himself.

"That's too bad."

"I can tell that you're really broken up over it."

After the initial shock had worn off, he'd actually thought Julia and Wyatt wouldn't last. Julia was beautiful in a classic way, but definitely high maintenance. He could see that clearly after being around Lola. As for Wyatt, well, he'd never had a serious girlfriend. He'd always preferred playing the field, as he called it.

"I'm sincerely sorry it didn't work out. Is that all?"

"Colt, stop being so mean." She sounded close to tears. She glanced around to make sure no one had heard her. "I feel so bad about what I did to you."

"You shouldn't." He realized he meant it. For a while, he'd hoped she choked on the guilt daily. Now he didn't feel vindictive. He realized he no longer cared.

"I know how hurt you must be."

"I was hurt, Julia. That was one crushing blow you delivered, but I've moved on."

"With that woman you were with the other day? Are you in love with her?"

Now there was the question, wasn't it? "It's complicated."

"It doesn't have to be." She reached across the table and covered his hand.

He pulled his free. "Are you suggesting what I think you are?"

She looked at him as if to say, *No one can be this dense.* "I want you back. I'll do anything." She definitely sounded desperate.

Colt had played with this exact scheme in his mind on those long nights in the desert after she'd dumped him. It had been like a salve that made him feel better. Julia begging to come back to him. Him loving every minute of it before he turned her down flat.

Now it made him feel uncomfortable because he no longer wanted to hurt her. If anything, he felt indifferent and wondered what he'd ever seen in this woman. He couldn't help comparing her to Lola. Julia came up way short.

"Julia, you and I are never getting back together. Truthfully, I doubt we would have made it to the altar."

"How can you say that?" she demanded. "You asked me to marry you."

"I did. But I didn't realize then how wrong we were for each other. I overlooked things, thinking they would change once we were married. Now I know better. I'm sure it was the same for you. Otherwise, how could you have fallen so quickly in love with another man?"

She seemed at a loss for words.

"So I imagine we both would have realized we weren't right for each other before we made a huge mistake."

Julia stared at him as if looking at a stranger. "I don't believe this."

Had she expected him to take her back at the snap of her fingers? The flutter of her eyelashes? She really hadn't known him. Even if he'd never met Lola, he wouldn't have taken Julia back. She'd proved the kind of woman she was—not the kind a man could ever trust.

Colt got to his feet. "You should try to work things out with Wyatt. Now that I think about it, you two belong together."

Her eyes widened, then narrowed dangerously. "Do you realize what you're throwing away? And for what? That…that…woman I saw you with the other day?" She made a distasteful face.

"Easy, Julia," he said, lowering his voice. "You really don't want to say anything about the mother of my child."

"What?" she sputtered.

"Lola and I have a beautiful daughter together."

Openmouthed, she stared at him. "Lola? That's not possible. You can't have known her long enough to… Are you going to *marry* her?"

"I haven't asked her yet, but you know me. I like to take my time. Also, I'm a little gun-shy after my last engagement."

Julia pushed to her feet. He'd never seen her so angry. It made him want to laugh because he realized, with no small amount of relief, that had he married her, he would have seen her like this a lot.

The one thing he did know was that he was completely over her. No hard feelings. No need for retribution. No need to ever see this woman again.

"This never happened," she said with a flip of her head. "You hear me? You're right. Wyatt and I are perfect together. We're going to get married and be happy."

He smiled. "So you and Wyatt aren't broken up." He let out a bark of a laugh. "Good to see that you haven't changed. Give Wyatt my regards."

Julia stormed out. Colt finished his coffee and threw away the cups Julia had left behind. He smiled as he headed for the door. He couldn't wait to get home to Lola and Grace.

CHAPTER FIFTEEN

LOLA SAW THE change in Colt the moment he walked in the door. It was as if a weight had been lifted off his shoulders. He was smiling and seemed…happy.

"I guess I don't need to ask how it went." Her heart had been pounding ever since Julia's phone call. A woman knows. Julia wanted more than Colt's forgiveness. A woman like that would try to hold on to him, to keep him in the wings—if she didn't already want him back.

Colt met her gaze. "She wants me back."

It felt as if a fist had closed around her heart, but she fought not to let him see her pain. "That must seem like a dream come true."

He laughed. "I'll admit at one time it would have been. But no," he said with a shake of his head as he stepped to her. "It would never have happened even if I hadn't met you. But now that I have…" He leaned down to kiss her softly on the mouth. As he drew back, he saw that she was frowning.

"I don't want you giving up the woman you love because of me and Grace," she said quickly. "I told you. We can take care of ourselves."

"That wasn't what I meant." His blue-eyed gaze locked with hers and she felt a bolt of heat shoot to her core. "Julia is the last person on earth that I want."

She swallowed. "But you asked her to marry you."

"I did." He chuckled. "And I have no idea why I did. Honestly, I feel as if I dodged a bullet. But I don't want to talk about her. I want you," he said as he drew her close again. "Is Grace sleeping?"

While he'd been gone, Lola had practiced what she was going to say to him. But when she looked up into his blue gaze and saw the desire burning there, it ignited the blaze inside her.

She told herself that they could have a serious talk later. There was time. Colt was in such a good mood, she didn't want to bring him down. She cared too much about him. But that was the problem, wasn't it? She was falling in love with him. And that was why she and Grace had to leave before Colt did something stupid like ask her to stay.

LATER, AFTER MAKING LOVE and falling into a sated sleep, Colt heard Grace wake up from her nap and slipped out of bed to go see to her. "Hi, sweetheart," he said as he picked her up and carried her over to the changing table. As he changed her, he talked to her, telling her how pretty and sweet she was.

She was Lola in miniature, from her pert nose to her bow-shaped mouth to her violet eyes. And yet, he saw some of himself in the baby—and knew it might be only because he wanted it to be true. They hadn't gotten the DNA results, not that he was worried.

What bothered him was how much he wanted to see himself in Grace. How much he wanted to tell her about all the things he'd teach her as she grew up. What he wanted to do was talk about the future with Grace—and Lola.

Getting Lola's baby back was one thing, but seeing himself in this equation? He would have said the last thing he needed was a family. He was selling the ranch and going back into the service. That had been his plan and he'd always had a plan.

Now he felt rudderless and aloft, not knowing if he was up or down. What would he do if not go back to flying choppers for the Army? Ranch?

He stared into Grace's adorable face, feeling his heart ache at the thought of being away from her. He picked her up, holding her as he felt his heart pounding next to hers. Fatherhood had always been so far off in the future. But now here it was looking back at him with so much trust… He thought of his own father, his parents' disastrous marriage, how disconnected he'd felt from both of them.

He knew nothing about being a father or a husband. A part of him felt guilty for asking Julia to marry him. True, he'd put her off for years. It had come down to break up or marry her. He'd thought it was what he'd wanted.

Now, though, he knew his heart hadn't been in it. What he'd told Julia earlier had been true. He doubted they would have made it to the altar. After he'd put that diamond—she'd picked it out herself—on her finger, all she'd talked about was the big wedding they would have, the big house, the big life.

He'd let her talk, not really taking her seriously. He should have, though.

While Lola… Well, she was different. Her heart was so filled with love for their child that she'd risked her life numerous times. He'd never met anyone like her. And Grace… She smiled and cooed up at him, her gaze meeting his, and he felt her steal another piece of his heart if she hadn't already taken it all.

"Does she need changing?" Lola asked from the doorway.

"All taken care of. She just smiled at me."

Lola laughed. "I saw that." She'd been watching from the doorway, he realized. He wondered how long she'd been there. She was wearing one of his shirts and, he'd bet, nothing under it. She couldn't have looked sexier.

His cell phone rang. Lola moved to him to take the baby.

After pulling out his phone, Colt felt a start when he saw that it was Margaret Barnes, his Realtor, calling. He'd forgotten about her, about listing the ranch. All that seemed like ages ago.

"Hello?" he said as he headed out of the nursery.

"Colt, I have some good news for you. I have a buyer for your ranch."

For a moment he couldn't speak. He looked back at Lola and Grace from the doorway. Lola was rocking the baby in her arms, smiling down at her, and Grace was cooing and smiling up at her mother—just as she had done moments before with her father.

"Colt, are you there?"

"Yes." He saw Lola look up as if she heard something in his voice.

"You said to find a buyer as quickly as I could. If you have some time today, stop by my office. I can get the paperwork all ready. The buyer is fine with your asking price and would like to take possession as soon as possible."

He felt as if the earth was crumbling under his feet. Yes, he'd told her to find a buyer and as quickly as possible. But that had been before. Before Lola had shown up at his door in the middle of the night. Before he'd known about Grace.

"What is it?" Lola asked, seeing his distress as she joined him in the living room. "Bad news?"

He stood holding his phone after disconnecting. "That was the Realtor."

Lola hadn't asked about the for-sale sign on the road into the ranch and he hadn't brought it up. But Lola knew what his plans had been months ago. The night they'd met he'd told her he was going to accept another Army assignment rather than resign his commission, like he'd been planning before that night, to marry Julia.

"Does she have a buyer for the ranch?" Lola asked, giving nothing away.

He wasn't sure what kind of reaction he'd been expecting. His gaze went to Grace in her arms. He felt his heart breaking. Lately, his only concern had been protecting Lola, getting Grace back and making sure that horrible Jonas didn't have either of them.

He hadn't thought about the future. Hadn't let himself. "I think we should talk about—" His phone rang again. He checked it, hoping it was the Realtor calling again. He'd tell her he needed more time.

It was the doctor calling. He glanced at Lola and then picked up. "Doc?" he said into the phone.

"Your test results are back. You're welcome to come by and I would be happy to explain anything you didn't understand about DNA testing."

"Let's just cut to the chase, Doc."

Silence hung on the other end of the line for a long few moments. "The infant is a match for both Lola and you, Colt."

"Thanks, Doc." He looked to Lola, who didn't appear all that interested. Because she'd known all along.

"Are you all right?" she asked.

He nodded, but he wasn't. Grace had fallen back to sleep in her arms. Had there ever been a more beautiful, ethereal-looking child? No wonder Jonas had wanted her. Wanted her and Lola.

If he looked like a man in pain, he was. Lola and the baby had taken his already topsy-turvy life and given it a tailspin. All he'd wanted just days ago was to get out of this town, out of this state, out from under the ranch his father had left him and the responsibility that came with it.

Now, though, he no longer wanted to run. He wanted to plant roots. He wanted to make them a family. "I think we should get married." The words were out and he wasn't sorry to hear them. But he should have done something romantic, not just blurted them out like that.

To his surprise, Lola smiled at him. "That's sweet, but…it's too early, isn't it?"

Too early? Like in the morning or—

"We hardly know each other."

"I'd say we know each other quite well," he said as he picked up the tail end of his shirt she was wearing.

She laughed and playfully slapped his hand away as she headed for the spare room that they'd made into a makeshift nursery. "You know what I mean."

He followed her and watched as she put Grace down in the crib. "We have a daughter."

"Yes, we do. But we can't get married just for Grace. You know that wouldn't work."

"But neither can I let the two of you walk out that door," he said.

"Colt, that door will soon be someone else's."

She had a point.

"I won't sell the ranch."

She gave him a pointed look. "I owe you my life and Grace's. But I also owe you something else. Freedom. Grace and I can take care of ourselves now. Jonas is no longer a problem. He isn't going to bother us, not after the sheriff saw our daughter and knows that Jonas lied about keeping her from me. My parents set aside money for me should I ever need it and I saved the money I made teaching. Grace and I will be fine."

"But *I* won't be fine."

She looked at him, sympathy in her gaze.

"Lola, I need you. I need you and our daughter. I want us to be a family."

Tears welled in her eyes as she tried to pass him. "Colt."

He took her in his arms. "I know we haven't known each other long. But the night we met, we connected in a way that neither of us had before, right?" She nodded, though reluctantly it seemed. "And we've been through more than any couple can ever imagine, and yet we worked together and pulled it off against incredible odds. If any two people can make this work, it's you and me."

She smiled sweetly, but he could tell she wasn't convinced. "We're good together, I won't deny that. But, Colt, you don't want to ranch. You admitted that to me the first night we met. Now you're talking about keeping the ranch just to make a home for me and Grace? No, Colt. You would grow to resent us for tying you down. I see how your eyes light up when you talk about flying helicopters. That's what you love. That's where you need to be."

He wanted to argue, but he couldn't. She'd listened to him. She knew him better than even he knew himself. "Still—"

"No," she said as she moved down the hallway to the room that they now shared. She began to pick up her clothing. "This is best and we both know it."

It didn't feel like the best thing to do. He'd come to look forward to seeing Lola's face each morning, hear her singing to the baby at night and spending his days with the two of them.

"Promise you won't leave just yet," he said, panicking at the sight of her getting her things ready.

She stopped and looked at him. "I'll stay until the ranch closes so you can spend as much time with Grace as possible. But then we have to go."

"It isn't just Grace I want to spend time with," he said as he drew her close. He kissed her and told himself he'd figure out something. He had to. Because he couldn't bear the thought of either of them walking out of his life.

JONAS STUDIED THE woman before him, letting her wait. Sister Rebecca was what was known as a handsome woman. She stood almost six feet tall with straight brown hair cut chin-length. Close to his own age, she wasn't pretty, never had been. If anything, she was nondescript. You could pass her on the street and not see her.

That was one reason she'd worked out so well all these years. She didn't look dangerous. A person hardly noticed her. Until it was too late.

Studying her, Jonas admitted that he'd come to care very deeply for her. He had depended on her. Her betrayal cut him deeper even than Lola's. Fury gripped him like fingers around his throat.

Along with guilt, he saw something else in her face now. She knew that he knew what she'd done.

"Rebecca?"

She raised her gaze slowly. The moment she met his eyes, her face seemed to crumble. She rushed to him to fall to her knees in front of his chair. "Forgive me, Father," she said, head bowed. "Please forgive me."

He didn't speak for a moment, couldn't. "For almost getting me killed or for letting Lola get away with the baby?"

She raised her head again. While pleas for forgiveness had streamed from her mouth, there was no sign of regret in her eyes.

"You stupid, foolish woman," he said with disgust, and pushed her away.

She fell back, landing hard. He watched as she slowly got to her feet. Her dark eyes were hard, her smile brittle. Defiance burned behind her gaze, a blaze that he saw had been burning for some time. Why hadn't he seen it? Because he'd been so consumed with Lola for so long.

"I have done whatever you've asked of me for years," she said, anger making her words sharp as knives hurled at him.

"As you should, as one of my followers," he snapped.

She let out a humorous laugh that sent a chill up his spine. "I wasn't just one of your followers."

He felt for his phone and realized he'd left it over on the table, out of his reach. Zack had said he would be right outside the door. But would he be able to get in quickly enough if Rebecca attacked? Jonas knew he wasn't strong enough to fight her off. Rebecca probably knew it, too.

"Many times you were wrong, but still I did what you asked without question," she continued as she moved closer and closer until she was standing over him. "All these years, I've followed you, looked up to you, trusted that you were doing what was best for our community, best for me."

He swallowed, afraid he'd created a monster. If he was being honest, and now seemed like a good time for it, he'd let her think that one day the two of them would run SLS. He'd trusted her above all others, even Zack.

"You didn't sound the alarm when you found the crib empty," he said, trying to regain control and get the conversation back on safer ground.

She shook her head. "No, when I found Sister Amelia standing next to the empty crib, I told her to go back to bed and let me handle it. I thought about sounding the alarm, but then I didn't. In truth? I was overjoyed to see the brat gone, along with her mother."

"That wasn't your decision to make."

She smiled at that. "You would destroy everything for that woman? You would take her bastard and raise it as your own? I thought of you as a god, but now I see that you are nothing but a man with a man's weaknesses."

The truth pierced his heart and he instantly recoiled. "You will not speak to me like this or there will be serious consequences."

A chuckle seemed to rise deep in her, coming out on a ragged breath. "Will you have the sisters chant more over me? You've already locked me up. Or…" Her gaze was hard as the stone Lola had used to try to bash his head in. "Will you have me killed? It wouldn't be the first time you've had a follower killed, would it?"

The threat was clear in her gaze, in her words. Rebecca knew too much. She could never leave this compound alive, and they both knew it.

He grabbed for his phone, but she reached it first. She held the phone away from him, stepping back, daring him to try to take it from her.

"This is ridiculous, Sister Rebecca. You would throw away everything we have worked so hard for out of simple jealousy?"

She raised a brow, but when she spoke her voice betrayed how close she was to tears again. This was breaking her heart as much as his own. "I know you. After all these years, I know you better than you know yourself. You'll go after her and that baby. You'll have her one way or another even if it means destroying everything."

He stared at her, hearing the truth in her words and realizing that he'd let her get too close. She *did* know him.

She looked down at the phone in her hand, then up at him. She pushed the alarm. The air on the mountaintop filled with the scream of the siren.

When Zack burst through the door, she threw Jonas his phone and, with one final look, turned and let Zack take her roughly by the arm and lead her back to her prison.

She wouldn't be locked up there long, Jonas thought. He owed her that at least, he thought as he sounded the all clear signal. But things weren't all right at all and he feared they never would be again.

CHAPTER SIXTEEN

COLT HAD BEEN worried that the sheriff was right, that Jonas wasn't going to take what had happened lying down. Hearing that Jonas had been released from the hospital, he'd almost been expecting a visit from the SLS leader.

He'd been ready, a shotgun beside the door. But the day had passed without incident and so had the next and the next.

The days seemed to fly by since he'd signed the ranch papers and deposited a partial down payment from the buyer. He'd kept busy selling off the cattle and planning the auction for the farm equipment. He tried not to think about the liquidation of his father's legacy, telling himself his old man knew how much he hated ranching. It was his own fault for leaving Colt the ranch.

He was in the barn when he heard footfalls behind him and turned to see Lola. "So the buyer doesn't want any of this?" she asked.

"No, I believe he plans to subdivide the property. It won't be a ranch at all anymore."

"And the house?"

"Demo it and put in a rental probably."

Lola said nothing, but when he saw her looking out the barn door toward the mountains, there was a wistfulness to her he couldn't ignore.

"I'm not leaving Montana. This will always be my home. I'm just not ranching. With what I got from the sale, I can do anything I want." But that was it. He didn't know what he wanted. His heart pulled him one way, then another.

"How long has your family owned this property?" she asked.

"My great-grandfather homesteaded it," he said. "I know it must sound disrespectful of me to sell it."

She shook her head. "It's yours to do with whatever you want, right?"

"Yes." He didn't bother to tell her that the three-month stipulation his father had put on it was over. "You were right. I'm not a rancher. I have no interest."

"But you're a cowboy."

He laughed. "That I will always be. I'm as at home on a horse as I am behind the controls of a helicopter. Ranching is a different animal altogether. Most ranchers now lease their land and let someone else worry about the critters, the drought, the price of hay. Few of them move cattle on horseback. They ride four-wheelers. Everyone seems to think ranching is romantic." He laughed at that. "It's the most boring job I've ever done in my life."

"That's why you're selling," she said with a smile. "It's the right thing."

He hadn't needed her permission, but he was thankful for it. As much as he denied it, there was guilt over selling something his father had fought for years to keep.

Nor had he contacted the Army about his next assignment, putting that off, as well. He still had plenty of leave, so there was time.

He'd also put off his Realtor about when the new

owners could take possession. It sounded as if they hoped to raze the house as soon as he moved out.

He knew he couldn't keep avoiding giving a firm date and time, but once that happened Lola and Grace would be gone.

"Where will you go?" he asked Lola.

"Probably back to California. At least for a while." The car she'd ordered had come, and she'd been able to get to her funds and make sure Jonas couldn't access them. She'd had to get a new driver's license since Jonas had taken her purse with hers inside, along with her passport and checkbook and credit cards.

Colt had heard her on the phone taking care of all that. No wonder he could feel the days slipping away until not only this ranch and the house he'd grown up in were gone, but also Lola and the baby. He worried that once he went back to the Army, this would feel like nothing more than a dream.

Yet, he knew that he would ache for Lola and Grace the rest of his life—if he let them get away. He'd always see their faces and yearn for them.

He'd never felt so confused in his life. What would he do if not go back to the Army? He was almost thirty-three. He couldn't retire even if he wanted to, which he didn't. He wanted to fly. But he couldn't ask Lola and Grace to wait for him for the next two to five years. He couldn't bear the thought of her worrying about him, or the worst happening and him never making it back.

His cell phone rang. Margaret again. "I'd better take this," he said to Lola. As she walked back toward the house, he picked up. "Margaret, I might have changed my mind."

Silence. "It's too late for that and you know it. Colt, what is this about?"

A woman and a child. The rest of my life. Regrets.

"If you're having second thoughts about selling the ranch—"

"I'm not. I just need a little more time to get off the property."

More silence. "I'll see what I can do but, Colt, they are getting very impatient. I need to tell these buyers something concrete. I can't keep putting them off or they are going to change their minds or fine you, which they can under the contract you signed." She sounded angry. He couldn't blame her.

As he looked out at the land, he had a thought. "I'll be in first thing in the morning."

"What does that mean?" she asked after a moment.

"I have an idea."

She groaned. "Could you be a touch more specific?"

"I'm selling the ranch, but there's something I need."

"Okay," she said slowly. "Why don't we sit down with them in the morning, if you're sure you won't change your mind."

He pocketed his phone and watched Lola as she slipped in the back door of the house. Taking off his Stetson, he wiped the sweat from his brow with his sleeve. "Do something," he said to himself. "Do something before it's too late."

SHE'S STAYING ON the ranch with Colt McCloud," Zack told Jonas later that afternoon.

"Is the baby with them?"

"I've had the place watched as you ordered. They

took the baby into town the next morning, bought baby clothes and supplies, and returned to the ranch."

So they were settling in. They thought it was over. "What kind of security?"

"No security system on the house. But I would imagine he has guns and knows how to use them since he's a major in the Army."

"I'm sure he does." That's why they would strike when the cowboy least expected it. He looked past Zack toward the main building below him on the hill. "You led church this morning?"

He nodded.

"What is the mood?"

Zack seemed to consider that. "Quite a few of them are upset over Sister Rebecca."

He'd suspected as much. "I'll lead the service tonight." Zack didn't appear to think that was going to make a difference. Jonas thought about the things that Rebecca had said and ground his teeth. He still had a headache, and while his wound was healing, it was a constant reminder of what Lola had done to him. Worse, she'd bewitched him, put a spell on him as if sent by the devil to bring him down.

Did he really want her back, or did he just want to retaliate? Did it matter in the long run? His memory was getting worse. The pills didn't seem to be working. He couldn't be sure how long he had until he was a blubbering old fool locked up in some rest home.

He shook his head. He wasn't going out that way. "I don't want Lola or the baby injured."

"What about McCloud?"

"Kill him and dispose of his body. I know the perfect place. If possible, leave no evidence that we were there."

COLT LEFT THE barn headed for the house, suddenly excited that his idea just might be the perfect plan. "Lola?" he cried as he burst through the back door.

"Colt?" She was standing in the kitchen wearing an apron that had belonged to his mother. He hadn't seen it in years. She must have found it in a drawer he and his father had obviously never bothered to look in.

"What?" she asked, seeing the way he was looking at her.

"You look so cute in that apron, that's all." He stepped to her. "I'm selling the ranch."

"I know."

"You were right. I'd make a terrible rancher, always did. This was my father's dream, not mine. I'm a helicopter pilot."

She nodded. "I thought we already knew this. So you're going to take the commission the Army is offering you."

"No."

She tilted her head. "No?"

"No," he said, smiling. "For years, my friend Tommy and I have talked about starting our own helicopter service here in the state. We're good at what we do. With the money from the ranch, I can invest in the birds we'll need."

"That sounds right up your alley. But are you sure?"

He nodded. "Come here." He put his arm around her waist and ushered her over to the window. "Look out there. See that."

"Yes? That mountainside?"

"Imagine a house in that grove of aspens and pines. The view from there is incredible. Now imagine an office down by the road and a helipad. The office would be just a hop, skip and a jump from the house. We'd have everything we need for Grace and any other children we have."

LOLA SMILED AT HIM, caught up in his enthusiasm. "Isn't that land part of the ranch?"

He grinned. "I'm going to buy it back."

"Aren't you being a little impulsive?"

"Not at all. I've been thinking about this for years." He seemed to see what she meant and turned her to face him. "And I've been thinking about being with you since that first night. With you and Grace here... Lola, I've fallen for you and Grace..." He shook his head. "It was love at first sight even before I knew for certain that Grace was mine. I want you to stay. I want us to be a family."

"Colt, do you know what you're saying?" But it was what he wasn't saying that had her stomach in knots. She knew he wanted her and Grace, but she wouldn't let herself go into a loveless marriage just to give her daughter a home.

She said as much to him.

He stared at her. "Damn it, Lola, I love you."

She blinked in surprise. All their lovemaking, their quiet times together, those moments with Grace. She'd waited to hear those words. Well, maybe not the "damn it, Lola" part. But definitely the "I love you" part. Her heart had assured her that he loved her and Grace. And yet, she wouldn't let herself believe it was true until he finally told her.

"I love you," he repeated as if they were the most honest words he'd ever spoken. "I've only said those words twice to a woman. With Julia, it was over two years before I said them. I don't think it was a coincidence that I held off. With you... I've been wanting to say them for days now."

"Oh, Colt, I've been waiting to hear them. I love you, too."

He reached into his pocket and pulled out a small velvet box.

Lola gave a small gasp.

"This ring was handed down from my great-great-grandmother to my great-grandmother to my grandmother. When my grandmother gave it to me, she made me promise only to give it to a woman who was my equal." He opened the box.

She looked down at a beautiful thick gold band circled in diamonds. "Oh, Colt." Her gaze went to his. "I don't understand. Julia—"

"I didn't give it to her."

"Why?"

He shrugged. "I don't know. It didn't seem...right for her. She picked out one she liked uptown."

Her heart went out to him. Julia had hurt him badly in so many ways, only proving how wrong she was for him almost from the start.

"Now I realize that I was saving this ring so I could live up to the promise I made my grandmother," he said. "I want you to wear it." He dropped to one knee. "Will you marry me, Lola Dayton, and be my wife and the mother to my children?"

She smiled through the burn of tears. "Yes."

He slipped the ring on her finger. It fit perfectly. "Now what is the chance of that?" he said to her, only making her cry and laugh at the same time.

Swinging her up into his arms, he spun her around

and set her down gently. "For the first time in so long, I am excited about the future."

She could see that he'd been dragged down by the ranch, Julia and the past, as well as his need to do what he did so well—fly.

Colt kissed her softly on the mouth. She felt heat rush through her and, cupping his face in her hands, kissed him with the passion the man evoked in her.

He swung her up in his arms again, only this time he didn't put her down until they reached the bedroom.

THAT EVENING, JONAS held church in the main building. He'd gathered them all together to give them the news. He could feel the tension in the air. There'd been a time when he'd stood up here and felt as if he really was a god sent to this earth to lead desperate people looking for at least peace, if not salvation.

As he looked over his flock, though, all he felt was sad. His father used to say that all good things end. In this case, the preacher was right.

"Brothers and sisters. I have some sad news. As you know, Sister Rebecca has chosen to leave us. It is with a heavy heart that I had to let her go." He wondered how many of them knew the truth. Too many of them probably. He was glad he'd had Zack bury her far away from the compound.

"But that isn't the only news. I have decided that it is time to leave Montana." His words were followed by a murmur of concern that spread through his congregation. "As many of you know, I'm in poor health. My heart… I'm going to have to step down as your leader."

The murmurs rose. One woman called out, "What's to become of us?"

He'd bilked them out of all their money. A lot of them were old enough now that they would have a hard time getting a job. He didn't need this crowd turning on him as Sister Rebecca had.

"Brother Zack will be taking those who want to go to property I've purchased in Arizona. It's farmable land, so you can maintain a life there. Each of you will be given a check to help with your expenses."

The murmur in the main building grew louder. "If you have any questions, please give those to Brother Zack. I trust him to make sure that each and every one of you will be taken care of." That quieted them down, either because they were assured or because they knew how Zack had taken care of other parishioners who'd became troublesome.

"It is with a heavy heart that I must step down, but I know that you all will be fine. You will leave tomorrow. Go with Godspeed." He turned and walked away, anxious to get back to his cabin and pack. The sale of his property would be enough to pay off his followers—not that he would be around to hear any complaints after tonight.

He rang for Zack. Since he'd told Zack of his plan, the man had been more than excited. Jonas had recognized that frenzied look in Zack's eyes. He'd seen it in his own. Zack would be Father Zack. God help his followers.

"I need you to pick about six brothers and a few sisters for a special mission," he told Zack. It would be one of their last missions under him.

Zack nodded, clearly understanding that he needed to pick those who would still kill for their leader.

"Make sure one of them is Brother Elmer."

"Are you sure? I mean—"

"Already questioning my authority?" he asked with a chuckle.

"No, of course not."

"Good. I have my reasons."

"I'll get right on it," Zack said, and left him alone.

Jonas looked around the cabin. He'd had such hopes when he'd moved his flock to Montana. He couldn't get maudlin now. He had to think about his future. He stepped to the safe he had hidden in the wall, opened it and took out the large case he kept there full of cash and his passport. Next to it was Lola's purse.

He took that out, as well, and thumbed through it even though he knew exactly what was in it since he'd often looked through it. He liked touching her things. He found her passport. Good, it was up-to-date. He'd deal with getting the baby out of the country when it came time.

After putting Lola's passport beside his own into his case, he closed the safe. There was nothing keeping him here after tonight. He would have everything he'd ever dreamed of, including a small fortune waiting in foreign banks across the world.

He thought of his father, wishing he could see him now. "Go ahead, say it. You were right about me, you arrogant old sanctimonious fool. I was your worst nightmare and so much more. But you haven't seen anything yet."

CHAPTER SEVENTEEN

COLT WOKE TO the sound of both outside doors bursting open. The sudden noise woke the baby. Grace began to cry in the room down the hall. Lola stirred next to him and Colt, realizing what was happening, grabbed for his gun in the nightstand next to him.

Moments before he had lain in bed, with Lola beside him.

They were on him before he could draw the gun. They swept into the room, both men and women. Colt fought off the first couple of men, but a blow to the back of his head sent him to the floor and then they were on him, binding his hands behind him, gagging him, trussing his ankles and dragging him out of the house.

He tried to see Lola, but there was a group of women around her, helping her dress. In the baby's room, he heard Grace quiet and knew they had her, as well.

The strike had been so swift, so organized, that Colt realized he'd underestimated Zack—the only ex-military man in SLS. Clearly he had more experience at these kinds of maneuvers than Colt had thought.

Still stunned from the blow to his head, he was half carried, half dragged to a waiting van.

"Take care of him, Brother Elmer," he heard Zack say, the threat clear in the man's tone. Zack must have known that Brother Elmer was a weak link. "Brother

Carl will go with you to make sure the job is done properly."

The van door slammed. Elmer started the engine and pulled away. The whole operation had taken less than ten minutes.

"DON'T HURT HIM!" Lola had cried as Colt was being dragged from the bedroom. Three women blocked her way to keep her from going after the men.

"Dress!" Sister Caroline ordered.

"My baby?"

"Grace will be safe as long as you do what we ask," Sister Amelia said. But there was something in Amelia's tone, a sadness that said not even she believed it.

Lola had no choice. They had Colt. They had Grace. She dressed quickly in a blouse and jeans, pulled on her sneakers and let the women lead her outside to a waiting van.

Sister Shelly was already in the van and holding Grace.

"Let me hold her," Lola said, steel in her voice.

The women looked at one another.

"Give the baby to Lola," Sister Amelia said and Shelly complied.

She sat holding the now-fussing Grace as the van pulled away. "Where are they taking Colt?"

No one answered. Her heart fell. Hadn't she feared that Jonas would retaliate? He'd be humiliated and would have to strike back. Isn't that what the sheriff had warned them about?

But what could he hope to achieve by this? The sheriff would know who took them. The first place Flint Cahill would look was the compound.

She remembered something she'd overheard while a prisoner at SLS. Some of the women had been worried that Jonas wasn't himself, that his memory seemed to be failing him. He often called them by the wrong names, got lost in the middle of a sermon. They questioned in hushed voices if it was his heart or something else, since they'd seem him taking pills for it.

"What is going on?" Lola asked, sensing something different about the group of women.

"We're leaving Montana," Sister Amelia said, and the other sisters tried to hush her. "She'll know soon enough," Amelia argued. "Father Jonas announced it earlier. He's selling the land here. Some are going to a new home in Arizona. Others..." Her voice broke. "I don't know where they're going."

Lola realized that their leader wasn't here. "Where is Sister Rebecca?" The question was met with silence. "Amelia?"

"She's gone."

"Everyone is leaving," Sister Shelly said, sounding near tears. "Father Jonas... He's letting Brother Zack lead the group in Arizona. He will be Father Zack now."

Lola couldn't believe what she was hearing as the van reached the highway and headed toward the compound. "He's putting Zack in charge?" She knew that the women in this van must feel the same way she did about Zack. "Did Jonas say what he is planning to do?"

Silence. Lola hugged Grace to her, her fear mounting with each passing mile as the van turned onto the road up to the mountain. Lola saw no other taillights ahead. No headlights behind them. Where had they taken Colt?

COLT COULDN'T SEE OUT, but he could tell that Elmer and Carl weren't taking him to the compound. He had a pretty good idea what their orders had been when Zack had told Elmer to take care of him.

He was furious with himself. He'd thought Jonas would have no choice but to give up. He should have known better. He should have taken more precautions. Against so many, he knew he and Lola hadn't stood a chance.

When they'd gone to the compound and rescued Grace, he'd thought this could be settled without bloodshed. It was why he hadn't taken a gun to the compound the first time that night. He didn't want to kill one of Jonas's sheep. They were just following orders, though blindly, true enough. But he hadn't wanted trouble with the law.

Now, though, he saw there was no way out of this. Jonas had taken Lola and Grace. Nothing was going to stop him. He was going to end this once and for all no matter whom he had to kill.

Colt rolled to his side. They'd bound his wrists with plastic ties. He worked to slip his hands under him. If he could get a foot into the cuffs, he knew he could break free.

As he did, he watched the men in the front seat. Neither turned around to check on him. He got the feeling they didn't like being awakened in the middle of the night for this any more than Colt had. And now they had been ordered to kill someone. They had to be questioning Jonas and the SLS. He already knew that Brother Elmer had a weak spot for Lola and her baby.

He managed to get his hands past his butt. He lay on his back, catching his breath for a moment before he pushed himself up. Once he had his hands in front of him…

The van slowed. Elmer shifted down and turned onto a bumpy road that jarred every muscle in Colt's body. Colt caught a glimpse of something out the back window and realized where they were taking him. The old gravel pits outside of Gilt Edge. He caught the scent of the water through the partially opened windows up front. It was the perfect place to dump a body. Weighted down, there was a good chance the remains would never be found.

He felt his heart pound as he worked to free his wrists. The plastic restraints popped—but not louder than the rattle of the van on the rough road. Colt went to work on the ones binding his ankles.

As the van came to a stop, he resumed his original position, his hands behind him, feet together as he lay on his side facing the door.

Both men got out. He waited, wondering if either of them was armed or if the plan had been simply to drown him.

The van door opened noisily. "Can you get him out?" Elmer asked his companion.

Carl grunted but reached for him.

Colt swung his feet around and kicked the man in the chest, sending Carl sprawling in the dirt. He followed with a quick jab to Elmer's jaw. The older man stumbled and sat down hard on the ground.

So far, Colt hadn't seen a weapon, but as he jumped out, he saw Carl fumbling for something behind him. The man came up with a pistol. Right away, Colt saw that he wasn't comfortable using it. But that didn't mean that Carl wouldn't get lucky and blow Colt's head off.

He rushed around the back of the van to the driver's side. Grabbing open the door, he leaped in and started the van. As he threw the engine into Reverse, he saw Carl trying to get a clear shot. Elmer had stumbled to his feet and was blocking Carl's way—either accidentally or on purpose.

Colt didn't try to figure out which as he hit the gas. The van shot back. He cranked the wheel hard, swinging the back end toward the two men.

Carl got off two shots. One bullet shattered the back window of the van. The other took out Colt's side window, showering him with glass, and just missing his head before burying itself in the passenger-side door.

Elmer had parked the van close to the edge of the gravel pit, no doubt to make unloading his body easier.

As Colt swung the van at the two men, they tried to move out of the way. But Elmer was old and lost his footing. He was the first to go tumbling down the steep embankment and splash into the cold, clear water.

Carl had been busy trying to hit his target with the gun so he was caught unaware when the back of the van hit him and knocked him backward into the gravel pit. He let out a yell as he fell, the sound dying off in a loud splash.

Colt shifted into first gear and tore off down the bumpy road, thankful to be alive. He hoped both men could swim. If so, they had a long swim across the pit to where they would be able to climb out.

If either of their cell phones still worked after that, they might be able to warn Jonas. Not that it would matter.

Colt sped toward his house to get what he needed. This time he was taking weapons—and no prisoners.

FOR LOLA, WALKING into Jonas's cabin with the bundle in her arms felt a little like déjà vu. Only this time, there was a precious sleeping baby instead of rocks in her arms. As she entered, propelled by Brother Zack, she told herself that she would die protecting her daughter. Did Jonas know that, as well?

"Leave her," Jonas ordered. Zack started to argue, but one look at their leader and he left, saying he would be right outside the door if he was needed. The sisters scattered, and the door closed, leaving Lola and Grace alone with Jonas.

He still had a bandage on the side of his head, but she knew better than to think his injury might slow him down.

"You are a very difficult woman."

"Only when someone tries to force me into doing something I don't want to do or they take my child from me."

He glanced at the bundle in her arms. "May I see her?"

Lola didn't move. "What do you hope to get out of this?" she demanded.

"I thought I was clear from the beginning. I want you. It's what your parents wanted—"

"I don't believe that. I heard from my father before he…died. He wanted out of SLS. He was trying to convince my mother to leave. I believe that's why you killed them both."

Jonas shook his head. "Are we back to that?"

"You're a fraud. This is no church. And you are no god. All this is only about your ego. It's a bad joke."

"Are you purposely trying to rile me?"

"I thought maybe it was time you heard the truth

from someone instead of Sister Rebecca telling you how wonderful you are."

"Sister Rebecca is no longer with us."

"So I heard. Did you kill her yourself or make one of your sheep do it?" She knew he could not let Rebecca simply walk away. She'd been with him from the beginning. She'd done things for him, knew things.

"Why do you torment me? I cared about Rebecca."

"And yet you had her killed. I don't like the way you care about people."

At the sound of vehicles and activity on the mountain below them, Lola moved cautiously to the window, careful not to turn her back on Jonas.

She frowned as she saw everyone appearing to be packing up and moving. Fear coursed through her. "What's going on? I thought they weren't leaving until tomorrow?"

"Our time in Montana has come to an end. We are abandoning our church here."

What Amelia had told her was true. "So they're scurrying away like rats fleeing a sinking ship. You're really going to let them go?"

"All good things must end."

She thought of Colt as she had on the ride to the compound. Something told her that he hadn't been brought here. "Where is Colt?"

Jonas shook his head. "As I said, all good things must end."

Tears burned her eyes. "If you hurt him—"

'What will you do? Kill me? They will put you in prison, take away your baby. No, it is time you realized that you have never been in control. You are mine. You will always be mine. I will go to any lengths, including having Grace taken away so you never see her again if that's what it takes to keep you with me."

Fear turned her blood to ice as she looked into his eyes and understood he wasn't bluffing.

"You have only one choice. Come with me willingly and Grace will join us once we are settled."

No, she screamed silently. She didn't trust this man. But she also knew she couldn't keep someone like Zack from ripping Grace from her arms. Just as she knew that Jonas wasn't making an empty threat. She'd known this man was dangerous, but she hadn't realized how much he was willing to give up to have her—and Grace.

"You have only a few minutes to make up your mind, Lola." He had his phone in his hand. "Once I push this button, Zack will take Grace. If you ever want to see her again, you will agree to go with me."

"Where?" She knew she was stalling, fighting to find a way out of this. Colt. If he was dead, did she care what happened to her as long as she had his baby with her?

"Europe, South America. I haven't decided yet. Somewhere far away from all this. I have money. We will live well. We will be a family."

She thought of the family Colt had promised her and felt the ring on her finger.

Jonas's gaze went to her left hand. His face contorted in anger. "Take that off. Take that off now!"

CHAPTER EIGHTEEN

Colt dialed the number quickly, knowing he had no choice even if he ended up behind bars. It would be worth it as long as Lola and Grace were safe from Jonas Emanuel once and for all.

"I need to borrow a helicopter," he said, the moment his friend answered.

"Mind if I ask what for?" Tommy Garrett asked, sounding like a man dragged from sleep in the wee hours of the morning. Tommy worked as a helicopter mechanic outside of Great Falls. Colt had served with him in Afghanistan and trusted the man with his life— and Lola's and Grace's.

"A madman has the woman I love and my baby daughter."

There was a beat of silence before Tommy said, "You planning to do this alone?"

"Better that way. I'll leave you out of it."

"Like hell. Tell me where you are. Outside my shop I have a Bell UH-1 Huey that needs its shakedown. The old workhorse is being used to fight forest fires. I'm on my way."

Colt knew the Huey could do up to 120 mph. But a safe cruising speed for helicopters was around a hundred. Without having to deal with traffic, road speeds or winding highways, the response time in a helicopter was considerably faster than anything on the ground. It was one reason Colt loved flying them.

So he wasn't surprised when Tommy landed in the pasture next to Colt's house thirty minutes later. The sun was coming up, chasing away the last of the dark. He could make out the mountains in the distance. Within a matter of minutes, they would be at the compound. He tried not think about what they would find.

"How much trouble is this going to get you in?" Colt asked his friend as he loaded the weapons in the back and climbed into the left seat, the crew chief seat.

"You just worry about what happens when we put this bird down," Tommy said in the adjacent seat at the controls.

As they headed for the mountaintop in the distance, Colt told him everything that had happened from that moment in the hotel in Billings to earlier that night.

When he finished, Tommy said, "So this woman is the one?"

For a moment, Colt could only nod around the lump in this throat. "I've never met anyone like her."

"Apparently this cult leader hasn't, either. Tell me you have a plan." He swore when Colt didn't answer right away.

"There will be armed guards who are under the control of the cult leader, Jonas Emanuel. But we don't have time to sneak up on them. You don't have to land. Just get close enough to the ground that I can jump," Colt said as he began to strap on one of the weapons he'd brought. "Did I mention that these people are like zombies?"

"Great, you know how I love zombies. Except you can't kill zombies."

"These are religious zealots. I suspect they will be as hard to kill as zombies."

"This just keeps getting better and better," Tommy joked.

Colt looked over at him. "Thank you."

"Thank me after we get out with this woman you've fallen in love with and your daughter." He shook his head. "You never did anything like normal people."

"No, I never did. There's the road that goes up to the compound."

Tommy swooped down, skimming just over the tops of the pines, and Colt saw something he hadn't expected.

"What the hell?" As they got closer to the mountain, Colt spotted the line of vans coming off the mountain. He felt a chill. "Something's going on. Fly closer to those vehicles," he said to Tommy, who immediately dipped down.

Inside the vans, he saw the faces of Jonas followers. There were a dozen vans. As each passed, he saw the pale faces, the fear in their eyes.

"Where do you think they're going?" Tommy asked.

"I have no idea. Leaving for good, from the looks of it. What is Jonas up to? Are these people decoys or are they really clearing out?" He thought of Lola and the baby. How crazy was Jonas? Would he kill them and then kill himself, determined that Colt would never have either of them?

"Up there," Colt said, pointing to the mountaintop. Tommy swung the helicopter in the direction he pointed. Within a few minutes, the buildings came into sight. Colt didn't see any guards. He didn't see anyone. The place looked deserted. Had everyone left?

Not everyone, he noticed. There was a large black SUV sitting in front of Jonas's cabin.

"Think you can put her into that clearing in front of the cabin?"

"Seriously?" Tommy said. "You forget who you're talking to. Give me a dime and I can set her down on it." Colt chuckled because he knew it was true.

LOLA LOOKED DOWN at the antique ring that Colt had put on her finger. She swore she would never take it off. It felt so right on her finger. Colt felt so right.

Jonas moved faster than she thought he could after his injury. He grabbed the baby from her arms and shoved her. She fell back, coming down hard on the floor. "I told you to take if off. Now!"

"Give me Grace."

"Her name is Angel, and if you don't do what I say this moment…"

Lola pulled off the ring. She knew it was silly. Colt was probably dead. She'd lost so much. What did a ring matter at this point? The one thing she couldn't lose was Grace, and yet she felt as if she already had in more ways than one. Jonas had them captive. He could do whatever he wanted with Grace. Just as he could do whatever he wanted with her now.

"Happy?" she asked, still clutching the ring in her fist.

"Throw it away." He pointed toward the fireplace and the cold ashes filling it.

She hesitated again.

"Do as I say!" Jonas bellowed at her, waking up Grace. The baby began to cry.

Lola tossed the ring toward the fireplace. It was a

lazy, bad throw, one that made Jonas's already furious face cloud over even more. The ring missed the fireplace opening, pinged off the rock and rolled under the couch. She looked at Jonas. If he really did have a bad heart, she realized his agitation right now could kill him. She doubted she would get that lucky, though.

He seemed to be trying to calm down. Grace kept crying and she could tell it was getting on his nerves.

She got to her feet. "Let me have her. She'll quit crying for me."

He shook his head. "I'm not sure I can trust you," he said slowly.

Colt was gone. The ring was gone. But Jonas had something much more precious. He had Grace. But Lola wasn't giving up.

"How do I know I can trust *you*?" she said.

The question surprised him. He'd expected her to cower, to promise him anything. She knew better than to do that. Jonas was surrounded by people who bowed down to him. Lola never had and maybe that's why he was so determined to have her.

She approached him. "You hurt my baby and I will kill you. I'll cut your throat in your sleep. Or push you down a flight of stairs. Or poison your food. It might take me a while to get the opportunity, but believe me, I will do it."

He chuckled as his gaze met hers. "I do believe you. I've always loved your spirit. Your mother told me what a headstrong young woman you were. She wasn't wrong."

It hurt to have him mention her mother. Was it possible that Jonas could get away with the murders he'd committed? She feared it was. She thought of Colt and felt a sob rise in her throat. She forced it back down. She couldn't show weakness, not now, especially not for Colt. She had to think about Grace.

"We seem to be at an impasse," Jonas said. "What do you suggest we do?"

"I suggest you give me my baby and let me leave here."

He shook his head. "Not happening. Neither you or your baby will be leaving here—except with me."

"So what are you waiting for?" she demanded.

Jonas chuckled as he tilted his head as if to listen. "We're waiting for Colt. I just have a feeling he will somehow manage to try to save you one more time."

Lola listened as her heart thumped against her rib cage. Colt? He was alive? She thought she heard what sounded like a helicopter headed this way.

"I believe that's him now."

COLT FOUGHT THE bad feeling that had settled in the pit of his stomach. Jonas was playing hardball this time. He wasn't going to let Lola and Grace go—not without a fight to the death. That's if they were still alive.

"Change of plans," he said to Tommy. He felt as if time was running out for Lola and Grace. "Put us down and wait for me," he said, fear making his voice sound strained as he passed Tommy a handgun. "I hope you won't have to use this. It appears that the guards have left, but I've already underestimated Jonas once and I don't want to do it again. I'm hoping this won't take long."

As Colt started to jump out, Tommy grabbed his sleeve. "Be careful."

Colt nodded. "You, too."

"I'll be here. Good luck."

Colt knew that if there was anyone he wanted on his side in a war it was Tommy Garrett—and this was war. These soldiers would die for their leader. They were just as devoted to dying for their cause as the ones he'd fought in Afghanistan.

The moment the chopper touched the ground, he leaped out and ran up the mountainside to where a large black SUV sat, the engine running and Brother Zack behind the wheel. Behind him, he heard Tommy shut down the engine. The rotors began to slow.

Colt looked around. The only person he'd seen so far was Zack, but that didn't mean that another of the guards hadn't stayed behind.

As he approached the SUV, he could hear the bass coming from the stereo. Closer, he saw that Zack had on headphones and was rockin' out. He must have had the stereo cranked, which explained why he hadn't heard the helicopter land. Nor had he heard him approach.

Colt yanked open the door. A surprised Zack turned. Colt grabbed him by his shirt and hauled him out. Unfortunately, Zack was carrying and he went for his gun. Zack was strong and combat trained. But Colt was fighting for Lola's and Grace's lives.

Colt managed to get hold of the man's arm, twisting it to the point of snapping as they struggled for the weapon. When the shot went off, it was muffled— just like Zack's grunt. Blood blossomed on the front of Zack's white shirt. The gun dropped, falling under the SUV.

As the man slumped, Colt shoved him back inside the vehicle, shut off the stereo and slammed the door before turning to Jonas's cabin. He'd seen suitcases in the back of the SUV and suspected the sheep weren't the only ones fleeing.

Colt pulled his holstered gun and climbed the steps. He had another gun stuck in the back of his jeans under his jacket. He always liked to be prepared—especially against someone like Jonas Emanuel.

He could still hear the sweep of the helicopter's rotors as they continued to slow. The wooden porch floor creaked under his boots. He braced himself and reached for the doorknob.

Before he could turn it, Lola opened the door. Her face had lost all its color. Her violet eyes appeared huge. He could see that she'd been crying. The sight froze him in place for moment. What had Jonas done to her? To Grace?

"Where is Jonas?" Colt asked quietly. Suddenly there wasn't a sound, not even a meadowlark from the grass or a breeze moaning in the pines. The eerie quiet sent a chill up his spine. "Lola?" The word came in a whisper.

"I'm leaving with Jonas," she said.

"Like hell." He could see that Jonas had put the fear into her and used Grace to do it. He'd never wanted to strangle anyone with his bare hands more than he did the cult leader at this moment.

"Please, it's what I want." Her words said one thing; her blue eyes pleaded with him to save Grace.

He pushed past her to find Jonas sitting in a chair just yards away. He was holding Grace in such a way that it stopped Colt cold.

JONAS RELISHED THE expression on Colt's handsome face. It almost made everything worth what he was going to have to give up. The cowboy thought he could just bust in here and take Lola and the baby? Not this time.

"Lola is going with me and so is her baby," he said as he turned the baby so she was facing her biological father and dangling from his fingers. He wanted Colt to see the baby's face and realize what he would be risking if he didn't back off.

"I don't think so," Colt said, but without much conviction. Jonas was ready to throw the baby against the rock fireplace if Colt took another step. The cowboy wasn't stupid. He'd figured that out right away. But he'd been stupid enough to come up here again. The man should have been dead.

Idly, Jonas wondered what had gone wrong at the gravel pit. He'd known he couldn't depend on Elmer, but he was disposable. Brother Carl had inspired more faith that he would get the job done. Jonas had assumed that Carl would have to kill both Elmer and Colt. Clearly, the job had been too much for him.

"Has he hurt you?" Colt asked Lola.

She shook her head.

Jonas was touched by the cowboy's concern, but quickly getting bored with all this. "Elmer and Carl?" he asked, curious.

"Swimming, that is, if either of them knows how," Colt answered.

"And Brother Zack?"

"No longer listening to music in your big SUV."

So he couldn't depend on Zack to come to his rescue. Another surprise. Everyone was letting him down. Just as well that he was packing it all in. He'd grown tired of the squabbling among the sisters and the backbiting of the brothers. Human nature really was malicious.

Still, he would miss Zack. And now who would lead his people to the promised land of Arizona? He chuckled to himself since he didn't own any land in Arizona. But they wouldn't know that until they got there, would they?

He saw the cowboy shoot a look at Lola. She was standing off to Colt's left as if she didn't know what to do. He could see the tension in her face. She wasn't being so smart-mouthed now, was she? As much as he was enjoying this, he didn't have to ask what she was hoping would happen here.

But, this time, she'd been outplayed. The cowboy was going to lose. It was simply a matter of how much he would have to lose before this was over. Did he realize that he wasn't getting out of here alive? At this point, Jonas wasn't sure he cared if Lola and the baby survived either, though he still wanted the woman, and damned if he wouldn't have her—dead or alive. The thought didn't even surprise him. His father used to say that one day he would reach rock bottom. Was this it?

"Why would you want a woman who doesn't love you?" Colt asked conversationally, as if they were old friends discussing the weather—and took a step closer.

"Because I can have her. I can have anything I want, and I want her. The baby is optional. I guess that's up to you."

"How's that?"

"You can't reach me before I hurl your baby into the rock fireplace. But if you try, I will, and then we will only be talking about Lola. The thing is, I don't think she will love you anymore, not after you got her baby killed," Jonas said. "Want to take a chance on that? Take another step..."

COLT COULD SEE that Jonas's arms were tiring from holding Grace up the way he was. He was using the baby like a shield. There was no way Colt could get a shot off with Jonas sitting and the baby out in front of him. Nor could he chance that, as he fired, Jonas wouldn't throw Grace into the rocks.

One glance at Lola and he knew that what they both feared was a real possibility—Jonas could drop the baby at any moment. Or, worse, throw Grace against the rock fireplace as he was threatening.

"Colt, I'll go with him. It's the only way," Lola pleaded as she stepped to him, grabbing his arm.

It was a strange thing for her to do and for a moment he didn't understand. Then he felt her reach behind him to the pistol he had at his back. She must have seen the bulk of it under his shirt. She freed the gun and dropped her hands to her sides, keeping turned so Jonas couldn't see what she held. Then she began to cry.

"You heard her," Jonas said. "Leave before someone gets hurt. Before you get hurt." His arms were shaking visibly. "If you care anything about this child…"

Jonas knew Colt wasn't leaving without Lola and Grace. Saying he could walk away was all bluff. Did he have a weapon handy? Colt suspected so.

Lola was still halfway facing him so she could keep the gun in her hand hidden. Colt feared what she planned to do, but he could feel time running out. Jonas was losing patience. Worse, his arms were shaking now. He couldn't hold the baby much longer—and he couldn't back down. Wouldn't.

"Tell him, Jonas," she cried, suddenly running toward the cult leader and dropping to her knees only feet from him after sticking the gun in the waist of her jeans. "Tell him I'm going with you, and that it's true and to leave."

The cult leader hadn't expected her to do that. For a moment, it looked as if he was going to throw the baby. Before he could, Lola grabbed for Grace with her left hand. At the same time, she pulled the pistol from behind her with her right. She had hold of Grace's chubby little leg and wasn't letting go.

Everything happened fast after that. Colt, seeing what Lola had planned, took the shot the moment Lola managed to pull the baby down and away from Jonas's smug face. Colt had always been an expert shot. Even during the most stressful situations.

He missed. Jonas had fallen forward just enough that the shot went over his head and lodged in the back of the chair. Before he could fire again, he heard Lola fire. She'd taken the shot from the floor, shooting under Grace to hit the man low in the stomach. He saw Jonas release Grace as he grabbed for his bleeding belly.

Lola dropped the gun and pulled Grace into her arms. They were both crying. As Colt rushed to the cult leader, his gun leveled at the man's head, Lola scrambled away from Jonas with Grace tucked in her arms.

Jonas was holding his stomach with one hand and fumbling for something in the chair with the other. Colt was aiming to shoot, to finish Jonas, when he saw that it wasn't a gun the cult leader was going for. It was the man's phone.

He watched Jonas punch at the screen, his bloody fingers slippery, his hands shaking. It took a moment for the alert to sound. Jonas seemed to wait, one bloody hand on his stomach, the other on his phone. He stared at the front door, expecting it to come flying open as one of the guards burst in.

Seconds passed, then several minutes. Nothing happened. Jonas looked wild-eyed at the door as if he couldn't believe it.

"They've all left," Colt said. "There is no one to help you."

Jonas looked down at his phone. With trembling fingers he made several attempts to key in 9-1-1 and finally gave up. "You have to call an ambulance. It's the humane thing to do."

"This from the man who was about to kill my baby daughter?"

"You would let me bleed to death?"

Colt looked over at Lola, huddled in the corner with Grace. Their gazes met. He pulled out his own phone and keyed in 9-1-1. He asked to speak to the sheriff.

When he was connected with Flint, he said, "You were right. Jonas hit us in the middle of the night. He sent two men to kill me. I left them in the old gravel pits. He took Lola and Grace, but they are both safe now. Unfortunately, one of his guards tried to shoot me. He's dead outside here on the compound and Jonas is wounded, so you'll need an ambulance and a—" He was going to say *coroner*, but before he could get the word out, the front door of the cabin banged open.

He spun around in time to see Zack bleeding and barely able to stand, but the man could still shoot. He fired the weapon in his hand in a barrage of bullets before Colt could pull the trigger.

LOLA SCREAMED. GRACE WAILED. It happened so fast. She'd thought it was all over. Finally. She'd thought they were finally safe. And so had Colt. He hadn't expected Zack to be alive—let alone come in shooting—any more than she had.

Colt threw himself in Grace's and her direction. As he did, he brought up the weapon he'd been holding on Jonas. The air filled with the loud reports of gunfire.

Lola laid her body over Grace's to protect her, knowing that Colt had thrown himself toward them to do the same. It took her a few moments to realize that the firing had stopped. She peeked out, terrified that she would find Colt lying dead at her feet.

Colt lay on his side, his back to her. She put Grace down long enough to reach for him. He was holding his leg, blood oozing out from between his fingers. He looked up at her.

"Are you and Grace—"

"We're fine. But you're bleeding," Lola cried.

"It's just a flesh wound," Colt said. "Don't worry about me. As long as you and Grace are all right…" He grimaced as he tried to get to his feet.

In the doorway, Zack lay crumpled on the floor. Lola couldn't tell if he was breathing or not. Her gaze swung to Jonas. He had tumbled out of his chair. He wasn't breathing, given that the top of his head was missing. She looked away quickly.

Grace's wailing was the only sound in the room. She rushed to her. As she did, she saw Colt's cell phone on the floor and picked it up. The sheriff was still there.

"We need an ambulance. Colt is wounded. Zack and Jonas are dead."

"Tommy," Colt said, trying to get to his feet. "He would have seen Zack heading for the cabin…" He limped to the door and pushed it open. Beyond it, he saw Tommy slumped over the controls of the helicopter. "There isn't time to wait for an ambulance. Tell the sheriff we'll be at the hospital."

As she related to the sheriff what Colt had said, she hurried to the couch. Squatting down, she fished her ring from under it. Her gentle toss of it hadn't hurt the ring or the diamonds. She slipped it on her finger, feeling as if now she could face anything again. Then, holding Grace in her arms, she ran after Colt to the helicopter sitting like a big dark bird in the middle of the compound.

COLT IGNORED THE pain as he ran to the helicopter. When he reached Tommy, he hurriedly felt for a pulse. For a moment, he thought his friend was dead, and yet he didn't see any blood. He found a pulse and felt a wave of relief. He'd dragged his friend into this. The last thing he wanted to do was get him killed.

On closer inspection, he could see a bump the size of a goose egg on Tommy's head. He figured Zack must have ambushed him before coming up to the cabin to finish things.

"Is he…?" Lola asked from behind him. She held a crying Grace in her arms and was trying to soothe her.

"He's alive, but we need to get him to the hospital. Come around the other side and climb in the back with Grace." Colt helped them in and then slid into the seat and took over the controls. He started up the motor. The rotors began to turn and then spin. A few minutes later, he lifted off and headed for Gilt Edge.

The helicopter swept over the tops of the pines and

out of the mountains. Colt glanced over at Tommy. He seemed to be coming around. In the back, Lola had calmed Grace down and she now slept in her mother's arms.

He told himself that all was right with the world. Lola and Grace were safe. Tommy was going to make it. But he was feeling the effects of his blood loss as he saw the hospital's helipad in the distance. He'd never lost a bird. He told himself he wasn't going to lose this one— especially with the precious cargo he was carrying.

Colt set the chopper down and turned off the engine. After that, everything became a blur. He knew he'd lost a lot of blood and was light-headed, but it wasn't until he'd shut down the chopper and tried to get out that he realized how weak he was.

The last thing he remembered was seeing hospital staff rushing toward the helicopter pushing two gurneys.

CHAPTER NINETEEN

COLT WOKE TO find Lola and Grace beside his bed. He tried to sit up, but Lola gently pushed him back down.

"Tommy is fine," she told him as if knowing exactly what he needed to hear. "A mild concussion. The doctor is having a terrible time keeping him in bed. We're all fine now."

Colt relaxed back on the pillows and smiled. "I was so worried. But everyone's all right?"

She nodded. "I was worried about you." She pushed a lock of hair back from his forehead and looked into his eyes. "You lost so much blood, but the doctor says you're going to be fine."

He glanced over at the IV attached to his arm. "I remember flying the chopper to the hospital but not much after that." He took her hand and squeezed it. "How is Grace?"

"Sleeping." Lola pointed to the bassinet the nurses had brought in for her. "I refused to leave until I knew you were all right." They'd also brought in a cot for Lola, he saw. "I've just been going back and forth from your room to Tommy's."

Colt smiled, took her hand and squeezed it. "I almost lost you. Again."

"But you saved me. Again. Aren't you getting tired of it?"

He shook his head. "Never." He glanced down at the ring on her finger. When he'd come into the cabin, he'd seen her rubbing the spot on her left hand where it had been. He hadn't been surprised Jonas hadn't liked seeing the ring on her finger. "When are you going to marry me?"

"You name the day. But right now you're in the middle of selling your ranch and holding an auction, and the doctor isn't going to let you out of here for a while. The bullet missed bone, but your leg is going to take some time to heal. Also, I believe you missed your appointment with your Realtor."

Colt grimaced. "Margaret. She is going to be furious."

"I called her. Apparently, ending up in the hospital bought you some time."

"I need to talk to Tommy, but I want to talk to him about my plan for the future, for *our* future."

The hospital-room door opened and Sheriff Flint Cahill stuck his head in. "Our patient awake? I hate to interrupt, but I need to talk to Colt if he's up to it."

Colt pulled Lola down for a kiss. "I'll talk to the sheriff. You can leave Grace. If she wakes up, I'll take care of her."

She nodded. "I know you will." She said hello to the sheriff. "I'll just be down the hall."

Flint took off his Stetson and pulled up a chair. "I've already spoken with Tom Garrett and Lola. I have their statements, but I need yours. I have two dead men up on the mountain, two suffering from dehydration and two more in the hospital. Elmer and Carl have been picked up. They both said they were the ones who almost got killed, not you." He pulled out his notebook and pen. "Said you knocked them into the gravel pit."

Colt nodded. "After they took me from my house in the middle of the night, tied me up and planned to kill me and dump me in the pit. They probably didn't mention that."

"Actually, Elmer confessed this morning. They're both behind bars." The sheriff sighed. "Just give me the basics. You'll have to come down to the office when you're released."

Colt related everything from the time he was awakened by the cult members breaking into the house until he landed the helicopter at the hospital.

"It would have been nice if you'd given me a call," Flint said.

"Jonas would have killed them. He was so close to hurting Grace…" His voice broke. "If Lola hadn't acted when she did…"

"Jonas had one bullet in him from a gun registered to you, but all the others were from a gun registered to Jonas himself. We found it next to Zack's body. Why would Zack kill his own leader?"

Colt shook his head. "He came in firing. When I jumped out of the way, he kept firing…"

"He's the one who wounded you?"

"Yes. And the one who knocked out Tommy, but he might have already told you that."

"Actually," the sheriff said. "He didn't see who or what hit him."

"Zack was the only guard left. Everyone else vacated the property."

"Lola said that most of them were headed to Arizona, where Jonas had promised them a place to live, but we can't find any property owned by him or SLS," Flint said. "We did, though, find a variety of places where he has stashed their money, a lot of it. I would imagine there'll be lawsuits against his estate."

"Lola thinks he murdered her parents. They're buried on the compound."

The sheriff raked a hand through his hair. "We saw that there is a new grave in the woods. We were able to contact a couple of SLS followers who didn't make it any farther than town. They said they think he killed Sister Rebecca and that she is buried in the new grave." He shook his head. "He had me fooled."

"Me, too. For a while," Colt admitted.

Grace began to whimper next to his bed.

The sheriff put away his notebook and pen as he rose. "I'll let you see to your daughter." He tipped his Stetson as he left.

THE STORY HIT the local paper the next day. SLS members were spilling their guts about what had gone on up at the compound. A half dozen had already filed lawsuits against the fortune Jonas had amassed.

The article made Colt and Tommy sound like heroes. Colt figured that was Lola's doing since she'd told him she'd been interviewed by a reporter. She'd said she was anxious for her story—and that of her parents— to get out.

"Maybe it will keep other people from getting taken in by men like Jonas," she'd said. "He caught my parents at a vulnerable time in their lives. But if they could be fooled, then anyone can."

Lola picked him up after the doctor released him from the hospital.

He sat in the passenger seat of the SUV she'd had delivered to his house. The woman was damned independent, but he liked that about her. Grace grinned at him from the car seat as they drove out to the ranch. Drove home. Well, home for a while anyway. All he'd been able to think about was getting back to that old ranch house that had felt like a prison before Lola. Now it felt like home.

Not that he was going to get sentimental and hang on to the house. Or the ranch. He wanted a new start for his little family.

They'd been home for a while when Tommy stopped by the house to see how he was doing before taking his helicopter home.

"You've met Lola," Colt said.

Tommy nodded.

"We got to know each other while we were waiting on you to get well. I had to thank him for all he did in helping us." She turned to the man from where she was making cookies in the kitchen. "We owe you. If you can stick around for twelve minutes, I will have a batch of chocolate chip cookies coming out of the oven. It's not much, given what you did for us."

"I'm just glad you're all right," Tommy said, looking bashful. "Anyway, I owe your husband. He saved my life. I'd do anything for him. I got to tell you, I think our boy Colt has done good this time," his friend said, grinning at Lola, then Colt. "You got yourself a good one," he said with a wink. "So what's this plan you wanted to talk to me about?"

"You're not mad at me for almost getting you killed?" Colt asked.

Tommy looked embarrassed. "I let some cult member sneak up on me."

"Zack was ex-military."

"That makes me feel a little better, but let's keep it to ourselves, okay? So what's up?" he asked as he took the chair he was offered at the kitchen table. Lola checked the cookies. Grace was watching her from her carrier on the counter. Colt liked watching Lola cook. He just liked watching her and marveling at how lucky he'd gotten.

"Colt?" Tommy said, grinning as he drew his attention again.

He laughed, then got serious. "Remember all the times we talked about starting our own helicopter service?" Colt and Tommy had spent hours at night in Afghanistan planning what they would do when they got out of the Army. Only Colt had stayed in, so their dream of owning their own flight company had been put off indefinitely.

"You still thinking about it?" Tommy asked.

"I know you're doing great with your repair business. I know you might not be interested in starting a company with me, but I've sold the ranch. I have money to invest. You don't have to answer right now. Take a few days to—"

"I don't need a few days. Absolutely," his friend said. "Where were you thinking of headquartering it?"

"There's a piece of land close by I'd like to build a house on. Right down the road from it would be the ideal place for the office, with lots of room for the shops and landing any number of birds."

Tommy laughed. "You really have been thinking about this." He glanced past Colt to Lola, who was busy taking the cookies out of the oven. "What about the military?" he asked, his gaze shifting back to Colt.

"I've decided not to take the upcoming assignment and resign my commission. I'm getting married. I have a family now. I don't want to be away from them."

"I get it," Tommy said as he took the warm cookie Lola offered him. "How soon?"

"I can make an offer on the land and we can get construction going on the shops and hangers—"

"How long before you get married?" Tommy asked with a laugh and took a bite of the cookie, before complimenting Lola.

"In three weeks. That was something else I needed to talk to you about," Colt said. "I need a best man."

LOLA WANTED TO pinch herself. She couldn't believe she was getting married. She'd never been so happy. She was glad they'd put off the wedding for a few weeks. There'd been a lot of questions about everything that had happened up on the mountain. The investigation, though, had finally ended.

It had taken a while for the bodies of her parents and Sister Rebecca to be exhumed. Just as she'd suspected, autopsies revealed that both of her parents had been poisoned. So had Rebecca. Lola made arrangements to have their remains flown to California and reinterred in the plots next to her sister's.

"You have nothing to feel guilty about," Colt had assured her.

"But if I'd come straight home after university and tried to get them out of that place—"

"You know it wouldn't have done any good. They were determined that you join them, right?"

She'd nodded. "But if I'd come right home when I got my father's letter, maybe I could have—"

"You know how Jonas operated. It wouldn't have made a difference. You said yourself that your mother adored Jonas. You couldn't have gotten her to leave and your father wouldn't have left without her, right?"

She'd known he was right. Still, she hated that she hadn't been able to save them. She was just grateful to Colt. If it hadn't been for him…

Lola looked down at her sleeping daughter. Yes, if it hadn't been for him there would have been no Grace.

COLT WANDERED THROUGH the days afterward, more content than he had ever been. He and Lola went horseback riding. She took to it so well that she made him promise he would teach Grace when she was old enough.

"I'll teach all of the kids."

"All of the kids?" she'd asked with one raised eyebrow.

He'd smiled as he'd pulled her to him. "Tell me you wouldn't mind having a couple more."

"You want a son."

"I want whatever you give me," he'd said, nuzzling her neck and making her laugh. "I'll be taking all girls if that's what you've got for me."

Lola had kissed him, promising to give him as many children as he wanted.

"And I'll teach them all to fly. Which reminds me, anytime you want to go for a ride… The helicopters will be coming in right after the wedding."

The new owners of the ranch had allowed Colt to stay on with his family until he was able to get a mobile home put on the land he'd bought back from them.

"We'll live in it until the house is finished, then maybe use it for the office until the office building is done."

Lola seemed as excited as he was about the business they were starting with Tommy. She kept busy with her new friends Lillie and Mariah. They were actually talking playdates for the kids.

He ran into Wyatt a couple more times in town. He hadn't wanted to slug him. Actually, he'd wanted to thank him. The thought had made him laugh.

Also, Colt hadn't been that surprised when Julia called. He almost hadn't answered. "Hello?"

"Colt, it's Julia. I saw your engagement announcement in the newspaper not long after that story came out. What a story."

He didn't know what to say.

"Wyatt and I are over. I know you don't care, but I wanted you to hear it from me first."

"I'm sorry." He really was. He no longer had any ill will toward either of them and said as much.

"I won't bother you again. I'm actually leaving town. But I had to ask you something..." She seemed to hesitate. "It's amazing what you did for this Lola woman. You really put up a fight to save her and the baby."

He waited, wondering where she was going with this.

"Why..." Her voice broke. "Why didn't you put up a fight for me?"

It had never crossed his mind to try to keep Julia from marrying Wyatt. She was right. He hadn't put up a fight. He'd been hurt, he'd been angry, but he hadn't made some grandiose effort like riding a horse into the church to stop the wedding—if it had ever gone that far.

"I hope you find what you're looking for," he said, because there wasn't anything else he could say.

"And I hope you're unhappy as hell." She disconnected.

He looked over at Lola and laughed.

"Julia," she said.

"Yep, she called to say she liked the article."

Lola smiled. "You're a terrible liar."

"She's leaving town."

"Really?" She didn't seem unhappy to hear that.

"She wished us well."

"Now I know you're lying," she said as he pulled her close.

THE WEDDING TOOK PLACE in a field of flowers surrounded by the four mountain ranges. Colt had purchased the property just days before. He'd had to scramble to get everything moved in for the ceremony.

What had started as a small wedding had grown, as old and new friends wanted to be a part of it.

"Lola, I know this isn't what we planned," Colt had apologized. They'd agreed to a small wedding, and somehow it had gone awry.

She had laughed. "I love that all these people care about you and want to be there. They're becoming my friends, as well." Lillie and Mariah had given her a baby shower, the three becoming instant friends.

He kissed her. "I just want it to be the best day of your life."

"That day was when I met you."

Colt couldn't believe how many people had helped to make the day special. Calls came in from around the world from men he'd served with. A dozen of them flew in for the ceremony. The guest list had continued to grow right up until the wedding.

"Let us cater it for you," Lillie and Mariah had suggested. "Darby insists. And the Stagecoach Saloon is all yours for the reception, if it rains."

Lola had hugged her new friends, eyes glistening and Colt thought he couldn't be more blessed. Lola had accepted their kind offer and added, "Only if the two of you will agree to be my matrons of honor."

So much had been going on that the weeks leading up to the wedding had flown by. Colt wished his father was alive to see this—his only son changing diapers, getting up for middle-of-the-night feedings, bathing the baby in the kitchen sink, and all the while loving every minute of it.

Tommy always chuckled when he came by and caught Colt being a father. "If the guys could see you now," he'd joked. But Colt had seen his friend's wistful looks. He hoped Tommy found someone he could love as much as Colt loved Lola.

She'd continued to amaze him, taking everything in her stride as the ranch auction was held and the sale of the ranch continued. She'd had her things shipped from where they'd been in storage and helped him start packing up what he planned to keep at the house.

He'd felt overwhelmed sometimes, but Lola was always cool and calm. He often thought of that woman he'd met in Billings—and the one he'd found on his doorstep in the middle of the night. Often he didn't feel he was good enough for her. But then she would find him, put her arms around him and rest her head on his shoulder, and he would breathe in the scent of her and know that this was meant to be.

Like standing here now in a field of flowers next

to Lola with all their friends and the preacher ready to marry them. If this was a dream, he didn't want to wake up.

LOLA COULDN'T BELIEVE all the people who had come into her life because of Colt. She looked over at him. He was so handsome in his Western suit and boots. He was looking at her, his blue eyes shining. He smiled as the preacher said, "Do you take this woman—"

"I sure do," he said, and everyone laughed.

Lola hardly remembered the rest of the ceremony. She felt so blissfully happy that she wasn't even sure her feet had touched the ground all day.

But she remembered the kiss. Colt had pulled her to him, taking his time as he looked into her eyes. "I love you, Lola," he'd whispered.

She'd nodded through her tears and then he'd kissed her. The crowd had broken into applause. Cowboy hats and Army caps had been thrown into the air. Somewhere beyond the crowd, a band began to play.

Lillie hugged her before handing her Grace. Lola looked up from the infant she held in her arms, her eyes full of tears. Colt put his arm around both of them as they took their first steps as Mr. and Mrs. Colt McCloud.

* * * * *